Everyone Burns

John Dolan hails from a small town in the North-East of England. Before turning to writing, his career encompassed law and finance. He has run businesses in Europe, South and Central America, Africa and Asia. He and his wife Fiona currently divide their time between Thailand and the UK.

Everyone Burns is the first book in the *Time, Blood and Karma* series.

The *Time Blood and Karma* series

Everyone Burns

Hungry Ghosts

A Poison Tree

The fourth book in the series, *Running on Emptiness*, will be published by
Tention Publishing Limited

EVERYONE

BURNS

John Dolan

TENTION BOOKS

TENTION BOOKS

EVERYONE BURNS published by Tention Publishing Limited
Copyright © John David Dolan 2012

John David Dolan has asserted his right under the Copyright, Designs and Patents Act 1988 to be identified as the author of this work

Tention Publishing Limited Reg. No. 8098036
Unit 4 Provender Mill, Belvedere Road,
Faversham ME13 7LD,
United Kingdom
www.tentionpublishing.com

A CIP catalogue record for this book
is available from the British Library

ISBN 978-0-9573256-0-9

For my mother Margaret Dolan
and for my wife Fiona
who somehow still manages
to put up with me

AUTHOR'S PREFACE

The events in this book take place on the island of Samui and in Bangkok over seventeen days from 25th January to 10th February 2005.

At this time, Thailand was still in a state of shock following the tsunami of 26th December 2004 which caused so much damage and loss of life on the country's Andaman Coast. Against this backdrop, the National Elections were held on 6th February and the eve of the Chinese New Year fell on 8th February.

From 10th January until 11th February, less than 4mm of rain fell on Samui, temperatures averaged in the high twenties and the mean humidity hovered around eighty percent. Bangkok fared similarly.

The picture of Koh Samui that is painted here is partly accurate, and partly the product of my over-active imagination. Wat Son does not exist and neither do the specific bars and restaurants to which I make reference. Bophut Police Station is located where mentioned, but it is not the architectural eyesore that I describe. I have taken some liberties with the organization of the Royal Thai Police, and the activities of the fictitious police officers in this entertainment should not be taken as representative of reality.

None of the characters herein are real people.

"How can there be laughter, how can there be pleasure,
when the whole world is burning?
When you are in deep darkness, will you not ask for a lamp?"
Lord Buddha, The Dhammapada

1

"One must imagine Sisyphus happy."
Albert Camus, The Myth of Sisyphus

Oh, bugger. I had been hoping for a quiet evening.

As the broken cue spins up off the pool table, the jagged end just misses my left eye, cutting a gash in the skin below. I duck as a ferrety-looking drunk in an *I Love Thailand* tee-shirt takes a clumsy swing at my head. Swivelling to the side I bring my right fist in hard towards his stomach, but my timing is off and I hit his lower ribs.

All hell is now breaking loose. On Koh Samui, bar fights are pretty rare. They are usually sparked by jealousy, a racist remark, or some sexual insult. Fists, bottles and bar furniture then start to fly, fuelled by cheap alcohol. Tonight is typical. Some overly-lubricated European had mistaken one of the pool-playing *katoeys* for a bona fide female, and had reacted violently when he realised his error. In fairness May, the katoey in question, *is* rather gorgeous, especially tonight in her red figure-hugging dress. However, when bad-mouthed by an inebriated *farang*, she is not averse to striking out with pool cues, glasses, bottles or any other suitable object that presents itself to her beautifully-manicured hand. So it had proved this evening, and with a shower of glass and loud oaths, the more macho patrons of the bar began wading into each other. The less oiled customers and the (inevitably more sensible) females meantime disappeared quicker than a Scotsman's generosity.

How do people pick which individual they are going to punch at such times? Interesting question. Maybe a Chaos Theory specialist could explain it. Something to do with the fluttering of a butterfly's wings perhaps, or maybe in this case the fluttering of false eyelashes. Suffice to say, however, that as I bring my elbow in hard contact with the side of the ferrety-one's jaw and he goes crashing off over a table, this action is not going to endear me to his drinking companions.

Two of the more overweight of them rush at me, although one is slowed down momentarily by an airborne bar stool. The first one – whose face bears an uncanny resemblance to the actor Geoffrey Rush (and in fact he swears at me in an Australian accent) – manages to pin me against the wall, dislodging a framed portrait of King Rama IX of Thailand, which promptly shatters on the tiled floor. Out of the corner of my eye I see the second charmer – a bearded, Jerry-Garcia-Grateful-Dead-type – break the neck off a bottle as he works his way through the flailing bodies towards me.

"You're screwed, mate," says Geoffrey Rush.

But apparently I am not. For at that moment help arrives in the unlikely form of a gigantic shaven-headed Russian, who flattens Jerry Garcia with a single punch to the jaw, before grinning widely at me. I notice two other pulped guys at the Russian's feet. My Australian assailant gulps and his face turns a fetching shade of corpse.

"Need some help?" asks the jolly giant.

"No, I'm fine, thanks," I reply, freeing myself with a sneaky knee to Geoffrey Rush's privates, and a rabbit-punch to the nose.

Surveying the human and non-human debris, I see the bar fight is effectively over. It's ended as quickly as it began. Clearly, the bruising and bone-cracking having ceased, it is now the appropriate time for the local police to arrive.

The Thai Boys in Blue are represented on this occasion by 'PC' and his sidekick 'DTs'. PC (real name: Preechap Chaldrakun) has the build of a Maori rugby player – his neck being the thickness of a local girl's waist – and the humanitarian features of a Japanese prison guard. His nickname is somewhat ironic since he is about as un-PC as anyone I've ever met, and he views every *farang* with suspicion. On the other hand, I suppose 'PC' has a certain ring to it as a policeman's moniker.

His partner, DTs (real name: Daeng Tathip) is a snake of a man with darting eyes, bad skin and a serious drink problem. PC does the physical stuff and I imagine DTs does the paperwork, assuming he can keep his shaking hand still long enough to wield the pen.

PC looks at me sullenly. He would probably like to arrest me, but he knows I'm friendly with his boss. Then his shark's eyes fix on the shattered picture of His Majesty Bhumibol Adulyadej.

"Who did this?" he demands.

The big Russian waggles a thumb in the direction of the Australian who is still lying on the floor with his hands to his crotch and a pained expression on his sweaty features. My earlier dancing partner, ferret-face, has vanished, so I point to the ex Grateful Dead member propped against a wall and spitting out what looks like a tooth.

"These two," I say.

This decides PC. For him, busting up a bar is one thing, but disrespecting the Thai Royal Family is on an altogether different scale. He uses his cuffs on the temporary eunuch and snatches DT's cuffs for use on Jerry Garcia. Then with hands like bunches of bananas he hauls the miscreants up and out of the bar.

I light the Russian and myself a cigarette, and we follow the circus outside to the waiting police car. While DTs stands twitching, PC bundles the two protesting farangs into the back of the vehicle. With a final glowering look at me, PC barks "Get in!" to DTs and his partner hastily complies. The car speeds off, rather faster than this crowded street of Chaweng warrants.

I turn to the Russian. "The name's Braddock, by the way," I say proffering my hand.

"Vladimir. Vlad," he answers, grasping my hand with a tattooed bear's paw. "Our police friends will now play with the rubber hoses, yes?"

"They don't use rubber hoses here."

"What do they use?"

"You don't want to know."

We wander back into the much quieter Mosquito Bar, where the barman is already clearing up. He shrugs, indicates his despoiled kingdom with a weary gesture, and offers us beers on the house. We gracefully accept. May and a couple of other katoeys, are attending to their makeup, but their faces radiate happiness at the sight of Vlad and myself. There is much *wai*-ing, smiling, hugging and general congratulatory behaviour, along with offers of obscene acts of gratitude. My companion takes this in good part. The cheerleaders dispersing, we find a couple of undamaged stools and sit at the bar.

"I saw you kick-boxing in Lamai last week," I venture to the behemoth sitting beside me. "You kicked the crap out of some local guy."

Vlad laughs and claps me on the shoulder, rather harder than necessary. "What can I say? Everyone needs a hobby, yes?" His smile, which includes two gold teeth, is slightly insane, and I notice the dilation of his pupils which suggests a recent acquaintance with some illegal substance.

I sip my beer. "Thanks for the intervention."

"Is no problem, my friend. I am Russian. When there is a fight I always choose side of right," he says, rather morally. "Those other men disrespect May. May is a friend of some of my girls here, so whether he is man or woman, it makes no difference to me. I do not like disrespect." He spits. "So I join you." He laughs again.

"That's a very, um, refreshing attitude," I say, wondering how many girls he has here, and whether his relationship with them is of a social or a business nature.

"Incidentally," whispers the Russian stubbing out his cigarette, "You might want to know that your face is bleeding."

EVERYONE BURNS

*　　*　　*　　*　　*

Such is the reality, and now for the idealising and philosophising. Some stock-taking would appear to be in order.

David Braddock. A fortysomething educated Englishman. Well-built (allegedly), with a full head of dark, flecked-grey hair (certainly), and a slightly crooked nose from a rugby-playing youth. Hiding out, if you will, on a small island in the Gulf of Thailand. Living off the proceeds of earlier capitalist days and inherited money. Vacillating between poetry and profanity. Running a barely-viable Agency whose dual nature is difficult to describe. In short, me.

To some – mainly local Thais – I am perceived as an advisor and solver of personal problems. To others – mainly Europeans and North Americans – I am a private investigator primarily employed in the tracking of possibly-unfaithful girlfriends.

In my first capacity, I am usually to be found in a comfortable consulting room dispensing empathy and the occasional tissue to an emotionally-affected client. In my second capacity, I either sit in an adjacent office taking businesslike notes and making pithy remarks to my predominantly white clientele; or else I hang around in bars and alleys observing the antics of young Thai women. Hence my recent presence in the Mosquito Bar and accidental participation in tonight's fracas.

To summarise, my life is one of split personality. I am in two minds about it myself.

Nevertheless, down these narrow streets a man must walk, even if it is in flip-flops. But I am no Philip Marlowe, and Koh Samui is not film-noir USA. There is nothing of Hollywood's black and white morality on this most colourful of Thailand's islands. And long overcoats just make you sweat in the sun. Here the Postman Never Rings Twice, simply because he never rings at all. He has better things to do. Lamai's and Chaweng's adventurers generally pack a condom, not a gun.

5

Some of the streets are, however, genuinely narrow. These same streets may not be filled with machine-gun fire and the dramatic screech of violins, but they overflow with the invisible and innumerable longings of the human heart. Love continues to minister here, but betrayal still wears its perfidious face, hatred hollows out the weak man's breast, revenge pursues its self-defeating course; and the unfulfilled dreams of the multitude haunt the island like so many hungry ghosts.

Accordingly there is work to be done: often trivial and meaningless, sometimes absurd, but on occasion a difference can be made. *Occasionally* Sisyphus can push the rock to the top of the hill without its rolling back down.

Meantime, my bleeding cheek is throbbing, my shirt is ruined, and I must repair home to be myself repaired.

*   *   *   *   *

My weatherworn house is just outside Chaweng, at a sufficient distance from the tourist madness, towards the hills. It used to be in a cul-de-sac but developers eager to offer affordable chunks of the island dream extended and improved the route so that it now loops back on itself to Samui's Ring Road. It is still quiet however, and most of the surrounding coconut groves survive intact. Fortunately most of my immediate neighbours are Thai.

When my battered jeep pulls onto the drive around midnight, my wife, Claire, is nowhere to be found. Wayan however has been waiting up for me, and her brown Balinese eyes react with horror at the sight of my damaged face.

"Mr. David, what happened to you?"

"I had a disagreement with the wrong end of a pool cue. I'm OK."

She rushes off to the kitchen, returns with our medical kit and promptly sets about cleaning up my cheek.

Wayan's role in our household fits the broad category of 'housekeeper', but she is much more than that. Claire and I first met her over fifteen years ago during one of our regular holidays to Ubud in Bali, where she was working in a spa. We became friends and stayed in touch. Wayan had never married in spite of being very pretty and kind almost to the point of saintliness. I gathered there had been a romance with a Westerner at some stage in her life which had ended. She has never discussed the details, and I have found it prudent never to ask. She believes her *karma* is to be alone. Periodically I have tried reasoning with her on this point but she remains firm. Now in her early forties, aside from the slightly fuller waist, she still looks to me the same young woman I met in Bali.

Her mother – her only family – died a few years ago, around the time I was decamping to Samui. I asked her to run the house here and she accepted. Getting her Thai paperwork sorted out was not easy, but I have some influence, a greedy friend in immigration, and cash in my wallet. Generally speaking, I find in South East Asia most bureaucratic problems have a monetary solution.

She looks concerned. "You should have stitches in this," she says.

"No way. The doctor would laugh at me and tell me I was being a baby. Besides, *Scarface Braddock* is a great name for a private detective."

She does not find this funny.

I notice the book she has been reading before I arrived. It is *Alice's Adventures in Wonderland.*

"Why are you reading this?" I ask.

"I need to improve my English."

This is nonsense, of course, as her English is very good, albeit with intermittent confusion of past and present tenses. I may not be able to converse with her on the more abstruse aspects of Quantum Mechanics, but then again why would I want to?

"Today I met a little Thai boy whose father was late collecting him from

7

the English School. I stayed with him until his father arrived, so we started talking. *This* is the book he is studying in English class. He said it was good so I bought a copy."

This is archetypal Wayan as Good Samaritan. "You were lucky to find a copy of this in the local bookshop."

"They buy for the school. I find it a difficult book. Is it meant to teach children about not taking drugs? Otherwise I cannot understand why they would give this to children to read."

She finishes her ministrations and peers at her work critically.

"That is the best I can do."

"Thank you, Wayan."

She puts a hand on my arm. "Mr. David," she says, her voice taking on a serious tone, "last night I had one of those dreams I have sometimes. You know about my dreams?" I nod. "I dreamed I could see you but you could not talk to me. I do not think *this* is the meaning of the dream," she indicates the cut, "but I think that something bad is coming. Perhaps this is the beginning of something bad."

I take her hand and squeeze it. I am hardly the superstitious type, but I have learned to take seriously Wayan's lucid dreaming. My theory is that, being supremely empathetic, she taps into feelings at a subconscious level – usually mine – and reflects back hopes, concerns and fears like a magic mirror. Her explanation is, naturally, quite different, and involves the elemental forces of Balinese gods and demons.

"Wayan," I say gently, "This dream can have many meanings, not all of them necessarily bad. You mustn't worry about me, or you will get wrinkles." Still no smile. "I *am* a fully grown man and I *can* look after myself." She looks doubtful, but is too polite to say anything.

"Anyway, thanks for waiting up. You get off to bed. I'll be turning in soon."

"Don't stay up too late."

8

"I won't, mother, I promise."

Finally Wayan smiles. She picks up her book and goes. I expect the psychedelic nature of her dreams will intensify the deeper she delves into Alice's adventures.

I drop my bloody shirt into the laundry basket, change into my dressing-gown and go out onto the upstairs balcony with my saxophone. The night sky being full of stars, my nearest neighbour being sufficiently far away, and my monkey mind being too restless for slumber, I blow some smooth, slow blues out into the still air. By one o'clock I am sufficiently chilled to smoke a final cigarette and turn in. There is still no sign of Claire.

My head hits the pillow and sleep instantly takes me. I dream I have fallen down a rabbit hole where I encounter a pool-playing Red Queen and a bald, grinning Cheshire-Cat with gold teeth.

2

"Oh, I've had such a curious dream!" said Alice.
Lewis Carroll, Alice's Adventures in Wonderland

Koh Samui sits in the Gulf of Thailand to the east of the Kra Isthmus. The island is (very) roughly round in shape, though featuring outcrops of land resembling drooping and erect penises enclosing the long, white sand beaches which act as a magnetic pull on the tired working mind. The interior rises as jungle-covered mountains, the highest of which, Khao Pom, reaches six hundred and thirty-five metres. To the north-east is the International Airport, and south of this at a distance of a few kilometres lies Chaweng, which functions as my base.

The heart of Chaweng is a long, narrow one-way street, crowded on both sides by shops, spas, hotels, restaurants and gaudy signage. Along the length of the street leaning electricity poles groan under the weight of rats' nests of cables hanging like grey/black dreadlocks. All the usual charmless Western suspects are to be found here dispensing junk food, overpriced ice cream and caffeine; along with more cheap tee-shirts, sarongs and general tourist tat than you could wish for. Dust, heat and motorbikes permeate the thoroughfare which rings to the hawkers' cries of "Taxi!" and (less loud, but more shrill) "Massage!"

To the east, obscured by the high street, but accessible by a myriad of pathways or via hotel lobbies, is the long beach. By day a baking tray for the sun-seeker, by night Chaweng beach transforms into a low-light stage of romance. On evenings where the breeze allows, paper Chinese fire lanterns float up into the black heavens. Here young couples dream of the years to come and old couples sigh for the years past; while the lapping waters of the Gulf echo an older rhythm than that of the drifting music from the bars and restaurants.

To the west of the main street is the lake, the far shore of which houses Girly Bar Heaven, the source – along with Lamai's town centre equivalent – of much of my income.

My office is located in a discreet concrete side road slightly to the north of the one-way system, an area where clients can generally visit undisturbed by the curious eyes of spouses and significant others.

It is already after 11.00am when I pass under the sign proclaiming the David Braddock Agency, climb the stairs to my first-floor offices, and am greeted by Da, my heavily-pregnant receptionist.

"Sàwàt-dii khâ."

"Sàwàt-dii khráp." I throw my straw hat at the hat rack and miss, as usual.

She notices the cut under my left eye. "Bad night?" she asks.

"I've had worse."

She hands me the mail: two bills and a flyer for a new restaurant. "I'm going to catch up on my emails before my appointment with Herr Vogel. No calls," I tell her.

Da leans forward as far as her bump will allow and says in a low voice, "Your emails may have to wait, *Khun* David. There is a lady here to see you."

I raise an eyebrow, "A lady?"

"Thai, mid-thirties. Well turned out. Nails immaculate, hair styled this morning. Expensive gold jewellery, authentic designer handbag. Speaks good English. Smokes. Since she wears a wedding ring, my guess would be it is a Matrimonial." She looks at me expectantly.

"Anything else?" I ask the trainee detective.

"She walks like she has had dance training. Also she is good at colour coordination." As an afterthought she adds, "And I like her shoes."

"Did she give a name?"

Da consults her pad, "*Miss Noi*, although I do not think that is her real

11

name. I showed her into the East Office. She has been waiting about fifteen minutes."

When I open the office door, a lady in an ash-grey dress is sitting with her back to me.

"Sàwàt-dii khráp. Miss Noi, I apologise for keeping you waiting. I am David Braddock."

My client rises gracefully and we give a respectful wai to each other. I indicate for her to sit as I take the easy chair opposite her, and find her scrutinising my eyes to see if I have recognised her. Which I have, but I am wearing my poker face. She is Nittha Rattanakorn, the wife of Thongchai Rattanakorn, the biggest gangster on the island. This may spell trouble.

She says, "Do you know who I am, Mr. Braddock?"

"No. *Miss Noi* will do fine. I find my clients tend to talk more freely if they feel our sessions are anonymous." I make open eye-contact and she seems satisfied.

"I will need to take you into my confidence as to my identity at some point," she says.

"Well, let's make that later, shall we. Would you like something to drink?"

"No, thank you."

"If you feel you would like to have another cigarette, it's OK."

"I haven't been smoking in here. What makes you think I smoke?"

I shrug, "Trick of the trade," and offer my pack of Marlboros.

"I prefer my own," she says taking out a gold cigarette-case.

I give her a light and light up one for myself. I fish out an ashtray, put it on the coffee-table between us and wait for her to begin.

"You come very highly recommended, Mr. Braddock," she says finally. "I hear that you are discreet and know how to keep matters ... um ... confidential."

"I have that reputation, I believe."

There is silence for a few moments as she smokes and composes herself. When she exhales her voice trembles slightly. I notice her shapely breasts and wonder if they are real.

"This is more difficult than I thought it would be. I am so stupid, stupid."

"Take your time."

She takes a deep breath.

"I have been married for twelve years. Although my husband has always been good to me, for most of that time he has also not been faithful. I think I have finally had enough."

This I do not want to hear. I need a job investigating a gangster like I need a hole in the head. In fact if I take this case there is a very good chance I will end up with a hole in the head.

I do not say any of this. Instead, I say gently, "Go on."

"He is the only man I have ever been with. I knew he had been with many women before me, but that did not matter. He was kind and made me feel special." She pauses a moment before continuing. "We have been through good times and bad times together, and while I knew he was looking elsewhere from time to time, I at least believed he would always come back to me." She trails off.

"You know for sure he has been unfaithful?"

Nittha Rattanakorn smiles sadly, "A wife always knows."

Not necessarily true, I think. And if you already know all you need to know, what are you doing here? Do you need your husband to bump off a farang as proof of his devotion to you?

"What sort of women does he like? Sorry, I need to ask."

"Married ones usually."

"Hmmn. So presumably he is either addicted to risk, or chooses his mistresses on the basis of no long term commitment?"

She blinks at me, "I never thought of it that way."

I assume an earnest expression. "I know of no perfect marriages, Miss

Noi. I know of only two kinds. There are those where the partners stay together because they love each other, whatever else is going on in their lives. Then there are those where the partners stay together for reasons of money, cowardice, laziness and/or family. I'm aware that's a broad category, but it excludes the *love* reason, which is the key point. Which type is your marriage, do you think? Or perhaps there is a third type which I am missing?"

"I feel like a ridiculous jealous woman." There are tears in her eyes now and I hand her a tissue.

"Miss Noi –" I begin.

"Please, Mr. Braddock, at least call me by my real name. I am Nittha –"

I interrupt quickly before she can get to the family name, "All right Nittha. And in that case, I am David." I sit back in my seat and do my best to look wise. I study her face for a few moments.

"Nittha, as you probably know, I run two practices here, and their purposes are very different. In my first practice I conduct investigations, usually into some form of sexual infidelity. In my second practice, which I run from *this* room, I have a more subtle role: to help people find out what it is that they really want. I think you came here today to talk to the investigator, but I wonder instead whether you should be speaking to the counsellor."

She is looking at me closely, "Why do you say that?"

"Well, let me make some observations. The first thing you tell me is that your husband has always been good to you. This suggests to me that you still have some respect for him, and perhaps affection. Then when you are upset, I see emotion but not bitterness. Your tears are sorrowful, but not angry. In your eyes I see regret and hurt, and maybe therefore, love."

I have her attention.

"I am guessing that since his infidelity over the years has been with various women, there has been no 'special' one. Is that correct?"

She nods, "Yes."

"Is it still correct? Or is there a 'special' someone for him now?"

"No, I don't think so."

"Then I ask myself: if this behaviour of his has been going on for some time, and you have, in a sense, anyway, accepted it – then what has changed recently to bring you here? Has something altered for him, or has something changed in *your* life?"

She blinks and runs a pink tongue over her lips. I decide to run with a hunch.

"May I see your cell phone?"

"My cell phone?"

"Please."

She takes the cell phone from her handbag and passes it to me. I take it with one hand and catch her hand with the other. She does not struggle. I see avoidance in her eyes, though she tries to hold my gaze. I look at the phone, as if trying to decipher a puzzle, then I look back at her. I am still holding her hand. I am now banking on a little showmanship and Thai superstition to take me forward.

"Nittha," I say slowly, "I am sensing there is something here that should not be here." I pause. The room is silent apart from the soft purr of the aircon.

She looks at me and lets out a long sigh. "Yes," she says, "there is a number in there that has no place in my phone."

"A man's number?"

"Yes. But nothing has happened with him. I swear."

I put the phone down and cup her hand between both of mine.

"What is it that you want?" I ask softly.

"I don't know."

I release her and sit back. She looks at the phone, and ashamedly puts it back in her handbag.

15

"You must think me a hypocrite," she says sadly.

I shake my head, "No, not at all. I think you are a woman who loves her husband. You worry that he does not love you back. And that is all I think. In the meantime, you have felt flattered by someone who is paying you attention. That is just human. But it is also, as I am sure you are aware, dangerous."

I pour her a glass of water and she takes it thoughtfully. I keep silent and let her think awhile. Eventually she says, "And you worked all that out in a few minutes and through holding my hand. You are as insightful as they say you are." She relaxes and folds over a long, shapely leg.

"Perhaps. Although I'm not sure who 'they' are."

She puts a finger to her lips, "I cannot say."

"By the way," I tell her, "that's a nice leg."

She giggles, "I've got another one just like it."

"I noticed. Your husband would be a very foolish man to lose a woman with legs like that."

She puts down the glass of water. "Thank you, David. I need to do some thinking. Can I come and see you again?"

"Of course. It might be better if you made an appointment next time, though."

"As Miss Noi?"

"As whomever you like. Names are not important when we're in *this* room. It's only in the PI room next door that we have to be specific about names."

"I understand. I'd like to come and see you again in *this* room. Unless of course," she adds coquettishly, "you'd like to meet me somewhere else."

I smile. "Then I'd likely become part of the problem, rather than part of the solution. Don't you think?"

"Not necessarily. Is my makeup smudged?"

"A little. There's a washroom through that door you can use."

"I bet you have lots of women who cry in here."

"Some. Most women only cry with me in the bedroom. Usually out of disappointment."

When she emerges, perfect once more, from the washroom, I hand her a card. "If you need me just whistle. You know how to whistle, don't you?"

"I do. Goodbye, David."

"Goodbye, Nittha."

She glides out to reception. I hear her exchange a few words and some Baht with Da, then she is gone.

Da puts her head around the door. "Was it a Matrimonial?" she asks.

"Not exactly. But you were right about the smoking. And the shoes."

"Nice breasts too, don't you think?" she says mischievously.

"The best that money can buy."

"I don't suppose mine will look like that after the baby."

"No comment. Go file something."

I indulge myself in a moment of self-congratulation at having avoided a surveillance job on Godfather Rattanakorn and at also perhaps having helped his wife – although the flirting was probably a bad idea.

I now have to shift mental gears to PI mode, and I pass through the connecting door to the more austere West Office where I see my PI clients. A desk, three chairs, a filing cabinet, an aircon, and a discreetly concealed bottle of Bells. That's about it. I have an hour checking emails and updating a report for a client on my laptop before Da announces the arrival of my first official appointment for the day.

"Herr Vogel."

There are some people you warm to at first sight: you just *know* they are going to be fun to be around. Klaus Vogel is not one of those people. Neither does he match the profile of my average PI client, which is overweight, over forty and over-anxious (and, of course, over here). Vogel looks like a Nazi propaganda pin-up boy from the 1930s: severely cut blond hair, broad-shouldered and unquestionably fit. When he removes his Gucci shades, his eyes are cold and blue as anti-freeze. He sports an expensive-looking watch, fine linen shirt and trousers and hand-made Italian shoes. His tastefully-undone top buttons reveal a tasteless gold medallion and the upper part of a hairless torso. I'm betting he waxes.

"Klaus Vogel," he says unnecessarily through humourless lips.

"David Braddock," I reply, suppressing the urge to click my heels.

He sits down without waiting to be asked, quickly scanning the bare room with an obvious air of distaste. He places a slim black folder on my desk and centres it, as any good anal retentive would. I am unsure whether to pick it up or not. I decide on balance to leave it where it is.

"So, Mr. Vogel, what can I do for you?" (I have decided to drop the 'Herr' bit.)

"Mr. Braddock, I understand you specialise in private investigations, and you have been in business here on the island for some years." The voice is precise and flat, like an Englishman impersonating a German speaking English.

"That's what the advertisement says, yes."

"And you operate a discreet service, is that correct?"

"Like a Catholic priest in a confessional."

"That means nothing to me. I am not a Catholic."

This is going to be hard work. I decide to cut out the levity and assume an air of gravitas. I place my elbows deliberately on the desk and rest my forearms on its surface.

"Merely a metaphor," I say. "Whatever is said in this room never leaves the room. I wouldn't stay in business long, Mr. Vogel, if I blabbed around my clients' personal affairs. This is a small island. Reputation counts for a lot."

"Quite so." He looks at me with x-ray eyes for a moment. I hold his gaze and he nods curtly.

"Well then, to business."

"I should explain my fee and expenses structure to you –"

He holds up a hand. "Thank you, that is not necessary. I have already questioned your secretary on this matter and I am quite satisfied."

Da and I have a system on PI fees. If the client is well-off but unpleasant, he is quoted Scale B (expensive); otherwise Scale A (not so expensive – just about keeps my car in petrol). It's my own little island version of socialism. Da is a shrewd judge of character so I'm laying a wager Vogel is on Scale B.

"I wish you to observe a young woman for me." He pauses to see my reaction but there isn't one, so he pushes the black folder forward and indicates for me to open it. "It is all in there," he says. "You may study it at your leisure."

"Before I open your file and start taking your money, I need to ask you one or two questions."

He stiffens, "Really? Why?"

"It's part of my procedures."

He relates to *procedures* and relaxes a little.

"Very well."

"First, I need to know your interest in this girl and how long you have known her."

"I have known her for a week. As to my interest in her –" he purses his thin lips somewhat priggishly, "– let us say she has some charm and certain talents which intrigue me."

And they say romance is dead.

"Does she work in a bar?"

"Yes."

"I should tell you, Mr. Vogel, based on my experience of bar girls, there is a 95% probability that she will be sleeping with someone else within 48 hours of your leaving the island. However much 'allowance' you have promised her, she can earn several times that by staying on the market – meanwhile pocketing your 'allowance'."

"She does not strike me as that type of girl."

"Yet you still want me to follow her. Check for boyfriends, suitors, people paying her attention – that sort of thing, presumably?"

"Yes. I need to be sure."

"I see."

Actually, I don't see. It's a puzzle why this guy would be interested in a bar girl. With his looks – if you discount for a moment his character – he should have no problem picking up females. On the other hand, his personality could be a very effective form of contraception. *Could* he be in love? With someone besides himself, that is? I plough on.

"Where does she work?"

"In the Ocean Pearl."

"That's a proper bar," I remark with some surprise. "It's not in Girly Bar Heaven. It's not even a girly bar."

"I know," he says.

"Your chances just got better."

"My chances of what?"

"Your chances of a happy ending." I realise I could have phrased this better, but the word-play is lost on him anyway.

"Read the file, Mr. Braddock," he says. "All you need to know is in there. There are also photographs of the girl. Her name is Wiwattanee Lamphongchat, although she prefers to be called 'Jingjai'."

"*True Heart.*"

"I'm sorry?"

"In Thai, 'jing' means 'true' or 'real', and 'jai' means 'heart' or 'soul'. Hence *True Heart.*"

"I see. True Heart. Yes."

I open the folder: two word-processed pages of data – her address, the address of the bar, lots of other sundry details – and four photographs of a cute if somewhat tomboyish Thai girl. She is not familiar to me, which may be good news for Vogel. Meanwhile Romeo drones on.

"I have included an email address for me, although I doubt you will need it. I do not give out my cell phone number to people I do not know well. No offense."

"None taken."

"I will be back in Samui in seven to ten days, and you can give me a report then. I will leave a week's retainer for you with your secretary. I can pay any balance on my return. I trust that is satisfactory?"

"Perfectly."

"And cash is acceptable?"

"Always."

"Good. I will of course need a receipt. Business expenses," he says without a trace of embarrassment.

"My secretary, Miss Da, will furnish you with the necessaries."

"Then I will say goodbye, My Braddock. Please be efficient on my behalf, and invisible. I do not wish the girl to think I mistrust her."

And so, managing to be quaintly polite, pointedly rude, and unintentionally ironic all in one speech, my paradoxical client leaves, taking his medallion and his charisma with him. I make a mental note to introduce a Fee Scale C for especially odious bastards. Thank the powers that not all Germans are like Vogel. Generally I like German people. Actually, most of the male ones I've met remind me of me. Although I recognise that is not necessarily a compliment.

A few minutes later Da appears.

"I charged your last client at the B Rate," she says.

"Good girl."

"He paid in cash. It looks as though we will be eating this week. Speaking of eating, Wayan called. She wants to know if you will be home for dinner this evening."

"No, I don't think so."

"Romantic dinner for two with Miss Noi?"

"Don't let the door hit your bump on the way out. I'm going to lunch."

*   *   *   *   *

It has not rained for days and the dusty streets lie prone beneath the sun's relentless assault. *Sometime too hot the eye of heaven shines*, as the Bard observed in one of his sonnets. But in spite of the surrender of the cracked earth, humanity is astir in the town. The Beautiful and the Damned have emerged from their lairs and troop or stoop their way respectively along the pavements, carrying shopping and hangovers. Another day in Paradise.

Lunch comprises a gin and tonic, a bottle of imported water and a few cigarettes. I sit under a large umbrella facing the beach and glittering sea. Having only one appointment this afternoon, I permit myself some people-watching and reflection time.

The day's discussions thus far have proved interesting if somewhat puzzling. Nittha Rattanakorn is a particularly worrying client. True I don't know for certain that Thongchai Rattanakorn puts horses' heads under bedsheets or his enemies' feet in concrete galoshes, but the criminal activities with which he is (allegedly) associated suggest a mild slap on the wrist would not be his preferred method of punishment. I justify my flirting with the wife of one of Thailand's *jâo phâw* on the basis that I have not yet established whether she is a PI client (in which case the flirting is ethically OK as far as I am concerned) or a therapy client (in which case it is not). Self-delusional as I may be on occasion, I can nonetheless see this distinction is pretty thin. *Do not under any circumstances meet Nittha Rattanakorn outside of the office*, I inscribe in my mental Not-To-Do-List.

Vogel is more of an enigma. Many lovelorn farangs have passed through my under-varnished doors over the last few years, seeking confirmation that their vision of love, sex and happiness is not a mirage. Usually they are disappointed, but at least initially they travel in hope; and with passion, fire, fear, doubt – all the human qualities so patently absent from my cold-blooded, control-freaky client of today. Something is missing from this picture at present, but I will paint in the details eventually.

On my way back to the office I pass a beggar huddled in the doorway of a shuttered shop, sheltering from the heat. This is an unusual sight in Samui, as itinerants are normally moved on quickly by the police to keep them from the eyes of tourists. This guy is filthy and looks about at the end of his rope. His skin colour and facial characteristics suggest he is from one of the Northern tribes, presumably having made his way to the island via Bangkok in search of work. Clearly, he has not found any. I hand him a fistful of Baht and he nods and gives me a smile displaying a mouthful of stained teeth.

"Good luck."

*　　*　　*　　*　　*

I am back in familiar territory with my afternoon appointment. Harold Jayne, a procurement officer with a haulage company in Slough, is reassuringly fat, balding, middle-aged and with a face like a marguerita pizza. On his podgy wrist is clamped a fake Rolex (the scratches on the glass are a dead giveaway), and, as a final nice touch, the armpits of his *Samui Heaven* tee-shirt are drenched in sweat. However, Harold is a man on a mission. He is almost certain he has found True Love: he simply needs my final reassurance.

"I saw your billboard when I left the airport, Mr. Braddock," he says in his Slough lilt. "I never thought I'd need to see you when I came to Samui, but here I am. Wow! What a holiday it's been!"

"I'm pleased you've had a good time. Now perhaps we could discuss the lady?"

"Ah, yes. Well, her name is Ting. Ting Saksri. She works in the Rubber Bar. And she's gorgeous. I brought a couple of photos, look. I downloaded them from my camera and printed them out at the PixShop in town."

I decide to give him a break.

"Are you a fan of Kipling, Mr. Jayne?"

He looks puzzled. "The cakes, you mean?"

"No, the author."

A blank.

"Wrote *The Jungle Book*?" I prompt.

"Oh. I saw the film when I was a kid."

"Never mind. Let me ask you: do you believe a leopard can change its spots?"

"Into what? Are you telling me Ting has a leopard or something?"

I pass a weary hand across my forehead.

"Your Miss Ting has previous form," I articulate patiently. "I have already had her under surveillance for two previous clients, and the results were not good. As I recall, one of the clients referred to her afterwards as 'Ching-Ching Ting', as in the sound of a cash register."

"Are you sure it's the same girl?"

"I know the name and your photographs confirm it." I tap one of the photos. "My, but that *is* a fine cleavage."

Harold looks crestfallen, and his face mutates from pizza to collapsed sponge cake.

"Harold –" I say, "– may I call you Harold?" He nods. "Look Harold, people do change sometimes. Perhaps Miss Ting has changed since I investigated her last about three months ago. Perhaps she would be perfectly content and would make an ideal companion living with you in your house in Slough –"

"I live with my parents at the moment."

"Right. All I'm saying is that there is a good chance this relationship will not work out well for you. I am, on the other hand, happy to take your money and report to you accordingly. But my services are not cheap. Man to man, I'm just trying to save you some heartache and currency here."

I slide a laminated sheet of my charges – Fee Scale A – across the desk, and he pauses for thought. His heart struggles with his head.

"You are sure –"

"Yes, Harold, I am sure it is the same girl. Wait." I rummage in my filing cabinet and find some earlier photographs of Miss Ting in a folder. Harold looks at them miserably. I watch his dream fade.

"Why not have this consultation on me as a freebie."

Two minutes later Harold has gone, and Da storms into my office.

"A *freebie* indeed!" she emotes, none too pleasantly. "What am I supposed to feed my baby on when he is born?"

"Show the guy some heart, Da," I say. "He's just had a big disappointment." I wag a finger at her. "Remember not everyone is as lucky in love as you. You have a perfect husband in Tong and you will no doubt have a sickeningly perfect baby. You get on with your in-laws, and you have a boss who always pays your salary on the nail, however little there is in the business bank account."

At the mention of her beloved Tong, Da's face lights up. "I love my Tong," she says.

"Now we have no more appointments today so bugger off home and dilate or something," I growl. "And go steady on that bike."

She kisses me on the forehead. "You are such a sweetie. I'll finish up a few things and then I'll be off."

I take the bottle of Bells from a desk drawer, pour myself a whisky and splash in a little water.

At some point I will have to address the problem of Da's replacement. This will not be easy. She is ludicrously over-qualified for her job, speaks perfect English – with colloquialisms thrown in for good measure – and knows how to handle people by applying that judicious degree of Asian submissiveness which many clients find so appealing: not that *I* ever see much of it. In her pre-pregnancy days, I would occasionally take her out with me on assignments, and she was showing the makings of a good detective. Motherhood and other priorities may, however, take her from that particular career path. She has had at least two proposals of marriage from visitors to the office that I know of, but her love for her childhood sweetheart Tong – now her husband – burns as a bright and unquenchable flame. She must have said *no* to a lot of men in the last few years. *And thus shines a good deed in a dark world.*

I drain the glass and feel a pleasurable burn. Then, for want of anything more pressing to do, I flip open Vogel's black folder on Jingjai. Neatly spaced and printed out on two pages are details of her date of birth, place of birth (Bangkok), height, weight, vital statistics, eye colour, hair colour, skin tone, distinguishing features (diamond in one of her teeth), siblings (none), apartment address, cell phone number, email, workplace, working hours, date she first came to Samui, where she spends her evening off each week, along with a heap of other stuff about how she dresses, etc, etc. At the bottom of the second sheet is Vogel's email address. Call me a prude, but this level of detail is all very creepy, like a stalker's crib-sheet on a victim. I do have clients who can be obsessive about their girlfriends, but this is on a whole new level. I try to envisage a romantic setting with Vogel eliciting this information from the girl while typing it into his laptop. *Yes, darling, your eyes look very beautiful this evening. What colour would you say they were? Hazel or darker? (Tap, tap, tap, tap ...) And how would you describe your skin tone? Please start without me, your soup is getting cold. (Tap, tap, tap, tap ...)*

The validity of some of this information is also questionable if it came from the girl herself. And why give me her email address? Does Vogel expect me to hack into her account?

For my purposes, the job details and her address are of most use. Her apartment, I note, is in a good block: perhaps expensive for a girl who only works behind a bar – but I suspend judgment, for now. Also helpful to know where she spends her evening off (if true).

I look at the photographs: Vogel is not in any of them. It is just the girl striking somewhat artificial poses with a backdrop which I imagine is the interior of the Ocean Pearl. In one image a diamond winks at the camera from her wide smile. She looks genuinely happy. Maybe she likes creeps.

*　　*　　*　　*　　*

Given the heat of the day and a desire for my armpits not to emulate those of Harold Jayne, I decide to drive home for a quick shower and change of clothing before the evening's surveillance. It also affords me the opportunity to drop off my laptop rather than risk having it lifted out of the jeep: I've already lost one laptop that way.

I find Wayan on the sofa watching one of the Thai TV soap operas, or *likay*, to which, I suspect sadly, she is becoming addicted. When we first came to Samui I thought these shows were awful, but now that I am fluent in Thai I realise that they are way beyond awful. As Wayan's Thai improves, I am hoping she will reach the same conclusion. But maybe not.

"Mr. David, Da said you would not be home for dinner."

"It's OK, Wayan, I'm not staying. I have to go out again."

"But I am glad you are home. I have something you can help me with."

"Oh?"

She produces the Lewis Carroll work and indicates a book-marked page. *"Why is a raven like a writing-desk?"* she asks, presumably thinking this is a suitable question for a detective. "I believe it is a riddle."

"I haven't the slightest idea," I say.

"That is what the Hatter says. They are always drinking tea because time stands still at six o'clock. It is a *very* strange book. Are you sure it is not about drugs?"

I reassure her on this score, attempt to explain the English concept of *nonsense*, fail, and go upstairs for a shower. The bedroom has been cleaned and sparkles in the sunlight. All of Claire's perfumery, lotions and potions, are arranged neatly on the dressing table. I put a squirt of her favourite Chanel on my wrist, close my eyes and inhale deeply, savouring the woman, not the couture. I open the sliding door to the big wardrobe where Claire's dresses hang next to my own clothes, select an anonymous outfit for my evening's observations, and lay it out on the bed. From the balcony I look down into the garden and see Wayan arranging incense sticks in the *san phra poom*, or spirit house. She is ensuring the spirits are not offended by making offerings. Given that she has already done this in the morning, and that there are more incense sticks than usual, I think perhaps her dreams are troubling her. I wonder whether Thailand's invisible beings are listening or, failing that, whether the Balinese gods' benevolent powers extend this far north. I certainly hope so.

Why IS a raven like a writing-desk?

*   *   *   *   *

Early evening finds me sitting at an outside table in a restaurant opposite the Ocean Pearl while the Bangles' 'Eternal Flame' plays in the background. Later I have more serious business at Girly Bar Heaven, but for now curiosity to see Jingjai – albeit at a distance – has brought me here. I needed to eat anyway, and this place is expensive, so better that it is on Vogel's tab. My trusty telephoto lens has already captured a few images of the girl and so far she is doing nothing more than the job warrants. She does, however, give the barmen a run for their money when it comes to mixing cocktails: she can flip the bottles and glasses around and shake with the best of them: all the while displaying a smiling *panache*.

I have just put a piece of stir-fried steak in my mouth when an unmistakably Geordie voice close by exclaims, "It's David Braddock, isn't it? Aye, it is you, isn't it?"

I have to swallow the mouthful of meat before I reply, "It is."

Leaning over the floral trough that separates the restaurant from the pavement is a stubbly, weather-beaten head that looks only vaguely familiar. No name comes into my mind. I see sun faded clothing and socks worn with sandals. Not a good look. The speaker senses my puzzlement and says in a gravelly voice, "Sinclair. Kenneth Sinclair. 'Geordie' to my mates. We met a couple of years back, if you remember."

I nod an 'ah' politely, although I have no recollection of where or how we met.

"Well, that's a coincidence. I don't see you for two years, and then the same day I decide to come and see you, I bump into you like this. It's champion, man." He notices my long lens camera. "Oh, I see you're working. Listen, I don't want to interrupt –" he says sitting down at my table interrupting, "– but I've got a bit of a problem that you might be able to help me with."

I want to say, *Listen, I've had a tiring day and I've a long evening ahead of me. The last thing I need right now is some blunt Northern-type spoiling my dinner. I'm very choosy about whom I accept as a client and at this moment my general impression of you is not favourable.* Instead, I say, "Uh-huh."

"You see, I was talking to your maid and she said you're the best man on the island for a job like this."

"My *maid*? I don't have a maid."

"The Balinese lady. Wayan, isn't it?"

"She's not my maid."

"Oh, isn't she? What is she then?"

I let this go. "Why were you speaking to Wayan?"

"Ah, well, bit of a cock-up on my side. I was late collecting my nine-year-old from school, and she saw the lad was on his own, and she, well, sort of kept him company until I showed up. We just got chatting. Wayan reckons you're quite a detective, sort of Samui's answer to Sherlock Holmes. Although perhaps she exaggerates a bit, eh?"

"Well let's see." I lay down my fork, pause, and look at him. "Shall we try some deduction?"

"If you like," he says.

I pause another moment or two for effect, and then I say, "Alice,"

"What?"

"Your boy is reading *Alice's Adventures in Wonderland* at the moment."

"Is he? That's more than I know."

"Yes, he is."

"How do you know that?"

"Just very simple deduction," I say smoothly. "I happen to know the manager of the local bookshop. About three weeks ago I was in there and he had just had a big delivery of *Alice in Wonderland* books. When I asked him about it, he said it was an order for Year 4 at the English School. If your son is nine, that puts him in Year 4, and given that Wayan never ventures any further than Chaweng, and always follows the same route into town, she probably met him outside the English School. In these circumstances, he is reading *Alice in Wonderland*. I could also add – although this is only a guess – that given the ethnic mix of children at the school, there is a high probability that your wife is Thai, and, given your son's age, at least ten years your junior. Finally, having observed the stain on your shirt, I surmise that you may have had spaghetti for dinner."

Sinclair is staring at me. "Bloody hell," he says.

"Impressed?"

"Very."

"Before you get too impressed perhaps you should ask your son if he really is reading that book."

I resume my meal and try to look nonchalant.

"You like them mouse shit peppers?" he asks irrelevantly, indicating the *prik knee noo* on my plate. "Too hot for me."

I nod, and Sinclair scratches his chin thinking of what to say next.

Since my uninvited companion shows no sign of moving, and is obviously too thick-skinned to take a subtle hint, I look over toward the Ocean Pearl and abruptly take on the aspect of a man who has just seen something important. I snatch up my camera, mumble an 'excuse me' and start snapping shots. He finally takes the hint. "Oh, well, I can see you're busy. Erm ... sorry."

Keeping my attention focused, so to speak, on the camera, I produce a business card and hold it out to him. "It's OK, I'm afraid I need to concentrate on this. Call my office. My assistant will schedule an appointment at the office and we can talk properly."

He takes the card. "Ah yes, well, I might feel a bit awkward coming to your office in broad daylight, and I was wondering ..." He tails off as I continue to be highly attentive to my camerawork.

Eventually he says, "I'll call then. Goodnight, Mr. Braddock."

"Goodnight, Mr. Sinclair."

I stay in position until I am sure he has gone, then I delete all the meaningless photos I've just taken and turn back to my steak; but I have lost my appetite. I tell the waiter to take away the plate. I order a cappuccino and light up a cigarette. David Bowie's 'Ashes to Ashes' starts playing.

I muse on how ridiculously easy it is to impress some people, at least some of the time. How desperately they want to believe in magic. Maybe we all do. Conceivably we'd all be a lot happier if the world were made up entirely of smoke and mirrors. Logic is, after all, an unsatisfying substitute

31

for a magician's wand. If Sinclair had applied Occam's Razor, he could easily have concluded that my 'deductions' had come principally from a conversation with Wayan and that, accordingly, I am a second-rate detective but a first-rate psychologist. How often – I continue reflecting – is it that we see what we want to see, rather than what is *really* before our eyes. In the trade we call this *confirmation bias*, and our brains are riddled with it. We take a position on something and thereafter only see whatever confirms that position, ignoring all evidence to the contrary. Still, three cheers – or at least two – for confirmation bias: without it I wouldn't have a business. Monkey thinks 'detective', monkey sees 'detective'. Not that I'm labelling all Geordies as monkeys. Just the ones who interrupt my dinner while wearing socks with sandals.

Across the road Jingjai is still mixing drinks. While she smiles and jokes with the customers, she does not seem inclined to engage with any particular one. Perhaps she is too busy at the moment. Perhaps they are not her type. Perhaps it is too early in the evening. Perhaps this job is making me overly-cynical. I ask for the bill.

*   *   *   *   *

When I arrive home around 11.30pm Wayan has already turned in, but Claire is still awake in the bedroom.

"Hello my darling," she says, "you look tired."

"A little." I dump my camera on the dressing table.

"It must be awful for you taking photographs of pretty Thai girls all evening."

"It's hell. Unfortunately, my tastes only run to flame-haired English women."

She laughs. "You're such a liar. Let me see your war wound."

"It's just a scratch and it's healing already. Shame, really. *Scarface*

32

Braddock had a ring to it. I'll have to come up with some other marketing ploy."

"Or get into another fight."

"Or get into another fight. That would work."

I rub my eyes and sit down on the bed.

Claire says, "Seriously, are you all right? Tell me about your day."

I tell her about the emotional gangster's wife, the unemotional German, the broken-hearted Slough-dweller, the rude Geordie, and the latter part of my evening in Girly Bar Heaven, snooping around and clicking a woman with thick ankles.

"That is *not* chivalrous," she lectures me sternly.

I feel chastened, but unburdened. "Tell me about *your* day."

She sighs. "My day? What transpired for me today? What would you guess? Everything and nothing as usual. Waiting, waiting, waiting for something to happen. Good, bad, anything. Anything old, anything new, anything borrowed, anything blue. But nothing happens. Ever. Most days I may as well be dead."

"That's not funny, Claire."

"No," she says, "Sorry. Sorry to be so ... enigmatic. But you know, my love, I can't *really* tell you about my day if you don't already know. You understand that, don't you?"

I don't reply.

"Come to bed, David," she says gently.

"I can't," I reply curtly. "I wouldn't be able to sleep now. Anyway, I need to get some photos downloaded and finish up a report."

"But you look exhausted."

"I'll only be half an hour."

"I need to sleep now, even if you don't."

"It's OK, you sleep. We can talk tomorrow."

"Yes, tomorrow. There's always tomorrow."

I pick up my camera. "Goodnight, Claire."

"Goodnight, David."

I go downstairs to my study and fire up the laptop. I download tonight's pictures of Miss K from the camera: pictures of Miss K leaving her house with her Thai husband, riding with him on his motorbike, kissing and fondling him in a bar. Each photograph displays a time and date stamp. I save them into a file with earlier pictures of her and attach the file as an annex to my report.

The report is addressed to a Canadian client, Joe Mears. Joe is a gentle fiftysomething widower from Toronto with a ruddy, kind face and silver-grey hair. His more streetwise younger brother (whose name I forget) had brought him on an extended holiday to South East Asia to 'show him some real life'. While in Samui, Joe had met Kung, a thirty-five-year-old divorcee, and, much to his surprise, had fallen for her. His brother, a more experienced Asian traveller, had forseen problems and brought Joe along to see me.

I read through my draft report on Miss K. I always use initials in my reports: my viewpoint is that it helps to depersonalise what is a very personal issue, and starts a distancing process when the news is bad – as it usually is. I also strive to keep the language objective and the content factual. The human element from myself I reserve for the accompanying email.

The summary reads:

> As instructed, Miss K has been under investigation
> and surveillance from [date1] to [date2].
> Inquiries have revealed that Miss K is not a divorcee,
> as represented, but is in fact still married. Her
> husband, Tai Tanchan, is employed as the restaurant

manager in the Sea Garden in Bophut. They have no children.

Mr. and Mrs. Tanchan own a house on the northern outskirts of Chaweng, where they live with Mr. Tanchan's elderly mother. The address is [address1]. Inquiries into the apartment address [address2] of Miss K given to this Agency by the client, reveal that it is let out to Miss K on a short-term rental basis.

Miss K has been observed on three separate occasions entering the apartment late at night with different Caucasian males. In each case the male in question did not leave the apartment until the following morning.

Annex 1 gives details with times and dates of our observations.

Annex 2 contains various surveillance photographs of Miss K. Such photographs are time-stamped for cross-reference to Annex 1.

We can include as Annex 3 copies of any relevant certificates, filings and other documentation, but since these are in the Thai language and client does not read Thai, no Annex 3 is included. These can, however, be supplied on request, with an English translation at extra cost.

It looks OK. I fill in the square-bracketed dates and addresses and save it as a final version.

When I open my emails, however, I find I have just wasted the last twenty minutes.

There is a mail from Joe.

Dear David,

I recently received an email from Kung explaining that she and her ex-husband have decided to give their relationship another try. While this is sad news for me, I appreciate her honesty.

Naturally this makes your efforts on my behalf redundant. There is no need for you to send me a report.

Please keep any balance on your retainer. If there are any further costs, let me know your bank account details and I will organise a transfer.

Kind regards, Joe

The romantic in me says that Kung had an attack of conscience and felt unable to take further advantage of this sweet guy. The pragmatist in me says she was tipped off about my surveillance, or saw me snapping photos, and decided the game was up. Either way, I am happy not to have to send Joe my report. We all need our little illusions. Or do I mean 'delusions'?

I reply.

Dear Joe,

I understand. I am sorry things did not work out for you.

There are no further costs to my account. If I can be of service to you at any time, please do not hesitate to contact me.

Best wishes, David

I attach the report file and annexes and forward the email to Da.

Da

If you are not in labour, please convert attached to
PDF and file under Closed Cases.

David

I logoff and power down.

As I switch off the study light and emerge into the hall, I notice a white
envelope on the floor by the front door. I pick it up. My name is written on it
in a hand I have seen before.

I take it into the study and open an anonymous-looking folder I had
tucked away at the bottom of a locked drawer. From the folder I remove
another envelope and compare the two. The envelopes are the same – cheap,
white and obtainable anywhere on the island. On both my name is written in
capital letters with a black pen in a style that looks either childish, or the
way a right-handed person might write with their left hand.

I spread my handkerchief out on the desk and place the second envelope
on it. After putting on some surgical gloves, I take out some dusting powder
and a small brush and carefully check the envelope for fingerprints. Other
than my own on the corners, there are none. I slit the envelope open with a
paper-knife. If this was *CSI*, I could check the gummed flap for the writer's
DNA. But this is *KSI* (*Koh Samui Investigator*), and I have no such technology
at my disposal. I carefully extract a single sheet of paper and repeat the
dusting procedure. Nothing.

I shake off the powder and lay out the paper beside the letter from the
first envelope. I am comparing two A4-sized sheets of cheap photocopying
paper. Both have been neatly folded twice, and the printing on both is in
Ariel Bold from a lazerjet printer.

The first letter says

HOW DO YOU SLEEP AT NIGHT?

The second says

WIVES CAN BE A PROBLEM

I put the envelopes and letters into the folder, and the folder back in the bottom of the desk drawer. I tidy up, lock the drawer and put out the light.

3

"and what I want to know is
how do you like your blueeyed boy
Mister Death"
E.E. Cummings, Selected Poems

This morning I go to the temple for one of my regular spiritual cleansing sessions.

Wat Son is a small but colourful Buddhist temple clinging to the hillside not far from my house. The wat is not on the standard tourists' itinerary so there I can meditate without being surrounded by gawping visitors or plagued by souvenir sellers. The only wares on offer here are merit and the necessary paraphernalia of devotion. I have rarely seen another white face there, and that suits me just fine.

Aside from the main temple building, the complex comprises a courtyard, some outbuildings, a walled garden and the monks' quarters. One of the outbuildings houses a glass case which contains a mummified monk dressed in traditional robes. In his cupped hands he holds a painted wooden lotus, the eponymous symbol of Buddhism. Some wag – I suspect the Old Monk who is in charge of the temple – has put a pair of mirrored sunglasses on the mummy. The devout claim this is so that you can see your own *karma* reflected back at you. I think it's just to demonstrate even Thai monks have a sense of humour. Or perhaps someone thought it was nicer to look at than a corpse's sewn-up eyelids.

The day's heat is already gathering strength when I arrive, and the courtyard is quiet – only a few locals and one young, orange-robed monk sitting on the wall, his head buried in a newspaper. As I pass by him I see he is reading the football results. "Manchester United wins again," he says brightly, giving me the thumbs-up.

39

I buy incense, flowers and gold leaf to rub on the Buddha statues, slip off my shoes and enter the temple, passing under a large stone arch in the form of a nāga, or serpent. Although there is no-one around, many incense sticks are burning and the sunlight streams through the windows exposing the peeling paint and setting alight the dust particles in the air. I experience one of those moments where time's arrow is suddenly halted in mid-flight, or seems to be. In the centre of the temple, the larger-than-lifesize golden Buddha sits impassive and I can feel around me the world of *samsara* crumbling before his blind gaze. *I am not a god,* he had said, *I am simply awake.*

I light a bundle of incense sticks and holding them between my palms, bow several times to the statue, before kneeling and bringing my forehead to the temple floor. After this, I present the rest of the incense, along with the flowers and gold leaf, before walking backwards respectfully out of the space. I slip on my shoes and go in search of the Old Monk.

I find him sitting beneath a tree in the garden, his bright eyes fixed on some point in the middle distance. While I wait for him to finish his meditation, I look around the garden. Although Thai Buddhism follows the Theravada tradition, there is something of Zen in this garden: not so much colour and many rocks, even some raked gravel shaped into lines and circles. But then the Old Monk, who exercises a hypnotic influence over the others here, is impatient with such sectarian distinctions, and I have heard him quote from Mahayana and Chán scriptures. He even likes kōans – paradoxical riddles which have no universal 'right' answer. *Buddha is Buddha,* he proclaims. *Although there is really no Buddha to be found at all,* he adds with a Zen twinkle.

At length, he notices me. "Ah, the White Tathagata returns," he says to me in Thai. (We always converse in Thai although we both know very well he speaks English.)

"Old Monk," I give him a high wai.

"Are you looking to pierce the veil of reality this morning?"

"That would be good. However, I fear it is beyond me today."

"Nonsense. Sit with me and meditate awhile."

"It's too hot for me out here to meditate," I say wiping away the perspiration from my neck and face with a handkerchief. "I'm burning."

"The whole world is burning," he responds tersely, rising to his feet. "Have you not read the *Fire Sermon*? Everything is burning, everything is aflame. The eye is aflame, the ear, nose and tongue, all the senses. Your body, even your mind is aflame. And you worry about a little sunshine? The sun is *there* to make us disenchanted with the corporeal world."

"Thus have I heard."

His eyes flash suddenly, "So why have you come here today, mmn? Is it to show your farang skin so that you will impress the ignorant ones here and they will come and do business with you?"

It's worked out well that way so far, I muse to myself. But I say, "I don't think anything. I come here *not* to think."

"Hrmph," he grunts. "Better. I don't believe a word of it. But better. Give me one of your cigarettes."

I light us both a cigarette, although I'm pretty sure we shouldn't be doing this.

He looks at me for a while. "Your mind is cloudy and swirling with too many inappropriate thoughts. Like the proverbial teacup, full to the brim. You first need to empty it before you try to pour in anything else."

I have heard this speech before. "You are so right."

"Walk with me. Walk slowly: you should always walk slowly. And do not talk. If you do this you might learn something of use to you."

I follow him out of the garden and along a narrow track that winds upwards through the trees. He takes a final puff on his cigarette and crushes the butt beneath his sandal. I do the same with mine: everything is dry and I do not want to start a forest fire.

A few minutes later we emerge into a small clearing with a view out to the sea above the tree-line. In a shaded spot there is a small wooden bench and he indicates for me to sit on it. I watch his bony frame draped in orange as he stands, unmoving, gazing out over the dazzling sea, looking for all the world like a prophet of the Old Testament. I start to relax.

I allow my eyes to de-focus, then close them and feel the slowing of my heartbeat. I concentrate on my breathing and the space between the inbreath and the outbreath. The moving light images behind my eyelids steady their dance and I imagine them coalesce into a single candle flame. Because I am so wired this morning, I struggle to eliminate intrusive thoughts and my meditation is shallow and fragmentary. I become aware of sweat droplets running down my face, but I am partially detached, afloat on a strange sea. There is an incomplete melting of the barrier between *I* and *Other*, but at least I feel some sort of inner stabilising. Today I know, however, I will not experience that mysterious and inexplicable interpenetration, and the gateless gate will remain closed to me.

I hear the Old Monk clear his throat and take this as a signal to reopen my eyes. In spite of my inability to achieve any depth in my practice, the tension in my neck and shoulders has disappeared. The colours I see are brighter, almost luminous, and my ears are attuned to the smallest sounds. Slowly, time starts to move again.

After a few minutes more, without a word and careless of whether I am following him, the Old Monk sets off back down the path. When we reach the garden he stops and turns to me.

"Is your mind clearer now?"

"Much clearer."

"It can be better not to talk. Sometimes words can mislead."

"Yes."

"And did you hear?"

"Hear what?"

"Did you hear the sound of one hand clapping?"

"No."

He shakes his head. "That is because you listen only with your ears."

*   *   *   *   *

Now it's later, it's quiet apart from the distant boom of dance music, and I'm alone in my office. Night has dropped over the island like a wizard's cloak. I'm seated at my desk, finishing my second whisky, looking at the framed photograph of my flame-haired wife and flame-haired teenage daughter. The picture is about ten years old, taken on holiday with a backdrop of Balinese rice terraces. I can almost smell the happiness mingling with the scent of frangipani. I light a Marlboro and reflect on the events of the last few hours.

The day was all downhill after my meeting with the Old Monk. To appreciate why that was the case, it is necessary to understand a little of my history and the way I go about my business.

When someone reads my somewhat lurid advertisements and billboards – which are designed to sow the seeds of doubt in the farang mind as to the fidelity of his new girlfriend – that someone may well conclude that I am offering my services as a private investigator. So far, so good. They are intended to create that impression. However, nowhere will the reader find the words *private investigator* or *detective* on any of my hoardings or literature, and that is for a very good reason. I am unregistered, and have no PI licence or qualifications. Unless you consider the two-week course I did over the internet, and my library of Mickey Spillane, Raymond Chandler and Conan Doyle as sufficient evidence of professional standing, you would have to conclude I am not a suitable applicant for the status of PI Registered Practitioner. And you would be right. You may suppose, therefore, with some reason that my investigations business operates in something of a legal grey area. As to why I chose this way of making a living for the first time on my arrival in Samui – having previously run car dealerships and import-export and property businesses – is a tale which will have to keep for another time. For now, let's just say I was ready for a change. As are many who wash up on these shores.

Furthermore, if you are curious at this point about my qualifications to act as a therapist, I should perhaps enlighten you that in the UK, *hypno*therapy is a largely unregulated profession, and a three-week course will avail you of the relevant certificates to frame and hang on the walls of your consulting room. Take out some readily-available insurance, print some business cards, and, voilà, you're away. Just don't call yourself *doctor* or sleep with your clients.

However, while a couple of courses and some marketing bumph may get you into these businesses, they will not keep you in business – as many less-successful impostors in Thailand have discovered. For me, the threat of unmasking as an unqualified fraud has receded with time. The longer you go on playing a role, the more it becomes you: and one day you wake up and discover you are in fact the person you have been pretending to be. Nor are my dual identities as PI and therapist as diverse as they appear to be. The thriving PI and the winning therapist share many common features, including the ability to create empathy, to project professionalism and discretion, and to probe and analyse logically. I may be lacking in some relevant paperwork, but these are the types of skills I honed in my years running various businesses, and they have stood me in good stead in my time on the island; along with my obsessive appetite for new experiences, tendency to gallows humour, and my sincerity. As someone once said, *sincerity* is the single most important human characteristic. So once you can fake *that*, you're made.

In truth, when I first came here I had no plans to be doing what I am doing now. I had bought into a small import-export concern in Bangkok through a contact of my father's and had thought to potter between the island and the capital. But I soon became bored and started experimenting first with a therapy practice and later, almost by accident, with investigations work. As a foreigner, drifting into business, in a country like Thailand, is generally discouraged. For a start, there is the little matter of the appropriate work permit – the absence of which can get you deported – as well as a whole other string of quotidian matters designed to trip up the unwary or those with a disregard for the niceties of South East Asian bureaucracy. I most decidedly belong to this camp. In fact I would be a fully-paid-up member of the *I Hate Paperwork Club* if I could summon the enthusiasm to fill in the application form.

I suspect my activities here would not have survived long without an idea, the germ of which came from a conversation with Charlie Rorabaugh, a New Yorker who owns a restaurant and jazz bar in Fisherman's Village. Charlie is an invaluable source of information on the island and its inhabitants, and it was he who told me that Police Chief Charoenkul had a *mia nói*.

The system of *mia yài mia nói* – major wife, minor wife – has a long tradition in Thailand. Until 1934, believe it or not, there was no law in Siam prohibiting polygamy: indeed there used to be no word in Thai for 'polygamy'. All the Thai kings up to Mongkut in the nineteenth century had *sànŏm*; the royal version of mia nói. While this practice lives on today among jâo phâw, politicians and anyone else with money, a practitioner's primary wife may have a divergent view on its acceptability for *her* husband. Having met Mrs. Kat Charoenkul, I had a feeling that she would not be one of those who would be happy with her spouse's fondness for this particular facet of Thai culture. A plan began to form in my head.

I spent a few weeks tailing the Police Chief's black Mercedes, until I tracked down his mistress' address: a sizeable property in Lamai. His routine usually consisted of an arrival just after dark followed by 2-3 hours of presumably illicit behaviour, after which he drove home. I noted that the Chief left his car parked on the driveway, the entrance to which had gates that were invariably left unlocked. The blinds at the front of the house were closed after dark, and the main bedroom where any action took place was at the rear of the house. A bit of silent nosing around on the driveway also taught me that Charoenkul had a tendency to leave police files in the car in plain sight – so much for professionalism.

Accordingly, I came up with a scheme which ran thus: break into his car, steal some files, then go to the house, present the files and say I had caught some kid running out of the drive, challenged him, and he had dropped the files and fled. Of course I would feign surprise and shock when Charoenkul opened the door dressed only in a robe, but give him my assurance of discretion: neither the careless loss of the files, nor his unexplainable presence in some lady's house at 11pm would ever be mentioned. Amazingly, and in spite of Charoenkul's initial suspicion, the scam worked. By way of a return of favours, my papers were 'fixed'. At least they were fixed after a fashion. I still rely on the Chief's grudging benevolence for my continuing presence here. I am aware, however, that my hold over him has loosened with time, and in the cat-and-mouse game that goes on between us, he is the feline one. But this is only one of the reasons I am wary of Charoenkul.

The other reason is that I have slept with his wife.

The affair was brief, and conducted over several weekends in Bangkok. It began shortly after the scam, when Kat and I found ourselves seated next to each other at a charity dinner – Charoenkul having been called away on urgent police business. There was some outrageous flirting, and one thing eventually led to the other. When you have as little self-control as I do around attractive women, and the forbidden fruit is tasty enough, lust triumphs over reason – just as a Smith and Wesson beats four aces.

I certainly succumbed with Kat. Looking back, I must have been harbouring a death wish, or at the very least suffering from temporary insanity. Anyway, the congress may have been brief but it was memorable. This in large part was due to Kat's considerable skills in the bedroom. If I hadn't known that she was from a good family and that her interest in me was motivated by bored wife syndrome, I would have assumed her talents had been acquired in the soapy massage parlours of Patpong.

That is not to say that Kat is in any way slutty as to her demeanour. If anything, she comes across as at first meeting as stylish, but languid and a little remote. I deduce that this somewhat frosty surface is a manifestation of psychological armour after her years with Charoenkul. It cannot be an easy life with the Chief, and it is one in the public arena: certain behaviour is expected. Closer acquaintance, however, reveals a personality with an exuberant side and, given the right circumstances, one which can let fall the cold aloof exterior. At such moments, a mischievous spark at once illuminates those dark eyes, and a sensual metamorphosis takes place. All the more puzzling, therefore, that Charoenkul should need a mia nói. To my mind, his primary wife's appetites should be more than enough for any man. Assuming that those appetites are not solely reserved for fortysomething farangs (unlikely). Maybe she is just too much woman for him. Either that, or he does not know how to light the spark (more likely).

Once Kat and I had sufficiently scratched our sexual itches – although a few more scratches would have been nice – we parted on good terms. We remain friendly when we bump into each other, as we do occasionally.

Even before the events of today, it had flickered across my synapses that the anonymous letters I have received may relate to Kat. This possibility etched itself more concretely into my head around noon, when Da put her head around the door of the West Office and announced there were two policemen here to see me.

I just had time to bundle my Sudoku book into a drawer and take out an old dog-eared client file before the visitors were shown in. I felt my intestines shrivel as I looked up to see PC and DTs framed in the doorway, but I managed a blasé smile which I knew would annoy PC.

"Officers, please sit down," I said in Thai, "just give me a moment to finish this."

I scribbled a few meaningless squiggles in a margin then closed the file. They had not moved. PC looked like he would like to unzip his flies and urinate over my desk, and DTs was watching me narrowly.

"So what can I do for you today?"

"The Chief wants to see you," growled my least-favourite gorilla.

"Well, let me just check my diary –"

"Now," he said nastily.

I ignored this and called to Da. She squeezed past them and eyed me anxiously.

"*Khun* David?"

"Da, those two appointments this afternoon; we may have to reschedule them."

She and I both knew very well there was nothing in the appointment book and that an afternoon of Sudoku had been beckoning, but she went along with it.

"When shall I reschedule them to?" she asked.

"I don't know. How long do you think we will be, officers?"

PC was not having any of this. "When Chief Charoenkul has finished with you." He smiled unpleasantly. "Whenever that is."

"What's it about, Officer Tathip?" I asked DTs, catching him off-guard and further ruffling his partner.

PC took a pace forward and I could see his hands were itching to get around my throat. "Never mind what it's about, Braddock," he said hoarsely, "move yourself now."

I turned casually to Da. "Best to reschedule the appointments for tomorrow. Oh, and tell the ambassador I'll call him this evening," I added for

PC's benefit.

She nodded and slipped out. I grabbed my notebook and cell phone and stood up.

"Well, officers," I said with a carefree air, "it seems you have my full attention. Shall we go?"

*   *   *   *   *

It was only a few minutes' drive in the police car from my office to the station, but my mind was racing. Uppermost in my thoughts were the anonymous notes, especially the second one:

WIVES CAN BE A PROBLEM

When I had received the first letter, the inference as to a guilty conscience could have referred to anything: after all, I am not exactly an angel. Unless fallen ones count. The second letter *could* refer to Kat. Had she told Charoenkul about the affair? I doubted it. Had he found out somehow? That also seemed unlikely. On the other hand, if the letter-writer was referring to Kat, then he or she had managed to discover the affair somehow. Perhaps Kat had confided unwisely to a friend, and that friend had decided on some mischief-making or blackmail. But there was no inference of a demand for money in the letters: they were more enigmatic. A mischief-making motive would be unfathomable at this point. I presumed that Kat herself had not received any letters: surely she would have been in touch. Maybe it was someone with a grudge just flying a kite. A few dozen disgruntled bar girls would fit this category: although their grasp of the subtleties of English prose would hardly fit the writer's style. Or maybe the "problem wife" referred to was Claire, and this line of thought about Kat was a red herring. Or maybe, or perhaps ...

Perhaps I didn't have a clue, more likely. But I needed to gather my wits if I was going in to front up to Charoenkul.

I saw PC looking at me in the driver's mirror, and I smiled sweetly at him, as if I had not a concern in the world. Neither he nor DTs had spoken a word since we got into the car. Meantime, my insides hardened into a clutch of Gordian knots. The image of John Hurt's stomach bursting open in the film *Alien*, suddenly popped into my head – except that in this version we were in Charoenkul's office, not onboard the *Nostromo*, the stomach in question was mine, and the creature that emerged was smoking a Marlboro and saying, "That's right, this white man has violated your wife, Chief. Let the dirty animal have it."

I became aware we had almost arrived, and I quickly needed to prepare a face for the face I was about to meet.

Bophut Police Station – oddly named in my view since it is in a different town – is the nerve centre of law enforcement on the island. Located conveniently for Girly Bar Heaven on a right turning at the end of Chaweng's one-way system, it comprises three sinister pale grey edifices – each four stories of flat-roofed KGB architecture – surrounded by a high perimeter wall.

As we approached, I could see the Thai national flag fluttering forlornly on a high pole in an internal compound. It appeared to be the only thing moving.

The Old Monk once asked me, "Is it the flag that is moving or is it the wind that is moving?" When I said, "They are both moving", he said, "No, it is your mind that is moving." Before adding with a Zen chuckle, "Although, of course, really there is nothing to move."

Unfortunately, the place was not deserted. A uniformed Thai appeared to slide back the metal gate, which closed behind us with the clang of a prison door. DTs let me out of the car, being careful not to make eye contact. He was trembling slightly. I hoped I wasn't.

I followed the gruesome twosome through some nondescript double doors that led into a reception area where a number of locals were sitting round on plastic chairs looking sorry for themselves. I spotted the Geoffrey Rush look-alike hunched in a corner with a satisfyingly bruised nose for which I was responsible, and a black eye for which I was not. He showed no sign of recognition. The area smelled of apprehension and neglect, and the walls needed a new coat of paint. An overfilled notice board dominated one side, displaying wanted photographs, dire warnings to would-be criminals and, bizarrely, some rooms to rent. Overhead a strip-light flickered in a manner ideal for inducing an epileptic seizure.

Working the reception desk was a foxy-looking female police officer who waved us through, giving me a wink as she did so. It probably meant nothing: I doubted she had any idea why we were there.

We passed through another door, beyond which was a functioning lift. The three of us stood in silence, gazing ahead, as the lift ascended creakily to the top floor. A right turn took us to Charoenkul's ante-room where his skinny secretary was sitting picking her teeth.

"Is this Braddock?" she asked PC who nodded grimly, and we were promptly ushered into Charoenkul's office.

There he sat behind his desk, making notes in the margins of some dog-eared folder, presumably having slipped his Sudoku book into a drawer before we entered. There were the inevitable royal portraits hanging on the wall to the left, above a teak wood book cabinet holding a few books like its heart wasn't in it, and several framed photographs of Charoenkul himself in golf attire. To the right was a pristine whiteboard, presumably acquired to impress some visiting superior officer or dignitary. An air conditioner hummed on the wall behind him.

Charoenkul let us stand like suspects at a line-up for a good half a minute, apparently engrossed in his activity, before announcing without looking up, "You two can go." PC and DTs happily shuffled out, closing the door behind them.

At length, he put down his pen, leaned back in his chair and studied me with his predator's eyes. His uniform and general grooming were immaculate, as always. With his dyed-black hair and thin moustache, overpowering cologne and pot belly, Charoenkul was every bit the Asian peacock. Like many short men, he suffers from a Napoleon complex, in his case augmented by a paranoia that others are talking about him behind his back. He thinks his career has not gone far enough or fast enough; and this he attributes to professional jealousy which keeps him from his just deserts. His nickname – 'Papa Doc' – does not derive from any cuddly association with Bugs Bunny cartoons, but from character similarities with an infamous former dictator. His complexion may not be so black, but they share the same heartbeat of ruthlessness and corruption: brothers beneath the skin.

He patted a book on his desk and addressed me in the Anglo-Saxon tongue. "I have been reading that the word *Braddock* has its origin in old English. It means 'a broad-spreading oak'. Did you know that?"

I indicated a vague affirmative.

"Interesting that the branches of your family oak have now spread out as far as Thailand. Please sit."

I checked the chair was not attached to the mains, and then sat.

"It was good of you to come at such short notice."

"I wasn't aware I had a choice."

He smiled, showing his expensive dental work. "We always have choices in life, Braddock. It is simply a question of deciding whether we can live with the consequences of our choices."

I said nothing. With an experienced interrogator like Charoenkul, I have learned this is the best policy.

He sighed theatrically and rubbed his face before leaning forward and whispering confidentially, "My wife thinks I work too hard. What do you think of that?"

"She's probably right. Wives usually are."

A beat. Then, "Yes. Yes, they usually are."

He pushed back his chair, walked over to the bookcase and picked up a photograph of himself holding a golf trophy.

"I have so little time to myself these days. Responsibilities, you understand." He waved the frame at me. "I was Island Champion for three years running. A record. Now I scarcely have the time to play a round."

Of golf? Or with your mia nói?

He replaced the photograph wistfully and moving behind me put a hand on my shoulder.

"So I need to ask a favour of you."

"A favour?"

The hand stayed on the shoulder and squeezed slightly.

"For our friendship's sake."

Charoenkul shifted back behind the desk, positioned his elbows on it and made a steeple with his fingers.

"A situation has arisen. One which requires the utmost delicacy and discretion."

Here it comes, I thought.

"Oh?"

"I can rely on your discretion, Braddock? That our discussion is confidential?"

"Of course, Chief Charoenkul."

He paused again a moment, as if choosing his next words carefully. The aircon sounded very loud in that space, and in spite of its efforts I could feel the sweat under my arms and in the small of my back.

"Two days ago," he began, "the body of a farang was discovered in a coconut grove outside of Lamai. The body had some interesting and unusual characteristics. It was fully clothed and lying face down. The back of the head had been beaten in with a blunt metal object, and the corpse was severely burned."

"Sunburned, you mean?"

"No. I mean it had been doused with petrol and set alight."

"Not a suicide, then?"

He ignored this and went on, "Naturally, I have every confidence that my men could clear up this matter in due course. However, the Special Investigations Unit from Surat Thani is involved, as can happen in such cases. Consequently, they are carrying out an independent investigation, which is ... inconvenient, and bad for local morale among my force. We have been relegated to a minor co-ordination role in the proceedings. This I do not like."

I bet you don't.

"So far we have managed the situation with the media, but tomorrow the incident will appear in the newspapers. Perhaps it may even make it to national television. I expect the journalists will play up the sensational aspects in their usual irresponsible fashion, oblivious to the damage it will do to our tourist industry on the island. I can only imagine the populist headlines. Because of the Surat Thani involvement, I will not even be leading when we make press releases and – Buddha forbid – if we have to hold news conferences."

Ouch. That's got to hurt.

"It is bad for Samui," Charoenkul concluded.

"And not so good for the poor bastard who had his head beaten in either."

"No. That also, of course, is a tragedy," he responded with his trademark empathy. He continued on, having dismissed the victim as a barely-relevant annoyance. "The Surat Thani officer in charge of the investigation is an old colleague of mine. He has at his disposal forensic and other resources that are denied to us here at this remote outpost of the Royal Thai Police. Ah, what I could achieve here if we had that funding."

Clearly he doesn't like this 'old colleague'. Possibly he is a rival for the promotion that Charoenkul craves: a nice posting to Bangkok, where the money-making opportunities are greater. Although Papa Doc already has so many rackets his game should be tennis, not golf.

"However, we must deal with the world as it is, rather than as we would wish it to be," he intoned philosophically. "But I am neglecting my duties as a host. Let me get you some tea."

He barked loudly to his secretary, and my overstretched nerves caused me to jump in my chair, in spite of my intention not to appear intimidated. His secretary cautiously put her nose round the door, and he gave her the drinks order in his authoritarian fashion. The nose vanished.

"So, Braddock, in summary –" he smiled charmingly, "– I want to employ your services as an investigator." This smelled like a trap.

"But Chief Charoenkul," I said sweetly, "you know very well I am not an 'investigator'. I don't have the requisite papers."

He laughed. "Let us not split hairs, my friend. The permit I have so kindly arranged for you gives you a certain – shall we say – latitude. I merely want you to assist me on this matter."

"When you say *employ my services*, I presume you are not contemplating any financial arrangement."

"You presume correctly. This is one way you can repay your adopted country for all the benefits it has bestowed on you. Indeed, for all the benefits it may yet bestow. I feel sure you value my good offices with Immigration on your behalf, and you would not wish to disappoint me over such a small favour."

So there it was: help him or get booted unceremoniously out of Thailand.

(Incidentally, I am still not convinced this is not about Kat. Papa Doc could be playing a long game, while building a better and more powerful mousetrap. He appears to be viewing the *mia nói* secret as a closed episode, meaning that my bargaining chip has gone. Either that or his poker face is better than mine.)

His secretary appeared with the tea, and we sat in silence until she left. I sipped the tea thoughtfully as he watched me.

"Well?" he said.

"Well, forgive my candour, Chief, but if this Surat Thani professional is already investigating the case, I don't really see why you need me. Besides, won't he be pissed at my involvement? I am just some farang amateur, and murder is hardly my area of expertise."

"My colleague Katchai," he remarked acidly, looking like a bulldog chewing on a wasp, "will not be aware of your role in this matter. It will be our little secret." He let the silence hang heavy in the air.

"So what do you want me to do exactly?"

He relaxed and put down his tea. "Good. Braddock, you have a certain reputation as a man who knows about psychology, and you know how to keep your mouth shut. Furthermore, as a European, you may have some insight into the victim that we poor Thais lack. I want you to do some psychological profiling for me."

"Of the killer?"

"Yes, and of the victim. Both may be relevant. Know the victim and you may find the perpetrator. That is sound logic, is it not?"

"It may be. Unless, for instance, it is some random murder associated with a robbery, in which case the only connection of one to the other is that of time and place. Was the victim robbed?"

"No," he said thoughtfully, "he was not. A charred wallet was found on him, with quite a lot of burnt cash and two melted credit cards in it. The motive was not robbery." He paused.

"Why do I get the feeling you're not telling me something, Chief Charoenkul?"

"Ah," he grinned, "So at last I have awoken your detective instincts.

Excellent. As well as the profiling, I will welcome your insights in this matter."

I waited. He became more serious.

"The victim's name was Hannes Boehme, a 36-year-old Dutchman, in Samui on holiday on his own. He had been here about two weeks when he was killed. As far as we know, he had no criminal record and no known criminal associations. When a girl stumbled by chance over his body, he had been dead about a day-and-a-half. The night of his death, someone fitting his description was seen drinking in Chaweng, but we can't be sure it was him. We have no witnesses, and the forensic evidence is not very helpful since the body was so badly burned. The place where he was found was behind a tree, only a few metres from a dirt road; but the ground was hard from the lack of rain, so we have no information from tyre-tracks. That's about all we've got: a dead end."

"I'm sure you realise that if the murderer was a visitor to the island, he's probably long gone, and your chances of finding him are zero."

Papa Doc looked a little uncomfortable.

"We have reason to believe that the killer may live on the island."

"Why is that?"

He cleared his throat. "Because the murder bears a remarkable resemblance to another one we had here three months ago."

I was aghast. "You mean to tell me that someone else has had his head bashed in, and been set on fire? Another farang?"

Charoenkul nodded.

"But there was nothing about that in the papers. I'm sure I would remember. I would *definitely* remember."

"The incident never made the papers."

"You hushed it up?" I asked incredulously.

"It was not deemed to be in the best interests of the public to create a panic," he said stiffly. "The peak tourist season was coming up and we did not want visitors to be unnecessarily apprehensive. Samui is a safe place."

"Not for Hannes Boehme it wasn't."

"Well, we see that now, naturally."

"So let me get this clear. You dismiss the first killing as a one-off event and convince the mainland police of your viewpoint on this; all the while keeping it out of the press. Then there is a second murder – which can't be a copycat killing since no-one knows about the first – and you are forced to act. No wonder the Surat Thani boys are all over you like a rash."

Papa Doc looked discomfited. "That's a pretty crude summary," he snorted.

"But basically accurate?"

"You could say so."

"So will the first murder hit the press tomorrow also?"

"No. Only the second one. We don't want people thinking there is some Western-style serial killer on the loose."

"There may be a Western-style serial killer on the loose, for all you know." I thought for a moment. "Do you know of any connection between the dead men? Other than their both being *farangs*, presumably?"

He shook his head, "No. The first one was English, not Dutch. He was here with his brother on vacation. It was the brother that raised the alarm." Charoenkul looked annoyed for a moment. "His brother was troublesome and tried to get the newspapers involved. But in the end, good sense prevailed and the matter was kept quiet. Fortunately, the brother is no longer on Samui."

Troublesome? I'd be troublesome if someone had just murdered a member of my family.

"Anyway, now you know the story," he said finally, and with a matter-of-factness that irritated me.

"If I'm going to be any use in all this, I'll need more information," I muttered testily. "What else can you give me on the victims and the forensics?"

"I will have copies of the files sent round to you tomorrow. But I need your undertaking that you will treat them confidentially."

"Well, I won't be leaving them around on the back seat of my car, if that's what you mean," I spat out rather spitefully.

He recognised the unsubtle reference to our early acquaintance and said sulkily, "Of course not."

"And you're not expecting me to be part of some cover-up?"

His face looked outraged, and for a moment I thought I'd gone too far, but he controlled his temper and replied icily, "In the first place, as I explained, the investigation is not mine to run. My colleagues over at Surat Thani want this business cleared up properly. Secondly, given the fact that our local journalists are already on to the recent murder, a degree of transparency is inevitable from this point. There will be no cover-up."

"Although you haven't told the press about the first murder –"

"That is mere detail."

"– but you have told *me*."

He looked up with a start, as the realisation hit him that involving me may not have been such a good idea after all; that he may inadvertently have given me some leverage over him again.

I wondered whether Buddha's expression was like that when he saw the morning star and the thunderbolt of enlightenment hit him. I doubted it. Actually, Charoenkul looked more like he had eaten a bad oyster.

The Chief recovered quickly, however, and purred in his most insinuating tone, "Mr. Braddock, I know you are a man of integrity. We would not be having this conversation otherwise. I merely ask for some goodwill and assistance on your part."

I sipped at my tea, but it had gone cold. I put the cup down again. He was looking at me expectantly.

"Very well," I said resignedly, "I am your creature. How is this arrangement going to work?"

He rubbed his hands cheerfully.

"Secrecy is the essence of our endeavour. No-one must know about this little favour you are doing for me. It would not be good for either of us."

"That much I gathered."

"Then we are on the same page. As I've said, I'll let you have copies of the files, and share with you any progress that Katchai and his team make."

"You have a spy in headquarters at Surat Thani?"

"I have friends everywhere."

"I see."

"You will only report to me personally. However, two of my men here will act as liaison for you, open any doors that need opening, etcetera. I am assigning officers Chaldrakun and Tathip to assist with immediate effect."

Just great. PC's company is about as welcome as a turd in a fondue, and DTs will be less useful than a second appendix.

"Naturally they will have to carry on their normal duties, but feel free to call them any time you need anything." He handed me a sheet with their addresses and contact numbers, which I stuffed in my notebook.

"What do they know about the killings?" I asked.

"Very little. They are just regular policemen, and have not been involved in either investigation. However, both of them are very loyal to me. I have also made it clear that they must ensure not one word about your assignment leaks out. Their jobs depend on it."

"I'm sure that will endear me to them." *Small wonder they were more hacked off than usual when they arrived at my office.*

"I'm also having extracts of the case files translated into English for you today to speed things along. I wasn't sure how well you read Thai."

"Whom are you trusting with the translation?"

"My wife."

A tsunami of nausea rolled over me and somewhere in my head a red light started flashing. "Mrs. Charoenkul?" I said tightly, my mouth as dry as powdered alum.

"My wife has many virtues, Braddock, and many talents. It's better that no-one here is involved: better for your anonymity. See how I look after your interests? You'll see Mrs. Charoenkul later today, anyway."

"Will I?" I managed.

"I want Chaldrakun and Tathip to take you to the crime scene now for a preliminary look around. To help you with initial thoughts and impressions. To get your detective's antennae twitching, as it were." He gave a short laugh, pleased at his own witticism. He was back in control, his earlier wobble forgotten. "After that, I want the officers to bring you to my house for a quick debriefing. You will meet Kat there."

A warning siren cranked up in my head to accompany the flashing red light. This was screwing with my brain.

Hoping my face was as inscrutable as his, I said, "Wouldn't it be better for us to meet here?"

He stretched his arms above his head and gave a yawn. "No. I'd rather you weren't seen here again. Besides, later this afternoon I have promised myself a round of golf with friends. I think my wife is right: I have been working too hard lately. I'll be changing at home, so it's convenient for me to meet up there."

"I see." I decided to let the game play out. "I presume your officers are taking me to the most recent crime scene, and that we'll be visiting the other crime scene later."

Papa Doc blinked at me. "How remiss of me," he said, "I should have mentioned it earlier. There is only one crime scene. Both bodies were dumped at exactly the same place."

*　　*　　*　　*　　*

PC accompanied me out through the main glass doors of the police station while DTs brought the car around from the side compound. They had tried to take me out the way we had come in, but I demurred, saying I wanted a cigarette. I was feeling rebellious and strangely light-headed having escaped from Charoenkul's office with a complete set of genitalia and only minor brain damage. I even thought I might leave a business card with the attractive police woman on reception as we passed through, but unfortunately she had been replaced by some guy with big ears and a constipated expression. Geoffrey Rush had also gone.

Outside was like an oven, and the glare was blinding, but I lit up a cigarette anyway. PC lurked in the partly-shaded doorway.

Is it ever going to rain again?

DTs arrived with the car and PC squeezed himself into the passenger seat. While I was pointedly smoking the cigarette down to the butt, I phoned Da to let her know everything was fine, that I had not been arrested, and I was giving the local police some informal advice on a 'Westerner problem'.

"What sort of 'Westerner problem'?" she asked, half-relieved and half-suspicious.

"Well, apparently lots of European tourists have been demanding their money back, saying Samui girls are all ugly and not at all like the pictures in the brochures."

"Don't make jokes. I was worried. The way you were taken off, I thought there must be some burning issue."

How right you are, I thought.

"No. I'm just helping out with some cultural stuff: getting inside the farang mind sort of thing." This at least was vaguely true.

"Does that mean we get paid?"

"Don't be silly."

"Will you be coming back to the office today?"

"Is there anything in the diary?"

"You know there isn't."

"I'm not finished here yet. Let's see how the time goes. I'll call you later."

"Do you still want me to phone the ambassador?"

"Very funny."

I rang off, flicked away my dead cigarette, and climbed into the car.

DTs drove us slowly out of Chaweng, heading south. We were pressed in by pavements overflowing with brightly-coloured stalls, Indian tailors, racking stacked with glass bottles filled with petrol, women in polo shirts offering massages, double-parked motorbikes, panting dogs, and bemused tourists with peeling heads. The car bounced gently over dusty potholes as bikes weaved around us respectfully. PC read a newspaper while I tried to look inconspicuous. Being seen in the back of a police car is not a flattering character advertisement.

Reaching the Samui Ring Road, the tarmac widens, and the building frontages recede back, allowing the traffic to breathe. Tourist sellers give way to more workaday commercial premises selling furniture, building materials, insurance and groceries. Intermittently, locals' houses lean against each other for comfort, and spread naughtily into neighbouring vacant lots where greenery and cast-off rubbish grow and interbreed. As the road meanders slightly from side to side like a happy drunk, a view of sea will periodically break through on one side, and green hillsides muscle into sight above weather-worn roofs on the other.

Approaching Lamai, we passed a police box from where a bored policeman waved a greeting which my companions ignored. They were concentrating on their bearings.

"Just here," said PC pointing ahead and to the right.

DTs slowed the car and indicated, waiting for a gap in the oncoming traffic before turning gingerly onto a concrete side road.

There were no inhabited buildings immediately in the vicinity of the turning, merely scrubland and some unhealthy-looking coconut trees. The concrete ran out after about a hundred metres, having rounded the grey skeletal remains of an abandoned building project. Presumably the road had been put in by the same overly-optimistic developer. The workmen having long since departed, nature was reasserting herself, and the unroofed structures were losing the struggle to stay above the rampant greenery. Part of the perimeter wall was, however, intact, although starting to crumble against the combined onslaught of plant and insect. It was behind this wall that the road stopped and, after a few metres, the ground began its climb towards the hills, and the coconut grove proper began.

DTs stopped the car on the concrete, put on the handbrake and left the engine running. He and PC both turned simultaneously to look at me. I looked back. "Well?" I said.

"Straight ahead," grunted PC. "Even you can't miss it."

"Aren't you coming?"

"No. We're going for some lunch. We'll be back in about an hour to pick you up."

I slammed the door closed. DTs turned the car around and drove off.

Now what?

I was alone under the early afternoon sun, equipped only with a cell phone, notebook, pen and full bladder. First things first. I relieved myself against the wall and, mindful of my karma, opted against flooding the teeming termite nest beside me. I lit a cigarette and took in my surroundings.

The wall and the trees concealed the clearing from the Samui Ring Road. Though it was close enough to hear the traffic, the sound was muffled. There was no sign of any functioning human habitation. The tree-covered land rose quickly towards the hills. Surprisingly for an island cul-de-sac, there was no discarded litter, prophylactics or dumped dead electrical devices –

which suggested the locals avoided the place.

Where the road ended, the earth was packed hard and dry as the Gobi. No imprint of tyre tracks, no cigarette butts, zilch. A few metres ahead of me the trees began, and I could see coloured tape marking out the crime scene. Here there were some cigarette ends, but these could have been dropped by bored or cogitating policemen. The dry grass and undergrowth had been trampled by several pairs of feet, and any trail from a dragged corpse obliterated accordingly.

I ducked under the tape and examined the ground. Next to one of the trees, the grass was blackened and scorched over an area about the size of a tall man's body. The killer must have used a fair bit of petrol because the flames had licked up the bark of the tree.

The victim had either been bludgeoned to death here, or killed beforehand and dragged into the trees for the bonfire. Given where the body was found either hypothesis was credible. I hoped the file Charoenkul was preparing for me might provide some illumination on this point.

I lobbed fallen coconuts ahead of me to alert any snakes, and wandered around under the trees awhile looking for God-knows-what. I was grateful for the shade, and wished I had a bottle of water with me. I thought about the Chief, my benefactor, and tried to piece together the chain of events that had brought me here.

Assuming Papa Doc was not playing mind-games with me over his wife, he must be desperate. Why else involve an unqualified Brit in a murder investigation? I racked my brains for what I knew of the Royal Thai Police. If I remembered correctly, the organisation was headed up by a Commissioner-General, and was broadly structured along military lines: all the ranks above constable were army classifications. Leaving aside the special units which dealt with threats to national security, border patrols and the policing of Bangkok, domestic law enforcement fell primarily under the Provincial Police Division. The Division was geographically subdivided into 9 Regions, to whom significant powers had been delegated from Bangkok as part of a reorganisation to improve effectiveness. As the Chief had said, Samui came under the Surat Thai Region ('Region 8'), and the HQ was on the mainland in Surat Thani Town. I vaguely recollected some recent bribery scandal over police entry examinations held there.

After Charoenkul's balls-up over the first murder, his superiors at HQ were evidently breathing down his neck; and the fact that they had sent in an investigation team must be a heavy blow to his prestige and promotion prospects. Now he could not 'officially' investigate the case – or rather cases. If, however, with my help he 'stumbled' over the solution, he could not be criticised for acting against orders, and his reputation would be restored. That, of course, was a big *if*.

Wondering whether to light up another Marlboro, I found I was standing on a narrow dirt track that wound through the trees. It must have spurred off from the concrete road, but I had overlooked it because of the dried-out earth. Having nothing better to do, I decided to follow it.

It snaked its way west, rising quickly with the ground, and after a short way, rounded a very large boulder, the product of some prehistoric landslip. Atop the rock was perched a dilapidated wooden structure, sitting above the tree-line. I could see now it was to this shack that the path led. I scrambled up, sweating, and was surprised to see the building's inhabitant.

On the dusty porch, soaking up the sun, sat an ancient-looking Thai man. His emaciated body was shirtless, his lower half wrapped in a faded sarong, and he wore mirrored sun-shades. He turned his head as I approached.

"Sàwàt-dii khráp," I said rather breathlessly.

He returned my greeting without getting up. I could see he didn't have many teeth left, and on closer acquaintance his skin was like a wrinkled walnut. Also his left foot was malformed: a *devil's hoof* it would have been called in less enlightened times.

"I'm sorry to disturb you," I panted in Thai, "but do you have any water?

It's a thirsty climb up here."

"Yes," he gave a short smile, "I don't have many visitors. Help yourself, there's water inside."

I passed behind him into the wooden hovel, which smelled of heat and old age. There was one multi-purpose room which served as kitchen, dining room and lounge; a curtain presumably screening off a sleeping area; and a partially-open door revealing a primitive toilet. Small gaps in the roof let in some sunlight and, I surmised, rain during less dry days. The place was ramshackle but clean, and the floor had been recently swept. There were small shelves around the walls, on which were piled carved wooden boats with intricate markings of lotus flowers and demons. A very large plastic bottle of water stood on the side, next to a gas ring and some neatly stacked pots, pans, plates and cups. I gave one of the cups a quick dusting with my handkerchief and splashed in some water. It was tepid, but refreshing enough. I could hardly expect ice-cubes: the place had no electricity.

I strolled back out onto the porch. The old man had not moved and seemed unconcerned with the presence of a stranger.

"This water's very welcome," I said. "My name is Braddock."

"You speak Thai well for a farang," he responded. "I am Yai."

From this vantage point, the sea was visible beyond the greenery and the roofs of Lamai. The abandoned development and the concrete road were hidden by the coconut trees, much to my disappointment. There was no other building close by that I could see.

"You have a good view of the sea from here," I remarked.

He chuckled at some private joke, and said, "I like to look at the sea, yes."

"It's unusual to find a Thai who likes sunbathing."

He shrugged. "I am an old man, Mr. Braddock. I want to feel the sun on my body while I can. I do not know how much longer I have to enjoy it."

The world was quiet while I sipped the water and thought about what to say next.

67

"I used to be a boat-builder," he said, breaking the silence, "but I cannot do that anymore. Now I carve miniature boats for the tourists."

"You live alone? It must get very lonely up here."

He shrugged. "I like the quiet. My grand-daughter brings me food and supplies and cleans up. No other islanders will live around here. They think the place is cursed."

"Why is that?"

A look of sadness flickered across his face. "Some thirteen years ago a man died in the coconut grove. Local people think his demon haunts the trees. And there have been things that have happened since." He paused. "You saw the half-built houses?"

"Yes."

"A businessman bought the land cheap because nobody else wanted it. He thought he would make a lot of money from the foreigners. But from the start there were problems. Local people were reluctant to do the building work. Two workers were bitten by snakes while they were clearing the land. Then a labourer died on the site of a heart attack. Finally the businessman went bankrupt, and the project stopped. More bad things have happened recently. Everyone thinks it is the work of the demon. You know we Thais are superstitious. You will not find anyone around here after the sun has gone down."

"Yet you are not afraid to live here."

"If there is a demon he will not harm me." He paused again, and then said sadly, "The man who died was my son."

"I'm sorry. I'm sorry for your loss."

At this point, I thought the old man was going to break down, but he choked back the emotion and recovered himself.

"So, whether or not he is a demon, I should like to meet him. That's why I live here; in the hope that he will come to me, one last time. So that I can comfort his restless spirit. I have been waiting for thirteen years. I will go on waiting."

"But you've never seen anything?" I asked rather lamely.

The old man laughed suddenly. "That would be difficult." He removed his sunglasses and showed me his opaque eyes. "As you see, Mr. Braddock, I am blind."

I tried to hide my shock, then realised I did not need to.

"Cataracts?" I said.

"Yes, cataracts."

"You know there is a simple operation –"

He interrupted me with a wave of the hand, and put on his glasses. "Who can afford such things? At my age, it would be a waste of money. Better that my grand-daughter has whatever money we make. My only regret is that I have not seen her since she grew up. Although my hands tell me her face is beautiful."

We let the words float in the air awhile. Then I said gently, "Yai, I am not exactly here on a social visit. I am a private investigator and I am looking into some recent events that took place nearby." He was silent. "I am not the police," I said as reassuringly as I could. More silence. "You mentioned some bad things that happened in the grove recently," I prompted.

"Yes," he said eventually.

"What do you know about them?"

He sighed, and his small body seemed to shrink further.

"The police came to see me three times," he said. "The first time was about three months ago; then twice in the last few days. Different policemen. They told me not to talk to anyone about it."

"I can imagine. But it's OK. I already know. Two dead men have been found in the grove."

He nodded. "My grand-daughter found the second one. I don't know who found the first. The police questioned her too. She was very frightened."

"Yai," I said softly coming close to the old man, "do you think your grand-daughter would talk to me?"

"I don't think she will be able to help you, Mr. Braddock. And I cannot either. I heard nothing." He snorted bitterly, "Obviously I saw nothing."

"Nonetheless, I would like to talk to her. With your permission, of course. I swear I will not frighten her."

He thought about it.

"I could meet her here, if you prefer. I would not ask if I did not think it important."

Finally he shrugged. "I will speak to her, but I cannot promise anything. It is her decision."

I put a card into his hand. "Thank you. Please ask her to call me soon. In the next day or so if possible."

I put the cup back in his shack and left him sitting there like the hero of Eliot's *Gerontion*: the old man in the dry month waiting for rain. Except that Yai was not waiting for rain. He was waiting for something altogether different.

*   *   *   *   *

Charoenkul's house is on the hillside above Bophut, on the north of the island and close to the Samui Golf Club. It is an impressive, two-storey villa with well-kept grounds and an air of superiority not unlike that of its owner. Clearly it cost more than an honest copper could afford.

The trip there from Lamai was quick, mainly because PC was driving; and by the urgency of his manner I took it that we were working to the Chief's tee-off time.

My companions stayed in the car while I was shown into the sanctum by some lady-retainer. Kat Charoenkul was pouring tea.

"Ah, Mr. Braddock," she said rising and greeting me in the grand European manner, "It has been a long time. How are you?"

"I'm well thank you, Mrs. Charoenkul."

As always, she looked like she had just stepped out of a beauty salon. Her hair was not the usual Thai black but coloured sandy-brown, and cut in a style that suited her exquisite cheekbones and Modigliani-like features. Her sky-blue dress hugged that toned body like it did not want to let go. And who could blame it. It made me want to lie on the grass and look up at the blue sky above me. Actually, it made me want to lie on the grass and look up at that sky-blue dress above me; but I needed to keep those thoughts out of my head.

"What happened to your face?" she asked indicating the scar under my eye.

"Occupational hazard."

"Some bar girl's fingernail, perhaps?" she suggested, a mischievous smile playing around her red lips.

Knowing I may only have a moment before Charoenkul appeared, I dropped the formality. "Listen Kat," I whispered urgently, "something has happened. I need to talk to you. Alone. Can you meet me somewhere this evening?"

"Not this evening, no. We have a dinner engagement. What is it?"

"I can't talk about it now. But we *need* to talk, trust me."

"A mystery, Mr. Braddock?" she smiled laconically. "How intriguing."

Before I could say anything further, Charoenkul arrived, looking dapper in his golf gear.

"Ah, Braddock, good. You're later than I expected. Let's go into the garden."

"I was just about to offer our guest something to drink, darling," protested Kat.

"No time. I have to be at the Club for tee-off on the hour. If I'm late it will be very embarrassing. Come on, Braddock." The Chief swept outside and I followed in his wake.

"We'll have some tea after you have finished, Mr. Braddock," Kat called after us, "and I apologise for my husband's bad manners."

The Chief led me into his sala which was furnished with large wicker chairs.

"We can talk here," he said. "So what do you have to tell me?"

"First of all, let me say this would have been a more useful exercise if I'd seen the reports beforehand."

"Yes, yes," he replied impatiently. "Just talk."

I tried to arrange my thoughts into some kind of order.

"Obviously I can't talk about the body or the method of killing, but there are one or two interesting things that strike me. The first is the location itself. Local people steer clear of it because it has an unsavoury reputation. There's a superstition about an evil spirit which is reputed to haunt the place. That suggests the killer may have some very specific local knowledge: he knew it was unlikely anyone would be around there, particularly at night. But why use exactly the same location for the second victim?"

Charoenkul didn't respond. He waited for me to go on. So I did.

"Well, one plausible explanation is that our man is just stupid and unimaginative. Another possibility is that, having seen the first murder go unreported and pretty much uninvestigated, the killer felt confident or arrogant enough to repeat his modus operandi."

"I trust you are not suggesting the Samui Police Force is responsible for the second murder," Papa Doc said flatly.

"I'm not suggesting anything, Chief. I'm just exploring the possibilities," I remarked breezily.

"You are also assuming that both murders were done by the same person."

"I'm assuming a lot of things until I've seen those files. It would be quite some coincidence, though, if these murders are not connected, don't you think?"

He relented. "Fair enough. What else?"

"I'm sure I'm not telling you anything you didn't already know –"

"Never mind about that. Incidentally, I didn't know about the local superstition. How did you find that out?"

"From an old man who lives in a shack nearby."

"The blind man?" He snorted. "He didn't mention that to us."

"He probably didn't want you to think he was crazy as well as blind."

"Perhaps," he said, not convinced. "Did he tell you it was his granddaughter that found Boehme's body?"

"Yes."

"Do you want me to have her picked up so you can talk to her?"

"No thanks." I didn't want Charoenkul's goons scaring the girl again. "I've already made arrangements myself to see her."

"As you wish. What else?"

"I'm curious about how the victims got there. Whether they travelled independently or with their killer. It's not exactly within walking distance of anywhere, and not somewhere you would go unless you had a specific reason."

He nodded.

"Let me study the files, try and put some ideas together and get back to you. Otherwise it's just guesswork. I also want to go back to the coconut grove after dark. I might be missing something important seeing it in daylight."

"Very well."

"I'd also like to speak to your original investigating officer, since I can't very well talk to Katchai, and Chaldrakun and Tathip don't know anything."

Charoenkul shook his head slowly. "I'm afraid that would not be a good idea. My investigating officer has become far too cosy with the Surat Thani team. His discretion may be compromised. Sorry, Braddock, but I cannot afford the risk of his talking to you." The Chief sighed. "It is a great shame. I fear my officer's promotion prospects may be damaged after Katchai's team have left the island. Anyway," he went on brightly, "his work has been fully documented, and the files will be in your hands tomorrow." He consulted his watch. "I have to go. We'll talk again soon."

I made to rise, but he indicated for me to remain in my chair.

"No, please stay. My wife seems very anxious to give you some tea before you leave, so you shouldn't disappoint her. You must have bewitched her with your English charm, Braddock," he said. "I wonder whether it is safe for me to leave her alone with you." His mouth was smiling, but the eyes were cold.

I began to mutter something self-deprecating, but he was already going. "I look forward to our next conversation," he called back over his shoulder.

Inscrutable.

I called Da on my cell phone to let her know I'd be coming back to the office soon. She informed me I had a new-client appointment the next morning ("So don't be late"), and that in addition Sinclair had called in to see me.

"I told him you were out on a case. He was quite insistent, even wanted your home address."

"The cheeky bastard."

"Anyway, he asked you to call him urgently. I can give you his number now if you like."

"I don't like. Let him wait, the bloody Northern Neanderthal."

"He's not so bad. I think he's quite shy really. Probably hiding his sensitivity underneath that brusque exterior."

"Thank you, Sigmund Freud."

I hung up and carefully examined the sala from top to bottom. I was inspecting the underside of the table when the lady of the house arrived accompanied by a tray-carrying maid. Kat raised a quizzical eyebrow but only said, "Refreshments, as promised, Mr. Braddock. Just set the tray down,

Sahli, I will pour."

After the maid had left, my hostess said, "What were you just doing, David?"

"Checking for hidden microphones."

"You are joking, of course."

"Not really, no."

She poured the tea and handed me a cup. "What is going on?"

"Have you received any strange phone calls recently, Kat?"

"No."

"Or anonymous letters?"

"No. Why?"

"I have."

"Really," she said, looking amused. "Another occupational hazard?"

"It's not funny."

"What do these anonymous letters say?"

"They're very vague. They might be about you."

"How flattering."

"Are you going to take me seriously at all today?"

"David, *tirak*, when I find you crawling around on all fours in my garden looking for hidden microphones, that is somewhat difficult." She took an elegant sip of tea. "Do you imagine my husband has lured you here to eavesdrop on our conversation? To find out whether we have been doing something inappropriate together?" she asked sardonically.

"It's possible. Has he been acting at all weird lately?"

"I can only think of one person I've seen recently who was acting weird," she chuckled.

"Well, I've been having a weird time," I huffed. "First I start getting anonymous letters then the Chief drags me into an 'unofficial' murder investigation. Finally, I discover you, of all people, are translating the reports on the murders. Doesn't that all strike you as a little odd?"

75

"All right, I'll be serious for a minute," Kat said. "Tell me what these anonymous letters say."

I told her. She was unimpressed.

"It sounds more like a prank to me. Your problem is you have a guilty conscience."

"So you don't think your husband knows about us," I pressed. "You haven't noticed anything different in his behaviour?"

"On the contrary," she replied, "recently his moods have been quite erratic. But that has nothing to do with you and me. It's this murder business. Deng is a very proud man and his standing in the Royal Thai Police is being undermined by this team from Surat Thani. He is under a lot of pressure," she said earnestly. "I am worried about him."

It caught me by surprise to hear Kat referring to the Chief fondly as 'Deng'.

"I need a cigarette," I said. "Do you mind?"

"You know I think it's a filthy habit, David. But if you must."

I lit up.

As if reading my thoughts, Kat said, "I know the two of you have a tense relationship, and I expect he's blackmailed you somehow into helping him. My husband is a difficult man, but he is my *husband*."

I hadn't seen this loyal side of her before, probably because I hadn't chosen to. When you're in bed with a beautiful woman, the last thing you want to dwell on is her relations with her pot-bellied husband.

"Is that why you agreed to do the translation?"

"It's one of the reasons."

"What are the others?"

"Boredom," she said. She gave me a girlish smile. "And once I knew who it was I was doing the translation *for*, well, that gave the job an added attraction."

"Now *I'm* flattered."

"I haven't seen you for a while. Plus you do still have a special place in my affections," she said teasingly, rubbing a foot against my leg. "You are the only man I've ever been unfaithful with."

I gave her an old-fashioned look and she laughed.

"Well, *nearly* the only man. Anyway, it's good to do something useful for a change. I wouldn't want you to think I'm only good for sitting in salons having my nails done."

"I'm still having trouble equating the Kat Charoenkul I know with the one who sits in a study working on police files. *Something* about you has changed, and I don't just mean your hairstyle. Which is very fetching, by the way."

She shrugged. "You'll work it out. You are a detective, after all. Do you want more tea?"

"No thanks. I have to go. So the files will be with me tomorrow?"

"Without fail," she said, giving a mock salute.

"Will you bring them over, or will it be one of the Chief's men?"

"Would you like me to?"

"If you have the time. I'll try to control myself."

"I hope you won't try too hard."

On the drive back to my office, I reflected on Kat's situation. She had hitched her hopes to Charoenkul's star, which in the early days of their marriage must have been burning bright. His luminous career was now in danger of transforming into a black hole. As an intelligent and cultured woman, Kat must have seen Samui as a temporary stop-over before elevation to the brighter lights of Bangkok. I imagined she felt like a caged animal, frustrated and confined on this small island. Small wonder she'd been propelled into the arms of a smooth-talking farang. I considered for the first time how much she personally had invested in her husband's elusive promotion. It wasn't even as though she had any children by way of

77

consolation. Ironically, Papa Doc was not a *papa*.

I also realised that my own situation here bears some sad parallels to Kat's. Leaving aside Claire, the Old Monk, and Charlie Rorabaugh of Bophut Jazz, my only sources of sophisticated conversation are the Police Chief and his wife; both of whom have been exposed to Western education.

Arriving back at the office in sombre mood, I asked Da to ring Wong's Home Delivery for some Chinese noodles to calm my rumbling stomach. I declined to call back Sinclair in spite of her obvious disapproval, and locked myself away in the West Office to jot down some thoughts and to cruise the internet for information on corpses, crime scenes and criminal psychology.

*   *   *   *   *

That was hours ago.

Da has long since gone, and the remnants of Wong's noodles sit cold and unappetising in the bin under my desk. The room smells like a cocktail of grease and cigarette butts with a dash of BO and Bells.

Nice.

I am no wiser, but much better informed about corpses, crime scenes and criminal psychology. I really should go home.

But before I do, I need a fix of Chinese wisdom. I unwrap the fortune-cookie that I've been saving and crack it open.

The slip of paper inside says

Like many Western men who settle in Thailand, you have an addiction to risk, questionable morals and a desire to have sex with as many women as possible; although in your case you prefer married ones.

Naw, I'm just messing around. It actually says

Be prepared. Something big is coming your way.

If fortune-cookies were really that accurate the world's policemen, social workers and psychiatrists would all be redundant. And so would I.

4

"Words are fools
Who follow blindly once they get a lead.
But thoughts are kingfishers that haunt the pools
Of quiet"
Siegfried Sassoon, Limitations

When I throw my straw hat at the hat rack and it actually stays on the peg, I feel a disproportionate rush of satisfaction. But this is snuffed out almost instantly when I see Da glowering at me from behind her desk.

"Khun David," she says in the strict tones of an experienced dominatrix, "The West Office smells like a smoky alcoholic abattoir this morning. It is disgusting. I've had to open all the windows. You cannot use it for clients today."

"Do I have any Western clients today?" I ask superciliously.

"You *should* have."

"How do you mean?"

"I mean are you going to ring Mr. Sinclair now?"

What is it with bloody Sinclair? Wayan was frosty with me over breakfast too. She'd bumped into the Geordie the previous day outside the school and he'd been moaning that I hadn't called back. The normally-diplomatic Wayan had even been tempted to confess that my 'brilliant deductions' about his son were just a sly confidence trick. Of course she hadn't – she's far too nice to drop me in it – but her displeasure made for an uncomfortable orange juice and muesli.

"Later," I say.

"I think that's very unprofessional, if you want my opinion."

"I don't." I shake my head. "What is this strange fascination you and Wayan have with this charmless oik?"

80

"He's shy and kind of vulnerable."

"Vulnerable my arse."

"Admittedly he doesn't have your sophisticated turn of phrase," she smiles acidly, "but he doesn't stand drooling over my breasts either."

Obviously Da and Wayan like him, and just as obviously I don't. I don't know why I don't, but I just don't.

"Give me his number," I say with bad grace.

I press the numbers on her desk phone, take a deep breath, and slide into my concerned professional voice. After a few rings he picks up.

"Mr. Sinclair? David Braddock here. I'm sorry I've not called back sooner."

To my surprise, he sounds happy to hear from me. I'd expected irritation, at the very least. I offer an appointment today, but he's too busy. Da mouths *be nice*, so I make an effort.

"Look, um, Mr. Sinclair," I say, knowing I'll regret the gesture I'm about to make, "tomorrow's Saturday. I don't normally meet clients at weekends, but I feel I've not given you much of a service so far. Would you like to come in tomorrow? Or I can come to you if it's awkward for you to come here."

"Could you come to me?" he says. "I have to stay in tomorrow morning, I've got a bloke coming about my trees. Shall we say around eleven o'clock?"

"Fine. Give me your address."

I jot it down and end the conversation. I replace the receiver and squint resentfully at Da. "Now I'm doing house calls. Happy?"

"Very. And that wasn't so hard, was it?" She thaws. "Go through and I'll make you a coffee. You've got plenty of time before your appointment. You're in much earlier than I expected."

"Well, I was missing you."

"No, you're here because Wayan was making you feel guilty about Mr. Sinclair, and you couldn't wait to get out of the house."

"Wayan rang you?" I say, appalled at this female conspiracy.

81

She nods.

"Unbelievable."

Da kisses my cheek fondly. "I'll get your coffee," she says.

I plonk myself down in the East Office with the English language newspaper and look at the front page.

Thoughts of Sinclair and the Monstrous Regiment of Women are banished from my mind as I read the headline *Dutch Tourist Found Murdered in Lamai*. While the content of the article is not so lurid as Charoenkul had feared, there is still more than enough to give the Chief apoplexy. The method of killing and the torching of the body are not mentioned, but the murder is described as 'brutal' and the coconut grove crime scene is identified. Worse for Papa Doc, there is a large flattering colour photograph of Katchai, who is named as the police officer heading up the investigation. His quoted words infer that the presence of his special team on the island is due to the investigation being beyond the expertise of the local boys. There is the usual puff that 'the full resources of the Royal Thai Police will be deployed to bring the perpetrator to justice', along with reassurances that Samui is a safe destination for tourists. It strikes me as naïve to imply that the murder is an isolated occurrence, even if it is good copy for the hotel trade. Katchai has already put himself in the same boat as the Chief: one with leaks in it. There is not the slightest hint about the first murder. Is the Royal Thai Police digging itself a deeper hole in which to bury some of its officers' careers? As I read on, I see there is some studied outrage from the journalist that such an event could occur here, but (as yet) no criticism of the law enforcement body. The article concludes with the helpful advice to 'be vigilant', and an appeal from Katchai for anyone with information to come forward.

I skim through the rest of the paper but there is no editorial on the incident.

Da puts down my coffee and asks if I've seen the headline. She remarks on what sort of a world she is bringing her baby into, and I pat her bump affectionately. As she waddles out, my cell phone rings. The display tells me it's Charoenkul.

"Have you seen the newspapers?" asks the annoyed Chief.

"Only the *Island Daily*."

"The others are just as bad."

"At least they've omitted the grisly details. It might be a marketing boost for petrol sales, but it's better not to put ideas into any impressionable heads. As a farang I have a vested interest in there being no more human bonfires."

"Quite," he says without a trace of concern.

I'm very tempted to ask him how his golf game went, but I bite my tongue. I'm pretty sure that given his state of mind his swing would have been all over the place. But there is no sense at this point in pouring trouble on oiled waters. Plus I'm not feeling especially brave today as far as the Chief is concerned. There is still the little matter of his wife to be considered.

"The files will be with you after lunch. Get working on them."

I'm about to tell him I have other things to do and a living to make, but he's already rung off.

I wonder whether Kat will bring in the files personally. Then I wish I'd put on a nicer shirt. Then I think about why I wish I'd put on a nicer shirt. Then I realise why I wish I'd put on a nicer shirt. And why I'm preening myself in the washroom. I press my forehead against the mirror and murmur an obscenity to myself. Next I take a good look at the idiot in the mirror. He shakes his head at me in sad disbelief, then splashes his face with cold water and tells me to get a grip.

I take his advice, put away the newspaper and wipe my mind clear of Police Chiefs' wives, anonymous letters and murder cases. I have a real live paying customer arriving in about half an hour, and I need to compose myself.

I return my empty coffee cup to Da and enquire about the client.

Da puts aside her baby magazine and consults the appointment book.

"Mr. Prasert Promsai," she replies. "He didn't say why he wanted to see you. He's a new client."

"Actually Da," I say mysteriously, heading back into the office and pausing at the threshold for dramatic effect, "he isn't." I close the door.

I reacquaint myself with Prasert Promsai's case notes. Far from being a new client, in fact he is one of my very first clients; preceding the arrival of Da at the David Braddock Agency. Although it is quite some time since I last saw him in a professional capacity, he attends the same temple as I do, and we wai each other on a regular basis.

Awaiting his arrival I sit cross-legged in the armchair, close my eyes and give attention to my breathing. By the time Da knocks on the door of the East Office I am the personification of calm.

Prasert Promsai and I greet each other in the traditional Thai manner. It is some weeks since I last saw him at the temple and he looks tired. He is a big man for a Thai, which is just as well because in the early days of his construction business he was the third man in the trench. He once told me that he is descended from Genghis Khan, and has the blue bruise on his buttocks to prove it. Of course if this urban legend of the bruise were true, then the Mongolian Conqueror must have impregnated a goodly proportion of the females of his Asian Empire and, from what I have read, genetics and evolutionary theory are against it. But like all good fairy stories, it persists.

There is, however, something decidedly un-Thai about my old client, even if there is no doubt about his devout Buddhism. Of the three Buddhist fires, his primary weakness is the fire of anger. When he first came to me his fiery temper was in danger of destroying his life. His short fuse had alienated his wife and most of his family, and was threatening to engulf his burgeoning business, in spite of the fact that he was known as the most honest and reliable builder on the island. For a proud Thai man to turn to a foreign counsellor about such a personal issue shows how desperate he had become, but over several sessions we worked through his anger management problem, and he learned techniques to overcome it. His marriage had survived and his business had continued to prosper. The last appointment with me had been an emotional one, and we had embraced unashamedly dewy-eyed at its conclusion.

I had expected him to keep our sessions private, but he had spread the good word about my little office to friends and colleagues at Wat Son and beyond, and accordingly many new Thai clients had beaten a path to me. In many ways my counselling business owes a big debt to Prasert, although quite why Samui islanders entrust their emotional well-being to the David Braddock Agency still remains a mystery to me. It seems a very un-Thai thing to do. I must ask the Old Monk about it sometime, if I can catch him in the right mood.

"Khun David."

"Khun Prasert."

"It is good to see you," he says.

We usually converse in Thai although his English is good, especially when he is waxing lyrical on columns, support beams, floating rafts and bathroom fittings.

"It is also good to see you, old friend, although I cannot help wishing it was at the temple and not in my office."

He nods sadly. "Yes, I need to call on your good services again."

"Tell me about it."

He takes a deep breath, and begins. "Since I last saw you here I have, as you know, learned how to control my bad temper. I must admit I have had the occasional lapse, but generally I can stay calm and keep my demon in check. However, lately I have felt a growing of the fire in me and I worry that my anger will once more explode and consume those that are dearest to me. I have exhausted the techniques you gave me without effect."

"Speaking of exhausted, you don't look as though you're sleeping."

"I'm not. When I do sleep my mind is not at rest. I'm sure I'm having bad dreams, but I can never remember them when I wake up. I go to the temple and make offerings, but nothing changes. My brain is so full of turmoil I cannot even meditate properly."

"If you've talked to Buddha and he can't help, what makes you think I can?" I ask with a smile.

"Buddha has helped," he says. "He told me to talk to you."

Not for the first time, this straightforward man makes me feel humble. I pour us both a glass of water from the jug Da has brought in. I think about Prasert's reference to his inner demon, and Yai's son's demon, and Wayan's offerings to appease the demonic spirits. To the average Western mind this is the mumbo-jumbo of the uncivilised, but I know that is simply labelling. The Freudian psychologist's *Ego* and *Id* are not so different to the idea of internal devils, and for the split personality, the depressive, the schizophrenic, and for a host of others tormented by the contents of their minds, the fears are just as concrete as if they possessed horns and teeth and bloody claws.

I do not say any of this to my client, however. Instead I say, "Prasert, you talk of the demon inside you. But we both know it is your own pain and apprehension that needs to be addressed. It is part of you, not some separate supernatural being that haunts you."

"Buddha said that too."

"Well I'm relieved Buddha and I are on the same page. Tell me what is happening to disturb you."

"It is my brother," he says, and I see the hurt in his eyes. "I have not spoken to you before about my brother Nikom, so I need to explain some things." He drinks some water then replaces the glass on the table, thinking how to begin. I remain silent.

"My brother is twelve years younger than me. My family's circumstances

86

were such that I had to care for him when he was young, and to look out for him when he was older. He was always getting into trouble: fights, drinking, unsuitable women. But his gambling was the worst. As you know gambling is one of the curses of my country, and many families have been impoverished or ruined by it. Our father was also a gambler."

He pauses and looks down at his hands awhile before continuing.

"Some years ago when my building company was taking off, I took my brother into the business. At first Nikom was hopeless, undisciplined and sloppy, but he gradually started to settle down and after a while I put him in charge of dealing with suppliers. However, even then he was more concerned with making money quickly. He got to know a local businessman who was fronting a property development for some Western investors. Against my better judgement, Nikom persuaded me to take on the building work on terms that were unusual. As you know, we builders normally expect to be put in funds by our customer for materials and labour, but with this deal I was outlaying my own money first and being reimbursed later. You can guess what happened. The businessman went bankrupt, the project was never completed, and I lost the money. It wasn't enough to drive my business under, but it was a big setback. Naturally my brother and I quarrelled bitterly about it, even to the point where punches were thrown."

He looks at me and manages a small smile. "This was some time before I came to see you. My self-control was not so good back then, as you know."

"I know."

"Anyway, we had a major falling-out, and he left for Bangkok."

"I take it your brother has a temper problem too."

He nods. "What a family, mmnnn?"

"Go on."

"Well, after a couple of years in Bangkok Nikom was in a mess. He'd got himself involved with a very bad crowd – I still don't really know what he was doing there, but I doubt it was legal. He owed money: mainly gambling debts. What could I do? He was still my brother. I paid off his debts and brought him back to Samui, to his old job in my office. We had an emotional reunion and he promised not to let me down again."

"And he has?"

Prasert lets out a deep sigh, and then becomes agitated. "I have learned recently that Nikom is taking bribes from some of our suppliers. My business of course ends up paying for this ultimately, since the suppliers charge higher prices to cover the payments to Nikom. Not only that, but my personal reputation suffers. How is anyone to know I am not pocketing some of this money; that I am not the one behind it?"

I can feel his rising frustration and see the tightening in his lips and throat. He clenches and unclenches his hands, and finally grabs the glass of water in front of him and drains it.

I wait a moment before asking him, "Are you sure your brother is taking kickbacks? Do you have any proof?"

"I am sure." He sounds bitter. "Many of my suppliers are old friends. We talk." He looks at me. "I am sure," he says definitively.

"And Nikom is still gambling?"

"Cock fighting. It is always his passion."

"Does your brother know that you know?"

Prasert gives a *who knows?* shrug.

"So you haven't tackled him about it?"

He shakes his head.

"Why not?"

My client rubs his eyes and I see the anger leave him, to be replaced with a sad helplessness.

"I am the only family my brother has. He has no wife, not even a regular girlfriend. Aside from my own children, he is my only living blood. Nikom may be deceitful and rash, but he is also a generous man. He loves and indulges my children like they are his own, and they love him."

"Forgive me, Prasert, but that hardly entitles him to rob you and to ruin your good name."

"I know this."

"What does your wife think about it?"

"She loves Nikom, but is also angry with him. Of course she does not know the whole story; but she knows most of it."

"Your wife is a very understanding lady."

"She has been with *me* for all this time, so that goes without saying."

I take a sip of water and consider his situation. He wants me to give him advice, but I cannot. All I can do is to help him to come to his own decision; one in accordance with his own needs and his own conscience.

"What options are you considering?" I ask.

Prasert chuckles suddenly and some of his anxiety falls away. "I knew you would not tell me what to do," he says.

I smile. *You know my methods, Watson*, I think.

"Prasert," I say, "My job is to assist you in finding the answer that is right for you. Not the answer that would be right for me."

He is silent. I think a little provocative behaviour on my part might be appropriate now.

"OK, I'll start," I say. "Option One: go to the police."

Prasert looks aghast. "I couldn't do that!"

"Why not?"

"He is my brother, Khun David."

"So?"

"The shame would be more than I can bear."

"I don't see why. Any shame is his, not yours."

"Absolutely not," he exclaims emphatically.

I sniff. "All right then. Option Two: kick him out of your business. That way he can't do any more damage. You'll stop feeling stressed and your business will be the better for it."

89

"I have already done that once. Look at how badly that ended."

"Prasert, your brother is a grown man. At some point he has to take responsibility for his own behaviour. As long as you keep parenting him he will never grow up."

He shakes his head. "I do not want to lose my brother again. When that happened before I was miserable."

"Which brings us to Option Three: do nothing."

"But how can I do nothing? I can't trust him. Lately I have even been thinking that perhaps this stealing from me started long ago. Perhaps he made money from the building project that collapsed and cost me so much. I have no peace in my mind about him." Prasert shakes his head dispiritedly. "I have considered all three of these options, Khun David," he says, "and none of them is acceptable to me. I do not know what to do."

"There is a saying about having the serenity to accept the things we cannot change, the courage to change the things we can, and the wisdom to know the difference."

"I have neither serenity nor courage right now," he murmurs, "and we builders are not famous for our wisdom."

I lean forward and touch him gently on the knee. "There is an Option Four," I say.

He looks up abruptly. "An Option Four? What is that?"

"Talk to him."

"*Talk to him?* I can't."

"You can. In fact you have no choice but to do so. Tell him what you know, what you suspect. But above all, tell him how you *feel*. Perhaps the decision of what happens next should not be your decision alone. Maybe it should be a decision for both of you to make."

"What happens if I become angry?"

"Only a saint never experiences some form of anger," I tell him. "However, we can work on that now while you're here, and reinforce the techniques you already know. But when you speak to your brother, focus your thoughts on your sadness and disappointment. Be honest with him. If he really is a good man at heart and has real feelings for you, you will know from the openness of his response. If not, then you will know what to do, and you won't need me to advise you."

I know he wants to say *BUT* and to raise a thousand objections. But instead he sits silent and mulls over my words. After a while he assents and we spend the next hour or so working on emotional triggers, anchoring, and some neuro-linguistic programming exercises.

At the end of the session Prasert taps his head, smiles, and tells me he feels like his brain has just had an upgrade. However, I have not finished with him just yet.

"So when will you talk to your brother?" I ask.

"Very soon," he says.

"Not good enough," I reply. "I need to know when exactly."

Prasert puffs his cheeks. "Is this what you farangs call 'tough love'?"

"This is what I call 'follow through', Prasert. You came here to fix a problem. I want to make sure it gets fixed."

"Very well," he says with resolve, "I will speak to him this weekend."

"Good. Call me on Monday to tell me how it went."

He laughs. "And if I don't call you, you will call me, is that right?"

"That's how it works."

"You are a hard taskmaster, Khun David. But Buddha was right to tell me to come and see you."

*   *   *   *   *

It's heartening to know I'm getting personal recommendations from Lord Buddha these days, but I'm not about to get too carried away. Nonetheless, enjoying my lunchtime Thai green curry on Chaweng beach, my mind is free of burned corpses and unfaithful bargirls. In a funny kind of way, it feels like I'm the one who has had the therapy session this morning. But then it's quite often like that. I have my own homespun hypothesis that the path to contentment may be through immersing yourself in the problems of others: for while you do this, your own problems don't exist. Some philosopher has no doubt already said this more eloquently. Pity I can't consistently put this into practice for myself. Maybe I should write a book, *Braddock's Enlightenment*.

On my walk back to the office I don't find the persistent calls of 'Taxi! Taxi!' quite so annoying as usual.

I see the tramp again in the same doorway, but this time a policeman is telling him none-too-kindly to move on. I hang around until the policeman has gone and give the guy some Baht notes. He gives me a high wai before shuffling off down the street, his scruffy baggage hung over his black undernourished shoulders.

* * * * *

Da is pleased with me. She says Mr. Prasert Promsai left much happier than when he arrived. After this she tells me I should be doing more counselling work and less hanging around in bars with a camera. I'm inclined to agree, were it not for the fact that sexual jealousy is what pays most of the bills. My therapist's halo, however, is already starting to fade as thoughts of self-preservation reassert themselves.

Yai's grand-daughter has not called, although I realise the blind man may not yet have passed on my message.

Da has just made me another coffee when the police files arrive in a large manila envelope. To my disappointment the person delivering them is not Kat Charoenkul but the unsmiling and nervous DTs. I presume his crime-fighting partner is outside in the car either reading the *Bangkok Post* or sulking.

The twitching one leaves and I try to put Kat out of my head, although that's difficult knowing the translation on my desk is her work. A handwritten note from her is pinned inside apologising for not delivering the files personally, but explaining that she has errands to run and that I should call her if I have any questions or if there is anything else I should like her to do. I re-read this last bit. I can think of several things I would like her to do, most of which involve exchanging bodily fluids. I go to the bathroom, wash my face in cold water, readjust my package and sit down again with Kat's package.

Inside the envelope there are two files labelled with the names of the dead men. I open the one titled *ANTHONY ASHLEY*, put to one side the photocopied Thai documents and photographs, and start reading the transcript.

Ashley was English, and forty years old when he died. He was the owner of an insulation business and was married with two step-children. This was not his first trip to Thailand, or even his first visit to Samui; although on previous occasions his wife had been with him. This time, however, Ashley was accompanied by his younger brother, Peter. The two were on holiday to mark Peter's leaving the British Army after twenty years of service. The transcript doesn't record how happy Mrs. Ashley was with the prospect of her husband flitting off to Thailand for a couple of weeks with his ex-squaddie sibling.

The two men had been staying at Lotus Blossom Villas, a three-star hotel on Chaweng beach; and according to the younger brother's statement hadn't ventured far. They'd hired a couple of motorbikes for the duration, but apart from an evening sortie into Lamai to watch the *Muay Thai* (Thai kick-boxing), one trip up to Big Buddha, and a boozy picnic at the Namvang Waterfall, the rest of their time had been spent around the restaurants, massage establishments and bars of Chaweng. So far, typical unattached

European male behaviour.

The younger Ashley was quite candid about his own experiences and pick-ups in the watering-holes of Girly Bar Heaven, but rather more coy about this brother's adventures. He insisted (somewhat improbably) that Anthony had done his drinking in the reputable bars of Chaweng – although there was a passing reference to his striking up a 'friendship' with an unnamed Thai girl. I'm guessing this was in deference to the feelings of Anthony's wife, not wishing her last memories of him to be of a whoremongering husband.

After nine nights on the island, Anthony Ashley had vanished. When Peter knocked on his door in the late morning of their tenth day on Samui there was no response. By mid-afternoon his brother had still not returned, and repeated calls to his cell phone were answered with the same message: cell phone switched off. Anthony's hired motorbike was in the hotel car park, and his passport, air ticket and traveller's cheques were still in the hotel safe. But of Anthony himself there was no sign. The police had been contacted and the usual bureaucratic nonsense followed.

According to his statement, Peter had last seen Anthony around 9.00pm the previous evening when the brothers had parted company after dinner at their hotel, each to go to his own separate pleasures. In Peter's case that meant picking up two girls at the Lolita Bar, paying their bar fines and taking them back to his room for a night of sweaty passion. The girls had corroborated Peter's story. But where Anthony had gone, his brother didn't know.

Photographs of the missing man were downloaded from Peter's digital camera and given to the police; but a time of frustration and anxiety was inevitable. Since the island police have seen it all before – the missing man who turns up a couple of days later after being holed up with some attractive girl – there is a waiting period before the lawmen will even fill in any paperwork, let alone start looking for a missing person.

As it happened, Anthony did turn up before the police started looking for him, but not in a good way.

A young Australian couple on a motorbike had taken a wrong turning off the Samui Ring Road outside Lamai, believing the concrete surface would lead them to one of the island's waterfalls. Instead it had lead to a dead end, and a grisly discovery among the coconut trees.

Peter had been called in to identify the body, which must have been quite a task considering its condition. There were a few things to go on: his brother had lost the tip of the little finger on his right hand, had a metal plate in his left leg as the result of a motorbike accident, and had prominent canine teeth. These points were enough for a preliminary identification. The burnt meat was Anthony Ashley.

There then appears to have been some desultory and half-hearted questioning of possible witnesses at the hotel and surrounding bars, but reading between the lines it looks as though Charoenkul and his boys were quietly burying an embarrassing episode which might be bad for the tourist trade. The interview with the old blind man is recorded, but as I already knew, he was oblivious to what had gone on.

I guess it might have been better if they could have fitted up the brother; but that would have been difficult, even assuming they'd intimidated the bar girls who'd supplied Peter's alibi. Hardly surprisingly, there is no mention of Peter's being 'troublesome' or of the considerable effort that must have gone into keeping the story out of the newspapers.

Forensics revealed that Anthony Ashley's death had been caused by repeated blows to the skull. From analysis of the damage, these hits had been delivered while he was lying face down. The body had been turned over onto its back, liberally soaked in standard-grade petrol and set alight. There was no trace of either the murder weapon or the receptacle(s) used for the gasoline. The report is silent on the subject of tyre-tracks, drag marks and footprints, and I'm guessing the inexperienced local plods had already contaminated the crime scene before anyone suitably professional had arrived. It doesn't say whether Ashley was killed in situ, or whether he was taken there already dead. There was no abandoned vehicle around and, as already mentioned, Ashley's hired motorbike was at his hotel.

In the absence of further trails to follow, the investigation had petered out.

According to the brother, so far as he knew, Anthony Ashley had no specific friends on Samui, and no business associates. He was simply your average tourist. Except that your average tourist doesn't end up as charcoal under a coconut tree.

I look at the photographs of the body and am glad I am not eating anything. The pictures of the face with the burned-off flesh are particularly gruesome. There are also pictures of the living version of Ashley, apparently taken recently in Samui. None of them has a Girly Bar Heaven backdrop as far as I can see, which does give some credence to the story that he had been behaving himself while he was here. Then again, maybe his brother had just been selective with the digital downloads. The images show a gaunt-faced man with slightly receding dark brown hair and pale skin. The prominent canine teeth give him a somewhat vampiric air. He is not, however, sporting a black, red-lined cape. A fuzzy copy of the passport page showing his photograph is included for good measure. Of course, that picture looks nothing like him.

The passport tells me he was born in London on 13th January 1964, which makes him a Capricorn in the Chinese Year of the Water Rabbit. The characteristics of Rabbits, if I remember correctly, are that they are fanciful, affectionate and very lucky. I stop myself mid-stream. I need to focus on rational issues and not get side-tracked into Sino-centric metaphysics. My brain also needs a break before I start on the second file.

I ask Da to make me another coffee, strong and black; but when I take out my Marlboros she banishes me outside. Clearly she has not yet forgiven me for the state of the East Office.

"Da, this is a three-cigarette problem," I protest, but this allusion to Sherlock Holmes is lost on her.

"Outside," she says firmly. "Your coffee will be here when you get back."

I go down the stairs, feel the sun's intensity, and recoil back into the shade of the doorway like a denizen of the undead. Under this Samui sun, a vampire would crumble to a heap of ash before you could say *suck my neck*.

How did I get on to vampires?

I flick my lighter and look at the flame.

Enough thinking, already.

I light up and enjoy my cigarette with an empty head, idly watching the smoke curl about itself as it rises up into the heated air.

My nicotine level thus topped up, I go back inside to the aircon, Da's coffee and the second transcript.

Hannes Boehme's file is thicker than Anthony Ashley's, reflecting a greater degree of professional thoroughness and interest than with the first investigation. There are lots of witness statements, a thick bundle of photographs and a businesslike forensic report which must have been rushed through more quickly than usual. I put aside the Thai documents and work systematically through Kat's English-language version.

The second victim was born in Utrecht, Holland on 10th October 1968, which makes him a Libran and an Earth Monkey (impish, enthusiastic and must do things his own way – in case you were wondering). Boehme was unmarried and worked as a trader in diamonds for a respected international organisation based in Amsterdam. He had been to Thailand a number of times before, but had not visited Samui for some years. So far as is known, he had no friends or contacts on the island, and was travelling alone. His arrival form into Thailand declared the reason for his visit as 'holiday'. He had flown from Amsterdam to Bangkok where he spent three days before flying on to Samui. He had pre-booked over the internet for two weeks' stay in a deluxe room at the plush Apsara Hotel, which sits on the hill to the north of Chaweng, overlooking the sea.

Eleven days after his arrival, Boehme's body was discovered in the same spot as Ashley's. The finder was Yai's grand-daughter, Bee, who was taking groceries up to the old man's shack.

The speed of response of Katchai's investigation team was impressive. They had done a thorough job interviewing all the hotel staff, as well as Yai and Bee. They had also started showing Boehme's photo around bars and restaurants in Chaweng. This last task was still ongoing due to the large number of establishments involved.

According to the hotel staff, the Dutchman had not brought any girls back to his room and had only eaten in their restaurant once. He had been polite but reserved, not mixing with the other guests. He was seen to swim in the hotel pool every morning before breakfast, after which he went out for the day in the car he had rented on first arriving. That same car had been found parked on the main street in Chaweng, so the officers had concentrated their efforts there.

As for the other interviewees, Yai and Bee, as I already knew, had nothing of value to add to the investigation. A barman in one of the better bars in Chaweng thought he *might* have seen Boehme on the night he had been killed, but he couldn't be sure. The manager of upmarket Zen Food said he had eaten there a couple of times but was vague about when. None of this struck me as terribly surprising: farang faces must all start to look the same in high season around here, and Boehme didn't seem the type to draw attention to himself.

The forensics showed that the Dutchman had been put to death under the trees by repeated blows to the back of the head. The murder weapon was identified as being made of metal and such was the ferocity of the attack that splinters of skull were found scattered around the grass by the body. Once dead, Boehme had been turned over onto his back with his arms out to the sides and thoroughly doused in petrol. He had not been robbed since, as Charoenkul had already told me, ashes of Baht notes and melted credit cards were found on the body.

I was also interested to note among the details that the Dutchman was a fairly big man (there were no such details in the first file), and the autopsy revealed the presence of some alcohol, but none of the more common drugs were found. He had been dead around a day and a half when Bee found him.

The only living picture of Boehme among the photographs was the one from his passport, which showed a rather serious-looking Germanic face topped with sandy hair. Some of the post mortem photos were truly stomach-turning, particularly the ones of what was left of the back of his head with the exposed residual mess of brain.

I close the files and put them back in the envelope. Risking Da's wrath, I light up a cigarette.

Two dead men, who had met the same nasty, brutish end. I consider what linked them other than the manner of their deaths. Both had visited Samui before and were of a similar age. Both Europeans. Both travelling without significant others: Ashley had left his wife behind in England and Boehme was unmarried. If the Dutchman had a girlfriend back in Holland, he had gone on his travels without her.

What brings unaccompanied farangs to this island? Business or girls, usually.

As to the former, if you want to do business here your choices are basically hospitality (bars, restaurants and small hotels) or property development. There's not much else unless you're resident and can keep a close eye on things. The victims' visits to the island were not sufficiently recent or frequent to suggest a business connection, and according to the transcripts neither man was known on Samui. If their interests were criminal, of course, that would be more difficult to track; but there is no rationale for following this speculative line.

Which moves us on to *girls*. This connection too looks problematical. According to Peter Ashley's statement, his brother was not here on a shag-fest, although for a cynic like me that's difficult to accept at face value. As the lead character in the TV series *House* says, *everybody lies*. However, even I have to accept there is no prima facie evidence of hanky-panky. Maybe the brothers did spend their days together and go their separate ways after nightfall. Again, according to the staff at Boehme's hotel, the Dutchman hadn't taken any girls back to his room – although there are other places here to make the beast with two backs.

Neither victim had been robbed. What other reasons are there for a killing?

I take out my notebook and brainstorm possible generic motives for a murder.

I write:

Money, Jealousy, Revenge, Envy

I look at the list for a while, which reads like a taster for the Seven Deadly Sins. No lights go on, so I get a little more fanciful:

Mistaken identity
Self-defence or defence of another
Acting while balance of mind is disturbed
To cover up another misdeed
Kidnapping that goes wrong
Blackmail

The last item on the list makes me think of my own recent experience with the anonymous letters. If I could find out who was sending them, I'd certainly be tempted to take a blunt instrument to the back of the bastard's head. I refocus. Nothing. Finding a reason for one killing is one thing, but for *two*? The logical part of my brain tells me this *should* be easier – just find the link between the two victims – but the emotional part of my brain is saying it's time for another cigarette. But what if there is no link between the victims other than one of time and place: the fact that they both encountered their killer? I add another motive to the list:

Because the murderer likes killing

Having drawn a blank on motive, I move on to method.
 I write:

Crude method of killing. Not a professional hit?
What instrument was used for the murders?
Was it the same one both times?
What is the significance of the location?
How did the victims get there?

It looks like methodology might provide some insight into the mentality of the killer, but I need to marinate these questions for a while. I also need another cigarette. I close the notebook and take the files into the West Office where I lock them away in a drawer of the filing cabinet.

I have to attend to my proper business for a few hours. I tell Da to have a good weekend, smoke a cigarette downstairs to clear my head of homicides, and climb into my jeep.

*   *   *   *   *

This murder investigation stuff is all very well, but it's not going to keep me in caviar. I have to clock up some time on Jingjai for Vogel, otherwise my German client will be wanting his advance back.

I park the jeep near the Ocean Pearl. At this time of the afternoon the bar will not be open, but the cleaning ladies should be in. The place is open-fronted, so I'm hoping to drop in casually for an 'unofficial' beer and see what I can find out.

There are two women there when I arrive, one sweeping the floor while the other wipes down tables. By night the bar looks quite hip, but in the stark sunlight it bears an altogether more worn and dusty appearance. The girl at the tables is chubby with cropped hair and a large dark skin discolouration by her left ear. She wears a faded red polo shirt, denim shorts and a sulky expression. I decide to try my luck with the old lady wielding the big broom. She looks shabby and gnarled, but at least has a twinkle in her eye.

I greet her charmingly in Thai and enquire politely if there is any chance of a cold *Chang* beer. And if so, would she and her fellow worker like one too? Her creased face brightens at this unexpected treat, and she moves quickly behind the bar and pops the tops off three bottles. The sulky one suddenly looks more cheerful too, and she acknowledges me shyly from a few tables away as the old woman thrusts a beer into her hand.

I invite the wrinkled lady to join me at my table, and she simpers and compliments me on my Thai. We chat about the heat, the lack of rain and other trivia for a few minutes before I move the conversation on to the subject of the Ocean Pearl.

"There is a very attractive young lady I've seen working here," I say. "She mixes a mean cocktail. Has a diamond in one of her teeth."

"Oh, you must mean Jingjai," replies the old woman with a wicked throaty chuckle. "You want to know about her?" she says craftily. "I wondered why you wanted to buy me a beer."

She is shrewd, this one. So much for my subtle strategy.

"I was just making conversation," I say unconvincingly. "I noticed her the other evening when I was out and –"

The crone pats my hand. "No, no," she says, "you are doing your homework first. That is good. Not many men are that smart." She laughs again. "But Dear is the one you should talk to," she says indicating the girl wiping the tables. "She knows Jingjai. Lucky you bought her a beer too."

She rattles off something fast to Dear, which I can't catch, and the girl flip-flops over to us. Again some quick colloquial Thai – I suspect obscene – is exchanged, and the chunky-thighed one giggles.

"This gentleman is interested in Jingjai," the mature lady says, once more speaking in a language I can follow.

I can feel myself blushing as I stammer out, "I wouldn't say I was interested in her exactly. I was just –" I shrug, as if that explains everything.

"Just checking to see if she is available?" smiles Dear putting a hand on my arm.

I laugh and shake my head as if I have been caught out.

"Well," says Dear cheerfully, her sulky mood forgotten, "she doesn't have a boyfriend at the moment. Not one that I know of, anyway. She used to hang out with a local musician, but I don't think that was anything serious, at least not on her side. I haven't seen him around for some time. Naturally she gets a lot of attention from the farang customers, but she's not interested in a holiday romance." She looks at me meaningfully. "But there are lots of girls in Chaweng who are."

"I'm sorry I got into this conversation," I say as humorously as I can.

They both grin and exchange knowing glances.

"I'd better pay for the beers and leave while I have some dignity left. Please don't say anything to Jingjai."

Fat chance, I think.

I pay up, leave a tip and saunter out into the sunshine.

103

*　　*　　*　　*　　*

"Before you say anything," I tell Wayan as I walk in through the front door, "I have phoned Mr. Sinclair."

It looks for a moment that Wayan is going to give me a spontaneous hug, but I'm not that lucky. Instead she regales me with one of her infectious smiles and says, "That is good, Mr. David. Mr. Sinclair is a nice man. He takes care of his boy."

Here we go again with the Saint Bloody Sinclair theme.

"Anyway, I am going to see him tomorrow."

"But you do not work tomorrow. It is the weekend."

"I know. I'm making an exception since it is the nice Mr. Sinclair." I try to keep the irony out of my voice, but Wayan picks up on it and wags a finger at me like I'm a naughty schoolboy.

"You are teasing me, but it is kind of you to do this on a Saturday."

Wayan is so utterly disarming, I decide to let the subject drop and bask awhile in her good opinion.

"I'm going out later, Wayan, but not for a few hours yet. Perhaps I could have something light to eat in the garden?"

"Certainly, Mr. David. What would you like?"

"Surprise me. I'm sure it will be delicious whatever it is."

I shower, change and go out into the garden with my laptop, taking refuge from the still-hot day in the shade of the sala. I type up some notes for Vogel, then wonder what to do next. On impulse I go into the study and return to the sala with my two-volume collection of Sherlock Holmes stories.

If Charoenkul could see me now he would wonder what sort of naïve nutter he had asked to help out in a murder investigation. Be that as it may, I flick through the books in search of inspiration. There is something I remember reading in one of the stories that is hovering on the fringes of my consciousness. I can't articulate what it is, but it is *something* and it is irritating me. I have some nagging intimation that it might be relevant to the murders. Don't ask me how. The subconscious mind, like the Good Lord, can work in a mysterious way, and mine has been known to work in a way that is completely unintelligible, if not downright barmy.

When I find what I am looking for, I fear my subconscious has been taking the Michael. It is a passage in the short story *Silver Blaze* about the curious incident of the dog in the night-time. The 'curious incident' was the fact that the dog did not bark when he should have. From this, Sherlock Holmes goes on to crack the case in high Victorian style.

I scratch the back of my head vigorously and try to work out what my sun-baked brain is trying to tell me. I fail.

It strikes me moreover that there is a problem at the heart of Holmes' deductive method: *when you have eliminated the impossible, whatever remains, however improbable, must be the truth.* The problem is that you need to have all the possible scenarios set out in front of you to start with. Then you knock them down one by one. The last one left standing is the solution to the riddle.

This might be fine in fiction, but with the burning murders I'm missing too much data for this to work. I need an intuitive leap and it isn't happening.

Wayan arrives with a tray laden with home-made *nasi goreng*, fresh mango and coconut milk. She has also thoughtfully brought an ashtray even though she doesn't approve of my smoking. I ask her to join me and she brings a banana and a glass of papaya juice from the kitchen.

Endeavouring to keep my mind off the obvious as she peels and eats the banana, I enquire as to whether she is still reading *Alice in Wonderland*. She nods.

"Oh, by the way," I say, "I worked out why a raven is like a writing desk."

"Why?" She looks at me expectantly.

"Because they both begin with the letter 'R', apart from writing desk."

"Are you being funny?" she asks.

"Obviously not," I reply.

*   *   *   *   *

I spray on mosquito repellent and slop around the garden until the sun disappears behind the hills. An hour after sunset and Claire has not put in an appearance. I sling the camera across my shoulder and ride my motorbike down to Chaweng: this will make it easier for me to follow Jingjai through the traffic after she finishes work.

The air is slowly cooling down and there is even a faint breeze as I leave the bike on the tourist-choked main street. I see Vladimir, the big Russian, cruising down the pavement with a tiny Thai girl under each of his overdeveloped arms.

"Hey, Braddock," he calls, "You want a girl? I have one extra. Or we can share the two."

"Thanks Vlad, but I'm working this evening."

"Ah, you take photographs of the naughty ones," he laughs, seeing my camera. "I hear you are a private consultant and you speak good Thai. Someday soon maybe I come to you on business. Not following young girls, I mean real business."

"Sure. Anytime."

"I am also working this evening." He squeezes the girls and they giggle. "But first, Muay Thai at Chaweng Arena." He indicates the sports bag over his back. "I will be on about ten o'clock. I am big kick-boxing star now in Samui: *Vlad the Impaler*. My girls know all about this, of course. Don't you, girls?" He puts his two companions in headlocks and they titter knowingly and roll their eyes. Freeing an arm, he hands me a complimentary ticket. "If you finish early perhaps you come and watch."

"Thanks," I say taking the ticket, "I'll see. But I think tonight will be a late one for me."

"Some other time then, Braddock. I have no plans to leave Samui for a while."

"Are you doing some business here?"

"Oh yes, but very secret." He winks. "See you soon."

I take the same table as previously over the road from the *Ocean Pearl*, and settle myself for a long evening on Vogel's expenses. I order *tom yum goong* and a mineral water. I have to pace my drinking if I'm going to stay on my bike later.

It is a boring evening. I take some photographs but nothing's happening. Jingjai is behaving herself concentrating on her work – which she needs to because the Pearl is busy. Some well-groomed Westerner at the bar spends hours trying to chat her up. She's friendly and polite, and serves his cocktails with a smile, but that looks to be as far as it's going.

I smoke lots of cigarettes, have a few beers and generally get fed up with the restaurant's limited musical fare as 'Putting out the Fire with Gasoline' comes round for the umpteenth time.

After my restaurant closes I move to the bar next door and wait for the *Pearl* to shut up shop.

When Jingjai puts on her motorcycle helmet, the Westerner who has been paying her attention climbs off his stool and waves farewell. I take this as a cue to climb on my bike. At a discreet distance I follow her weaving in and out of the now-sporadic traffic. She goes straight back to her apartment block and passes inside. I wait around smoking for an hour until I'm sure she's not coming back out again. Then I ride home.

*   *   *   *   *

I love Samui in the wee small hours. I especially love it on nights like this when the white moon stares down from the blackness like the pockmarked eye of a blind god. At such times, when the island's bright signs have paled to grey and the broom of sleep has swept the revellers to their beds, my mind's cynical crust cracks open a little, and some fanciful poetry leaks in. Then the dark hills appear to me as slumbering prehistoric leviathans, the clouds assume the air of restless ghosts, and the moon-dusted sea murmurs in some long forgotten tongue of the divine.

Fortunately I catch myself just in time before I dissolve completely into this *schmaltz*. I force myself to think about all sorts of horrible atrocities, giving special attention to man's worst inhumanities to man. That's better. Now the moon looks like the face of a drowned man and the shadows under the trees are just plain scary. Now I'm in a more suitable frame of mind for what follows.

I steer the jeep off the near-deserted ring road onto the concrete surface, pass slowly by the half-finished buildings and park with the headlights pointing at the police hazard tape that still marks the crime scene. I switch off the engine and the lights, and look up towards Yai's shack, but can see nothing. Then I realise how dumb it is to expect a blind man to have a lamp burning at night.

I also realise how spooky this place is. Even the insect noises sound hushed and hesitant. The unfinished columns of the abandoned structures stick up like grey, snapped bones and the lunar shadows look dark and threatening, as if concealing something monstrous. I switch the headlights back on.

Getting out of the car, I walk up the slight incline towards the tape. Yup. Plenty of light to see what you are doing.

The murderer would have needed to see what he was doing. His blows were savage, but precise. There was no damage to the spine or the shoulder bones of either victim. Only the backs of the heads had been smashed like eggshells. The men can't have been moving around or there would have been collateral damage. Maybe the first unexpected blow had rendered them unconscious and they were finished off on the ground. Or maybe they were already unconscious before their heads were pulped.

How had Ashley and Boehme got here? This remote grove is an unlikely spot for a rendezvous – unless you're a drug dealer – and the victims' bike and car respectively were found in a different town altogether. Had they driven here voluntarily with their killer in his car? They couldn't have come on a bike surely: how would the murderer have carried the petrol and the heavy blunt instrument?

Perhaps their killer had forced them to drive his car here at gunpoint or knifepoint. But if so, why not stab them or shoot them? Wouldn't a single gunshot just be taken for a backfiring car? Other than Yai, who would have heard it anyway?

I go on foot to the main road and look back towards the scene, confirming what I'd suspected: because of the topography the headlights are not really visible, *unless you're looking for them.*

I walk back to the jeep. From the back seat I take some old towels and a number of cardboard boxes folded flat. I carry them into the trees and scrunch the material into an untidy lump, hoping nothing in the grass bites me in the meantime.

As I straighten up, something whizzes past my head and I jerk with fright. The jeep's headlights catch a circling bat, and squinting upwards I see another one overhead. Not a winged spirit after all, but close. Easy to understand how superstitious locals might combine the death of Yai's son with the presence of these nocturnal predators to create a flying demon. (There is reputedly a small island off Samui where no dogs can live because the high-pitched noise of the large bat colony there drives canine critters mad. Mind you, that story could be just so much *guano*.)

I remove from the jeep three glass bottles of petrol and carry them to the mound of towels and cardboard.

If Charoenkul is trying to stitch me up, now would be the time for his policemen to leap out from behind the trees and arrest me for murder. Explaining my presence at a multiple crime scene carrying gasoline at three o'clock in the morning would be, to put it mildly, somewhat challenging. But no-one appears. Even the bats have gone.

I pour the contents of the bottles over the towels and drop a match. The resultant blaze will hardly mimic the burning of a human body, but that is not the point of the exercise.

I hurry to the car, taking my empties with me, and drive back to the main road. The glow of the fire can be seen, but would it cause anyone to stop and investigate? There are no live-in neighbours and certainly at this hour of the night little passing traffic.

My jeep reeks of gasoline. Unless the killer wanted his vehicle to smell the same he must have ditched the empty bottles quickly: I suspect one may find broken glass among the building site debris. But would that be of any forensic use?

Twenty minutes later I park the jeep on my drive, and leave all the windows open to get rid of the smell.

I doubt it will rain tonight.

5

"Four things happen to the thoughtless man
who takes another man's wife:
he lowers himself, his pleasure is restless,
he is blamed by others, he goes to hell."
Lord Buddha, The Dhammapada

Last night I had a bad dream. I know I did, even though I don't know what the dream was. When I awoke – which I did with a start, as though someone had hammered on my chest – the bedcovers were soaking and the sweat was running off me in rivulets. The alarm clock registered just after nine: I'd only slept for about four-and-a-half hours. I felt like crap.

I took a cold shower, shaved, dressed and went downstairs in search of headache pills. No Claire and no Wayan to be found. I drank two glasses of water from the cooler to rehydrate and swallowed a couple of tablets. Wayan had left out croissants from the French bakery, which I coated with butter and jam and swilled down with a glass of orange juice.

It was time to get over to Sinclair's. I hoped the pills would lessen my headache before I arrived since I needed to be in a positive frame of mind when I met the Geordie. *I could really do without this today*, I thought, feeling a smidgeon of annoyance at Da and Wayan. I was sure the discomfort would pass, however, as soon as I'd had my first cigarette of the day. Unfortunately my packet of Marlboros was empty.

I grabbed my notebook, checked my appearance in the mirror and tried a smile. Not very convincing. Last night's activities were etched in dark circles under my eyes, in artistic contrast to the scabbing scar on my left cheek. I was going to have to take a nap later if I was going to get through the day.

I put on my hat and went out to the jeep which, I was happy to note, did not smell of gasoline. The sun was already well up in the bright blue sky. No rain today, unsurprisingly.

I drove to the nearest convenience store and bought cigarettes, smoking one and checking Sinclair's address before I headed off.

Sinclair's house is near Na Thon on the far side of the island. Of course on Samui, 'far' is an extremely relative term. The whole Ring Road only measures about fifty-five kilometres, so in practice wherever you are you're pretty close to beer, seafood and female companionship.

As the light traffic pootled its way around, I tried to convince myself to adopt a more benevolent attitude to the Northerner. In truth, I couldn't think of any coherent reason why I should dislike him, aside from the fact that he'd once interrupted my meal – which, let's face it, is rather lame. There was just *something* about him. I'm usually a good judge of character, but then Da is too: so one of us is off in our reading of Sinclair. (Wayan tends to see the good in everyone, so I discount her viewpoint. I don't understand how she can maintain this outlook in the face of the overwhelming evidence that mankind is selfish, violent and screwed-up. But she does. Luckily, she has a cynic for an employer who can watch out for her.)

Sinclair's house was easy to find and I arrived a few minutes early. I parked the jeep alongside Sinclair's big black SUV, took a deep breath and ventured a warm-up smile in the rear-view mirror to see if my face would crack. It didn't. I got out of the car and knocked on the door.

The style and decor of the Northerner's house testified to the influence of a Thai wife with a taste for the traditional. Neither the wife nor the son appeared to be around this morning. Wives seem to go missing regularly on Samui, I've noticed.

An ancient maid showed me through into the large garden where Sinclair was deep in conversation with some horticulturalist. He wasn't wearing socks with his sandals today. He must be making a special sartorial effort just for me.

The subject of their discussion was the pests damaging his coconut trees. I tried to look interested as the expert waxed lyrical on the coconut hispine beetle, *Brontispa longissima* (which can be eradicated by releasing a beetle-eating insect called *Asecodes hispinarum* at the top of the tree), and the Rhinoceros beetle (which is countered by mixing grains of rice coated with the fungus *Metarhizium anisopliae* in the fertiliser you spread on your plantation). All fascinating stuff, no doubt, if you're into biological agents of mass destruction – which I'm not. From my perspective, I was inclined to think the biggest threat to coconut trees on the island came from some guy with a penchant for burning gasoline; but I kept this opinion to myself.

With a promise to contact the Surat Thani Pest Control Centre on his client's behalf, Sinclair's expert departed with a respectful wai.

"These Rhino beetles are bloody destructive," Sinclair opined taking the lid off a plastic box he had with him. "Look at the hardware on this bugger."

The insect did look, well, like a rhino: dark tough body armour and horns straight out of Africa. For a moment my mind zipped back to a holiday with Claire in Zambia where we'd seen the country's last two surviving white rhinos, presents from the South African government. Both dead now, killed by poachers for their horns.

"I've been plagued by these beetles recently. I don't know where they're all coming from. It's like somebody's bringing them in by the truckload and dumping them in my garden. You know in Northern Thailand the natives stage fights between Rhino beetles and bet on the outcome. They probably do it here too for all I know. Thais will bet on anything." He put the lid back on the box.

"You grow all sorts of stuff by the looks of it," I said indicating the surrounding flora and fauna.

"Aye," he said, "My missus got me interested in it." He gestured with an arm. "Over here I've got *sator* – 'stinky beans' to you. Very popular with the Thais even though they make you fart and give your pee an interesting smell. Pineapples and mangoes there, and over that way some durian trees. Can be tricky to get the durians to fruit. They're finicky: it's to do with their pollination system. You like durian? The 'King of Fruits', as they say. For me, eating a durian is like eating a creamy yoghurt while standing in a public toilet."

"I'm afraid the only thing I know about the durian is that the Thais pick them while they're on the trees while the Malays wait until they fall to the ground. Or so my father told me. He was a planter in Malaya after World War II. He attributed the difference to Malay laziness – they couldn't be bothered to climb the trees. Sounds a bit racist nowadays, of course."

Sinclair chuckled. "Well, I didn't know that. Let's go sit in the sala and I'll get you something cold to drink. We don't get that many people to the house so I'm out of practice at social hosting."

His sun-weathered body disappeared into the house, leaving me to my thoughts amid the luminescent greenery and fire-red Birds of Paradise. *Fire-red*. I didn't want to think about fire at the moment. Then a vision of Kat's naked body stretched across a bed came into my mind. I didn't want to think about that either. I lit a cigarette and let images of bats, coconut trees, non-barking dogs, rhinoceroses and fighting beetles meander through my head. And Claire was in there too. Claire when I first met her, Claire on our wedding day, Claire when Catherine was born, and later ...

"Coconuts," said Sinclair, interrupting my reverie. "It seemed appropriate." He set down a tray groaning with two enormous decapitated specimens with straws sticking out of them.

Since it's hard to look dignified and professional bent over a coconut sucking on a straw, I exchanged a few more pleasantries and finished the milk before proceeding to business.

"So," I said sitting back, "why did you want to see me, Mr. Sinclair?"

"Call me 'Geordie', please."

"Geordie."

He rubbed a hand over his head then scratched his stubble. I noticed how big his hands were, how callused, how the nails were bitten down: some internal stress was at work on him. His bonhomie had quickly drained away, the enthusiasm for his garden forgotten. He was no longer making eye contact. He cleared his throat and put his left hand on his chin.

"It's ... um ... it's a matter of trust."

"It usually is."

If he was a smoker he would have lit up now. But he wasn't. So he didn't. Instead he scratched his chin again.

"You presumably know I have three businesses: realty, car hire and a car repair shop. In each one I have a Thai partner. The car hire and the repair businesses are complimentary; as I'm sure you appreciate. My realty company, Euro-Siam Properties, is a bit of an oddity which I kind of fell into through contacts of my wife's. Property sales and long-term lets to Westerners. Not really my thing, but 'accidentally' starting businesses happens a lot on Samui."

"I know. It happened to me. It's unusual for anyone to have just one business here. Does Euro-Siam do any property development? Most Europeans dabble in it at some time."

He shook his head. "No. I had a bad experience with that once, so I've steered clear."

"Anyway," I ventured, "even if you're just selling real estate, you probably know a friend of mine, Prasert Promsai, the builder."

"Aye, I do. Genuine bloke. He's done some fixing-up for some of my clients. Quality work. I know his slimy little brother too."

I waited, but he didn't elaborate.

Instead Sinclair said, "Anyhow, it's not the property side I want to talk to you about: it's my car hire business, Smiley Cars Samui."

This dour-looking, grizzly Northern caveman was about the last person on the planet I'd imagine owning a business called Smiley Cars, but I kept a straight face and said, "Yes, I've seen your stand at the airport."

"Straightforward business," he sniffed. "I've always been in transport, one way or another. I had a haulage company back in Geordieland before I came to Samui. Though that seems like a lifetime ago now." He looked like he was about to say something significant, but then changed his mind and shrugged. "So, we cater for the tourists. Simple proposition: we guarantee a cheaper price than Avis, Hertz, the big boys. And our cars are properly maintained, not like some of the death-traps you can hire from the locals without even having to show a driving licence."

I waited patiently for the advertising to finish and for Sinclair to get to the point.

Eventually he blew his nose and went on, "A few months ago I gave a job to the nephew of my Thai partner. Nothing too responsible, you understand. He just looks after some of the paperwork and does routine checks on the vehicles. But this means he has access to the car keys. He can't hire out the cars – our systems are too tight for that – but I think he might be taking a car out once in a while."

"Where are the cars garaged when they're not hired out?"

"Well, certainly not at the airport, that'd be too damn expensive. No, we have a compound nearby at Bang Rak."

"Any CCTV?"

"Nothing so high tech. We have a security guard."

"So the guard would know if a car was being taken out?"

"He *would*, but I very much doubt he'd shop one of the bosses' nephews. Not to a farang. Even though I pay his wages."

I asked a few pertinent questions about the guards' shift rota and the nephew: Kwanchai Ramsuwan, twenty-eight years old, handsome, charming, and too clever by half for his current job. I made a few notes in my book then came to the more interesting questions.

"So what do you want me to do?"

"Catch the bugger taking a car out."

He leaned forward animatedly. "I've thought it through how you can catch him. You've got a laptop with an internet connection, right?"

I nodded.

"And a set of binoculars?"

"I *am* a private investigator," I replied somewhat testily.

"Then here's the plan. First, I give you read-only remote access into a limited section of our company database, so you can see which cars are hired out and therefore which ones should be in the compound."

"So I watch the compound and count wheels."

"Exactly."

"Before we get into discussing the logistics of 24-hour surveillance, I'll need to know exactly where this place is so I can find a suitable observation post."

Sinclair clasped my wrist and laughed, both of which irritated me.

"Already sorted, David. I presume I can call you 'David'?"

This also irritated me.

"Presume away."

"Right. Well, one of my property clients that I do lettings for is having his swimming pool re-done – by Prasert's company, as it happens. While that's going on, the house is empty. One of the back balconies overlooks my car park. You can sit out on the balcony and snap shots with your telephoto lens – I know you've got one of those."

"Sounds like you've thought it all through."

"Aye, it's the dog's bollocks, isn't it?" he said cheerily.

"The only problem is my time and the cost. Doing a stake-out like that will be expensive, unless you're happy for me to get one of my local boys that help me out to do it."

"No!" he said rather too loudly and quickly for my liking. "No, I want you to do it. Personally."

I told him my rates, but he didn't flinch. I really wanted to say, *If it's so easy why don't you do it yourself?* But I didn't want a roiling from Da and a month of burnt toast from Wayan.

However, as if he could read my thoughts, Sinclair went on, "You're probably wondering why I don't just do this on my own."

"It crossed my mind."

He looked nervous for a moment, and again dropped his gaze. "Well," he began slowly, "it's a delicate thing, what with my partner being the lad's uncle, and so on. If the evidence is put together by an 'independent' person, it's harder to dispute. That's why I want you to do it. You'll have credibility, which some Thai boy working for you won't have."

"I see."

I sat awhile and mulled it over. There was something decidedly odd about all this, and his arrangements were a bit too pat, but I was struggling to come up with a reason to say no. One that Da and Wayan would sign onto anyway.

Eventually I said, "I can do this, of course, but I have other cases at the moment. It would be a few days, maybe a week before I could start."

Sinclair looked relieved. "No problem. The key time for you to be on the job, as it were, is from about 6.00pm till 11.00pm, and there'll be no builders around then. If Kwanchai is going to take a car out, that'll be when it happens. You don't even need to do it every evening. If we liaise, I can tell you Kwanchai's plans, and which evenings are the most likely ones for his shenanigans. I don't even mind if it takes a few weeks, part-time like, as long as I get photos of him on a few different occasions."

He sensed my hesitancy, even then, and continued, "It's money for old rope, David. Get paid for sitting in the dark for a few hours each evening. That's all."

I smiled as sincerely as I could manage. "OK. But I'll need a photograph of the nephew. Presumably you'll let me have details of how to access your database; passwords and the like. And I don't want to be held responsible for crashing your systems, or to be blamed for someone hacking into them."

"Don't worry. It's all firewall-protected, and the data will be encrypted anyway. You'll only have access to a small area. I don't want you knowing how much money I make." He laughed a little uncertainly.

He took me into the house and provided me with a box file containing a highlighted map, system access instructions, keys to the house, and photographs of Kwanchai. He'd clearly anticipated my questions.

"I'd like to call by your office on some pretext and have a look at this guy in the flesh," I said. "Will he be in today?"

"He'll be around this afternoon, yes."

"OK. I'll be in touch."

"Just one thing afore you go. If we need to meet up I'd rather do it here or at your house. I don't want to go to your office in Chaweng. I can't say why, sorry, I'd just rather not."

I gave him my address and we shook hands. There was a distinctly guilty element to his demeanour that I couldn't figure out. In fact there were lots of things about Sinclair that I couldn't put my finger on. But sure as hell he wasn't being entirely straight with me.

I'd have staked my PI's licence on it, if I'd had one.

*   *   *   *   *

As I left Sinclair's house I checked my cell phone which I'd had on silent mode since last night. Two missed calls, both from local numbers, neither of which I recognised. Driving back onto the Samui Ring Road I pressed return call for the first number and a woman's voice answered.

"Hello, David, thank you for calling back."

"*Kat?* Is that you? This is not your usual number."

"Never mind about that now. I need to see you." She sounded less composed than at our last meeting.

"Of course, no problem."

"Can I meet you at your office?"

"Sure. Say in an hour, around one o'clock?"

"Make it three o'clock."

"OK. I'll leave the street door open. What's the mystery?"

"I can't talk now. I'll see you later."

She rang off.

I did not like the sound of this. Whatever was coming my way in three hours' time, it was not going to be good. I could feel my thumbs pricking.

I took a breath then called the second number. A young female voice greeted me.

"Hello, this is David Braddock," I said in Thai. "I think you were trying to call me."

"Wait a moment, please." I heard some chatter and traffic buzz then the sound of a door closing and the background noise stopped.

"Hello, Mr. Braddock, are you still there?"

"Yes."

"Sorry, I was in the shop. This is Bee. My grandfather asked me to call you." She sounded apprehensive.

"Ah, Bee, yes. Thank you for calling me. Listen, I'd be very grateful if I could meet you. There are some questions you may be able to help me with."

"Grandfather told me all about it. I have already told the police everything I know. I do not think I can help you."

"I know you've spoken to the police. Don't worry, I'm not going to make any trouble for you. Please meet me. Wherever you like and wherever is convenient for you."

I could feel the reluctance at the other end of the phone.

"Just to talk, that's all."

A sigh. Then, "OK. Tomorrow I will take some food to my grandfather. I will meet you there."

"Thank you, Bee. What time?"

"Say four o'clock. I have to go now, sorry."

"Perfect. I'll see you –"

She had already gone.

*   *   *   *   *

I didn't feel like driving home for lunch so I stopped at a convenience store for a sandwich and a warm chocolate bar to keep me going; and an instant coffee to keep me awake awhile.

I parked the jeep near Sinclair's office in Chaweng and went inside for a brief conversation with Kwanchai about some imaginary friend of mine who would need a car when he visited Samui next month. Normally I wouldn't want a target to be able to recognise me, but given the circumstances of the job and my growing distrust of the Northerner, I wanted to see this guy up close. To make sure he actually existed, for one thing. And it wasn't like he was going to spot me while I was lying in wait for him on a dark balcony.

Kwanchai was courteous and helpful, and didn't particularly seem the rascally-type, but then the joy-riding he was suspected of hardly made him Public Enemy Number One.

Afterwards I drove to my office hoping to catch a couple of hours' shut-eye before Kat pitched up, but there was too much static in my head, revved up by a sense of impending hubris.

So I just sat there in the East Office, waiting for Mrs. Charoenkul, while the second hand of my watch dragged itself around the face like a sleep-deprived tortoise. Einstein was exactly right about the relativity of time: when you're enjoying yourself it whizzes by, when you're miserable it all but stands still. Right now, I felt like the Mad Hatter at his never-ending tea-party. Although I probably looked more like the Dormouse.

Eventually I heard Kat's heels on the stairs and went out into reception to meet her.

She looked a good deal more composed than I had expected following our earlier conversation. She was wearing designer sunglasses, a white blouse and jeans. A Gucci bag hung over her shoulder.

"Hello, Kat."

"Hello, David." She pushed up the sunglasses onto her hair. "Which office do you want me in?"

"The West Office has the biggest desk."

She smiled. "Just as well I locked the street door behind me, then."

"Seriously, the East Office is more comfortable."

We went in and sat down.

"You look fabulous, as always," I said.

"And you, tirak, look like you haven't slept in a week."

"Thanks. I was up half the night wandering around a certain coconut grove."

"Poor baby."

"Anyway, I was expecting a distraught woman with runny mascara after your earlier call. Yet here you are as cool as a cucumber and ready for the catwalk," I protested irritably. "What's going on?"

"I'm sorry, David. I was a little panicky this morning. I've calmed down now."

"So I see. You got me panicking too. What happened?"

She reached into her bag and took out a white envelope which she put on the table.

"This happened," she said.

The envelope bore a local postmark and was addressed to *Mrs. K. Charoenkul*. The handwriting was unmistakable. My mouth felt suddenly dry and something hardened in my chest, like I'd had concrete poured into my lungs.

"We need to go next door," I said peremptorily and picked up the envelope by one of its corners, holding it out in front of me like it was noxious.

We passed into the East Office where I rummaged in the filing cabinet and took out my other dusting kit.

"My, you do have a big desk in here. Useful for all sorts of purposes I should think," said Kat in an attempt at humour.

I didn't answer. I spread out my handkerchief and placed the envelope on it, then put on a pair of surgical gloves. Kat looked at me dubiously like I was about to give her an internal examination. She was about to say something, but then thought better of it and mimed zipping her lips.

I worked silently on the envelope which, unsurprisingly, was covered in fingerprints.

"Has anyone else in your household touched this envelope? Your husband or the maid?"

"No. I collected the post. My finger marks will be on it though."

"I know. I'll need to take your fingerprints in a minute."

"You're not serious, David."

"I'm perfectly serious."

"How exciting."

I carefully removed the sheet of paper from the envelope. White, A4, two folds: as expected. The printing and font were also the same as in the previous letters. This one said

THE INDO-CHINA INTERNATIONAL, BANGKOK,
IS DAVID BRADDOCK'S FAVOURITE HOTEL

Kat and I looked at each other. Then I said, "OK, let's do your fingerprints now."

I took out an ink pad and card template then slowly and methodically pressed each of Kat's fingers in turn onto the pad and card. She watched me closely, a half-smile on her lips. I tried to ignore her feline scent and the closeness of her body, but it wasn't easy.

Eventually she said, "You know, David, we should do this sort of thing more often."

"I'm so glad you find this entertaining."

She pressed her leg against mine and said, "Don't be so grumpy, tirak. Are you finished or are there any other parts of me you want to rub in ink?"

"I'm done. You'd better wash your hands: you can go through next door."

While she was out I dusted the letter and compared the prints with Kat's. They all matched hers. Some of the envelope prints matched hers too, obviously. I doubted whether any of the other prints were the writer's. He was too careful for that. I labelled Kat's fingerprint card and put the paraphernalia into a plastic wallet. Later this would all join my private paranoia collection at home.

Kat came back in and sat down opposite me. She looked at me across the desk and waited for me to say something.

When I didn't, she said, "So?"

"So what?"

"So what do you think?"

"I think we can safely assume the letters I've had are not part of some elaborate prank. In light of this," I waved at the folder, "they were clearly about you and me. Someone knows."

"And more," she said slowly, looking into my eyes.

"Like what?"

"Well, you can call me the jealous type if you like, David, but look at the wording. *The Indo-China International, Bangkok, is David Braddock's favourite hotel.*"

"Yes, well, you and I went there several times, so it would be."

"It sounds to me like the writer is telling me that I'm not the only woman you've taken there."

"That's ridiculous."

"Is it?"

"Yes."

"So you haven't taken anyone else there?"

"No. Absolutely not," I said firmly.

"You see, I've been thinking about this today – I've thought about little else – and it occurs to me that perhaps the writer is some other woman you seduced and then dumped. She's found out about us somehow and this is her way of getting revenge. *A woman scorned*. You know the saying."

"I haven't been to this hotel with any other woman, Kat, you're just being paranoid."

"If I am paranoid, David, I've caught it from you." She tapped her shoulder bag. "Do you know I cleared out my bag this morning to make sure I wasn't being bugged? This is what comes of finding my lover crawling around on his hands and knees in my sala looking for microphones. You've infected me with your madness."

I noted the use of the word *lover*, rather than *ex-lover*, then reached over the desk and took her hand.

"I'm sorry I got you into this, Kat," I said.

She snatched her hand away. "So you should be," she snapped angrily. Then she relented and took my hand again. "No, no, David it's all right. I'm a big girl. I knew what I was doing. I knew the risks." She smiled. "That doesn't mean you're not a bastard, though. Are you *sure* I'm the only one you've taken to that hotel?"

"Absolutely. All the other policemen's wives I've seduced I've had them in here, while Da was on her lunch break."

"Yes, right."

"I think we should be talking about your husband, not my non-existent affairs at the Indo-China International."

"I'm sure Deng doesn't know."

"Not yet maybe. But I doubt the letter-writer is going to stop now. The Chief *will* know; it's only a matter of time. The next letter may well be sent to him."

She shrugged. "Well, there's nothing we can do about that," she said evenly.

"Are you going to say anything to him?"

"Why would I? Whoever is writing these letters can't have any proof. We were very careful, David. If Deng ever confronts me about it, I shall deny everything. I shall say it is just mischief-making by someone with a grudge against the police or against him. And you mustn't say anything either. Don't go soft on me."

"However much I'm tortured in the cells at Bophut?"

"Don't be so melodramatic."

I sat back in my chair. "Well, you're a cool one, Kat, I'll give you that."

"There's nothing to be gained by feeling useless guilt. People get hurt that way."

"So tell me about your cell phone."

She looked puzzled. "My cell phone?"

"The number you called me from this morning is not your regular number. And it's not the number of the SIM card you used when we were seeing each other."

"I damaged that SIM card. It doesn't work anymore."

"So why did you feel the need for another number?"

"Perhaps I wanted to be able to ring you without anyone being able to trace that the call was from me. You know, like the old times, before you dumped me?"

"I did not dump you."

Kat laughed. "You're *so* serious."

"I'm *so* stressed. And I don't need you teasing me. I don't know what the hell's going on."

She leaned forward in mock concern. "You know, you look like an overworked headmaster sitting behind your desk." She fluttered her eyelashes theatrically, ran the tip of her tongue over her lips and whispered, "I could help you relax, tirak. I could pretend to be one of your students and crawl under your desk. If it would help my grades."

"You're bad. But what is worse, you're not serious."

"Are you sure?"

"Unfortunately, yes."

"Ah well." She signalled the end of the conversation by standing and putting her bag over her shoulder. "Perhaps some other time. If you can fit me into your busy schedule, that is. Meantime I'll call you if I receive any more letters."

"And I'll call you on your new number if I receive any."

We kissed, European-style, and she left. I listened to the *click-clack* of her heels descending the stairs, then the sound of the street door closing behind her.

Her perfume lingered heavily in the room, and the imprint of her presence lingered in my mind. *Why did I find it so hard to think straight when Kat was around?* Something about her voice and the ripeness of her body blocked the rational part of my brain and flooded the rest of me with naked carnality. I'd been kidding myself that I'd got her out of my system. Obviously I hadn't.

I took the plug out of the chemical bath of lust that my wits were soaking in and waited for it to empty. I smoked a cigarette while I contemplated the return of reason.

There was one person aside from me that had definite knowledge of Kat's affair with me. That person was Kat herself. I had to consider the possibility that Mrs. K. Charoenkul was the author of the anonymous letters. But if that were true, the only question was why. Could she have felt that I had 'dumped' her? She'd inferred it just now, although as far as I was concerned the ending of the affair was a mutual decision. And it was a long time ago: surely she'd have reacted sooner if she really felt that way.

However, the more I thought about it, the less I liked what I was thinking about. Kat knows where I live – she could certainly have dropped off the letters to me. And she could have posted the last one *to herself.*

Alternatively, supposing this were all a ruse to re-establish contact with me. Maybe Kat had suggested to Charoenkul that she translate the police files of the murders, knowing that they were intended for me.

There was something else I wasn't getting. Kat's reaction to the whole situation was altogether too calm, too detached. It was almost as if she didn't care if our affair was discovered. Her behaviour was like that of someone who either had nothing to lose, *or else had nothing to worry about.* This was in vivid contrast to how careful she had been during the course of the affair to ensure it stayed secret. Kat had changed, somehow.

You'll work it out. You are a detective, she'd said to me in her garden.

I also wondered if she knew, despite my protestations of innocence, that there *was* another woman I'd stayed with at the Indo-China International. That woman could not conceivably be the author of the letters: it was impossible. But she could be the cause of jealousy. Maybe Kat felt herself to be the *woman scorned*, to use her words.

As I curled up on one of the East Office chairs to catch some sleep, two things at least were obvious to my fuddled brain. The first was that I needed to get my sexual feelings for Kat under control. The second was that, until I knew more about her present motivations, I shouldn't trust her. Not one bit.

*   *   *   *   *

128

The fog lifts and I see myself hosting a TV game show called 'Whom Do You Trust?'

I am dressed as Sherlock Holmes, and standing on a set whose red walls are festooned with oversized guns, daggers and bludgeons. A backlit screen displays a succession of grainy pictures of notorious gangsters and serial-killers. The show's panel of contestants – all of whom are attired in black-and-white-striped prison garb – comprises Sinclair, Kat, Vladimir and Charoenkul. A terrified and naked Klaus Vogel is locked in a cage suspended over a huge fire pit.

As the opening music fades and the audience applause dies down, I welcome everyone to the show. "The only place on the planet where you can kill the people you don't like without guilt or consequences; and still go home with a cash prize," I announce.

Vogel screams from his swinging cage and the audience laughs.

"So here we go," I say. I take out a large magnifying glass which I use to read the quiz cards. "Geordie, you first."

"Right you are, David," says the Northerner cheerfully.

"Your question. It's about this job you've given me, trying to catch your employee taking out a car. The question is: why have you given it to me?"

"Because you're a smug, overly-intellectual twat, David, who needs taking down a peg or two."

"Right answer."

There is a metallic clang, and one of the chains holding up Vogel's cage drops away. Vogel cries out and the audience laughs again.

"Now, Kat," I say, "your question. Something about you is different. What's changed?"

"Well, David, since you passed on a sexually transmitted disease to me, I've adopted a whole new philosophy of life."

"Correct."

Another chain falls; another scream; more applause. There is now only one chain supporting the cage, which begins to rotate.

"Vladimir."

"Hello, Braddock, I have spare whore for you."

Guffaws from the crowd.

"Thank you, thank you, Vlad. Your question. What are you really doing here in Samui?"

"I like to fight and to boom-boom many girls."

A buzzer sounds loudly. There is a disappointed 'ahhh' from the audience.

"I'm sorry," I say, "I can't accept that answer."

"Is no problem. I kill you later," smiles Vladimir.

I turn to Charoenkul.

"Chief Charoenkul. Last chance to drop Vogel into the fire pit."

The spectators are hushed. The caged German is bug-eyed with fear. Papa Doc looks at me intently.

"Your question." I pause. "Do you know I've been sleeping with your wife?"

Charoenkul thinks a moment before responding.

"I do now," he says.

There is a roar of laughter from the audience, followed by loud enthusiastic applause drowning out Vogel's screams as the cage falls in slow-motion and vanishes into the flames. Fireworks are let off and sparks shoot everywhere. Papa Doc takes a bow.

As the hubbub quietens, I am about to wrap up the show when the Old Monk puts in an appearance. He is clad in white robes and sports sunglasses.

"Tathagata," he says, "we have a surprise in store."

There is a whirring of machinery and a second cage appears over the glowing pit, held by a single chain. In the cage is Claire. She looks at me sadly.

"The audience has a question for you, Mister Braddock," croaks the Old Monk. He takes out a scroll from his robes. With his other hand he lights a cigarette, taking a couple of drags before continuing.

"Your question." He pauses. "David Braddock, do you love your wife

Claire?"

I look at Claire. I remember the good times and the bad times and the times in between.

"I do," I say.

"Right answer."

The chain goes slack, the cage plummets downwards and ...

I wake up.

*   *   *   *   *

I heard Salvadore Dali used to swear by the recuperative powers of the micro-nap. Apparently he would hold a coin in his hand so that when he nodded off the noise of the coin hitting the floor would wake him up again. Yes, I know it's nuts. But notwithstanding my surreal dream, and the fact that I was only out for about an hour, I felt regenerated.

As I drove home I was marginally less obsessed with my own problems than usual and more aware of what was going on around me. What had crept up and escaped my attention (or at least only registered subliminally) was that the Thailand National Elections were now only eight days away and the Chinese New Year celebrations would follow a couple of days later. It was going to get noisy.

The election poster competition, it seemed to me, had started out modestly enough on the island, but was presently heating up, and the fly-bills were multiplying.

Prime Minister Thaksin Shinawatra's Phak Thai Rak Thai was expected to cling onto power with its coalition partner Phak Chart Thai. In spite of criticism last year of Thaksin's handling of the bird flu outbreak and the deaths of Muslim protesters in Southern Thailand, the government's swift reaction to the tsunami of 26th December which swept over Thailand's Andaman Sea coast, was widely praised, even by some of Thaksin's opponents.

The tsunami had effectively knocked the election out of the headlines and even currently, a month after the disaster, the reportage was still significant.

I preferred not to think about the tidal wave and its devastation: memories were still too raw. Since there was also little I could do to influence the outcome of the election (even assuming I had an opinion on the subject), my time was better spent thinking about the impending Chinese New Year and making sure we were adequately provisioned. I had no objection to firecrackers going off, just so long as no political hotheads were firing guns at the same time.

I decided on a detour to Mae Nam where some of Samui's Chinese community lives, and bought some *Ang Pao* – red envelopes to put money in as New Year gifts. On impulse, I also bought some firecrackers and a couple of mega rockets. To give some spiritual balance to my shopping, I purchased some frangipani-scented incense sticks, which might score some brownie points with Wayan.

When I arrived home I was still feeling buoyant. For us marginal manic depressives, good moods are rather like tsunamis – they come in big waves, unexpectedly and rarely. And like a big wave, the mood can recede just as quickly, so I needed to make the most of it.

I gave Wayan the incense sticks and a hug, took a shower and shut myself in the study to make some notes for Charoenkul before my personal preoccupations closed in again and put an end to any creative thinking. Kat's letter was filed with the others for another day.

I looked at my notes on the murders. The more I thought about it, the more I became convinced that to gain traction on the case I needed to answer two questions.

How had the victims been transported to the scene?

Why had the bodies been burned, yet identification left on them?

I tapped some notes for the Chief into my laptop, aware of the fact that my little essay seemed to deal more with logistics than the psychology of the victims and killer; which is what Papa Doc had wanted me to focus on.

I left out the superstitious stuff about the murder site (lest he think me whimsical) and the nagging voice in my head about the non-barking dog in the night-time (lest he think me unhinged). For good measure I put in some trendy psychobabble which was, to put it mildly, gibberish. After this I went out into the garden awhile to smoke three cigarettes and to ponder the mystery of *fire*.

Given that the purpose of burning the bodies did not appear to be primarily associated with the destruction of the victims' identities, I wondered whether there might be some ritualistic significance attached to it.

Fire has a deep and primal place in the human mind. I thought of the Greek myth of Prometheus who brought the gift of fire to man and incurred the wrath of Zeus who believed fire should be the preserve of the Gods. For his trouble, Prometheus was bound to a rock by adamantine chains, his innards pecked at eternally by an eagle. (It's amazing how a public-school education colonises your head with this Greek stuff; along with Latin ephemera. *Omnia Dicta Fortiori Si Dicta Latina.*)

Fire also resonates deeply in the world's religions, whether we consider the Judeo-Christian traditions involving candles and incense, the Three Fires of Buddhism, the Hindus' sacred *Agni*, or the Aztec, Mayan and Egyptian cultures' worship of the sun. In all these systems, fire represents light and life, but there is also a purification element; a searing of souls. Even non-religious, state-sponsored methods of corpse disposal encompass cremation.

The flame that enlightens, the fire that destroys.

This philosophy would be lost on the Chief, however. It was best I avoided anthropological meditations in my notes. I went back inside, tidied up the draft document and switched off the laptop.

I phoned Anna, Claire's sister. The seven-hour time difference between Thailand and the UK meant that it was now mid-morning there, and with luck Anna would be at home unless she was taking Jenny to one of those innumerable weekend activities that four-year-olds thrive on.

As well as being Claire's sister, Anna is one of my oldest friends: in fact I met her before I got to know Claire. She is in addition my confidante, personal shrink and chief cheerleader. Anna was widowed a few months before Jenny was born, but she shares with Wayan an indomitable optimism that things will turn out for the best. She's also the best damn editor in Bright Sparks Publishing.

To my delight she picks up.

"Anna Holland."

"Hi, Anna, it's David."

"David, how lovely to hear your voice."

"It's mutual, my dear. How are you? And how's Jenny?"

"We're both fine. Jenny's at a friend's this morning, and I was just wondering what to do with myself for the next few hours."

"Well, I can help you fill in some of that time, anyway."

"You sound happy."

"I don't always phone you when I'm miserable."

She laughed. "Not *always*, no. Just *usually*. What's happening with you?"

I told her about my involvement in the murder investigation, but not about the anonymous letters. There are some things you can't discuss with your sister-in-law.

She sounded a bit concerned at this news. "I thought you said you didn't trust the Thai police. 'Gangsters in uniform', I think was the term you used. Are you sure you should be getting involved in something like that?"

"It's a favour. Don't worry. Everything's OK."

"I do worry about you," she said. There was a pause and then she went on. "Are you and Claire still talking?"

"Sometimes," I replied. "I don't see much of Claire these days. She's rarely around."

"When did you last speak?"

"A couple of days ago."

"Oh, David."

"Hey, Anna, let's change the subject. I didn't phone to talk about me. I want to hear about you and Jenny."

We spoke for a while about the sorts of things that normal people talk about: work, school, family, the weather. It reminded me I'd once had a straightforward existence, although that seemed light years away from my current life.

"You have remembered it's your father's birthday tomorrow, David, yes?"

"Yes."

"And you will ring him?"

"Yes, I'll phone the old bugger."

"Promise? It's important. He wants to hear from you."

"I doubt that. But I will call him."

"When are you next coming over? I miss you, and so does Jenny."

"In a few months. I'll let you know when the flights are booked. By the way," I said, "I miss you too."

"I should hope so, Mr. Braddock."

After we'd finished I phoned Katie. I found my daughter at her desk at Croft Daniels, International Legal Advisors, dragged into the office at the weekend by some urgent litigation work.

"Hi, Dad."

"Hi, Katie, how are you?"

"Oh, same-same, you know. Still trying to tip the scales of justice in our clients' favour. Working on a couple of interesting cases, actually. How about you?"

"Helping out on a murder investigation."

"Sounds cool."

"How's the boyfriend?"

"He has a name, you know," she said huffily.

"Just teasing."

"He's fine. When are you back in the UK?"

"Soon. I'll call you."

"Dad, I have to go."

"OK, pumpkin."

"Don't forget to ring Grandpa tomorrow."

"I won't."

I wandered through to the kitchen where Wayan was doing some ironing and watching a soap on the small TV.

"Mr. David, would you like something to eat?"

"No thanks, Wayan, I'm eating out later." I gave her a hug.

This being her second hug of the day, she looked at me quizzically. "You are very happy today, Mr. David," she said.

"I am. Have you had any more dreams I should know about?"

Her face took on a serious expression and she put the iron down. "Last night I dreamed about you. You were running away from a big flying demon. He kept swooping over your head. You tried to keep him away with a stick."

Spooky. Especially as I had not mentioned to Wayan either my conversation with Yai or my nocturnal visit to the coconut grove.

"Did the demon get me?" I asked half-seriously.

"No. I woke myself up so he could not eat you."

"That's good. Actually, you know, I've been having some strange dreams myself in the last couple of days."

"Am I in your dreams?"

"No, Wayan, I don't need to have you in my dreams," I said reassuringly,

136

"you are here all the time looking after me when I am awake."

"Is Miss Claire in your dreams?"

"Sometimes, Wayan," I said. "Sometimes."

*   *   *   *   *

Watching Jingjai later was every bit as uneventful as I'd expected it to be. The smart Westerner I'd seen the other evening was back trying his luck again and obviously floundering. How many martini cocktails was this guy going to drink before he realised he was wasting his time?

When Bryan Ferry's cover version of 'Smoke Gets in Your Eyes' came on the restaurant sound system for the third time, I couldn't sit there any longer. A mélange of ennui and the afterglow of today's manic happiness attack combined to haul me out of my seat and across the road into the Ocean Pearl. I needed to have something to put in my report to Vogel, even if I had to act as an agent provocateur to produce a storyline.

I parked my behind on a barstool next to the Westerner who looked none-too-pleased at my appearance. His evening was about to get worse.

I targeted Jingjai with what I hoped was my most winning smile and beckoned her over.

"Yes, sir," she said in a husky voice that carried a slight lisp.

"What can you recommend, beautiful?" I asked.

"I'm afraid Happy Hour is over, sir."

"Never mind. I'm sure every hour I spend in this bar looking at you will be a Happy Hour anyway."

She smiled and I saw the diamond twinkle. The guy on the stool next to me grimaced but I ignored him.

"Well, let me see. How about Sex on the Beach, or shall we save that for later?"

She must hear this sort of corny chat-up every other evening, but she laughed good-naturedly. *I like this girl already,* I thought. *I hope she is on the level.*

"I'm only kidding," I said. "I'll have a Marguerita. Lots of salt. And can I get you a drink?"

"That's kind of you, sir, but I'm all right at the moment."

"Hey, you're turning down a drink? I must be uglier than I thought."

"I don't drink when I'm working, sir. But perhaps my customer will give me a nice tip at the end of the evening?"

"Smart girl. I'm David, by the way." I held out my hand and she took it.

"Jingjai."

"Pleased to meet you, Jingjai. Miss True Heart," I said in Thai.

She looked impressed. "You have a good Thai accent, Khun David."

"Let's speak Thai for the rest of the evening. I need the practice."

She went off to mix my drink and the other guy shifted on his stool uncomfortably. He wasn't even going to be able to follow the conversation from now on. Clearly he didn't speak any Thai.

To add to his discomfort I nudged him and said, "Nice girl."

"She *is*," he said pointedly, "A very nice girl."

"Your accent sounds Lancastrian. I'm guessing ... Manchester?"

"Yes."

"United or City?"

"I don't follow football," he said cutting off the conversation.

Jingjai came back with my drink. I took a good look at her. The breasts beneath the Ocean Pearl polo shirt had definitely had some work done on them, yet there was something androgynous about her body. Slim hips, rather like a boy's. She carried herself well though, and was nicely turned out, with her hair cut shorter than the norm. Her makeup could best be described as theatrical – a lot of black around the eyes, and the false eyelashes were not exactly to my taste. Not beautiful, not plain. Tomboyish, if you discounted the eye make-up. No visible tattoos, modest earrings. She could hold your gaze which testified to self-confidence, and her voice lacked the shrillness of your average bargirl. She was clearly *not* your average bargirl. Her manner was that of someone filling in time while she waited for something better to come along. I doubted that *something better* was a white man with a black wallet. So where and how did Vogel fit into this picture?

"You strike me as way too educated and sophisticated to be working in a bar," I said to her.

"Ah, if I told you about that, Khun David, I would have told you too much." She went off to serve another customer.

Two more Margueritas and a *Chang* beer later, and I was no nearer to veering our talk towards a rendezvous in my non-existent hotel room. The Mancunian at my side had become increasingly morose, but was obviously determined not to leave. I suspected a deep masochistic streak. But whatever, that was his problem.

Thankfully there was no live band playing at the *Pearl* – most of the bands on the island are awful, in my humble opinion – and the musical selection was fairly good, and not too loud. Robert Palmer's 'Addicted to Love' had just started playing when my cell phone rang and I had to ask the caller to wait while I stepped outside.

It was Nittha Rattanakorn.

"David, I'm ... I'm really sorry to call you so late, and on a Saturday too." Her voice sounded strained and intense.

"What is it, Nittha?"

"I'm ... erm ... David, can you meet me?"

"When, tomorrow?"

"Now."

"*Now?*" I looked at my watch: it was after 10.30pm.

"Yes, now. I'm sorry. Can you?"

I quickly flipped over the pages of my mental Not-To-Do-List. *Do not*

139

under any circumstances meet Nittha Rattanakorn outside of the office.

"At my office, OK? In ... let's see ... twenty minutes?"

"Thank you. I'll see you there."

Now what?

I should, of course, have said no. I should have been more professional, strict and objective. I should have told her that I had rules with clients, and that there were boundaries that had to be observed. I should have asked her whether it was a real emergency, or whether it could wait until Monday. I should have told myself that meeting the wife of a major mobster at night alone in my office was a bad idea. But I didn't do any of those things. Instead I remembered how attractive and vulnerable she'd looked when I first met her a few days ago. Then I went back into the Pearl, paid my bill, gave Jingjai a big tip, patted my sullen companion's shoulder condescendingly, and wished him good luck.

Riding my motorbike to the office I could have sworn for a moment I saw Klaus Vogel in the crowd surging into one of the nightclubs. But my eyes must have been playing tricks on me. Or maybe, because I'd been talking to Jingjai, the German was on my mind and it was my brain playing tricks.

After all, Vogel had no reason to be back in Samui just yet, did he?

*　　*　　*　　*　　*

Nittha Rattanakorn was in a state of considerable agitation.

I guided her to the two-seater sofa in the East Office and sat down beside her. She was trembling and her breathing came in shallow gasps as she struggled to contain her emotion.

When I touched her wrist gently the tears came, and they kept on coming. She put her head on my shoulder and I put a solicitous arm around her. When she rested a hand on my thigh, however, I must confess I felt an inappropriate stiffening of muscle in the groin area. I patted her arm in what I hoped would be taken as an avuncular gesture.

"Just let it flow, Nittha, it's all right."

When her sobbing subsided and she lifted her head, my shirt was sodden with her tears.

I made us green tea while she composed herself. When I brought in the tray I thought it prudent to sit opposite her, since with a coffee table between us we were both afforded a measure of protection.

She told me her husband had flown off the island today on a business trip. The man who had been giving her attention – and who was a business associate of her husband's – had seen this as an opportunity to take their relationship to a more physical level. When Nittha had made it plain that not only was that *not* going to happen, but that she didn't want to see him again, he had taken it badly and become abusive.

She was so shaken by the experience that she needed to talk to someone so she could unburden herself. *Cue David Braddock.*

I explained quietly and calmly that she'd done the right thing, and that she shouldn't feel embarrassed about crying in front of me. She took my hand, pressed it to her face and told me I was a good man.

I wasn't so sure about that. If she could have read my thoughts, she may well have had a different opinion: a fit woman's tears always make me feel protective and horny in equal measure. Fortunately she wasn't a mind-reader.

I considered the two women I'd seen in my office that day: Kat, confident and independent; and Nittha, unsure and needy. Of the two, I had to be most careful with Nittha. A therapeutic relationship can produce dependency on the side of the client, which carries the danger of boundary violations and a quick descent to naked romps in hotel bedrooms.

I didn't want to become a crutch for Nittha. Kat, on the other hand, had no need of a crutch – unless as a toy during unorthodox foreplay perhaps.

Before she left, Nittha said, "If I'm going to see you again, David, I think it's only fair to tell you who I am."

"I know who you are. You're Nittha Rattanakorn; Thongchai Rattanakorn's wife."

"How long have you known?"

"From the beginning."

*   *   *   *   *

"So you're working weekends now?" said Claire when I eventually arrived home.

"I had an emergency call this evening and had to go into the office."

"A woman, of course."

"An upset lady, yes. She needed to talk."

"That's very chivalrous of you, David. Was there any hugging involved?"

"A little."

"You will get yourself into trouble one of these days. It's lucky I'm so understanding."

"It is."

I sat on the bed.

"I called Anna today," I said.

"Anna?"

"Your sister."

"I know she's my sister. My question was rather *why* you had called her," she said tersely.

I shrugged. "We haven't spoken for a while."

"What did she have to say?"

"She's concerned about ... well, about these conversations we have. And where it's all going."

"I'm concerned about the conversations we have." She paused. "Maybe it's about time we stopped having them."

"Claire –"

"There was a time," she continued, "when Anna and I used to talk about everything; when we had no secrets; when nothing was off-limits. Same as you and I used to be. But we have to face it that six years ago that all changed. It will never be that way again, David."

I remained silent.

"I think it's time I moved out permanently," she said.

"Whoa, Claire."

"Let's face it, my darling, I'm only here some of the time anyway. A clean break would be better. I'm not just thinking of us; I'm thinking of Catherine too."

"Don't bring Katie into this," I said angrily.

"She is already *in this*. You want the wife you used to have and she wants the mother she used to have. But that woman no longer exists, David. Times have changed. We all have to move on."

"Claire, I'm not ready to let you go."

"I know that. But you must."

I looked into those beautiful sad eyes and said, "You are the love of my life. Whatever has happened, that doesn't change. That will never change."

"I'm the love of your last life, David. Now you have a new life. And I have somewhere else I should be too." Her voice softened. "My being here is making you ill, my darling. In your mind, it's making you ill. I *know* this. Just think about what I'm saying."

"I can't talk about this now, Claire. I'm sorry. I'm going for a cigarette."

I stepped out onto the balcony and lit up, waiting for the thudding in my heart to ease off.

After a few minutes I went back inside.

Claire was gone.

6

"Some are born to sweet delight,
Some are born to endless night."
William Blake, Auguries of Innocence

"You are not here either for devotion or meditation," said a voice from behind me. "That much is obvious."

I remained silent and motionless, so the Old Monk hit me across the back with his stick.

"Stop pretending," he ordered. "You are wasting Buddha's time. And mine."

We were in the Wat Son garden. He sat down beside me and bummed a cigarette. After we'd lit up, he looked at me quizzically.

"Why are you here?"

"Everybody has to be somewhere."

"That is not necessarily true. Perhaps you have come to think through your problems? To make them disappear?"

"Perhaps."

"I can help you there. I am good at making things disappear. For instance," he said, "You see that glass bottle?"

He pointed to the garden wall where a young monk was lounging against the other side, his back to us. The monk had evidently been sipping a cola drink and had placed the bottle on the wall while he buried his nose in a newspaper.

I nodded. "I see the bottle."

The Old Monk stared at it fiercely for a moment. Then he banged his stick twice on the ground and turned to me. "There you are," he said. "The bottle has gone."

The bottle hadn't moved.

"What is this?" I responded. "Jedi mind tricks?"

"I assure you," he said calmly, "there is no bottle."

He rose and walked over to the wall. He picked up the bottle.

"Do you imagine I now hold a bottle in my hand?"

"Yes," I said.

"And am I now looking at it?"

"Yes."

He rotated the bottle in his hand then dropped his half-smoked cigarette into it.

"How deluded you are."

He clipped the young monk behind the ear and handed him the bottle. "This stuff would rot your brains if you had any," he said.

The Old Monk walked back to me and sat down again. "You cannot solve your problems because you see them the same way you see the bottle. As discrete, as separate, as *other* to you. You fail to see that the bottle is not a thing *of itself.* The word 'bottle' is just a label attached for convenience. Yet you imagine there is such a thing as 'bottle-*ness*', that has intrinsic meaning?" He paused and sighed wearily. "I say again, there is no such thing as a bottle. It is because your mind is confused that you think you have problems."

"I do have problems. And all your metaphysics won't conjure them away."

"Very well," he said. "Supposing I humour you for the moment. What problems do you imagine you have?"

"For a start, I'm assisting on a murder investigation, and it's giving me a headache. That's highly confidential, by the way. The investigation I mean, not the headache."

"Ah, now you begin to interest me. So you are engaged in some *real* detecting?"

"Yes, I am," I said tetchily.

145

He traced a circle in the dust with the end of his stick. "You know Lord Buddha was a great detective?" he asked rhetorically. "He solved the greatest puzzle facing mankind: the cause of suffering, of *dukkha*, and how we can put an end to suffering. He sat under the Bodhi tree and resolved never to rise until he had found enlightenment. Such determination and single-mindedness were needed to solve this problem. These are the characteristics a great detective needs." He looked at me sardonically and tut-tutted. "Your mind is too scattered at the moment to solve mysteries. You lack focus and discipline."

The Old Monk had a point, I had to give him that. Out of the corner of my eye I could see the young monk dithering over whether to enter the garden and risk another whack. In the end he decided against and wandered off in the direction of the wat, presumably seeking shade from the midday sun. It was, inevitably, another dry day on Samui.

"Does Buddha have any more useful advice for unfocused detectives?"

"Oh yes," he said emphatically. "A lot of useful advice. Are you familiar with the *Kalama Sutra*? It has some good parallels for you."

I shook my head. While the Old Monk talked he continued to trace circles on the ground with his stick. His voice took on a dreamy quality, like a talking meditation.

"The *Kalama Sutra* is Lord Buddha's charter on free inquiry. Every private investigator should read it and memorise its messages. The Kalamas asked the Enlightened One for guidance on how to recognise whether teachings that were given to them were right or wrong. He told them: *Do not believe in anything simply because you have heard it; or because it is in your traditions; or because many speak about it; or because it is found in your religious books; or because your teachers and elders believe it; or because you have become attached to it from habit.*

"Buddha thus counselled a wise caution, a form of constructive cynicism, if you will. He went on to say that you should observe and analyse for yourself. If you find that your conclusions are in accord with reason, then you should accept those findings and live by them."

I thought about the source of my information on the murders. It was pretty much all Charoenkul and his boys, and of course his wife had done the translation and summary. *How objective was this information and how much of it was coloured by bias and error?* I really wanted to talk to Yai again, and to his grand-daughter.

I considered the anonymous letters in the same light. Other than the physical reality of the letters themselves, the remaining data I had to work on had all been generated inside my own head. If I couldn't trust what others told me, could I trust what I told myself?

The Old Monk had stopped tracing circles on the ground and was turning them alternately into smiley faces and sad faces.

"Did you know this person who was murdered?" he asked.

"No. And it's not just one person. Two people have been killed."

"Did they have families?"

"One did."

"So many problems in the world," he said quietly, as if to himself.

He was silent for a while. He appeared to be contemplating the four happy faces and the four sad faces he had traced in the dust. I wondered what they meant, assuming they meant anything. The world of duality, perhaps? The world of *appearances*; in Buddhism known as the realm of *samsara* where everything you experience is an illusion?

"If you are going to solve your most important problem," he said breaking the silence, "you will have to adopt the Right View."

"And what would that involve?" I asked.

The Old Monk looked at me with intensity, and spoke slowly. "Someday soon we should have a very specific conversation. There is something I need to communicate to you, but today is not the time. The ground of your mind is not prepared. Today we must speak of more mundane things, like death."

He let out a sigh. He seemed sad.

"Give me a cigarette," he said. He puffed for a minute before he continued.

"Lord Buddha spoke about the importance of reason; of working out things for yourself. His teaching he likened to a raft: useful to carry you across the river, but ultimately to be left behind when it became a burden. He was very pragmatic, and you must be too. You must apply reason and logic, but you must also be able to empty your mind of the clutter of labels and boxes and categories. Your tendency to compartmentalise your life and the world into neat *segments* will get in the way of your finding a solution. You will lose your appreciation of the bigger picture. That's what I meant by adopting the Right View."

"OK," I said, "so I should sweat the details, but not lose sight of the wood for the trees, right? I know that."

"I am talking about more than that. I'm saying that if you can free your mind of the artificial construct of *things*, you will see what is really happening in the world. A mind that is empty is *interconnected*. In Buddhism we sometimes use the image of the Jewel Net of Indra to illustrate this point. Imagine an immense three-dimensional net with a mirror attached at each and every connecting point. Each mirror would reflect the image of every other mirror and so on to infinity.

"You are one of those mirrors, but in a sense you are also all of those mirrors, because everything is a reflection of everything else. Because our mind and our self have no effective substance, we are all multi-centred and interconnected; like the reflections of mirrors in mirrors."

"That's a very pretty picture," I said, "But I don't see how it helps to tell me that the world as we know it is just a hotchpotch of unrelated images." I wagged my cigarette in what I hoped was an ironic fashion.

"If you would stop only listening with your ears you might understand better," he said gruffly. "Let me spell it out for you. The images are *not* unrelated. *Everything is connected. Everyone is connected. Everyone and everything is interconnected.* Crime, punishment, you, me, this island, the Three Fires of Buddhism, history, the weather, elephants, the National Elections, a cola bottle, *everything*. Your analysis of your problem will be based on individual *things*, but your solution will lie in the interdependency of *everything*."

He stubbed out his cigarette and looked suddenly tired; like a man daunted by the task before him. However, he rallied and went on. "Study the doctrine of *Dependent Origination*. Everything has a cause and everything has an effect. For me, this is the true meaning of karma."

"So, to summarise," I said brightly and somewhat flippantly, "first, I should trust no-one, because everybody lies, and instead I should make my own inquiries and observations. Second, I need to do an analysis of the facts, but I shouldn't get bogged down in them. Third, I am already somehow connected to the murderer; I just have to figure out how. You know, you should write a manual for murder detectives."

"As to that, I have no interest in murders. I offer a recipe for life, not for solving crimes."

I looked at him sharply. "I thought you were talking about the murder cases," I said.

The Old Monk snorted. "I don't know what gave you that idea," he said. "Your mind has an eccentric understanding of gravity: it circles a dead planet. I was referring to Your Problem."

"My problem is the murder cases."

"I think not." The Old Monk took his stick and scrubbed out the pictures of the faces.

"So what is *My Problem*?" I asked peevishly.

"Another time," he said rising.

I was annoyed now, and felt a juvenile impulse to retaliate. I tried quickly to think of something to say. This was the best I could come up with.

"So before we meet 'another time'," I said, "I have something for you to think about. Consider this. *Why is a raven like a writing-desk?*"

He bowed solemnly. "I shall give the question my full consideration."

*   *   *   *   *

I'd started the day early, staking out Jingjai's place as atonement for my lamentable failure of the previous evening to behave as a professional PI.

I was sitting outside her apartment block in the jeep by 8.00am, puffing on a Marlboro and sipping a takeaway coffee. Of course she *could* have had an overnight visitor who had left before that time, but I doubted it. Certainly not the dull-as-ditchwater Mancunian. I wondered if he'd be back in the *Pearl* again tonight, the poor bastard.

Around 10.30am Jingjai appeared on the street, alone and on foot. She wasn't wearing any makeup, was casually dressed and sported a baseball cap. She looked like a boy. She didn't notice me as she walked to a nearby fruit and vegetable stall, made a few purchases and chatted for a few minutes. Then she went back inside the apartment building. A couple of minutes later I saw curtains drawn back and her face briefly at the window. I could now identify her flat.

No farang had come out of the building in the two-and-a-half hours I'd been sitting around. I'd waited another hour for nothing to happen, then drove to the temple.

*   *   *   *   *

My temple visit and lecture from the Old Monk being over, I had some time to kill before my rendezvous with Bee. I drove half-way to Lamai and pulled the jeep off the road at a grass-roofed eating hole that overlooked the sea. I sat at a table made from driftwood, ordered a beer and lit up while I perused the interestingly-worded menu. It read *If you have ever had crabs, you will like it here. Our friendly staff is always ready to service you.*

My mind, however, soon drifted towards the words of the Old Monk. In spite of the fact that we'd spent several minutes talking at cross-purposes about 'My Problem' – whatever he imagined it to be – what he'd said about everything being connected had struck a chord.

I could sign up to the proposition of everything on the planet (and beyond) being in some way ultimately related to everything else. But so far as the murders were concerned, I had to work out which things were connected in a *significant way*; and which things were not significant, and therefore irrelevant.

As an exercise, I took out my notebook and started to draw a spider-web diagram; a sort of schematic micro-representation of the Jewel Net of Indra, Braddock-style. Names of people and *things*, I put inside circles and joined the circles with lines where I perceived a connection, however tenuous.

I put myself at the centre of the diagram, and expanded it outwards adding randomly, and sometimes fancifully as notions popped into my head. It was most certainly *not* a structured approach, more like a brain-dump. I realised after a while that the picture I was drawing was not solely related to the murders.

I put down my pen and looked at the web. A big chunk of my life had been reduced to circles, lines and letters.

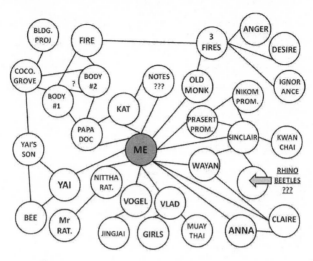

I scanned the paper, like some old-fashioned English archaeologist deciphering hieroglyphs. I searched for pattern and meaning, but found only randomness. The lines joining the circles denoted relationships, but not for the most part *causal links*. I was reminded of the quotation about history being just one damn thing after another.

I needed more data; but at least I could rearrange, expand, prune as necessary and annotate later. It was a start. I figured that if I looked at the problem from as many different angles as possible, something might stick out.

I lit another cigarette and became aware that a waiter was hovering at my shoulder hanging around to take my order. He'd probably been there a while, just too polite to cough. I ordered some steamed rice with the catch of the day and he lumbered off and left me to my thoughts.

My thoughts were about flames, and the Three Fires, and about what remains after the fire has burned out. I thought about ashes and I thought about cremations. And I thought about Claire and whether she would leave me. *The burnt-out ends of smoky days.*

'Everybody Hurts', by REM, started playing on the crackly music system. *Yeah*, I thought, *that would be about right*. Everybody hurts and everybody lies. And everybody burns.

*   *   *   *   *

Everybody might burn, but not everybody is burnt. But two people have been. I reminded myself that this was not a game, not some dry intellectual puzzle for my bored brain. Two people were dead. The Old Monk was right: I needed to regain control of my monkey mind and focus.

My mind, however, has ideas of its own. It is not accustomed to long stretches of enforced discipline. It will tolerate that regime for a while before it starts screaming at me that it needs creative space and that it needs to roam free.

If my mind were a dog, it would be the sort of dog that chews the furniture, chases cars and defecates on the neighbour's lawn. This afternoon I put my mind on a short leash. I made it sit, heel and roll over, then I tickled its tummy. It seemed inclined to behave itself, so I gave it the benefit of the doubt, but remained wary. Sooner or later I knew it would try to hump somebody's leg.

I arrived at the coconut grove a few minutes early, but someone else had arrived there before me.

A young Thai girl – I would guess her age at 18-20 years – was sitting on a motor scooter under the shade of the trees. She looked vulnerable and undernourished, and something about her posture suggested habituated disappointment. On her lap she clutched a basket covered with a crimson cloth. The scene put me in mind of Red Riding Hood. As I climbed out of the jeep she looked at me with nervous eyes, like I was the Wolf.

"You must be Bee," I said lightly in Thai, and made a wai.

She had risen respectfully and returned my greeting. "Mr. Braddock," she said bowing her head.

"I understood we were meeting at your grandfather's house."

"I thought perhaps we could talk here for a while first, before we see my grandfather."

She looked at me in a way that suggested that, while life had so far given her a good whipping, her spirit was not yet entirely broken.

"I am concerned for my grandfather and I do not wish to see him upset."

There were a couple of large boulders near to where we were standing and I suggested we sit down to talk. She nodded but continued to hug the basket to her like it was a magic charm to keep me at bay.

"Bee," I said, "I have no desire to distress either you or your grandfather. Why do you think our conversation might upset him?"

"It is personal. A family matter."

"And difficult to talk about to a farang?"

She nodded.

"Does it concern your father?"

She nodded again.

"Yai told me your father died here. I'm sorry. It must be hard for you having to come here knowing what happened."

Bee bit her lip. "Did grandfather tell you how he died? I mean, the circumstances of his death?"

"No."

She paused and then said, "It is a long time since I spoke about this to anyone. I'm not sure I have ever *really* talked about it."

"Perhaps it's time you did."

"But – here?" she said indicating the grove. "And to a stranger?" She shook her head. "No, no. It is impossible."

"It is not impossible. Our setting is a little strange, perhaps. But it's neither impossible nor ridiculous. Talk to me," I said. "Tell me about your father." I lit a cigarette to make it clear I wasn't going anywhere. "What was his name?"

"His name was Wasan," she said quietly.

154

"And was he a boat-builder like your grandfather?"

"Yes, he was. Although boat-building was not where his heart lay."

"You mean he was more interested in his family?"

She shook her head sadly.

"No, Mr. Braddock, that is not what I mean. My father provided for mother and me – even loved us in his own way – but we were not his real passion."

"What was?"

"My father was a political activist."

"Really? I shouldn't have thought there'd be too many of those on Koh Samui."

"There are some."

"Well, everyone needs something to live for."

"In my father's case it turned out to be something to die for." She hesitated and looked at me. What she saw must have reassured her because she continued. "How much do you know of the recent history of my country, Mr. Braddock?"

"Probably not as much as I should, given that I live here."

"Have you heard of 'Black May'?"

"I've heard of it, but I can't say I know much about it."

"Then I need to share some of our history with you, so you can understand." She began to recite, as if from a history book. "In Thailand there has been a long struggle for democracy over the years. Fourteen years ago, in February 1991, Army Commander Suchinda Kraprayoon led a coup d'état which overthrew the elected government. The coup-makers called themselves the National Peace-Keeping Council and appointed a former diplomat as interim Prime Minister. A new constitution was promulgated by the junta-dominated Assembly and elections were held in March 1992.

"General Suchinda who had orchestrated the coup – and was not even a Member of Parliament – was appointed Prime Minister, to the outrage of many Thai people. In a mood of anger, large-scale protests followed, and a strike was planned for 17th May, with an accompanying rally in Bangkok."

Bee put down her basket and stood up, agitated. As she continued she began to walk around, occasionally leaning on a tree for a moment or two before becoming restless and moving on. When she talked it was as if she were talking partly to herself. Perhaps she was.

"My father had been passionate about politics for some years. In 1976, a student friend of his had been beaten to death by the paramilitaries during the 6th of October Massacre at the University campus in Bangkok. The climax to the day's brutality was the burning of a heap of petrol-soaked bodies: the corpse of my father's friend was among them. It left a very deep impression on my father, as you can imagine.

"So when this new army-inspired injustice arose, my father felt he had to do something.

"Along with three of his friends he travelled to Bangkok for the rally. It was not easy to get there since the Interior Minister had ordered the provincial governors to prevent people from travelling. But by various means my father and his friends made their way to the capital.

"By the evening of the first day of protests some two hundred thousand people thronged Sanam Luang, spilling on to the surrounding streets. After darkness fell, the protesters began a march to Government House to demand the resignation of Suchinda.

"However, when they reached Phan Fa Bridge, they were met with a razor-wire barricade, water cannons and riot police armed with batons. Violence ensued, and shortly after midnight the government declared a state of emergency.

"By the morning the army had brought in more troops, M16 rifles were fired in the air, and the protests spread to other parts of the city. The violence escalated.

"My father and his friends were arrested and separated, and my father was taken to the grounds of a school in a truck with other protesters. There they were kicked and beaten with rifle-butts, tied up and left out in the hot sun without food or water."

Bee interrupted her narrative and took a deep breath. Her hands were shaking.

"Take a moment," I said.

"I heard all this from my mother," she said. "And it got worse. My father and a few other men were dragged into the centre of the school courtyard, and they had gasoline poured over them. The soldiers laughed at them and stood nearby smoking cigarettes and threatening to set them on fire if they didn't behave themselves.

"My father remembered what had happened to the student protesters sixteen years before, and he was terrified. After a few hours, the soldiers hosed the protesters down with water and let them go.

"My father learned later that the King had intervened and an amnesty had been declared for the protesters. A few days later, General Suchinda stood down as Prime Minister.

"Fifty-two deaths were *officially* acknowledged by the government, and there were hundreds of injuries. Some of the injured were women and children. In all, three and a half thousand people were arrested, and many said they had been tortured. No-one knows how many people 'disappeared'. A Special Committee concluded that excessive force had been used by the authorities, but to this day nobody has been prosecuted.

"My father's friends were never seen again: they became part of the 'disappeared' statistics. Only my father returned home to Samui, and he was a changed man, traumatised by what had happened. He felt guilty that his friends had died and he alone had survived."

"*Survivor's syndrome*," I said. "It must have been hard on you all."

"I was only six at the time," Bee replied. "I don't remember any of it. The responsibility all fell on my mother. In the months that followed, father became more and more withdrawn. He said that he should have died with his friends; that he was a coward and didn't deserve to live. He became obsessed with the idea of immolation – death by fire.

"One day he left our house and didn't come back. He came to this grove, sat down cross-legged on the ground over there –" she indicated the spot where the murders had taken place, "– poured gasoline over himself and struck a match."

"He burned himself to death?"

"Yes."

"On the same spot as you discovered the farang's body?"

"Exactly the same spot. That's how I noticed it. Every time I come to see my grandfather I look at the place my father died and say a silent prayer for him."

"What happened to your family after your father died?"

"Mother and grandfather rowed. Grandfather was very hurt and angry. He hadn't approved of my father getting involved in politics. He said it was mother's fault his son had died; that she hadn't cared for him and comforted him enough after Bangkok; that a 'real' wife would have been able to save him. He moved out to this wooden house here, so he could be near my father's spirit. Soon after his death, stories began circulating of a flying demon. You know how ignorant and cruel people can be sometimes," she said bitterly. "Shortly afterwards, grandfather went blind. His eyesight had been failing for some time."

"How do you and your mother manage?"

"Mother works in a spa, I work in a shop. We sell grandfather's carved boats. We get by. Every few days I bring supplies to grandfather."

"And your mother and grandfather still don't talk?"

"No. Mother would like to make peace but grandfather is stubborn and won't meet her. It is a great shame. We are the only family he has left."

I went to the jeep, brought back two bottles of water and handed one to

Bee. She had lapsed into silence and I realised how much older than her years she seemed. I imagined what it must be like for a young girl having all that pain turning around in her head from dawn to dusk.

"Thank you for sharing that with me," I said. "It can't have been easy."

"I don't know how it helps you," she replied, "But somehow I'm glad I told you." She drank from the bottle. "Thank *you*."

"Bee, did you talk to the policeman about your father's death? When they questioned you about the farang?"

"No."

"Doesn't it strike you as a strange coincidence that the farang's body was burned, like your father's? That they were found in the same place?"

She shook her head. It was a gesture of hopelessness. "There are so many things that cannot be explained in this life, Mr. Braddock. After all these years I still don't understand why my father had to die. How am I expected to understand the death of a stranger? Perhaps the people around here are right after all. Perhaps this place is cursed."

"You don't believe that any more than I do," I responded. "What can you tell me about the farang you found?"

She frowned at the memory. "He was lying on his back with his arms at his sides. His body was dreadfully charred, and the smell of burned meat was horrible. There were ants and insects on him. Even I could see he had been dead for some time." She shivered. "That's all I saw. That's all I wanted to see. I thought of my father." She paused. "Then I called the police."

"You didn't see anything else around? No bike, no glass bottles, no ... I don't know what."

"No. Nothing. Just the dead man under the coconut trees. That's all."

I felt a frustration arise inside me; but it was not due to anything associated with the murders. It was the anger I feel when I see needless suffering: in this case a family at war with itself through hurt, pride and stubbornness. I resolved to do something about it, however 'interfering' this might be.

Bee collected her basket and we trudged up the slope to her grandfather's shack; Red Riding Hood and the Wolf travelling in convoy.

The old man was out on his porch carving a toy boat. He was shirtless and his lap was covered in shavings, some of which stuck to his body which glistened in the sun.

Bee greeted him fondly and Yai visibly relaxed. He must have worried that her encounter with me would leave her upset. She took the basket into the house and began unpacking.

I hunkered down beside the old man and put my hand on his wrist. He stopped carving and turned his sightless eyes towards me. I steeled myself to be a hard-nosed SOB.

I asked him if it were true that he and his daughter-in-law no longer spoke and he grunted a 'yes'. Then I told him that he should be very proud of his grand-daughter; that she was a courageous girl; that she had integrity and that she loved him very much. I told him that she had shared with me the painful details of her father's death and its bitter aftermath.

"Bee met me in the coconut grove," I said, "because she didn't want to talk here and have me stir up memories that would be painful for you. She didn't want me to upset you.

"However, I am afraid, Yai, that I *am* going to upset you. You are not going to like hearing what I have to say."

Bee had finished unpacking her basket and was standing in the doorway looking at me with alarm. She began to protest, but the old man silenced her.

"What do you have to say, Mr. Braddock?"

"Just this. Your son is not coming back. There is no demonic spirit haunting the trees. Wasan was a troubled man at the end, but he is not the stuff that evil ghosts are made of. He had courage and he had a sense of justice. He may not have been able to see it that way, but that's how it was.

His tragedy is that he died needlessly. He fell into the darkness before his time."

"My son put his beliefs before his family," said the old man bluntly. "That's where it all went wrong."

"So tell me, Yai, how is that any different from what you are doing now?"

"What do you mean?" he asked indignantly.

"I mean that for years you have put your resentment before your family. I mean that you were blind before you ever lost your sight."

"And what do *you* know of my family?" he shouted angrily. "What gives you – a farang – the right to talk to me like this?"

"I have to be the one to talk to you like this because no-one else *can*. You have hidden yourself away here beyond the reach of family and friends; so that you can be alone with your grief.

"Have you ever stopped to consider your family's grief? What about your grand-daughter? What about your daughter-in-law? You abandoned them when you came here. You left a widow alone to bring up a child. You could have been a comfort to them instead of nursing your *own* pain and sense of loss.

"Yet in spite of all that, Bee still comes here to you; she cleans for you; brings you food; loves you. Do you not think *she* deserves better?"

Bee put her arms around Yai and wept with him. They were the bitter tears of lost years, and of remorse, and of deeply-buried pain.

"I thought you were a good man," the girl cried to me. "Why do you say these hurtful things? Do you not think we have suffered enough?"

"On the contrary," I said, "I think you have suffered too much. All of you. But your suffering is pointless. It has to stop." I put my hand back on the old man's wrist and he tried to pull away, but I held fast.

"Yai, listen to me. *You do not need to be blind.* You can still help your family. It is not too late. If you will allow me, I will arrange and pay for the operation to remove the cataracts from your eyes. The procedure is simple and straightforward. It will not cost you a Baht. You can have your sight back in a few days' time: the surgery can be performed here on Samui."

Bee looked at me anxiously. "Why would you do that?" she said.

"Why would I *not*?" I answered. "Yai, the doctors can restore your sight, but that is all they can do. That is the easy part. What happens after that is up to you."

Bee and I looked at the old man. I wasn't sure how he would respond. Bee whispered something in his ear and hugged him. He nodded to her and she said, "Grandfather agrees."

Yai rose unsteadily without acknowledging me, and took himself back into the shack. He had a lot to think about.

"You will have to give him some space," I said to Bee. "He is a proud man. This is not easy for him."

She shook her head and examined my face closely, as if trying to resolve a contradiction in her mind. "You believe in hard medicine, Mr. Braddock."

"I believe in what works," I replied. "My assistant, Miss Da, will call you tomorrow and start making arrangements with one of the local hospitals. Don't worry," I went on, "I will make good on my promise. But tell me, I'm curious. What did you say to him just now to get him to agree?"

"I asked him if he wanted to see my face."

*   *   *   *   *

I once visited a coffee factory in Bali which produces *kopi luwak*, a premium coffee that retails at about a thousand US dollars per kilo. The process employed is rather interesting. Civet cats are fed with the choicest coffee berries. While the berries are in the cat's stomach, the fleshy pulp is digested and enzymes mix with the beans – which makes them aromatic and less bitter. Ten to twelve hours later, the cats excrete the beans which are then washed, dried, roasted, bagged and sold on to coffee connoisseurs, many of whom probably have no idea they are drinking *hot civet shit*.

I mention this because working on my relationship with my father in some ways resembles the kopi luwak process – it is like trying to make something valuable out of cat poo: possible in theory, but unlikely in practice.

In the first place, my father, Edward James Braddock, is one of those people who have fallen under the poisonous and incurable spell of the Protestant Work Ethic. As a result of this, it is impossible for anyone – especially me – to work hard enough to satisfy Braddock Senior's exacting standards. *Consequently we are all wastrels.* (When I dropped out of university this was made abundantly clear to me.)

Secondly, he is an entrepreneur par excellence. Everything to which he has turned his hand has subsequently turned to gold; whether it was plantations in post-World War II Malaya, property, car dealerships, import-export, or whatever. Accordingly, he has a mind like a metal trap and the unforgiving memory of an elephant. Whatever the subject, he is always three steps ahead. I can't keep up.

Since we are not exactly close, conversations with him are always difficult. He is not the most family-centred of men, although he has an obvious soft spot for Katie and is devoted to Nang – his second wife and my step-mother.

My father and Nang's marriage is just about the strongest one I know. This is somewhat ironic given that Nang is Thai and my business is based on the premise that farang-Thai relationships don't work.

Nang's personality is a fascinating combination of steel and fluff. She has kicked my backside when necessary; but she has also been a real mother to me following the death of my own mother while I was still very young. Tragedy has dogged her own attempts at motherhood and after two stillborn baby girls, the risks to her physical and mental health were too great to continue trying for a family, however much Mr. and Mrs. Braddock might want one. Nang had borne this blow with fortitude. For me, strength of character coupled with femininity makes for a winning and attractive combination. It's not surprising my father fell for her. If I'd been twenty years older, I would have too. She's now in her sixties and still looks pretty good.

So this afternoon when I phoned the old sod on the occasion of his seventy-fifth birthday, I was pleased when Nang answered.

"David! How is my handsome boy?"

"Still handsome, Nang. How is my favourite, most elegant, and not-at-all-evil stepmother?"

She laughed.

"And how is the elderly curmudgeon today? Still drowning kittens and tearing the wings off butterflies?"

"David, don't be so naughty. Wait a moment and I will get your father. He'll be so happy to hear from you."

He so won't. The line went silent for a while then there was a click followed by Edward Braddock's gravelly, measured tones. "Hello, David, good of you to call."

"Happy birthday, Dad."

"Thank you. Kind of you to remember."

"Are you and Nang doing anything special to celebrate? I mean, seventy-five is a big one."

"Indeed it is. We'll be opening a bottle of ridiculously expensive champagne at Thorogood's later."

"Excellent."

There was a silence. Our conversations tend to be punctuated by them: the forced jollity collapses and it takes a while to pump it up again. I half-expect the talk to veer towards the indefatigable topic of 'when-are-you-coming-home-to-do-a-proper-job', but my father has clearly decided to be unusually restrained on his birthday.

"Katie phoned," he said. "She sent me flowers, of all things. A sweet thought."

"It was."

"So when do you next expect to be back in England?"

And so the words limped out in their own stilted way, like verbal gimps, until we could decently put our phones down and heave a sigh of relief that we wouldn't have to speak again for some time.

By the way, while we're on the subject of families, the civet cat isn't really a cat at all. It's a distant cousin of the mongoose. So kopi luwak is actually *mongoose turd coffee*. I'm not sure if that's better or worse.

*　*　*　*　*

As dusk was gathering, I drove over to the empty house at Bang Rak armed with a printout from Sinclair's Smiley Cars database. I told myself I was there to perform a dry run of observing the car park and matching the parked vehicles to the 'unhired cars' list.

I was really there because I was bored with the idea of observing Jingjai for another uneventful evening, so the dry run enabled me to defer this task for a couple of hours.

The neighbourhood was unlit and the property was big. Using Sinclair's spare set of keys I opened the padlock on the sliding gate and stepped onto the drive. The garden was a mess of broken concrete and stacked tiles. A large plastic bin, half-full of sand and cigarette butts, stood forlornly by the edge of the ruined pool. I let myself into the house and made my way onto the back balcony. A dog barked in the distance: no curious incidents in *this* night-time.

Sinclair was right. There was a perfect view of his car park; and although I was only able to make out some of the number plates, by comparing the

165

makes and colours I could deduce which car was which and match them to my list. There were no cars missing. Kwanchai was being good today.

As the waning light segued into a soothing darkness I lit a cigarette and relaxed into the moment. There was nothing more to be done, so I opened the trapdoor to my subconscious, climbed in, and had a root around.

My father was seventy-five. Yai was getting his sight back and Bee was getting her grandfather back. Somebody was sending anonymous letters. My wife was probably about to leave me. The Old Monk was being enigmatic and I was no nearer to solving the murders. There was still no rain.

I visualised myself pressing the 'locate' button on my Moral Global Positioning System. The display came up like a teleprompter.

I am a man who ... sleeps with another man's wife; and

I am a man who ... helps the blind to see; and

I am a man who ... thinks he can fix other people; and

I am a man who ... needs to fix himself.

I switched to Latin Mode. *In regione caecorum rex est luscus*. Except that, dear Erasmus, the one-eyed man is not always king.

Such were the thoughts rolling like tumbleweeds through my dry brain in this dry season.

* * * * *

Since I had no intention of following Jingjai home after her shift, and no conviction it would be necessary anyway, I took the jeep into Chaweng.

I discovered Vladimir sitting alone at a corner table in the Ocean Pearl and he was in a less-than-exuberant mood. Even in the Pearl's subdued lighting I could see the bruising on his face, and there were scratches on his neck which looked like they may have been made by fingernails.

Apparently his big fight on Friday night had not gone as well as

166

expected: against the odds, he had lost to a visiting boxer from Poland.

"He was big," said Vlad by way of explanation.

"Bigger than *you*?" I asked. "I'm surprised they could fit him in the arena."

"Is big disgrace for Russian losing to Polish," he said miserably. "This week I train hard, and next week I kick his Polish ass. We have *remash*."

"You mean 'rematch'."

"Yes."

"And how about the scratches?" I indicated his neck. "Girlfriend trouble too?"

He gave a non-committal shrug. "I stay away from girls for a while."

I decided to keep him company for an hour or two. There was no point in going home. Claire wouldn't be around for a few days, assuming she would ever be around again. I didn't want to think about Claire. I didn't really want to think about anything.

The Pearl was quieter than it had been recently. I stayed away from the bar although I snapped a few shots of Jingjai out of habit. The guy from Manchester was nowhere to be seen, and I surmised he'd finally taken the hint and given up. Maybe he'd lowered his sights and was knocking back watered-down spirits in Girly Bar Heaven.

Vlad was not exactly great company. He insisted on taking me kick-by-kick through the highlights of Friday's Muay Thai, although the technicalities were wasted on me. I slapped a phoney smile on my face, smoked, nodded at the appropriate points, and downed several beers and whisky chasers. The Russian was still reticent about the reason for his continued presence on the island, but I couldn't have cared less. I was happy to let my brain rot awhile; so I let him ramble on about the difference between his hometown women and Thai women, and how Mother Russia had regained her pride under Putin and was taking her rightful place in the world once more.

By midnight I'd had enough. Nobody was chatting up Jingjai and even after the alcohol infusion Vlad was boring me witless, so I took a slow walk along the beach to clear my head before turning back onto the main street.

Arriving back at the jeep, I saw the Thai tramp camped out for the night in an adjacent doorway. If anything, he looked to be in an even more pathetic state than when I'd last seen him. I was surprised he hadn't taken the hint from the police and left Samui, but then perhaps he just didn't have anywhere else to go; or maybe he was hanging on until Chinese New Year in the hope that fortune might smile and he might pick up a few red envelopes stuffed with money from festive locals.

Before driving slowly home to my big empty bed, I rummaged in my pockets for some Baht and handed it to him. I didn't think he'd mind the fact that the money wasn't in a red envelope.

"Good luck."

7

"Watchfulness is the path to immortality:
Unwatchfulness is the path of death.
Those who are watchful never die:
Those who do not watch are already as dead."
Lord Buddha, The Dhammapada

From the moment I open my eyes I have the feeling that today I need to be alert, and I already *feel* alert. Something is heading my way, something big and potentially unmanageable. I can sense it in my bones. I don't know what has put me in this twitchy mood. Maybe this is how a nervous breakdown starts; or maybe Wayan sneaked into my room last night and rubbed cocaine on my gums. Whatever, I am extremely wired. Lucky I don't carry a gun or I'd be popping a cap in somebody's ass.

The image of Wayan in my bedroom with her fingers in my mouth is still disturbingly in my mind as I have breakfast. She leans across the table to pour me some juice and I experience an almost uncontrollable urge to put my head between her breasts. I have a monster erection and I can feel the sweat breaking out on my brow. Wayan notices my discomfort and puts a hand on my forehead, which only makes matters worse.

"Is something up, Mr. David?"

It most certainly is, but I can't tell her what. I mumble something about feeling dehydrated.

As she moves away to get me a glass of water, I can't help noticing how sinuously her buttocks, thighs and hips move as she walks.

When did I last have sex? I can't remember. If Wayan touches me again ... It doesn't bear thinking about. I need to get out of the house.

When she returns, I gulp down the water as fast as I can and make a hurried exit hoping she doesn't notice the bulge in my chinos.

I wheel-spin the jeep off the drive, go a hundred metres down the road then brake too quickly as I stop the car, and clouds of dust rise up around me. I can feel my heart thudding like it's coming out of my chest. I wind down the window, light a cigarette and try to stop my hands from shaking.

Jesus, what's gotten into me? Am I having a heart attack? I sit by the side of the road taking deep breaths and hoping that Wayan doesn't come out of the front door; since from where I'm parked, I'm still visible from the house.

I smoke three cigarettes, one after the other, and the jerking in my limbs subsides. The adrenalin flood abates, and the psychotic ants stop crawling around my nervous system. I check whether I can hold an image of Wayan in my head without it triggering an erection. I find that I can, just about, provided I don't imagine her in a tight top. I rotate my neck to get rid of the crick, throw my cigarette butt out of the window and drive to the office.

When I arrive at the David Braddock Agency I am relieved that on seeing Da my brain does not fill up with images of penetration involving my third-trimester employee. The withering and somewhat scornful look I receive from my receptionist the instant I cross the threshold would in any event shrivel any residual erotic notions.

"Khun David, good morning," she says with heavy irony.

I know that tone. I throw my straw hat at the hat rack and miss.

"What have I done?" I say.

"Who can say?" she replies. "But you had an early visitor this morning. *Miss Noi* dropped by to settle the account for her 'emergency weekend therapy session', as she called it. She seemed disappointed you weren't here. She insisted on paying double the normal rate, *as it was so late on Saturday night when she had her session with you.*"

"And?" I say innocently.

Da squints at me suspiciously. "Are we providing a weekend call-out service now?" she asks. "Or should I say 'drop by service'?"

"Well ... this weekend I was seeing Sinclair anyway, so I thought 'in for a penny, in for a pound', as we Brits say."

"She paid double," Da says accusingly.

I spread my arms. "What can I say? Someone values my services."

"*Double*," she says again, as if the idea were incomprehensible. "And she looked smug about it."

"Do I detect a trace of the green-eyed monster? Surely not. But then again, what woman can resist the Braddock charms?"

Da points to herself. "This one. Probably many others also."

"Da, my dear," I say sweetly, "may your labour be long and your contractions exquisitely painful."

"Huh," she says.

I pat her shoulder condescendingly. "I remember vividly when Claire was pregnant with Katie. Claire was lying there screaming in agony and shouting *Get this thing out of me!*"

Da looks concerned. "So your daughter's birth was difficult?"

"The birth? No. I was talking about the conception."

"You are such a comedian, Khun David," she says stony-faced.

"Anyway, enough of this idle banter, Miss Da. I have some serious work for you to do."

I tell her about Yai, how I've volunteered to pay for the operation on his eyes, and that I want her to make the arrangements. She thinks I'm joking and it takes me a few minutes to convince her I'm not. I'm amused watching her facial expressions as she goes through various revisions to her opinion of me; starting with *bad taste joker* then mutating by degrees to *compassionate, misunderstood human being*.

When she's finally convinced I'm serious, she volunteers unbidden to make me a coffee, squeezes my arm affectionately and promises to phone each of the Samui hospitals to get me the best price. I give her Yai's and Bee's cell phone numbers so she can liaise with them, before I go into the East Office to email Sinclair.

I tell him that I've had a dry run observing the car park (without incident) and that I should be able to start in earnest tomorrow.

I've decided tonight will be my last evening watching Jingjai personally, unless something interesting happens. After this I'll get Prem – one of the Chaweng street urchins I employ periodically – to keep an eye on her and report back anything naughty.

After I've fired off Sinclair's email and scanned the newspapers, I have time for a lazy cigarette and a second cup of coffee before my appointment with the Widow Suttikul, a sweet if loquacious old lady who comes in periodically for advice on what she should do about her will. She has two sons, both of whom adore her, and neither of whom lives on the island; so she gets lonely and comes in to chat on the pretence of fussing over her post mortem dispositions. Da knows to charge her a 'special' rate. I'd really prefer to see her FOC, but Mrs. Suttikul won't hear of receiving any charity.

By the time the old lady has finished with me, my sexual adrenalin rush of this morning is long since forgotten.

Next I phone Prasert Promsai to find out how the heart-to-heart discussion with his brother went. The conversation almost instantly takes a disturbing and unexpected turn.

"The discussion went badly, Khun David. We both lost our tempers." Prasert sounds worried.

"Go on."

"I told him he was dishonest. He wouldn't own up to what he was doing, so I became annoyed. I even accused him of stealing from me during the failed property development outside Lamai; the one he'd got me involved in some years ago."

My ears prick up. "Wait a moment, Prasert. The property development that went bust was *outside of Lamai*?"

Prasert is confused. "Yes. But I don't see why that matters –"

"Never mind, it's probably nothing. What did Nikom say to that?"

"He was very angry, started shouting. He said that I was ungrateful and that he was working even now to get my money back on that investment. Said on my behalf he was still chasing the foreign investors who were behind it. All rubbish, of course. He was just blustering, trying to cover his tracks."

"Very probably. Did he say *how* he's pursuing the investors, or even who they *are*?"

"No. It's all nonsense anyway." He sighs. "Before our talk deteriorated Nikom admitted he was gambling again. Not only cock fighting. He's even been involved in organising beetle fights – some filthy racket he'd picked up from Northerners he'd met in Bangkok."

"Rhino beetles?" I ask. "The ones that eat the coconut trees?" This is getting weirder by the minute.

"Yes."

"So what happened next?"

"He said he would show me how wrong I was about him. He said again that he would get my money back. Then he left slamming the door behind him."

"Where is your brother now, Prasert?"

There is a pause. "I don't know. He's disappeared."

"Maybe he's just sulking."

"No, Khun David, he's gone. We rowed on Friday evening. He left and he hasn't been home since. I'm worried."

"Prasert, it's important that you call me straightaway if your brother gets in touch with you. Will you do that?"

He is mystified. "Of course. But I don't see why –"

"Never mind. Just call me, OK?"

"Very well."

"Have you told the police he's gone missing?"

"No. And I won't. This is family business. The police won't be involved."

I reassure him that he's done the right thing, and that the previous situation was untenable. He agrees wearily, but his voice is tinged with regret and hurt. I ring off.

Unknown foreign investors - Bankrupt property development –
Two dead farangs - A Thai with a grudge - Rhino beetles

My head is spinning. I flip open my notebook and look at the diagram of 'Braddock's Web'. I take a pencil, make some additional connections and colour in some of the circles.

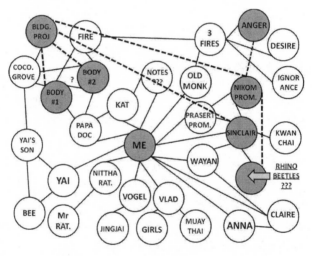

Supposing the dead men were investors in the failed property development and it was their failure to put in cash that resulted in the collapse? Ashley and Boehme had both spent time in Samui some years ago: it was conceivable they could be the anonymous backers.

If Nikom Promsai had lost out in the scheme, or he genuinely did have a desire to get his brother's money back, might he have gone after the men? If they knew him and trusted him, maybe he could have lured them to the grove on some pretence.

And there was something else. Geordie Sinclair knew Nikom – Prasert's 'slimy little brother' he'd called him. The Northerner had told me he steered clear of property investments following a *bad experience*. Sinclair's coconut trees were being destroyed by Rhino beetles, and Nikom was arranging beetle fights here on the island. If Sinclair had also been an investor, maybe the beetles were some kind of a warning, and Nikom could be going after him next.

I don't like the Geordie, but that's no reason he should get killed.

I ring his cell phone but there is no answer. I try again. Still no-one picks up. Worrying.

I'm just looking up the number for Sinclair's office when my own cell phone rings, and the tale takes another twist.

*　　*　　*　　*　　*

Everyone burns, but not everyone is burned. But someone else has been.

The caller is Charoenkul. A third body has been found. Papa Doc sounds like he doesn't know whether to be happy about it or pissed off. Happy because Investigator Katchai now has a bigger PR headache; pissed off because said Investigator may now have more clues and could therefore be nearer to finding the killer.

"I want you to go to the crime scene," barks the Chief.

"Yeah, that's fine," I say, "I'm dressed for a barbecue."

"Good. I want you to leave now."

"Isn't Katchai's team crawling all over the murder site? I don't see how I can just turn up and say, 'Hi I'm a curious Englishman; can I have a look at the body?'"

"Katchai's forensic team has finished their immediate work and gone. I suggested my officers supervise the transport of the body to the morgue, so there are three of my men at the scene. We'll have to move it soon, so you need to get over there *now*."

"Same place?"

"No. Our killer has switched locations. I've sent a car for you. It will be there in a few minutes."

"Fine. I'll just cancel all my appointments for today, shall I?" I say sarcastically.

"Yes, obviously," he replies. "And one more thing. Ring me as soon as you've finished, before you leave the scene, right?"

He cuts off without waiting for a response.

I call Sinclair's cell again. There is still no answer. I call his office: he hasn't called in today and no-one has seen him.

I'm wondering if he's dead.

*   *   *   *   *

It is an evasive and shaking DTs that drives me slowly to the scene: I assume his partner is one of the three policemen standing guard over the crispy stiff.

All the way there while my driver navigates twitchily and mutely through the traffic, I'm praying silently in my head that the body's not Sinclair. If it is, I know that sucker's ghost is going to squat on my shoulder for the rest of my natural. In the car I call the Northerner's phone another three times: nothing.

We take the Ring Road as it heads north, then circles west. About half-an-hour after we've left my office and we're through Mae Nam, DTs indicates left and we slip off the main route onto a dirt side road bordered by an unkempt scrubland of trees, wild grass and heaps of dumped rubbish. After a few metres the dirt road takes a sharp turn behind a derelict wooden store-house, and there our journey ends amidst more discarded junk, undergrowth and police warning tape. DTs parks next to the other police car, switches off the engine and looks nervously ahead, determined not to engage in conversation with me.

PC is leaning against a tree smoking and looking bad-tempered. There are two other policemen whom I don't recognise standing beside a plastic-covered shape that I'm also hoping I won't recognise. Happily there are no gawping spectators.

As I climb out of the car, PC flicks away his cigarette end with a gesture of contempt and says, "The ambulance will be here soon. You'll have to be quick."

"What can you tell me?" I ask.

"Nothing," he says helpfully. "I've not been here long, but these two –" he reluctantly indicates the other policemen, "– were here for some of the time while the forensics were busy." He walks off back to his tree and lights up again. DTs shrugs and turns his face away. *Thanks a lot, team.*

Fortunately the other two have been instructed by the Chief to be helpful to me, although clearly they are bemused as to what a foreigner is doing here. But if they are Charoenkul's 'men', I'm sure they get orders to do all sorts of things that they know better than to ask about.

The taller of the two – whom I notice drags his right foot as he walks – is the more talkative. He tells me the body was found yesterday evening, but he doesn't know by whom. Katchai's team had been called out as soon as it was realised it might be another 'burning' murder, and they'd been busy until about an hour ago. Listening in on their talk, he'd gathered the provisional opinion was that the victim had been killed sometime late on Saturday night or very early on Sunday morning.

"Anything else you can tell me?" I ask, scribbling in my notebook and putting off the moment when I'll have to look at the corpse.

"They found a hotel key on him from the *Samsara Hotel* in Chaweng, so it's probable he was a guest there."

It's not Sinclair. At least, probably not.

177

He goes on, "And a credit card."

"Was the name legible on the card?"

"Yes. Lewis Carroll."

"You're kidding me. *Lewis Carroll?*"

He looks puzzled. "Yes."

"Next you'll be telling me he's an Anglican deacon, writes nonsense poetry and books for children, and is over 170 years old. Not to mention that 'Lewis Carroll' is a pseudonym and his real name is Charles Lutwidge Dodgson." *Also, he was slain by a Jabberwock while the slithy toves did gyre and gimble in the wabe.* I don't say this last bit since it's not translatable into Thai.

The policeman looks at me like I'm mad.

I sigh. "Sorry, long story, bad day. Never mind. Let's have a look at him."

The shorter policeman pulls back the plastic sheet to reveal a sight that makes me want to dry retch. *Hi there, Lewis Carroll. Welcome to Wonderland.*

One good thing that can be said for the vision before me is that it is *not* Sinclair. That is in fact the *only* good thing that can be said for it.

Aware that four pairs of police eyes are scrutinising my face to gauge my reaction, I have to maintain a dispassionate air. I take out a small plastic jar of Vaseline from my trouser pocket and dab a couple of blobs under my nostrils. The tall policeman looks impressed. I offer him the jar but he shakes his head and steps back: he isn't planning on getting that near the dead man. I hunker down and look at the corpse which is lying on its back.

The face has been burned off. A few blows of something heavy has caved in the nasal bones and shattered a few front teeth, ruining some pricey dental work. Unburned hair behind the corpse's ears is brown in colour. I'm guessing he was maybe in his thirties, not younger. A farang, of course. Leaning down I can see the trademark shattering of the back of the skull and masses of coagulated blood, which has also soaked into the surrounding earth. Killed on his front, turned on his back. Just like the others.

The burning over the body is irregular. The hands and lower arms have been comprehensively torched – as has the face – but the torso and legs are lightly and patchily flamed: a half-hearted immolation.

The clothing is not standard-Samui-beach-issue. The shirt is linen, the trousers are chinos and the shoes are brown leather loafers, almost new. I inspect the charred hands: no wedding ring or jewellery of any kind. Impossible to tell whether the watch on the left wrist was a good one or not, it's too damaged.

I stand up and light a cigarette. The tall policeman looks at me expectantly.

"Yep," I say, "He's dead all right."

PC snorts cynically. DTs is still standing by the car looking at his feet, studiously avoiding eye contact with anyone, as usual.

I take some photographs of the late Lewis Carroll for later reference then tell the short policeman, "You can cover him up."

I look around. There are no dwellings close by. The derelict building conceals the immediate site from the road: no witnesses but the silent trees. The dirt road beneath my feet is compacted and hard from weeks without rain.

"Any tyre tracks?" I ask. "Or footprints?"

The tall policeman tells me the forensic team took some imprints, but he'd gathered from their conversation that they weren't very hopeful.

I remove the Vaseline from my nostrils and walk over to the ruined store-house to call Charoenkul. Before I can do so, my cell phone rings. The display tells me it's Sinclair. *Why the hell couldn't he have phoned me earlier and spared me the stress?*

"David Braddock here."

"Hello, David, it's Geordie." His mouth sounds like it's full of cotton wool. "I saw the missed calls from you. Sorry, I was at the dentist's. I chipped a lump out of one of my teeth yesterday and had to book an emergency appointment this morning. Excuse me if I sound as though I'm eating a pillow, but the anaesthetic hasn't worn off yet."

I'm relieved to hear his voice. Even if he is a git. At least he's not a dead git.

"Don't worry about it. I wanted to check if you'd received my email."

"Oh yes, I did. Glad the system works."

"Just while I've got you on the line," I add trying to sound casual, "perhaps you can help me with something."

"OK," he responds cautiously.

"You mentioned when we last spoke that you know Prasert Promsai's brother, Nikom. I wondered, Geordie, whether that was in connection with a property development?"

He makes a strangulated laughing sound. "Ha. No way I'd trust that weasel on a property investment. Naw, I got to know him through cock fighting. I used to be into that stuff a while back. Nikom's a guy who welches on his bets. It gets him into trouble."

"I see. It's just that you said you'd had a bad experience in property, and I was thinking perhaps it was that development outside Lamai that Nikom was involved with."

"No. I don't know anything about that. My property disaster was in Spain, donkey's years ago. But I've not been interested since. Once bitten, as the saying goes."

"I understand."

"Why?" he asks. "What's up with Nikom? Is he being a naughty boy again?"

"Maybe. He's fallen out with his brother." I consider it preferable *slightly* to betray a minor client confidence than to tell him what my real suspicions were. "Anyway," I continue, "thanks for calling back. I'll speak to you soon when you're not partially anaesthetised."

I end the call.

So much for that panic. Nikom's not after Sinclair. I open my mental Not-To-Do-List and add *Do not let your imagination run away with you* underneath the note on not meeting Nittha Rattanakorn outside of the office.

Now I can go back to being suspicious of the Geordie and disliking him guilt-free. The metaphorical conscience monkey jumps down from my shoulder and climbs to the top of a nearby coconut tree, from which vantage point he watches me sadly.

I select Charoenkul's number from my cell phone contacts list and press the button. He answers immediately.

"I'm finished here," I say. "Shall I come to your house? I can be there in about ten minutes."

"No," he replies. "I'll meet you at your house in an hour."

"At *my* house?" I ask, but he's already gone. I walk back to the car, where the twitching one continues to inspect his footwear. PC is deep in conversation with the other two policemen and ignores me.

"OK, driver, I'm done," I say to DTs. "Take me away from all this."

*   *   *   *   *

On the wall of my study hangs a large framed print of the Wheel of Becoming. The Wheel is a visual teaching aid and a summary in pictorial form of the Buddhist ideas on samsaric existence. The core concept is that the world as we perceive it is an illusion, and unless we can rid ourselves of our mistaken viewpoint and understand the true nature of reality, we will remain forever locked in a repeating cycle of death and rebirth.

Taking the Old Monk's advice, I examine the intricate and colourful painting before me. At the hub of the Wheel are the three motive forces of human behaviour that lead to suffering: ignorance, desire and hatred, represented respectively by a pig, a rooster and a snake. Surrounding this hub is a ring divided into two – a black half and a white half – with figures ascending or descending depending on whether their karmic habits were good or bad.

Radiating outward, next come the spokes of the Wheel partitioning the six samsaric realms into which we can be (re)born: the realms of gods, demons, animals, hell-beings, hungry ghosts and humans.

The rim of the Wheel is separated into twelve segments representing *Dependent Origination*, the chain of causation which ensures that the Wheel of Samsara keeps spinning; the dozen linked elements that lead from ignorance to suffering and death.

Holding the Wheel in its clawed hands is a monstrous apparition with three eyes and large fanged teeth. This is Yama, the Lord of Death, and on his head he wears a crown of human skulls. Yama has power over those who live in samsara: his hold can only be broken when we free ourselves from the delusions of this life.

I remember the Old Monk telling me once that the Wheel can also be seen as a mirror. We find our own reflection somewhere on it. Causation, logic, karmic action and reaction. *Paticcasamuppāda.*

Because of ignorance, volitions arise;
Because of volitions, consciousness arises;
Because of consciousness, mind and body arise;
Because of mind and body, the six senses arise;
Because of the six senses, contact arises;
Because of contact, feeling arises;
Because of feeling, desire arises;
Because of desire, attachment arises;
Because of attachment, becoming (worldly existence) arises;
Because of becoming, (re)birth arises;

Because of birth, decay, grief, lamentation, suffering, and despair arise.
Thus arises the entire mass of mankind's suffering.
And thus the Lord of Death has dominion over us.

Some analogous chain of causation has led to the deaths of three foreign men here on the island, has committed them to the embrace of Yama. Some feeling, some desire, some attachment is at work; some twisted mission serves to propel forward a deluded individual towards acts of obscene destruction. Someone out there is burning, aflame with a murderous obsession; and he is burning others because of it.

I try to remind myself that finding the killer is not *my* responsibility. I am only meant to be helping out. Catching this slayer is the work of the police. But I am not persuaded. It feels personal.

I scan the Wheel of Becoming for guidance, and I examine my own heart for clues by proxy as to what darkness may lie there.

*   *   *   *   *

As we sit in my study I observe Charoenkul's face and demeanour, and am put in mind of a tyre with a puncture. His usual bombast and arrogance are absent. There is something deflated about him, and for parts of our conversation his attention seems to be somewhere else entirely. The fact that he actually thanks Wayan for his cup of green tea puts me on high alert: this is not the Papa Doc I know.

I need to be careful as to how I voice my thoughts on the abandoned building project and its possible significance to the murders. Already today I have made one wholly unsupportable supposition about Sinclair and been proved wrong within hours. I do not want my speculative ruminations about a link between a failed property development, the Promsai brothers and three dead foreigners to result in Prasert and Nikom being fitted up by

Charoenkul for a hat-trick of murders. There is however, checking up which can be done by the police which may nudge my tentative hypothesis towards some kind of proof.

I am also anxious to avoid any discussion of Kat, since I am not *entirely* sure yet where the land lies with her husband on that subject.

I decide to start my report elsewhere.

"After seeing today's body, I've been re-examining the photographs of the first two victims," I tell the Chief. "I noticed something very curious that I hadn't spotted on first viewing."

I show him a selection of the photographs on my laptop that I'd downloaded from my camera earlier.

"Look at the pattern and intensity of burning on Lewis Carroll, the third victim. We may surmise that the murderer has judged the first killing site as now being too risky to use, and has had to find somewhere else to dispatch his prey. But consider: with this second site he is not so familiar. The screening from the main road is not so good and he is running a higher risk of discovery. *This time* he has to act very fast. The killing is the same method, but the precision is lacking. It is rushed, and a little panicky perhaps. The killer imagines he is short of time, every second counts. In those circumstances, he would only do what is absolutely necessary: ensure Carroll is dead, and burn only what needs to be burned."

Charoenkul sips his tea and says almost convivially, "Go on."

I point at the screen of my laptop.

"You can see care has been taken to ensure the hands and lower arms were completely burned, and the face has also been rendered unrecognisable. In Carroll's case the nose has additionally been smashed for good measure: this didn't happen with the other two. The rest of Carroll's body was only partially consumed by the flames; as if burning that was only of secondary importance."

I pull out the files on the first two men and extract a selection of the photographs.

"It's not so easy to see with these shots; but it does seem that the hands and faces of Ashley and Boehme were more comprehensively disfigured than the rest of their bodies. I wouldn't have noticed this were it not for today's discovery."

"So the killer was trying to remove the easily-identifiable aspects of his victims: face and possibly fingerprints," says Charoenkul. "I don't see what's so surprising about that."

"What's surprising about it is that he left credit cards and other personal items on the bodies, which would enable the authorities to identify the victims relatively quickly."

"Perhaps he assumed these would be unrecognisable after the fire too."

"Well, it's possible. However, it would have been much simpler and safer to have taken away the cards and other stuff and got rid of them. If Carroll's card was in his front trouser pocket, for instance, it may be virtually undamaged. Certainly Katchai's team could read it easily at the scene according to your man."

"So what's your theory?"

I scratch my chin. "It's like the killer only needed the body to be unidentifiable for a short time and after that it didn't matter. He didn't want the dead man's face to be seen by someone who could recognise him; didn't want a photograph of the face turning up in the next day's paper maybe."

"But why?"

"Beats me."

"And the burned hands, what is that about?"

"There are various possibilities. First, it could be some ritualistic thing – as could the facial work – but I don't know of any ritual that involves destruction of the hands in this manner. In some cultures there is the cutting off of a thief's hands, but burning them away? No. So I don't think that's it.

"Secondly, it could be done to eliminate evidence: the killer's skin under the victim's fingernails, for example."

"Like where the victim had scratched his attacker, you mean?"

"Yes. Although that would suggest all three victims had clawed their killer. Seems unlikely. As you said before, it could be to erase fingerprints, but that doesn't chime with my hypothesis on the non-removal of the credit cards."

"Perhaps the killer is just stupid, and there is no system at work here."

"He's not *that* stupid, or you would have caught him already."

Charoenkul lapses into silence and looks at his hands.

"There is another factor that suggests itself to me," I say when I can stand the quiet no longer. "The element of contempt. The face-down smashing of the head, the torching, the breaking of Carroll's nose. The victims were despatched brutally, without dignity. This guy either hates farangs generally, or at least he hated these three men specifically. Although there is a deliberate act involved here, it is not a cold execution. Some passion is at work."

"You're not about to give me a lecture on the Three Buddhist Fires, I trust," the Chief says drily, as if reading my mind.

"No," I reply defensively, "but I think the fire motif is significant. Did you know that some years back there was a suicide by fire on the same spot as the first two murders?"

"That could just be a coincidence."

"It *could*, but it would be a pretty strange coincidence, don't you think?"

He ponders this a moment, then says, "Have you questioned the daughter of the blind man yet?"

"Yes. As you surmised, that was a dead end." I have no intention of being responsible for Charoenkul's gorillas hauling in Bee and Yai for further questioning.

"This is all very well, Braddock," intones Papa Doc, sounding more like his usual unpleasant self, "but don't you have any more definite leads?"

I would like to remind him that my (unpaid) job here is to help with profiling, not to solve the case, but I bite my tongue. Now is the time to broach the subject I've been holding back.

"There is one avenue that may be worth pursuing," I suggest tentatively.

"Spit it out then."

"At the site of the first two killings there is a building project that was never finished. I gather it ran into financial trouble. I am further given to understand that the original backers were farangs."

The Chief's beady eyes fix on me and he seems interested, at last. "So you think someone here on the island may have lost money, and he's pursuing a revenge agenda; that the three victims may be investors and the killer holds them responsible?" He's way ahead of me.

"Of course, it's just an idea. I have no way of checking all that out – but *you* could."

Charoenkul rubs his hands and a sly smile creeps over his face. "Katchai's team is definitely *not* looking at that line of inquiry."

I continue, "Ashley and Boehme have visited the island before, some years back. I don't know about Carroll, obviously. It might explain something that's been annoying me – how the first two victims came to be at the grove. If they actually knew their killer, well ..."

"I'll do some checking. Interesting, Braddock, very interesting. Do you have anything else for me?"

"There is one thing, but I hesitate to mention it. You may think I'm crazy."

"I may think that anyway. Go on."

"OK, it's the victims' surnames: Ashley, Boehme and Carroll. A, B, C. They were killed in alphabetical order."

Charoenkul frowns. "I don't understand."

"A, B, C," I say again, hoping the Chief hasn't read Agatha Christie's *The*

ABC Murders. "If we're dealing with a serial killer rather than a disgruntled property investor, the alphabet may be his 'system'."

Papa Doc laughs. "Well, if that is the case, at least you're safe. He's already done 'B'."

"I told you before, murder investigations are not my speciality," I say testily.

"Calm down, Braddock," he urges. "I thought you British liked a joke. Maybe you are not so keen if it is a joke at your expense though, mmn?"

"Whatever." I hand him a slim bound file I'd put together earlier. "Anyway, here's my report. It covers the areas I've just discussed, and in rather more detail."

"Good. I'll make sure you are given details of any relevant findings on the Carroll death, particularly forensics." He winks. "Then you can update and expand your report."

"I'd rather hoped our business would now be finished."

"I am afraid not."

I expect him to get up and leave, but he doesn't. Ominously he asks whether my 'kind maid' could bring some more tea. I find Wayan in the kitchen and pass on the order.

When I return to the study carrying the tea myself, Charoenkul is standing with his back to me gazing out of the window.

I set down the tray on the low table, take a comfortable chair and invite him to join me. I don't know what's coming next, but I have a feeling it won't be enjoyable.

He sits and picks up the cup, sips distractedly, then settles back in his chair. He looks suddenly old and vulnerable, like some worn-out bureaucrat ground down by a lifetime of thankless activity and petty politicking. But I have to remind myself this is *Charoenkul*, after all. A man whose vindictiveness is legendary, and someone who remains dangerous to D. Braddock Esquire. He is still the police official with whose wife I have enjoyed carnal knowledge; a fact which, at some juncture, I expect him to become acquainted. I have to be careful. Papa Doc has bite in him yet. *'Tis better playing with a lion's whelp // Than with an old one dying.*

I wait for him to voice what is on his mind. He looks at me for what feels like an eternity before saying, "Mr. Braddock, how much can I rely on your discretion?"

"Chief, as I have already told you, so far as my involvement in this murder investigation is concerned –"

He raises a hand to cut me off.

"The matter I wish to discuss has nothing to do with the murder investigation."

I wait.

"It is a private matter," he says, selecting his words with care. "A personal ... issue."

I can feel that now-familiar tightening in my chest and my palms are beginning to sweat, but I maintain an outward composure and say mechanically, "Whatever you have to say stays in this room; if that's what you want."

"Didn't you wonder why I wanted to meet at your house today, rather than at my house?"

"It didn't strike me as important," I reply. "I assumed you had a reason."

"Indeed," he lets out a long sigh. "The matter I wish to talk to you about concerns my wife."

I can see him struggling to get out the words.

"I believe she may be having an affair."

I had unwisely taken a sip of tea, and it takes me a while to stop choking on it at this statement.

"Excuse me," I mutter hoarsely, trying to recover my aplomb, "but what makes you think Mrs. Charoenkul is having an affair?" For the second time today I can feel my heart trying to punch its way through my chest.

The Chief continues haltingly. "Until today I had some rather ... loose suspicions. My wife, you understand, enjoys considerable freedom to do as she pleases. Apart from some charitable activities, her time is her own. In recent months she has taken to going on shopping trips to Bangkok, naturally staying overnight. Sometimes she is out very late ... and there is a *change* in her that I cannot put my finger on. Until today, I only knew that something was *different* about her."

I don't want to ask, but I know I have to.

"What happened today?"

"I received this."

He takes out a white envelope and lays it carefully on the table.

"Posted on the island and addressed to me, as you can see," he explains. "An anonymous letter. Please open it."

Not only do I not want to open it, I don't want to touch it. I recognise the handwriting; the same hand that has already sent letters to me and to Kat. I am in deep, deep trouble.

"Don't worry," he prompts, "I've already checked for fingerprints. Nothing useful."

It's not the fingerprints that worry me, although once I've handled the envelope and inevitable-A4-sized-note inside, *my* fingerprints will be on the damn thing. But I have no choice.

I open the envelope and remove the letter. It says simply

YOUR WIFE IS UNFAITHFUL

I have the urge to laugh hysterically, but instead I sit back and take a sip of tea, being careful not to choke this time. I endeavour to look wise, virtuous, and above all, celibate.

"This is hardly conclusive," I say. "More like someone making mischief. Perhaps you should just ignore it. You have no evidence and, by the looks of it, neither does the writer of this poisonous little note."

Charoenkul shakes his head. "No," he says, "I can't sit by and do nothing. I need to act."

"Are you going to confront your wife? Talk through your suspicions?"

"Don't be ridiculous, Braddock. Confront her with what? This?" He snorts and points at the paper scornfully. Then he picks up the letter and envelope and puts them away in his pocket.

"Then what did you have in mind?"

"I want you to follow her."

Fortunately I have not just taken a sip of tea – otherwise the choking and coughing would have been even more pronounced.

"I can't do that," I say aghast.

"Why not?"

I can't think of a reason I can give him, even a lame one, but happily the Chief assumes I'm thinking about money.

"Don't worry," he says with bite, "I don't expect you to do *this* for free. You will be paid your usual rate. After all," he adds condescendingly, "trailing possibly-unfaithful partners is what you do. Is that not correct?"

I try to get this straight in my head. *Charoenkul is going to pay me, his wife's lover, to tail his wife and find out if she is having sex with anyone. All well and good until he receives the next anonymous letter naming me as her lover. Then Pandemonium ...*

I become aware that Papa Doc is still talking and is putting another sheet of paper on the table with information about Kat's movements. "Tomorrow she flies to Bangkok, and is supposedly meeting up with an old girl friend for two days of shopping. These are her flight details and the hotel where she is staying. I want you to go to Bangkok, follow her and report back. If she is up to no good, this trip will not be the innocent one it appears. Then I will know for certain."

I realise I am sitting with my mouth open like an idiot, so I close it. Then

I open it again to complain that I have appointments and commitments and I can't just drop everything; but Charoenkul is having none of it.

"Two days of your time," he asserts, "that's all."

To my disbelief I find myself agreeing to his request. I can only attribute this to being so relieved I don't have a bullet from Papa Doc's gun in my head that I would say yes to anything.

I hardly notice the Chief leave, I am so in shock. I'm still slumped in my chair staring into space when Wayan arrives a few minutes later to clear the cups.

I am vaguely aware of her recounting another dream involving me and a large flying demon ("This time he was flying away from you and down into a dark pit"), and I am thankful that I am not fantasising about her sexually at this moment. Although after the day I've had so far I don't see how that would be possible.

I ask her to get me a large whisky. As she leaves the room I check out her bottom and swaying hips. Attractive, as always; but I am comforted that there is no stirring in my loins.

I light a Marlboro and wonder how much more surreal my life can possibly become. Then I send a SMS to Kat; *Call me as soon as you are free to talk. VERY URGENT*

I down the whisky in one.

I wait for Kat's call.

*   *   *   *   *

Evening finds me at Charlie Rorabaugh's Bophut Jazz in Fisherman's Village, Bo Phut.

I've booked my flight to Bangkok, told a suspicious Da to reschedule my appointments, and informed Sinclair I'd be away in the capital for the next two nights so my observation of his employee is postponed. The Northerner was unfazed, and even seemed cheerful at the prospect: I'm beginning to wonder what I need to do to piss him off. I've checked that Wayan will be OK on her own while I'm away. Claire, of course, is not around to talk to, and I don't anticipate her being around for some time yet. I've set up Prem, my erstwhile street urchin employee to meet me at Bo Phut later; and I've asked him to bring me some weed and rolling papers. I need to mellow awhile.

The only person I've not spoken to is the one I really want to: Kat has not yet called me back. I'm not going to get panicky about it. Not yet anyway.

I'm anticipating an evening chilling out at Charlie's place will restore some badly-needed equilibrium in me. According to Vogel's notes, this is where Jingjai will be spending her evening off; so I can kill two birds with one stone – observe the girl in non-working mode and, at the same time, catch a good Australian beef steak. Maybe I'll even hear some good live music, although I'm decidedly sceptical about *that*.

I also have some notion of putting a third bird to death. Charlie Rorabaugh has been on the island a long time and is tuned in to all the Samui news and gossip: maybe he can dish me some dirt on Sinclair. Yes, I know. I'm becoming obsessed with the Neanderthal, even as the rest of my life is slowly disintegrating around me. But each time I interact with him I get more and more wary of what's going on inside that grizzled, stubbly skull.

Charlie is on good form tonight. He is never happier than when playing the role of short, fat, friendly host. He's wearing a bright red American sports shirt, stretched over his ample belly, and his thick curly hair looks freshly dyed (black). A Jewish native of the Bronx, Charlie has only two passions: good quality jazz and good quality beef. His decade on Samui has left him with a golden tan; appropriate since his loud exterior conceals a heart of gold.

"Hey, Davy," he calls out in his throaty New York brogue above the hubbub of Bophut Jazz, "Where the hell have you been hiding out? I was beginning to think you must have died."

"I had myself declared dead for tax reasons," I reply. "How are you doing, Charles?" We embrace and he gives me an enthusiastically hard hug: his fingers are like pork sausages – kosher ones, of course.

"Good man, real good. Where's your saxophone? It's, like, centuries since you played here. Come and have a drink at the bar."

The place is full, in anticipation of the live band later. Charlie Parker is playing over the music system, counterpointing nicely with the chatter and the sizzling of steaks on the big fire-grill. We elbow our way to the bar, down a couple of beers and exchange some island gossip.

"So what are you up to these days?" he asks.

"I'm doing some consulting work for the police."

"You're kidding me. Those bastards?" He looks like he'd spit if he had a bucket handy. Or there was room. "It's not on this farang murder by any chance, is it?"

"Could be," I say, "but keep it under your hat."

"Hey, Davy, you should be careful, man. Those guys are as bent as a Rio Carnival. Did I ever tell you the story of the infamous 'Chaweng Suicide' a few years back?"

"No. Amaze me."

"Some British ex pat was found floating face down in Chaweng Lake with lots of holes in his chest. The word was he'd had a big row with his *katoey* boyfriend and the ladyboy had done him in by stabbing him with a big kitchen knife, then dumped him in the lake. The police said the guy had drowned himself and called it suicide."

He pauses to bark some instruction at a waiter.

"Where was I? Oh, yes," he continues. "Some of the island ex pats kicked up such a stink that a special team was called in from Surat Thani to investigate. Guess what? Same conclusion: suicide. They're all as bad as each other, not interested in farang deaths. No money in it, you see."

"There's a team from Surat Thani over here now looking into things," I tell him. "Chief Charoenkul says they're doing a proper investigation."

Charlie snorts. "I doubt that, bro'. Watch your back."

"Anyway, Charlie, leaving aside dead farangs, I wanted to pick your brains on somebody; you being the fount of all knowledge on Samui ex pats."

"Buy me another beer and I'll tell you whatever you want to know. I'm a cheap date. Almost a tart, really."

I catch the barman's eye and set up some beers.

"Kenneth Sinclair," I say. "What do you know about him?"

"Geordie Sinclair, you mean? Looks like he should be working in a shipyard as a welder, yeah?"

"The same. He's asked me to do a job for him, but I think there's something fishy about it. I'm looking for some background on him. Discreetly, mind."

Charlie considers. "Let me see. Sinclair, Sinclair. He came to Samui around the same time I did. He's from Newcastle, UK, originally, but I guess you know that. He has a couple of businesses here: car hire and a realty firm, I think. I don't see much of him these days, he's become a bit of a recluse – but when he first came here, over ten years ago he was much more talkative, and very bitter too as I remember."

"Bitter about what?"

"About the break-up of his marriage. Real chip on his shoulder about it. His wife ran off with some younger English guy, and took the kids. She made it impossible for Sinclair to see them, so he came to Thailand to start over. Some women are bitches like that. His wife was called Joy: pretty ironic, huh? I can't remember the name of the guy, though I should, he talked about him enough. Called him 'Andy Arse-Wipe' or 'Andy Arse-Lay', something like that. Sinclair seemed to think his wife's lover was a bit, you know, on the feminine side. Quite a blow to his Northern manhood losing his woman to someone like that. Yes, he was certainly angry all right."

Charlie takes a pull on his beer, reminiscing.

"Geordie likes Northern folk music, or at least he did then. Especially that guy from the band Dire Straits. Mark Something. He used to bang on about a song of his, 'Sailing to Philadelphia'. I guess he thought that would make a connection with me. Though Philadelphia is kinda fucking awful. And no way am I going to have *folk music* in here. I'd rather die." He wrinkles his face in disgust.

"I see."

Charlie slaps me on the shoulder.

"Hey, that's not the most interesting part of the story. Less than a year into his time on the island he meets a local woman, Nok, and falls head over. Like really head over. Changes his life. And she's really keen on him too. No shit. A real love match.

"Anyway, they get married and have a kid. Geordie's settled down, put the past behind him, everything's sweet, then – bang! Nok gets killed by a hit-and-run driver and his world falls to pieces.

"He went completely nuts. Harassed the police – who were useless of course – trying to track down the driver responsible. He took out advertisements in all the papers offering a reward for information. Of course he got lots of leads and promises from con artists who saw a chance for some easy money, but nothing ever came of it.

"Eventually he pulled himself together. I guess he had to for the little boy's sake. Life is tough enough here for a *luk kreung* – a 'half child' – without his having a dead Thai mother *and* a crazy English father."

"So Sinclair's OK these days?" I ask.

"Well," Charlie hesitates. "I did hear that recently someone had contacted him and said he could identify the driver that had killed Nok 'for a price'. Sinclair got very excited about it."

"What happened?"

"I don't know. He hasn't been in here for a while. I expect it's just some ghoul trying to make some money from the guy's grief. Let's face it: the trail of the hit-and-run driver must be stone cold by now."

"Interesting stuff, anyhow. By the way, you wouldn't happen to know if he's ever been involved in any property development on the island here, would you?" I ask, still suspicious of anything Sinclair has told me.

"Not as far as I know." Charlie grins. "You don't like him, Davey, do you? Sinclair. I can tell."

"Maybe not. But he *is* a client."

Charlie somehow manages to squeeze me onto a small table after admonishing me for not booking ahead. I look around the restaurant but can't see Jingjai, although I do see a scrubbed-up PC in civvies scowling over a beer at the far side of the bar. An unlikely music lover, I'd have thought. I wonder if he's paying for the beer or if it's part of Charlie's 'police tax' arrangements.

After a few minutes the beaming host steps up to the microphone on the micro-stage to announce that *Silk Thais* will be performing their set shortly. I groan inside and hope the steak will be worth the assault on my eardrums.

Much to my surprise the music *is* good, really good. The six-piece Silk Thais look and sound every inch a professional outfit. Saxophone, rhythm guitar, electric piano, double bass, drums and vocalist – they launch into their opening number, 'Moondance'.

The real revelation for me however is the female vocalist. *It's Jingjai*. And blow me down, but she sounds like a combination of Diana Krall, Nora Jones and Nina Simone; though not all at the same time, obviously. The girl can flip between low-throaty-sexy or clear-and-ethereal, and she knows how to make love to a microphone. I look around the restaurant. Guys are sitting entranced, practically drooling: either that or they are telling their wives/girlfriends to shut up so they can listen. Best quality Australian beef steaks go cold on their plates.

When the band takes a short break and Jingjai takes over the keyboard to perform a solo version of 'Cry Me a River', Bophut Jazz's patrons break into loud, spontaneous applause. Even PC is clapping madly and smiling: a pretty gruesome sight. I snap some photos of the girl for Vogel. And for myself.

As the band finishes their set with an old Sade number I grab Charlie.

"Where did these guys come from, Charlie? They're fantastic."

"I don't know which hole you've been hiding in Davy, but they've been my Monday night regulars for the last three months. I'm surprised you've not heard of them."

"That singer works in a bar in Chaweng."

"You know her?"

"Slightly. Well, I thought I did. Now I'm not so sure. Her voice is amazing. Those musicians are first class too, especially the keyboard man."

"Yeah, yeah, well, everyone falls in love with Jingjai. Just keep that napkin over your lap, Davy. We don't want any accidents."

Afterwards I go to congratulate Jingjai. Up close her makeup looks as theatrical as it did that evening at the Ocean Pearl. Now I know why.

She recognises me and smiles, and the diamond flashes in the light.

"Khun David," she says, "how kind."

This time she lets me buy her a drink provided I buy one for the rest of the band too, which I do. They all toast my health apart from the tattooed rhythm guitarist who looks to be in a sulk.

Later Prem meets me at the near-deserted western end of Fisherman's Village. I hand him my second-best camera, show him a photograph of Jingjai and give him instructions for the next two evenings. He nods as if spying on girls is the most natural thing in the world for a teenage boy to do. Which of course it is.

He hands me a small clump of weed wrapped in cellophane and some rolling papers, and I hand him some cash. My fifteen-year-old dealer. He rides off happily on his bike smoking one of my Marlboros.

I walk to a deserted stretch of beach and sit down, careless of whether the sand gets into my pants.

The black sky has star-holes in it. A few fire lanterns are drifting gently out to sea on the faint breeze. Across the water rises the dark mass of Koh Phangan, its lower slopes dotted with tiny twinkling lights.

Using some tobacco from one of my cigarettes to mix with the weed, I make up a joint, light it and lie back on the sand. I allow my mind to empty.

I'm not sure how long I've been lying there when my cell phone rings. It's Kat. Finally.

Calmly I recount some of today's conversation with her husband, and explain I'll be tailing her tomorrow. We'll even be travelling on the same flight to Bangkok. The line goes quiet as Kat's bravado fails her for once. I hear myself reminding her to look surprised to see me at the airport. Then the absurdity of the whole situation suddenly overwhelms me and I start giggling.

"Are you stoned?" she asks crossly.

"If I'm not, I'm certainly getting there."

"You are a degenerate, David Braddock," Kat announces in mock-disapproval, "A disgraceful scoundrel."

"You may be right," I say. "Come and join me on Bo Phut beach and we'll put that theory to the test right now."

"Do you think you could manage it, David, really?"

"I've only had a couple of beers and one joint. I'm certainly happy to give it a try."

"I'll bet you are," she laughs. "Some other time, tirak."

"I might just hold you to that."

"I might just let you."

8

"In every man ... there is in the depths of his nature,
a mob of low and vulgar desires
which constitutes him an animal."
Arthur Schopenhauer, Counsels and Maxims

I dreamed I was walking alone through an apocalyptic landscape of burnt leafless trees sticking up from the ash-strewn earth like twisted black wires. Above me, dark swollen clouds hung low in the sky, faintly backlit in places by a red sun and random flickering bursts of sheet lighting. Distant booms of thunder were the only sounds: no birds, no insects, nothing living to cry out. The dead trees stretched off in all directions towards barren mountains, whose higher reaches were cloaked in grey mist. My feet crunched on dry branches buried beneath the snow-like ash, and occasionally on broken animal skulls and bones. Ahead of me a narrow plume of smoke rose almost vertically in the torpid air, and I resolved to head towards it.

As I neared, I could see the smoke was issuing from the chimney of a white weather-boarded house which was surrounded by a picket fence. The earth inside the fence was stained red. As I entered through the garden gate I noted with shock that the ground was swollen with blood, as if the land were delivered of some deep and fatal wound.

Sitting on a striped deck-chair in the midst of the garden was an ancient man. His yellowed skin was stretched like old parchment across his bent bones. A dirty cloth had been tied across his eyes and his faded clothing hung from him as nothing more than frayed rags.

I stepped cautiously toward him, feeling the ground suck at me, and trying as best I could to keep the sticky blood off my shoes. He turned his face towards me at my approach.

"What do you want?" he asked, with a voice that rasped like dried leaves.

"I am lost," I replied. "I need your help. Tell me what I must do."

He shook his head. "It is not yet time," he said.

"Not yet time?" I echoed. "Time for what?"

"It is not yet time," he repeated, pointing beyond me, "and you must leave the garden. You must leave the garden now."

After I wake I lie looking up at the ceiling fan's slightly wobbly rotation and am put in mind of the opening sequence of *Apocalypse Now*. Unlike Martin Sheen's character, however, I have no urge to climb out of bed, practice martial arts moves, drink alcohol, smash up the mirrors and end up with my blood all over the room. The mellow mood engendered by last night's two joints still lingers, my Daliesque dream notwithstanding. I can't even be bothered to light a cigarette.

The morning sunlight has crept under the curtains towards the foot of the bed, but is unable to progress further. I can hear the muffled noises of Wayan moving around downstairs, presumably preparing breakfast for her lazy boss. My bedside clock tells me there is no rush to get up since I have a couple of hours before I need to go to the airport and begin the unreal experience of following Kat to Bangkok to try and catch myself sleeping with her.

Eventually however my rumbling stomach and post-toke food cravings drag my indolent backside out of the pit and propel me towards the bathroom. On the way I slide back the wardrobe doors to check that Claire's clothes are still hanging inside. They are.

In the mirror my eyes look bloodshot and the skin on my face is blotchy and dry. I have a tepid shower under the strong jets, and watch the soapy water run down my body. There are some mosquito bites on my legs and a bruise on my hip that I have no idea how it got there. I close my eyes and the retinal images put me in mind of a spinning pool cue. I have a vague presentiment that it means something important, but like the Curious

Incident of the Dog in the Night-Time, my subconscious may be having a laugh at my expense. I try to think what it might mean, but fail. It probably means I shouldn't have had that second joint.

After shaving and brushing my teeth I look a little more respectable. I throw some overnight bits and pieces into a shoulder-bag and go downstairs.

"You seem more like yourself this morning, Mr. David," says Wayan pouring my coffee. She is wearing an outfit that makes her look like a Singapore Airlines flight attendant. At least she looks like that to me.

"Yesterday you seemed agitated. Is that the right word, 'agitated'?"

Well, Wayan my dear, if my craving to ravish you without mercy over the breakfast table among the fruit and cereals classifies me as 'agitated', then yes.

"I think I was running a bit of a fever yesterday."

Although I am not today seeing Wayan through the distorted lens of naked lust, I am nonetheless still stirred by her femininity and the charm of her movement. I recognise in myself a jarring chord of sexual frustration, like a swollen spot that needs to be squeezed.

Some may be surprised to learn, given my general track record, that I have *not* enjoyed the fragrant delight that is Wayan's body. Not yet anyway. So far I have managed to maintain that particular line in the shifting sands of my malleable principles. Of course I would hardly be the first Westerner in Asia to sleep with his domestic help. And I wouldn't be the last, that's for sure. But something about Wayan's gentle temperament and her almost sisterly attitude towards me, keeps me in check. I also tell myself that, so long as Claire is still part of my life, physical intimacy with Wayan can't be allowed to happen. That's what I tell myself, at any rate. But then I tell myself a lot of things, especially these days.

What was really going on in my mind when I brought Wayan here from Bali, I wonder. Friendship? Companionship? The need to have someone around me I can trust? A hope that some of her goodness might rub off on me? Making sure the windows got properly cleaned?

She probably knows me better than anyone else in my life – my ups and downs and in-between moods – and yet she was happy to pack up her life in Bali and come here. It's a bit strange when I think about it. She has never intimated any romantic feelings for me. Her behaviour has always been impeccable in that respect; unlike many other Asian women in her position who have been quick to exploit the libidinous weakness of their male employers.

In many respects Wayan and I resemble the long-married couple where the wife turns a blind eye to the husband's peccadilloes. We just don't have sex, that's all.

Wayan is a decent woman, I muse. Sometimes it might be better if she were either less attractive or less decent. Or if I were more decent. None of these things is going to happen anytime soon.

My Singapore Airlines stewardess lookalike pours me another coffee while I give her the details of my trip to Bangkok. This excludes the bit about my following Kat Charoenkul, naturally. That sorted, I pick up my bag and have a surreptitious peek at Wayan's cleavage as she bends forward to clear the table.

I close the front door behind me, throw my bag in the jeep and light a Marlboro.

*   *   *   *   *

Samui International Airport.

Sounds impressive, but in reality it's more cute than impressive. For a start it's largely open-air: concrete poles cunningly disguised to look like wood supporting grass roofs or something equally pastoral. After you've checked in for international flights, you go *back outside* and wander through

203

Samui Park Avenue, a shopping boulevard with fountains, trees and red and yellow flowers poking up through the greenery like small fires. The departure gate is more poles and grass roofs, a civilised outdoor smoking area, and free refreshments while you buy your last-minute tourist souvenirs from the kitsch gift shop. Vehicles reminiscent of 1960s Butlins then transport you unhurried to your plane.

My flight, however, is a domestic one, so I take a left turn after the elfin check-in girl has processed my boarding card and put up with my sad middle-aged flirting.

I really need to get laid. And soon. While my mental Not-To-Do-List contains a strict prohibition with regard to *Samui* bargirls, it is silent on the subject of *Bangkok* bargirls. Thus far I have managed to honour this distinction, despite frequent urges for good old-fashioned horizontal jogging sans commitment or boring preliminaries. My personal moral code draws an arbitrary boundary line once the Samui coastline is safely behind me; and Bangkok is well outside the fifty mile exclusion zone for reprehensible sexual behaviour with young women. Whether intercourse with mature women and/or married ones on Samui is allowable, is a somewhat grey area. However, I'm fairly confident I can convince myself this is OK, should the need ever arise.

I'm hoping I will be able to find some time while in the capital to visit Siam Welcomes You in Patpong – an unprepossessing little establishment where all customers are guaranteed both an enthusiastic greeting and a lighter wallet.

I'm early arriving at the departure gate and, as yet, there is no sign of Kat. I sit down with a coffee and a copy of today's Island Gazette.

The cadaver formerly known as Lewis Carroll has hit the headlines and, in contrast to the last murder, the writing has a slightly hysterical edge to it: *Another Tourist Found Dead*. Someone must have got careless because the burning of the body is mentioned. There is a map of the island showing the murder sites and a rather fuzzy photograph of bemused policemen at the most recent scene. Katchai has suddenly gone low-profile: no reassuring words from the investigation team, just some murmurings about examination of forensic evidence and interviewing being ongoing.

An editorial on page six questions whether visitors to Koh Samui are safe, but concludes with some 'no need for panic' statistics. The writer makes no outright criticism of the police, and the non-disclosure of Ashley's murder continues. I suspect pressure has been brought to bear behind the scenes; but there must be a limit as to what can be suppressed from now on.

If bodies keep turning up things are going to get nasty, and I don't mean just for the hoteliers.

"Why, it's Mr. Braddock," Kat says with a straight face for the benefit of anyone who might be watching. "You're going to Bangkok too?"

"Mrs. Charoenkul, what a pleasant surprise. Yes, a couple of days in the capital. Business, I'm afraid. No rest for the wicked."

We continue with this baloney for a couple of minutes, and I'm worried that the absurdity of our situation will get the better of me and I'll start laughing out loud. Fortunately the guy sitting on the other side of me stands up and wanders off. Kat and I maintain our formal body-postures but drop our voices and proceed to more pertinent matters.

"I need to know your schedule of movements over the next two days."

"Do you indeed."

"I do indeed."

"You are not seriously proposing to follow me around Bangkok, David, are you?"

"Not all the time, no, but I do need to find out if you're having sex with anyone. That *is* what your husband is paying me for."

"Anyone apart from you, you mean."

"I didn't mention it on the phone last night, but the Chief has received an anonymous letter. It's from the same author as the notes to us."

Kat looks disconcerted for a moment, but mindful of the public place we're in, she maintains her cool.

"What did it say?"

"That his wife is unfaithful."

"Is that all?"

"Yes."

"You know very well that's about *us*. You and me."

I run a hand over my forehead and wipe my eyes. "I know," I say wearily.

Kat goes off to get a fruit juice then sits back down.

"Do you know *why* I'm going to Bangkok?" she asks.

"The Chief says you'd told him it was a shopping trip."

"It is – partly. But a good friend of mine there is seriously ill. I'm going with her to the SIH Hospital this afternoon to get her test results. She hasn't told her husband yet and she wants me there."

"I see. And afterwards?"

"You are a prying bastard. For your information we're having dinner together. Then tomorrow we're going shopping. All right?"

"To celebrate or to commiserate, depending on the results?"

"Yes."

"So why not just tell your husband what you're doing?"

"I *have* told him," she says crossly. "Evidently he chooses not to believe me."

We sit in silence for a while until our flight is called.

"Just one thing before we separate," I say. "What time and where are you meeting your friend today?"

"Three thirty. We're meeting in the lobby of my hotel. *Why*," she intones icily, "are you coming with us?"

"I need to follow you and take some photographs."

She gives me a withering gaze.

"Look," I say matter-of-factly, "I have to get some innocuous shots of you and your friend so I can convince your husband you're not up to no good. Work with me on this, Kat."

She stares at me for a moment then she nods. "Very well, David."

"And after you get to your hotel and you're sprucing yourself up, leave your phone on."

"Why?"

"Because I might need to call you."

"Why?"

"Because I just might," I say petulantly. "God, you ask a lot of questions."

"That's because I don't get satisfactory answers."

"Well, welcome to my world."

She pauses and looks at me searchingly.

"I suppose you already know from Deng which hotel I'm staying at?"

"Yes. The Indo-China International. My favourite hotel, so rumour has it. I'm flattered. At least I would be if you'd asked me along with you."

Mrs. Charoenkul shakes her head disbelievingly. Then she rises and says formally. "I hope you enjoy your stay in Bangkok, Mr. Braddock."

*   *   *   *   *

As soon as the door is opened at Don Muang International Airport, Bangkok, I'm off the plane like a greyhound out of the traps. Kat is sitting way back, and I know she has checked luggage – *how much stuff does a woman have to pack for two days?* – so it's going to be a while before she gets out of the airport. This is good, because I want to get to her hotel before she does. I hurry through the airport, jump into a taxi and tell the driver I'll give him a good tip if he can get me to the Indo-China International fast. Accordingly he drives like a lunatic while talking to me over his shoulder about what a shame it is that Don Muang will close when the new Suvarnabhumi Airport opens next year. I think he's more worried about the renewal of his taxi licence than any emotional attachment to the former Royal Thai Air Force base.

The dirty concrete buildings and raised roadways of Bangkok's suburbs whizz by. They appear more scruffy than usual in the bright, hot sunlight, and the numerous advertising hoardings look faded and sad. Drying washing hangs over balconies and blackened air conditioning units cling to the sides of buildings, competing for space with satellite dishes and weather-eaten cables.

As we move into the centre of the city the election posters become more numerous. Pictures of Thaksin Shinawatra appear to be everywhere. His statesmanlike gaze beams out from a blue background, and he is wearing a sensible business suit, white shirt and pale blue tie. His smile appears to say *trust me, what other choice do you have?* The poster is topped and tailed with fiery red blocks: I have no idea what the writing on them says. The election is only five days away, but the excitement doesn't touch me: I have other things to worry about.

Like a number of the upmarket hotels in Bangkok, the Indo-China International is located on the Chao Phraya River so that the tourists can watch the charming and the not-so-charming water traffic, and, when they're bored with that, the setting sun. I tell my driver to drop me about a hundred metres from the hotel and hand him a nice tip. In return he hands me a card. I'll be sure to use him again the next time I have a desire to die in a head-on collision.

I stroll casually up the street and find a food stall parked on the corner of a side-road almost directly opposite the hotel entrance. I buy some fresh mango and stand chatting to the vendor as I eat, all the while keeping an eye on the hotel. A furtive looking Thai with a pronounced limp is hovering outside the Indo-China, chain-smoking and watching who gets out of taxis, occasionally referring to a photograph he pulls from his jacket pocket. At first I think it is the policeman I met at Carroll's murder scene, but realise it isn't. Whoever it is, he is looking for someone, and I don't think it's to greet them.

A few minutes later the taxi containing Kat pulls up, and as the lady alights the limping one looks excited while trying not to. Of course, the mere sight of Kat is generally enough to get any red-blooded male excited, but it may be more sinister than that. I am not reassured when, as she disappears into the lobby, the man consults his watch, takes out a small notepad and scribbles on it.

I light a Marlboro and give Kat ten minutes to check in and arrive in her room before I call her mobile.

"David, I haven't even unpacked yet."

"Never mind that. I need you to do something. Go back down into the lobby, and when you come out of the hotel turn right and walk to the 24 Hour Store. It's about 100 metres. Buy a bottle of water and walk back to the hotel. If you see me, don't acknowledge me, and don't look behind you."

"*Walk?*" she says in an outraged tone. "David, tirak, I don't *walk*. Anyway, it's hot and I'm in high heels."

"Christ, Kat. Then change into some flat shoes."

"I don't have any flat shoes with me. Why do I have to do this?"

I make an exasperated noise and she relents.

Shortly thereafter she appears through the revolving door and does as instructed. The suspicious-looking Thai quickly stubs out a cigarette he's just lit and follows her at a distance. As Kat begins her walk back he pretends to talk into a phone until she has passed him then watches her re-enter the hotel, before taking up his original position. He writes something else down.

I phone Kat again.

"You have a tail," I say. Then I add, "Quite appropriate for a *Kat*, really."

"I thought you were my tail."

"I thought so too. Can you think of anyone other than your husband who would be having you followed?"

"No."

"OK, sit tight. I'll call you in a little while."

"Mind if I get changed now?" she asks archly. "I'm all hot after that walk."

"Carry on. I'll be following you later, after I've got rid of the other guy."

I buzz Charoenkul who answers immediately.

"If you are going to get someone else to follow your wife, I suggest you hire a private investigator that doesn't have a peg-leg. If I can spot him a mile away, I'm sure Mrs. Charoenkul will too, and then everything's blown."

Papa Doc is quiet.

"Call him off. Let me do my job," I say. "You don't need two guys following her around like some sad music hall duo."

He sighs. "Very well."

"Make the call."

I hang up.

A short time later, the Thai Long John Silver gets a call on his cell phone. He nods, puts the phone in his pocket and limps away. I hang around until I'm sure he's gone then I walk to my (much more modest) hotel situated above the 24 Hour Store.

I unpack and throw a few essentials into my camera bag then I go back down into the street to look for a biker who wants to make some money. I find a likely candidate called "X", who sports a Brazil football shirt and a large collection of tattoos. We hang around smoking at the food stall until Kat appears with her friend, a rather mumsy Thai lady. I take a couple of photos before they step into a taxi.

"Follow that cab," I say to X, somewhat over-dramatically. "And make sure they don't know we're trailing them."

We travel slowly through the steamy heat of the city, stopping regularly and choking on traffic fumes. My shirt is soaked in sweat when the ladies' taxi arrives at the SIH Hospital. X parks a respectable distance away and I climb off the bike. I have time to snap a few shots of their backs before they vanish inside the main building.

Shortly afterwards I receive a SMS from Kat: *Will probably be two hours. Don't worry we'll come out the front door*

I send a message back: *SMS me when you are done, am going for a cool drink*

Since X can't leave his bike on the main thoroughfare, he puts it in an adjacent side-road, and we have a couple of beers in a lean-to establishment across the way from the hospital. X doesn't have much conversation, so I send him off to get me a *Bangkok Post* and a packet of Marlboros.

I light up, open the paper and see Mr. Carroll has made the national news. Not the headlines, but enough inside coverage to give my police friends on Samui some serious heartburn. The phone lines from the island to Surat Thani must be glowing.

It's after 6.00pm when I receive a message from Kat: *Finished, not good*

I pay the bill and tell X to get the bike.

Kat and her friend emerge arm-in-arm from the hospital. Kat looks grim and her friend is in tears. They make their way to an upmarket coffee shop nearby and sit down at a corner table. Kat looks to be comforting her companion, who seems to recover for a spell before breaking down again. I take a couple of heartless photographs for Charoenkul.

After a while I can't bear to watch this anymore, so I send Kat a text for her to call me later, and get X to take me back to my hotel. I take his cell phone number, book him for tomorrow and pay him for today. Then I go shower and change into cool, dry clothing while I wait for Kat's call.

She calls around seven-thirty.

"Where are you?" she asks in a voice that sounds strained.

"In my hotel room, not far away."

"Why don't you come over? I could do with some company. Sumalee has calmed down, but she's decided to talk to her husband this evening; and she thinks it best I'm not there. Can you come? I'm in Room 415."

"I'll be there in ten minutes."

I check no-one is hanging around outside the Indo-China, but as a double precaution I take the lift to the fifth floor and walk down one floor of steps to Room 415.

"You've brought your camera bag?" Kat says opening the door.

"Professional habit."

Although she's obviously been through an emotional couple of hours, she's changed and scrubbed up well. We chat for a little while, and I proffer a few weak jokes on inconsequential subjects, after which she's almost back to her usual self.

We have a couple of drinks from her mini-bar then unexpectedly Kat throws a towel at me.

"Take a shower," she says.

"Why?" I ask.

"Because you're not having sex with me until you've showered," she replies.

"Are we having sex then? After what you've been through this afternoon? God, you're a resilient woman."

She shrugs. "We may as well," she smiles. "Since you're here. I *do* have an itch that needs to be scratched, and I don't feel like doing it myself. Besides which, it will take my mind off things. Do you have any condoms?"

"Only a dozen or so."

"I'll try to pretend you didn't anticipate this. That way I won't feel taken for granted."

I strip and step under the shower. Kat disrobes, ties back her hair and joins me. She turns the shower setting onto 'narrow pulse' mode and the hot water hits my skin like tiny needles.

"When did you last come?" she asks as the water splashes off us and the glass walls begin to steam up.

"Centuries ago."

"Are you sure? You haven't been riding any dirty little bargirls recently?"

"Scouts honour."

Kat puts her arms around my neck and kisses me slowly on the mouth. Then she draws her face back a few inches and says softly, "I don't want you coming straightaway, tirak, I need you to last. Turn around and put your hands on the wall."

I do as I'm told.

She presses her body against my back, and I feel the hardness of her nipples as she rubs against me. She moves my legs slightly apart with her foot, and I know what's next. She places her left hand on my chest, and pulls herself against me. She uses her lips and teeth on my shoulder and with her right hand she begins to masturbate me.

"Is that nice, Daddy David?" (There is something a wee bit sick about Kat at times, but I can't pretend I don't like it.)

"I think you know it is, Mrs. Charoenkul."

"You're such a sweet one," she says, wanking me very hard. "Come for your little Katty."

She bites my shoulder hard and I cry out as I come.

"That's my good boy."

"Jesus," I gasp.

She lets the water wash the semen from her hand, and says in a businesslike manner, "My turn next."

She soaps me all over, and I reciprocate. In spite of the fact that I've just come, my cock is at half-mast as we step out of the shower. In the bedroom we dry each other with soft white towels, and I kneel down to dry her legs, like a supplicant before the altar of her ripe body. She offers me a foot to kiss and I oblige.

"You've done well," she says. "I'm dry everywhere apart from one place. You can lick that dry." She grasps my hair and we fall onto the bed. She pushes my head down over her smooth stomach and waxed pubis, guiding my mouth towards her sex. "Eat me, tirak. Eat me deep. Taste your little Katty."

I gently part Kat's velvety thighs and insert the tip of my tongue into her. She is already wet, and I savour her taste. I peel back the labia with my fingers so that I can penetrate deeper, and I hear her sharp intake of breath. Her fingers tighten in my hair, and she begins to move my head rhythmically against her. My tongue seeks out her clitoris, and I suck on her. She pulls back my head.

"Gently, David, gently. Slowly, darling. I don't want to come yet."

But I can't stop now, and I eat her greedily, her juices flowing into my mouth and down my chin. As she approaches climax, her hips rise and fall and she thrusts herself against my lips. I have to be careful not to bite her.

"You – greedy – bastard," she pants, and suddenly she releases my head and arches her back. As she comes I wrap my arms around her thighs and press them against the side of my head, burying my wet face into her. I continue feasting on her more slowly until she shoves my head away.

"Enough, David. That's enough."

She pulls me on top of her and kisses me hard on the mouth. Then she wipes my face with her hand and observes, "I don't think you've licked me dry, my pet. Just the opposite, in fact."

"Sorry about that."

"So you should be." She rolls me off her, slaps my shoulder and says in mock disapproval, "I ask for gentleness and you eat me like some wild beast."

"You love it."

"Fuck you," she says, and kisses me hard on the mouth again. "I didn't want to come that quickly."

"Next time will be longer."

She looks down at my penis which is hard again and the glistening end is against her thigh, making it sticky.

"Are you ready for some serious penetration?" I ask.

She smiles and brushes back a strand of hair. "I need to ring my husband first," she says.

"You're not serious."

"Oh but I am."

She stretches her body across me to take the cell phone from her bag.

"Do you expect me to lie here while you call the Chief?" I say incredulously.

"Why not? I'll only be a minute. Otherwise he might get suspicious."

She presses some buttons with one hand and strokes my cock with the other. Then lying on my shoulder she proceeds to have a conversation about her friend and how she'll be spending some money on the credit cards tomorrow to cheer her up. Charoenkul doesn't argue.

Towards the end, she slides down me, still talking.

"No," she says to her husband, "I haven't eaten yet. I thought I'd have something in my room." Her mouth hovers over my penis and she looks at me naughtily. She licks her lips and raises an eyebrow. "Oh, I don't know," she says into the phone, "something hot I think. I feel the need for something warm inside me."

She hangs up. I pull her head away from my groin area and pin her down while I slip on a studded condom.

"How romantic," Kat whispers. "You do care after all."

She slaps me and bites my neck, then pulls back suddenly.

"Now David," she says seriously, "I want you to fuck me very, very hard. Very hard. Do you understand?" Her eyes flash.

"Yes, Mrs. Charoenkul."

She puts her mouth to mine and we go at each other like animals.

As I shower afterwards, I notice Kat has drawn blood from me in several

215

places. There are scratches on my back, sides and abdomen from her nails and teeth marks on my neck, the inside of my right thigh and on my left forearm. My lower lip is swollen where she was chewing it over-enthusiastically. It looks like I've just been in a fight. Which in a sense, I have.

The lady herself, of course, is completely unmarked; although she may have some internal bruising in one particular location.

I'd put my cell phone on silent prior to our session, and now I see I have two missed calls; one from Charoenkul and one from Wayan. I tell Kat I need to make a few calls and I'll be slipping out for a short while. Kat is too busy reapplying her makeup to be bothered about this.

"Hurry back, tirak," she says distractedly examining her mascara.

Before I leave the room I stealthily switch on the recording device that is in my camera bag, and leave the bag on the desk behind a vase holding lilies, roses and baby breath flowers.

Outside and away from the hotel entrance the street is dark and stuffy, but, as always there are people about. The mango seller is chatting to a friend, and a couple of bored taxi drivers are smoking in their cabs. There is no sign of the limping man.

I call Wayan and her voice has a frightened edge. She tells me there is a car parked on the unlit road opposite our house, and she thinks she has heard someone moving around outside. Given that Wayan is not given to imaginary fears, I am immediately concerned. I tell her to stay indoors and ensure all the doors are locked and the windows closed, and that I will call her back in five minutes.

Then I ring Charoenkul.

"How is it going?" he asks.

"Nothing happening, as I thought," I reply. "Your wife went to the hospital with her friend and returned to the hotel a couple of hours ago. She's still there. I'm outside the Indo-China now."

He wants to chat further but I cut him off.

"Listen," I say. "I think there is a prowler at my house. I want you to send a car around. There is a woman in my house on her own."

He snorts. "Do you think my policemen have got nothing better to do? Your maid is probably just being hysterical."

"My *housekeeper* never gets hysterical," I shout down the phone at this slur on Wayan. "If she's anxious, it will be because she has good cause. And if I wasn't doing this favour for you, *I'd* be there now to sort it out. I want a patrol car sent to my house *immediately*, and I want it to stay there until morning."

"My, my, we are tetchy this evening, Braddock. I'll see what I can do."

"I want you to do better than that," I say firmly. "I'm calling my housekeeper back now, and I'll stay on the line until your car gets there. Otherwise our deal is off, and you can get the guy with the limp to watch your wife."

I can sense him pursing his lips in disapproval at this farang insolence, but after a beat he says, "All right, I'll send a car. But it's probably nothing."

I redial Wayan's number and tell her a police car is on the way. She is instantly apologetic, but I tell her not to worry and that I want her to stay on the phone until the car arrives.

I talk in a soothing voice about nothing much in particular. After about ten minutes she reports the patrol car has turned up; and the other car has driven off as it was arriving. One of the police officers comes to the front door and I instruct Wayan to hand him the phone.

I tell the officer in my most commanding Thai that I am a personal friend of the Chief and that I want him outside my house and awake until morning. I don't give him much chance to speak other than to say a compliant *very well, I understand, sir,* at the end of the call. Then I tell Wayan to go to bed: I will leave my phone on all night and she is to call me if she is at all worried.

"Thank you, Mr. David. I am sorry I cause such a problem for you."

"It is no problem, my dear. Now go and get some rest. I'll ring you tomorrow morning."

Back in Kat's room, she has changed into a black silk negligee and there is a bottle of champagne on ice.

"Why did you put your makeup on again?" I ask. "You know it's going to get smudged."

She laughs.

"You wish."

*   *   *   *   *

The digital clock says 02:47, and I become aware that Kat is not in bed beside me. The curtains to the sliding door are partially open and through the glass I can see her outline on the balcony. She is wearing one of the white hotel robes and is leaning over the railing with her back to me.

I slip on a robe and join her. I put my hands around her waist, and as she turns I can see she has been crying.

"Kat," I say alarmed, "what is it? What's wrong?"

"Give me a cigarette," she says.

"But you don't smoke."

"Just give me a cigarette."

I fetch my Marlboros and light one for each of us.

"What's the matter, darling?" I ask softly.

She shakes her head slowly then rests her body against me.

"My best friend is dying," she says quietly. "We treat life like a game, and we laugh at it. But it's serious. You know? We can't joke about it forever. There comes a time when –"

She stops and wipes away the tears from her face.

I have never seen her vulnerable before. I pull her to me and kiss the top of her head. I don't know what to say.

218

We stand like this, smoking in silence until she throws her cigarette over the balcony towards the river. Then she takes my cigarette and throws that away too.

Kat wraps my arms tightly around her and looks up into my eyes.

"David," she whispers, "I would like you to hold me and make love to me gently. I know you don't love me. I know that. But just for an hour I'd like you to pretend that you do. Will you do that for me? Please?"

9

"In the morning they wore each other's face"
Ted Hughes, Lovesong

Some people are straightforward. What you see is indeed what you get. Their words have no subtext and their hearts are open. Such individuals possess a naïveté which is both striking and humbling, and which inspires trust in others because these people are themselves trusting. They see life essentially through childlike eyes and, because of that, the more cynical members of the human race often consider them foolish and unsophisticated. Those more experienced in the ways of the world view them as easy marks, such stuff as the con-man's wet dreams are made on.

Straightforward people are very much in the minority, and in today's world where idealism has become unfashionable and the concept of self-sacrifice unfathomable, they are in all likelihood an endangered species.

For the rest of us, lying and deception is a necessary social skill. One we practice every day. Those – like myself – suckled at the breast of Perfidious Albion especially see the public expression of vulnerability as anathema. We harbour an abhorrence for emotional weakness; and we Brits are by no means the only ones. On a dog-eat-dog planet if you are to thrive, you have to be in control of yourself. Or at least appear to be.

So we wear masks. We hide behind them. We feel naked without them. They are our public face. So far as our acquaintances are concerned they *are* us. Sometimes we even fool ourselves, at least for a while.

Our mask is like an energy shield, fabricated of our own deep insecurities and fears. But the cost of maintaining the shields day after day is high. Without someone with whom we feel safe to remove the mask and power down the shields, we exhaust ourselves. Absent a trusted loved one and the respite from role-playing they can bring, there is always the risk of neurotic collapse: the mask is torn away and the exposed human face is presented to a mocking world.

Last night Kat's mask slipped. For an hour I glimpsed the real woman who dwells behind the façade of the Police Chief's wife; a flesh-and-blood person with fears and complexities and needs. But by this morning she had disappeared again. The energy shield was once more firmly in place, and the tenderness of the moonlight consigned to the land of never-was.

She booted me unceremoniously out of her bed and sent me to my own hotel for a shower, shave and change of clothing. Trust was manifestly not on her agenda at this juncture, neither was a desire to repeat our intimacy of the hours before.

On the issue of trust, maybe she had a point. While she was attending to her toilet the previous evening I had lifted from her mobile phone the numbers she had called yesterday, and switched off the recording device, slipping it to the bottom of the camera bag for later playback.

Now sitting in my hotel room I reflect that she had called three phone numbers. Judging from the time of the calls, I'm guessing the first call was to her friend Sumalee; the second (of course) was to her husband. As for the third? Well, the time of the third call was when I was outside on the phone to Wayan and sorting out a police car. With luck my recording device – which is pretty sensitive, the best the private surveillance industry can offer – has captured one side of the third conversation. I rewind the tape and switch it onto 'play'.

For the first couple of minutes there is just the sound of Kat moving around the room, humming to herself. Then she makes a call. I can't hear the voice at the other end, but from the tone of her voice and the words that follow I know it's a Thai man.

Hello, tirak. I'm so sorry ... Yes, I know, it's not exactly what I had in mind either. My friend has just had some really bad news ... She's very upset, I'm going to have to stay with her tonight, but tomorrow I'll see you, I promise ... I know, I know ... I'm going shopping with Sumalee tomorrow morning to cheer her up, but I should be able come to you, my dear, say around three o'clock ... Yes, to your room. I can't wait to see it, I've never stayed in a penthouse before, especially one frequented by members of Arabian royal families ... Good view of the river? Even from the Jacuzzi? Sounds wonderful! I wish I could be with you tonight, but I can't ... I know ... Oh, not far. You're only a couple of hundred metres from my hotel. I might even walk to you ... [sound of Kat's laughter] ... I'll be wearing high heels, don't worry, and something black ... Ha ha, you're a naughty boy ... Of course, I'll stay tomorrow night ... Yes, ALL night. So you'd better get plenty of rest tonight, you'll need all your strength tomorrow ... [Kat laughs again] ... Oh, that's so bad ... Now you will leave a key card for me at reception, won't you? I don't want to have to call your room from the lobby like some common prostitute ... You are outrageous ... ha.

There is only one Sheikh-friendly hotel on the river with a penthouse close to the Indo-China. The outrageously expensive Carlsson Sharifah. The lobby has a truly enormous water feature you could drown an elephant in, the manager is reputedly a baron and the bell-boys all wear Prada. Nice: somebody's got some cash to splash. Oh frailty, thy name sure is woman. One woman, at least. Plus she might even *walk*. Kat volunteering to walk, for goodness' sake. Must be quite some guy she's seeing.

I listen to the rest of the tape then erase everything from the end of her phone conversation.

I check my watch: time to ring Wayan, she should be up and dressed by now.

"Mr. David?"

"Wayan, are you OK?"

"Yes, yes, I am fine. You don't have to worry about me. The policemen have gone now. Everything is all right."

"I *do* worry about you. Did you manage to get some sleep?"

"I am fine, Mr. David. Yes, I have slept. Now I have to go and do some shopping."

"Do you want me to come home today? I'm not sure I want you to be alone tonight."

"It is not necessary."

"I can have the police car back again."

For sure I want a police car back there again tonight.

"Please, I do not want to make a fuss," she says, embarrassed.

"Well, I'll call you later."

I consider what to do about Mrs. Charoenkul. But then she calls me.

"David, tirak, how are we going to handle today?"

"How do you mean, Kat?" I ask with my best innocent voice.

"Well, Sumalee will be here shortly. She's just phoned me. We're going to go shopping, we'll have a good girls' chat and then later I'm going to her house. I'll probably stay the night there."

"Sounds like a good idea. I'm sure she could do with your support."

"Exactly. She spoke to her husband last night and – well, I don't want to bore you with all this."

I have to hand it to Mrs. C: it's not everyone that could use an old friend's terminal illness as cover for adultery without *some* pang of guilt. But she carries it off beautifully.

"Listen, Kat, there's no point in my following you around today," I say doing my own bit of bare-faced lying. "Your shopping will be sufficient evidence of how you've spent the day without my needing to take photographs. Besides, the Chief can check out the credit card receipts for himself if he's not satisfied."

"That's right, he can," she says, sounding relieved.

"I've got other stuff I'd like to do today, so just call me later and let me know which shops you've been to so we can co-ordinate our stories in case the Chief rings. I'll then see you on the flight back tomorrow."

"OK, tirak, that sounds like a plan. Are you going over to Patpong today to see some girlies, then?"

"That's hardly likely. My penis looks like a cheese grater's been at it. Actually most of my body does. I'll need a couple of days to recover before I go anywhere near a woman again."

"You say the sweetest things. I'll call you later."

"Looking forward to it. Missing you already," I say in my best American accent.

Kat smacks me a kiss and hangs up.

There is a powerful smell of mendacity in the air. Kat and I are both such good liars, we really should be married. Either that or in politics together.

I feel ever so slightly miffed, although I have no right to be. It's not like Kat owes me anything; not even an honest account of the real reason for her presence in Bangkok. It's the Chief who should be miffed, having a wife who betrays him with two men simultaneously (well, not *exactly* simultaneously, but you get my drift). Of course, that poor bastard doesn't have a clue what's going on. Moreover he's not about to learn the truth from me.

My only consoling thought is that Kat's lover will be stirring *my* porridge, not the other way round. Anyway, leaving all that seamy stuff aside it's time for a scrub up and a good breakfast. I didn't eat much yesterday – if you discount Mrs. C – and I'm hungry.

I jump on the back of X's bike and we roar off into the Bangkok traffic. I've told him to ride like we're being followed and I want to lose the tail. That's because I've started wondering if I *am* being followed – not by the limping one, that would be too obvious; but by *somebody*. This may be paranoia, but of course just because you're paranoid doesn't mean someone isn't out to get you.

X takes his instruction seriously and tears between the cars and other bikes, giving a hair's breadth clearance at times. I get the impression he's done this before. Maybe he's related to the taxi driver I had yesterday. He cuts up a tuk-tuk driver who yells something obscene at him. X merely gives him the finger. I could get to like this guy.

The rushing air against my face is hot and seemingly devoid of oxygen. The capital is baking hot already. The fumes, heat, noise, dust and overweening presence of excess humanity combine to evoke a world straight off one of Hieronymus Bosch's canvases: hell on earth.

How I love Bangkok! It's so teeming with everything that should be forbidden. I'm not just talking about the sex trade. I also mean the ways of driving, the ways of putting up buildings, environmental management arrangements, the continual attention of con artists and snatch-thieves, and the quaint local custom of peeing in side-streets. This urban potpourri currently incorporates election posters splattered onto any unguarded vertical surface and coloured lights and other decorations sprouting up ahead of the Chinese New Year festivities. If I could get enough air into my lungs I would laugh with joy.

X drops me at the Krung Thep Plaza off Sukhumvit Road. I don't want to hang around here too long. There is always the remote chance that Kat's shopping spree will bring her here at some point in the day and I don't want to bump into her accidentally. I'm keen not to arouse any suspicions that I might be following her, otherwise my task becomes doubly difficult. However, as I'm in Bangkok I want to use the opportunity to drop in on my partner at our shop, Sutra Arts.

Asda Nueng, the working half of our partnership, is busy charming an elderly American couple with his knowledge of Buddhist statuary. He is, as always, immaculately turned out (and I'd say looking handsome, if I were a woman). An attractive (I'd say) Russian girl is examining a display containing an oversize bronze *mudra*, presumably awaiting the arrival of her sugar daddy and his credit card.

I'm always struck by the tasteful and expensive feel of Sutra Arts, from the gorgeous tapestries and fabrics to the Asian religious iconography: Asda is not only a wizard at selling and buying but also at displaying. I remember once suggesting to him we stock some Timor primitive sculptures and he looked at me and wrinkled his nose like I'd suggested I sleep with his wife. *I think not, David,* he said drily. *That would not be in keeping with what we are trying to achieve here.* I leave it up to him.

He hands over the Americans to his female assistant to complete some shipping paperwork, asks solicitously if he can help the Eastern European Barbie, then comes over to greet me.

"Hey, Asda," I say, "you finally sold the giant Garuda."

He smiles. "David, surely you had no doubt I would sell it?"

"None whatsoever."

We talk business for a little while, with occasional interruptions from wide-eyed customers. The Russian sugar daddy arrives and the mudra is sold, along with a large Siva statue and an ornate hanging from Northern India. The assistant makes us a coffee, but the street door keeps swinging relentlessly open.

"Business is brisk, Asda," I observe. "I'll leave you to it. I'm just in the way."

"If you stay around long enough, David, I can sell *you*. Many of our clients like old, interesting pieces."

"I'll be back in a few weeks for a proper visit," I tell him. "I have other work to do today. I just wanted to drop by while I was in town."

"Next time you have to come to my house for dinner," he says. "The family would love to see you. It's been too long, my friend."

As I step outside my cell phone rings: it's Da.

"Aren't you on your way to have that kid yet?"

"I believed he was coming early this morning," she replies. "I thought my contractions were starting but it turned out to be a false alarm."

I *really* have to start thinking about Da's replacement soon.

"You take care."

"Always. Now listen, Khun David, I've telephoned all the hospitals about Khun Yai's eye operation, and sorted out which one has the best price. He'll be going in for an examination tomorrow and his grand-daughter will go with him. If all is well, they'll do the operation next week. I've taken money out of the petty cash box to pay for the consultation. I assume that's OK?"

"Well done."

"I had a long chat with Bee over the phone. She sounds nice, I liked her. I assume you like her too."

"Yes."

"What does she look like?"

"Older than her years."

"But she has a nice body, yes? She must have surely."

"For your information, not *every* woman I talk to –" I begin indignantly, but give up. "Oh, never mind. Listen, Da, I need you to do something else for me."

"Anything that my current medical condition will allow."

"I want you to book a hotel for Wayan to stay at tonight."

"I don't understand."

"There was a car parked outside my house last night and Wayan thought she heard someone moving around out there. I had the police station a patrol vehicle there until morning. It might be nothing, but I don't want to take a chance. I can't get back to Samui just yet and I don't want Wayan staying on her own tonight."

If I were talking about some other female, Da would make some smutty remark at this point, but she respects Wayan, even if she has a particular viewpoint about me.

"Is Wayan OK?" she asks concerned.

"She's fine."

"What sort of standard of hotel do you want me to book?"

"Book a nice one, but not somewhere she's going to feel awkward. Try the Lotus Blossom Villas. This is *Wayan* we're talking about. I don't want her in some cockroach-infested hovel with a backpacker banging a bargirl up against the wall next door."

"Understood."

"Then ring Wayan and give her the details. I'll call her in the meantime and let her know you'll be in touch. Oh, and one more thing. If you suspect anyone is watching the office or there is anyone hanging around outside looking suspicious, I want you to lock up and go home straightaway. I'm probably over-reacting, but, well –"

"Khun David, you know you can be so sweet sometimes."

"Thank you for the *sometimes*. SMS me when you've made the booking."

After I end the call it occurs to me that the Lotus Blossom Villas is where Ashley and his brother stayed. But I'm not the superstitious type. Besides, Wayan is not a middle-aged male European. She's much more appealing than that.

I call her, explain the situation and tell her to take some money from our cash drawer at home to pay for the hotel room. As expected, she thinks this is all unnecessary, but I am firm with her and eventually she relents.

Now if I was to catch the last flight back to Samui tonight I could surprise Wayan at the hotel and we could have a drink together and ... And then my life would be in even more of a mess. Stick to the plan, Braddock.

I need to go somewhere not too far from my hotel and where I won't run into Kat. Somewhere where she wouldn't be seen dead, preferably. I know just the spot.

I have X take me to a small eating place on the north bank of the Chao Phraya River. It's decidedly downmarket, but it's popular with locals (usually a good sign), well shaded and has a distant view of the Temple of the Dawn, *Wat Arun*, which right now is shimmering in the haze. The iridescent river is full of busy little boats and rusting, crammed-full ferries, some of which pull in at the nearby pier.

I find a dusty corner table, order some vegetable rice and beer and light up a cigarette. There are quite a few people around and some of them are looking at me curiously. It may be because I am the only farang in the joint, but I still have this itchy feeling at the back of my neck that I am under observation; and not just casual observation by inquisitive locals. The crackly sound system switches from traditional Thai music to Billy Joel's 'We Didn't Start the Fire', and I wonder if this is in my honour.

We didn't start the fire,
It was always burning since the world's been turning ...

My cold beer arrives and I watch the condensation form into small streams and run down the outside of the glass. It's so chilled it sets the nerves jangling in my bottom teeth as I take a pull.

I have time to kill.

Time. So much of our human experience is bound up in time, I muse. It reflects in our everyday colloquialisms, and drives so much of our activities. Yet this obsession with the passing of the hours is a relatively modern phenomenon; an inevitable product of the Industrial Revolution, and its fixation on efficiency. A new master exported by England across the globe, so that in the developed world at least everyone has one wrist on which is clamped the new and unforgiving shackle we call a watch. In less pressurised days, men observed the ageing of the universe through the more sedate changing of the seasons. But no more. Now the hour is king, or the minute and sometimes even the second. We are all people in a rush, where speed is of the essence, and *slow* is often deployed as a term of abuse.

Time to spare. Not enough time. A time to sow and a time to reap. Time on our hands. The time of our lives. Time to decide. The wrong time, the right time. Quality time. The thief of time.

Time as the great healer: although I don't quite see it that way. I see it

229

more as a vehicle to transport me away from painful memories, when mere distance is not enough. Where burns the hope that one day my pursuing furies will eventually tire and falter, and I will find some kind of peace. But that time is not yet upon me. Would that it were.

I light a Marlboro and put aside these contemplations.

I return to my enduring obsession: Kenneth Sinclair.

There are about a zillion other things I should be thinking about, I know. Like who is writing these anonymous letters to me, to Kat and to Charoenkul? Like what on earth is Kat playing at seeing someone else right under her husband's nose when she knows he is already suspicious? Like what on earth is Kat playing at seeing someone else right under *my* nose? Like what will Charoenkul do if he finds out I've been having sex with his wife *while he was paying me to watch her*? Like who was watching my house last night? Like Claire ...?

Sod all that. What I really want to think about is Sinclair and what he's up to. This paying me to spy on his employee, I just don't buy it.

In spite of the fact that Prasert Promsai's brother Nikom is currently top of my list of possible farang killers, I decide to indulge my dislike for Sinclair by contemplating how I might fit him up for the three burning murders. Now let me see. Supposing he were to be the murderer, what would be his motive? I consider what I know about the Northern Neanderthal.

His first wife dumped him for somebody else; that's what Charlie R told me. Someone effeminate, or at least our macho Geordie considered him so. Although it occurs to me that Sinclair might consider anyone who uses toilet paper effeminate, perhaps I exaggerate. Moving on. His first wife's lover was affectionately referred to as 'Arse-wipe' or 'Arse-lay' according to my Bronx friend's sometime reliable memory. What if this was a word-play on 'Ashley', the surname of the initial burning victim? What if Sinclair had by chance discovered his former love-rival on holiday on Samui and beaten his brains out? Losing your spouse and access to your kids could be a powerful motive for murder. Sinclair certainly has the brawn to do the deed. He would have little difficulty wielding a blunt weapon. Indeed he might uncharitably be described as a blunt weapon himself. It would also explain the contemptuous nature of the torching.

But how to explain the other two murders? One of the more exotic murder motives that I list is *to cover up another misdeed*. He could have done in the other two guys to cover up the first killing, so that the whole thing looks like some serial murder spree when in fact the real crime is a straightforward revenge job.

But why would he bother? The first murder didn't even make the papers, and it must have been obvious that the police weren't going to put themselves out investigating it. Carrying out more killings would just attract attention and increase the hitherto negligible risk of getting caught. And aside from anything else, the whole situation with Sinclair's first wife was over ten years ago. Since then the Geordie has found a new life, fallen in love, remarried and started a second family ...

Wait a minute.

The Neanderthal has also lost his beloved second wife. In circumstances which, anti-Sinclair that I am, even I can appreciate must have been painful. *He went mad*, Charlie said, and recently he'd been excited again when someone had raised his expectations that his wife's hit-and-run killer might be identified. But how would I jump from *that* to the burning murders? I don't know. But the coincidence of timing is interesting.

Of course what I should really be considering about Sinclair is why I dislike him. But I don't want to think about this.

So far as the murders are concerned, my money still has to be on Nikom Promsai. But only a little bit of money, at least until such time as Charoenkul has run a check on the property development angle and Nikom has turned up again. Assuming he does turn up again. Assuming he's not dead and I've somehow managed to get this whole thing arse about face.

Smoke another cigarette, Braddock, and think about something else. Watch the pretty boats on the river and listen to the music. Aha. When I do pay attention I note the sound system is crunching out Elvis singing 'Burning Love'. Someone somewhere is trying to tell me something. Wayan would be so proud. Psychedelic dreams, flying demons, spinning pool cues and non-barking dogs in the night-time. Either I'm beginning to embrace primitive religion, or there is only thing that's barking in the night-time, and that's *me*.

*   *   *   *   *

A quarter to three in the afternoon sees me sitting at the coffee shop in the marble-columned foyer of the Carlsson Sharifah, hiding behind a newspaper. I've succumbed to one of the wicked calorie-laden cakes off the display to accompany my cappuccino, despite the fact that my stomach still feels bloated from the rice and beer I had at lunchtime.

From my position I can watch the revolving doors for the arrival of Kat. I hope I've got my facts right and this is the correct hotel, otherwise the chances of tracking my shady lady to her love-nest are slim.

She'd called me around one-thirty to give me a list of all the shops she and Sumalee had been to and what she'd bought there: Charoenkul's credit cards had clearly taken a severe battering. She told me she was going back to the hotel shortly to drop off her shopping, change and pick up a few things before heading over to her friend's house where she would spend the night.

"I'll need to know your friend's address and how to get there," I said.

"*Why?*" asked Kat sharply.

"Because if I'm supposed to have followed you there, I'll need to be able to give a convincing account to your husband of exactly where it is I've been."

232

"Oh, I see," she said, sounding relieved.

She gave me the details and we double-checked our stories. She then asked me what I would be doing for the rest of the day and expressed her fervent hope that I wouldn't be going off to Patpong to spend time with dirty women. I reassured her on that score, pointing out my body was in no state to be getting involved in anything like that; all the while thinking what a bloody cheek she had.

I see the hands of my watch have already passed the hour and there is still no sign of Mrs. C. I would expect her to be fashionably late, but by the same token a small puff of resentment inside me says that she will nonetheless be anxious to see her lover. Especially as she has already had to forgo one night with him, courtesy of David Braddock.

At ten after the hour she appears looking radiant and makes her way over to the desk where she presumably collects her key-card before proceeding to the lifts. She doesn't once glance in my direction.

Using as cover the lobby's grotesquely-sized water feature – which has been making me want to pee for the last fifteen minutes – I see Kat enter one of the lifts, and watch the display above signal the ascent to the top floor. Bingo.

I pay my bill at the coffee bar and proceed up the glamorous main staircase to the first floor. The corridors are empty, so I go up another flight and I find what I am looking for: a bribable chamber-maid. This one is in her forties, overweight and seems to have an asthmatic condition. After some charming preamble, I tell her if she can find out the name of the man staying in the penthouse I will make it worth her while. I reassure her that I am not a criminal, she will in no way get into trouble and that I will treat the source of my information with the strictest confidence. She remains unconvinced until I mention how much I will give her. Then she is extremely convinced.

She tells me she has a good friend on reception: she will get the information and meet me at the nearby pier after she finishes work for the day at four o'clock.

I thank her, kiss her podgy hand gallantly and make my way back down into the lobby, past the bored uniformed flunkeys and out into the stifling air.

One hour later my chamber-maid waddles into sight. I hand her the Baht and she hands me a slip of paper. I look at the name on the paper. Then I fold the paper, put it in my pocket and go looking for X.

*   *   *   *   *

The sky is already dark when X drops me off in Patpong.

Since my rendezvous with the ample chamber-maid, I've had a SMS from Da confirming Wayan's booking, been back to my claustrophobic hotel room, taken a cold shower (because there was no hot water) and changed into some dry clothing. I've also called Wayan to make sure she has checked into the Lotus Blossom Villas, which she has albeit reluctantly. I suggested she take dinner in the restaurant, a suggestion which I'm sure she will discreetly ignore.

I gave Charoenkul the agreed story on his wife's movements for the day and told him that, having seen Mrs. C safely inside her friend's house, I was knocking off for the day. He didn't particularly react, even when I advised him he should sit down before opening his next credit card statement. I said I could supply him with more details when I gave him my bill. This at least drew a resigned sigh from the other end of the phone.

I hand X his bounty for the day and tell him he doesn't need to hang around, since I'll take a taxi back to my hotel later.

"Why don't you enjoy yourself while you're here," I say. "The night is young."

"I don't drink," he replies stiffly, "and I have a regular girlfriend, so I don't mix with these whores."

234

"Good for you," I respond through gritted teeth.

And so the moral tattooed biker rides home to his domestic idyll while the immoral middle-aged businessman makes his way on foot through Patpong's bright lights, hawkers, pimps and girls. I turn into a rubbish-strewn and evil-smelling side-alley and climb a flight of peeling stairs at the top of which is my destination, Siam Welcomes You.

The interior is darker than the outside alley. The concealed lighting is only just about bright enough to enable you to make your way from the entrance to the bar where an eerie blue glow illumines the face of the resident bartender. To the right and left are large couches with low tables. A small pole-dancing stage nestles unsubtly, and currently unlit, in one corner. The sound system plays Tina Turner's 'Private Dancer'; the irony of the lyrics apparently lost on the room's occupants. It is still early so there are only two customers on the barstools and two more on the sofas: each has a girl draped over him. Three bored-looking girls are examining their cell phones at the far end of the bar: they haven't noticed me yet.

The eagle-eyes of the establishment's owner have, however, clocked my entrance, and she comes over to greet me.

"Mr. David, Mr. David," she croons. "How wonderful to see you back with us again."

'Mama-san' is in her sixties, a portly hard-nosed Thai businesswoman who rules her small kingdom with a rod of iron. She operates some very strict policies – no drugs, no violence, no rowdy drunks and no credit. At least both the girls and the clients know where they are, and the girls seem to stick around so I guess she's doing something right. I gather she was given her title by a Japanese client many years before when she was on the game herself. I have no idea what her real name is. I'm not sure anybody here knows it.

Unusually for this sort of 'club', Siam Welcomes You has a couple of bedrooms upstairs, for the use of Mama-san's *special* customers. I feature among this august body; and indeed a couple of years ago I found myself holed up in one of those rooms for an entire weekend operating a rota system with five of Mama-san's girls. I'm not bragging mind you: the girls did most of the work, sometimes two-at-a-time as I recall. To commemorate this expensive and sinful occasion, I painted a sign for them which is still displayed behind the bar: *BAR TABS CAUSE AMNESIA: SORRY NO CREDIT*.

I recognise two of the three girls at the bar, and give them a wave, but I don't see my favourite one around.

"Mama-san," I say, "is Pichaya not working today?"

Pichaya is a statuesque, and remarkably pale-skinned beauty from Chiang Mai, who has the most perfect set of white teeth I've ever come across. I used to call her 'Sìp Jèt' which incidentally has nothing to do with powerful oral suction, but is rather the Thai word for 'seventeen' – a throwback to when I first met her and Mama-san had given each girl a number (a practice I'm happy that she has since dispensed with). Pichaya has a young son back in her village who is looked after by her mother: she's never even hinted at wanting money for him, unlike many in her situation. Pichaya also doesn't do the fluttering eyelashes thing which personally I find a bit of a turn-off.

"Pichaya is not available, Mr. David, it is her time of the month. I am so sorry. But we have many other beautiful girls as you know."

"I *do* know. But I did want to see Pichaya, even if only for a drink. Is she back in Chiang Mai or is she around?"

Mama-san laughs obscenely and nudges me in the ribs. "Oh, I *see*, Mr. David. I know what you want Pichaya to drink! You want her drink you, yes?"

That wasn't really what I had in mind, but I can't be bothered to argue. Mama-san goes off to ring her.

About twenty minutes and a couple of beers and cigarettes later Pichaya arrives and gives me a friendly hug. Mama-san ushers the pair of us upstairs into one of the pink boudoirs with its many mirrors. She winks and leaves.

I explain to Pichaya in Thai (her English being not-so-great) that, contrary to Mama-san's assumption, I'd just like to lie in bed with her, look at her butterfly tattoo and cuddle awhile.

We undress and she looks in alarm at all the bruises and scratches on my body.

"I was in a scrap with a large cat," I explain.

"A cat that had breasts, I think," she laughs.

"You could be right."

She snuggles up to me in bed and we clink our beer bottles.

We lie there contentedly listening to the humming of the air conditioner.

I think about the slip of paper the chamber-maid gave to me and the name she had written on it: Thongchai Rattanakorn. Nittha's husband.

10

"The gods are just, and of our pleasant vices
Make instruments to plague us"
William Shakespeare, King Lear

On my taxi ride to Don Muang Airport I call Da to let her know her I'll drop by the office later after I've checked on Wayan. She tells me she's spoken to Wayan this morning and she's already home, preferring to breakfast there rather than at the hotel ("Nice though it is.").

"There's no need to rush in," she says. "There's nothing in the appointment book for today; or for tomorrow for that matter."

"How are you?" I ask. "No more twinges?"

"No," she replies. "I think my baby must be a boy. Only a man could come this late."

I repress the urge to say something smutty. "Yeah, right."

"Khun David," she says rather sternly, "What are you going to do about my replacement when the baby comes? You cannot put off this decision forever. I have told you I will come back to work as soon as I can, but you will need someone to cover for me while I'm off."

"We'll talk about that later."

"I might be in hospital later. Do you want me to talk to my cousin?"

"Like I say, we'll talk this afternoon. If the baby starts coming in the meantime, just cross your legs and take a painkiller."

Da sighs. "You are so irresponsible sometimes," she says.

"Procrastination," I reply, "Is a boss' prerogative."

"By the way," she responds ignoring my comment, "you never told me exactly why you are in Bangkok."

"Didn't I? That was thoughtless of me. See you later."

I hang up.

My taxi is negotiating its way through the overheated streets of the capital slowly. I half-wish I'd used the kamikaze driver who'd brought me from the airport since I feel an urgency to shake the dust and sin of the city from me quickly.

I always behave badly when I come here. There is just too much temptation around for my feeble willpower. It's like Krung Thep expects its visitors to indulge in dubious antics, and some of us are only too happy to oblige.

If I were a better man I would describe the sensation I'm feeling now as *shame*. But I'm not, so I don't. I experience more a sense of needing a prolonged shower, as if soapy water alone could wash away all my misdeeds.

I tell my driver to turn up the aircon.

When Kat arrives at the departure gate she is looking more demure than is her custom; more natural, less businesslike. She seems quieter, more reflective. If I didn't know her better I'd say she was feeling a bit *guilty*. But then I remind myself that Kat is a great actress and finds it easy to conceal herself behind whatever persona she chooses to wear. Today she is the Police Chief's Wife, while I have on the expression of the Bored Private Investigator.

However, in spite of my external diffidence inside I find myself seething. It is alarming how Kat's body has taken my mind hostage. I may not be able to experience shame, but the sharp bite of jealousy I feel clamping down in my innards is unmistakeable. My head is flooded with explicit imaginings of Kat's flesh in intimate congress with the other man. Just as last night, when I inevitably surrendered to Pichaya putting her lips to my skin, it was Kat's mouth I felt consuming me.

I am losing control. I sense a massive collision rushing towards me. If there is light at the end of this tunnel, it is almost certainly an oncoming train.

Kat lies to me that she spent an emotional evening with her friend and accordingly feels wrung out. I lie to her that I had dinner at my business partner's house and we stayed up drinking until late.

Our masks are securely in place, even if the worms are wriggling in the meat beneath.

"I think it would be a good idea if you spent time with your husband for the next few days," I suggest soberly.

She nods. "You are probably right," she says quietly.

"Probably better if you don't call me for a while too. Unless something serious happens."

Kat looks at me for a time. "Are you angry with me about something, David?" she asks.

I smile convincingly. "Of course not, Kat. Why would I be? I'm just concerned about how all this will turn out. And exactly what I'm going to tell your husband. Also I'm a bit hung over. Ignore me."

"Everything will be fine, tirak, don't worry."

She squeezes my hand discreetly.

The flight is busy and we are sitting well apart. When we land in Samui I stride straight through Arrivals without a backward glance.

*   *   *   *   *

The thought that something could have happened to Wayan, that she could have been put in peril because of my recklessness gnaws at me on my drive home. It is one thing for me to be careless of my own wellbeing; but putting someone I care about, someone as decent as her in danger is just downright wrong. I drive faster than I should because I need to satisfy myself she is safe.

Of course, she is, thankfully.

When I arrive she is doing some tidying in the kitchen, looking serene and unfazed. I want to put my arms around her and apologise for compromising her safety through my thoughtlessness. At the sight of her, the implications of what might have happened – suppressed for the last two days – fester up into my full consciousness. While I was in Bangkok, thinking about getting laid, she could have been attacked or worse. Just the idea turns my insides to ice and I feel sick. Da is right: I am irresponsible.

"Hello, Mr. David, would you like something to eat?"

The uncomplicated domesticity of this scene, compared with the lying, cheating and lewdness of the last forty-eight hours, almost brings tears of relief to my eyes. How far my life has strayed from normalcy.

"Are you OK?"

"I'm fine, really. There was no need for you to put me in a hotel."

"I was worried. I had to. I wanted you safe. I'm sorry. I shouldn't have left you on your own," I stammer, my face flushing with embarrassment.

Wayan touches my arm soothingly. "Mr. David, *I'm fine*. You can't worry about me every time you have to go away on business. Please, I'm OK."

There are so many things I'd like to say to her. But I don't want to alarm her or cause any awkwardness between us, so instead I nod, mutter some platitude and squeeze her shoulder in a non-intimate fashion.

I dump my bag, shower and calm down.

We lunch together in the garden, in the shade and fan-induced cool of the sala. I probably look at Wayan too much, like someone who has lost something precious, but then found it again. She doesn't seem to notice this, or if she does she doesn't say anything about it.

Wayan recounts that she is still having dreams about flying demons, or to be more accurate, one large flying demon in particular. She urges me to be careful since she fears the evil spirit is pursuing *me*. I don't tell her I have so many fiends chasing me already that one more won't make much of a difference.

After lunch I retire to my study to catch up on my emails and scan the local paper for anything about the burning murders. Yesterday's edition contains an editorial and interviews with some of the island's ex pats on whether they feel 'threatened'. I notice they haven't spoken to any tourists about *their* feelings on the matter: but then those poor buggers probably don't have a notion of what has been happening. Katchai must be under increasing pressure to get a result. Charoenkul may be unhappy at the thought of having a wayward wife, but he must be rubbing his hands in glee at the Investigator's discomfort.

Among my emails is one from Vogel. He will be back in Chaweng for Chinese New Year and wants to come and see me. I reply for him to ring my cell phone when he arrives since I am minded to close the office for a few days.

I smoke a cigarette and prioritise the rest of my day. At some stage I also need to prioritise the rest of my life, but I have to start somewhere, so it might as well be with today. Let me see.

Burning murders

Anonymous letters

Claire

Kat/Charoenkul/Rattanakorn

I have to do something about the Kat/Charoenkul/Rattanakorn thing, and I have to do it soon. This is no time for Hamlet-type self-reflection and dithering. The rest will have to wait.

Duller would I be than the fat weed that rots itself in ease on the Lethe wharf, if I do not stir in this, as one grounded in Elizabethan tragedy might say.

If I do not begin to take my own self-preservation more seriously, bad things are going to happen. And not just to me, but potentially also to those closest to me. Wayan, for example, might get sucked down into the sink-hole.

I further reflect that, given the 3D minefield into which I have blundered, it is debatable which will end first; my sanity or my life. (Mythologically speaking, of course, those whom the gods would destroy, they first make mad.) The only reason I'm not already bouncing off the walls of some rubber room must be that my mind has such a high tolerance of ambiguity: however there has to be a limit. We can all live with a degree of ambivalence, but I sense the imminent arrival of a time when I won't be able to cope, and the whole edifice of my life will reach its tipping point.

I don't want Wayan buried under the rubble.

But – to use another metaphor – before I can start draining the swamp, I have to wade deeper in. Up to my neck, in fact. I have to ring Rattanakorn. And then I have to meet him.

In doing so I will be putting myself between Scylla and Charybdis: I'm not sure whether the gangster is the cliff and the Police Chief is the whirlpool, or vice versa. It's comforting to know nonetheless that a classical education can provide solace when one is contemplating one's position between a rock and a hard place. *Or not.* Let's be honest, my situation is more Homer Simpson than Homer.

Hum, about my brains.

I look at the two cell phone numbers I'd lifted from Kat's phone. Which one to ring first? Eeny meeny miny moe. *Just do it.* I hit the buttons.

A female voice answers: Sumalee, presumably. I apologise and say I've called the wrong number.

I dial the second number.

A cautious male voice answers, "Yes?"

"Mr. Rattanakorn?"

"Who is this?"

"My name is David Braddock. I'm calling from Chaweng."

"How did you get this number?"

"That's not important right now. I'm a private investigator." I pause a moment to let this sink in, then say, "I think we should meet."

"I don't know you."

He sounds like he is about to hang up, so I say quickly, "I believe it is in your interests that we meet. You see, you left something behind at the Carlsson Sharifah."

"I don't know what you're talking about."

"I think you do."

There is a long silence at the other end of the phone. Then he says, "What do you want?"

"Just to talk. I can't say what I have to say over the phone. Do you have time to see me today or tomorrow?"

He considers this for a few seconds. I can sense him trying to work out what is going on. He's probably thinking *blackmail*.

"Not today or tomorrow, no. What did you say your name was?" He's buying time to do some research of his own *on me*.

"David Braddock. Are you already back on the island? Can we meet on Saturday?"

He ignores my first question. "You can come to my office at one o'clock on Saturday. As you're a private investigator, you presumably know where that is."

He cuts the line.

My hands are shaking as I light a cigarette. I may have just made an enemy of a jâo phâw. It's not a pleasant thought. I can feel the swamp water reaching my bottom lip. I hope Rattanakorn won't have me bumped off until he's heard what I have to say, but I can't be certain.

I set off for my office and put a Meatloaf CD in the jeep's player. 'I'd Do Anything for Love' comes on. It's not heavy metal enough to drive my jitters away, so I select 'Bat out of Hell', a song about someone dying in a road accident. Perfect. I turn the volume up loud.

*   *   *   *   *

An acne-faced yob in a baseball cap is sitting in reception playing with his cell phone when I arrive at the office. His legs are covered in mosquito bites and he is wearing a lime green tee-shirt with a cartoon drawing of a dead cat on a dinner plate. The logo beneath reads *I Eat Pussy*. I take an instant dislike to him even before he's opened his mouth. Something about him reminds me of Sinclair, and it's not the BO.

Da rolls her eyes and says, "Mr. Braddock, this is Mr. Mitchell. He's just arrived and wondered if he could see you for a few minutes. He says it's urgent." Her expression says *we have nothing else in the book, and I'll shortly have a baby to feed*.

Oh, what the hell. I could do with a short distraction.

I usher the foot-dragging throwback into the West Office and take some details. Trevor ("Trev to my friends") Mitchell wants me to keep a close eye on his 'squeeze' for him after he returns to his family estate in Millwall. The squeeze in question turns out to be my old friend Ting. She certainly doesn't waste any time. Trev is no lovelorn Harold Jayne, and therefore I'm inclined to take his money without giving him the gypsy's warning. He looks aghast when I tell him the cost of my retainer, but he coughs up the cash anyway. I'm beginning to think I should offer Ting a partnership since she brings so much business my way. It could be a mutually beneficial arrangement.

"Nice man," utters my now-whale-like assistant ironically once the bad smell has left the office. "English. Nice."

"Aren't you *ever* going to drop this kid?" I ask gruffly at this slur on my nation.

"I will as soon as we've organised my temporary replacement."

"Not that line again."

"At least let my cousin fill in until you can find someone more suitable."

"Just how *unsuitable* is your cousin? Can she speak English?"

"A little."

I groan.

"Anyway, Khun David," she says trying to get comfortable in her seat, "I have two pieces of good news for you."

"Well, I could do with some of that."

"First, I've organised us some free publicity. I'm very confident it will bring us some new business."

"How exactly have you done that?" I ask suspiciously.

"I called the *Island Daily* and told them about how the David Braddock Agency was paying for old man Yai's eye operation as a way of giving back to the community. They'll be running the story next week."

I groan again.

"I knew there was no point asking them to send a photographer, because you'd refuse to co-operate, so I gave them one of your old photographs instead."

"How old?"

She hesitates. "Quite old," she says.

"Great."

"Think of the business."

"Think of the begging letters."

"You know I'm right."

I sigh. "You're always right. What's the second bit of good news? I hope it's better than the first."

Da reaches under the desk and produces a carved wooden boat. "This. Bee called in the office and dropped it off for you, as a way of saying thank you."

I examine the boat. It's quite a work of art, and beautifully painted, with large eyes on the bow to ward off evil spirits.

"A gift from Charon," I say.

"Sharon?" Da asks, puzzled. "I thought her name was Bee."

"Not *Sh*aron. *Ch*aron. He's the boatman who ferries the dead across the River Styx to the Underworld, at least according to the Ancient Greeks."

"Oh really?" says Da, uninterested.

I go on regardless. "As you probably know, American films usually depict him as a skeleton or death-like figure, but actually he's an old man in a loincloth. I can't stand that sort of American inaccuracy. It bugs me. It's like when they show coins put on the eyes of the dead man to pay for his passage, when in fact the Greeks would usually put the coin in the corpse's mouth."

"I have no idea what you're talking about."

"I'm educating you. Did you ever see the film *Gladiator*?"

"Russell Crowe, yes. Quite a man. Big muscles."

"Never mind that. You know when the Emperor gives the 'thumb down' for the defeated gladiator to be killed?"

"Yes," she says cautiously.

"It's rubbish. The 'thumb down' actually was a sign for the gladiator to be spared, not killed. It's an urban myth, and it's not right. Ridley Scott, the director, knew what he was showing was inaccurate, but stuck with it anyway, thinking he might confuse his audience. At least nobody can ever accuse Hollywood film-makers of being *educators*."

"Have you finished educating me?"

I'm rambling. Let's get back on track. Da doesn't give a stuff about this crap.

"For now."

Da shuffles around in her seat again. "Bee's quite plain, isn't she? Poor thing. She needs feeding. Or the love of a good man, like my Tong. I liked her, though."

I ignore all this. "I guess I'd better call her or Yai. See how the consultation went. It was this morning, right? Or is it this afternoon?"

"This morning."

I take the boat into the East Office and find a suitable display position for it.

I'm not sure what Yai's attitude to me is following my rather aggressive approach at our last meeting. Saving face is almost as important to the Thais as it is to the Chinese, and I've probably bruised his dignity. I'd like to think I'm usually more culturally sensitive, but on this occasion ...

I decide to call Bee to test the waters.

She is at home, and sounds excited. The consultation went well and Yai is being scheduled in for the op next week. She is almost as happy about the fact that Yai is there with her, and he and her mother are talking finally. I hear some gabbling in the background and Bee conveys to me that her mother would like me to join them for a meal at their house during the Chinese New Year celebrations. I thank them for the invitation and for the boat, and say I will sort out the hospital payment direct so everything should go smoothly. I also suggest tentatively that, if Yai is at home tomorrow, I will drop by and see him some time in the afternoon.

"Grandfather says that will be fine," Bee replies after some chatter. "He would like to see you."

Since there's nothing in the appointment book, I tell Da I've decided to close the office until after Chinese New Year, with immediate effect.

"That gives you almost a week to have the baby," I say. "Even you should be able to manage that. And before you ask, yes, I will pay you for the days."

"And I can call my cousin about filling in temporarily?"

"If you must. And ring me, or have Tong ring me, when the wee one finally puts in an appearance." I hand her a red envelope with some cash inside. "Here, this is for the little bugger."

Da rises with some difficulty and squeezes my arm.

"Thank you, boss," she says smiling. "If it's a boy perhaps we'll call him David."

"Don't you bloody dare. Now go home."

"You still haven't told me what you were *really* doing in Bangkok."

My cell phone rings. "Some other time," I say heading back into the office. "Sorry, I have to take this. Go home."

I close the door behind me.

"Yes, Chief Charoenkul," I say. "What can I do for you?"

Twenty minutes later I'm parking the jeep on the patch of sun hardened waste ground next to Bophut Police Station.

In spite of Charoenkul's view of a few days ago that he didn't want us to meet here he's changed his fickle mind. Or something else has changed. I walk towards the public entrance with a deepening sense of dread. He sounded spiky on the phone and was in no mood to tell me *why* I'd been summoned, so I'm expecting the worst. Actually, I'm not even sure what the worst *is* any more.

Self-preservation. Think self-preservation, Braddock. Be confident and assertive. Lie boldly. Get your story straight and don't over-elaborate. Otherwise Papa Doc will chew you up and spit you out.

The public waiting area is every bit as depressing as I remember it. The strip-light still hasn't been repaired, and the smell of the unwashed hangs heavy in the stale air. The foxy female police officer is manning the desk again. I state my name and hand her one of my business cards.

"If you ever need any therapy, or if you need someone to keep an eye on a wandering husband, give me a call," I say, more as a reflex than with any serious seductive intent.

"I'm not married," she says meaningfully before asking some other officer to take me up to the boss. I am expected.

The lift is out of commission so we take the stairs, which makes me feel more depressed. I do however have sufficient presence of mind to plant an assured expression on my face and to straighten my back before I plunge into the Chief's lair, moving past his skeletal tooth-picking secretary on the way.

Deng Charoenkul is standing with his hands behind his back looking out of the window. After a moment he turns and gives an impatient flick of the head to indicate my police escort should leave. His eyes have an angry look and his voice is clipped when he says to me, "Sit down, Braddock."

I sit. He remains standing, peering at me through those piggy little eyes.

To break the silence I remark, "I thought you didn't want us to meet here again, Chief Charoenkul."

He gives a dismissive wave as if the matter is not worth discussing before lowering himself gingerly onto his chair; on which I notice there is a thick padded cushion. A brief spasm of discomfort flicks across his face as he completes the manoeuvre.

"Are you in pain?" I ask somewhat unnecessarily.

"You could say that," he replies tight-lipped.

"Haemorrhoids?" I proffer.

He glowers at me. "If you must know, yes," he hisses.

"That's a bummer."

"Are you trying to be amusing?" he asks nastily.

"No, Chief, sorry. Unfortunate phrase. Very unpleasant condition, not a joking matter. My apologies."

He adjusts his position and winces slightly.

"Flares up now and again. And I've got an important bloody golf game on Sunday. It's very inconvenient."

"You're playing golf on the day of the election?"

"What did you expect me to be doing? Roaming the streets with my officers harassing voters?"

"Of course not, I –"

250

"Thailand is a democratic country, Braddock. The Police Chief doesn't need to be on duty on election day, it's a routine matter."

I say nothing.

He eases himself back in his chair and appears to relax slightly although I know he's fully alert. Hard not to be when you're suffering from piles.

"So give me a full report on the last two days."

I run through my prepared speech while he sits, motionless and watchful, never taking his eyes from my face.

"So you're certain nothing happened?" he asks.

"Look," I reply, "your wife went with her sick friend to the hospital. She stayed at her friend's house. They went shopping. End of story."

He looks unconvinced.

"Of course," I suggest, "it may be that she banged some junior doctor in a broom cupboard while her friend was having her consultation, but on the whole I'd consider it unlikely."

"That's enough of that," he snaps. "This is *my wife* you're talking about."

"And someone who, in my humble opinion, is under suspicion unfairly," I state without the hint of a blush. "Based on what I've observed, Mrs. Charoenkul is *not* fooling around." If I pull this off I really should be in line for an Oscar.

Charoenkul emits a non-committal grunt.

"Do you want me to go on following her?"

"No."

"Do you want me to give you a written report?"

"No."

"Do you want copies of the photographs I took? They're pretty boring, but you're entitled."

"No."

"Then can I ask you one more question?"

"What?" he barks at me impatiently.

"Why did you consider it necessary to employ a second private investigator to watch your wife? And a second-rate one at that? Do you doubt my competence or my integrity?" I hope I sound more annoyed than nervous.

"Listen, Braddock," he says heavily, "When a man gets the idea that his wife might be unfaithful rationality flies away. You make your living out of people's jealousy. You of all men should know that. I wanted some insurance, that's all, a second opinion."

I continue to look at Papa Doc like someone whose professional pride has been hurt.

"Anyway," he intones gruffly, "I called him off as you asked. I don't know why you're so offended."

"So can I give you my bill now?"

He reaches into the top drawer of his desk, takes out a wad of thousand-Baht notes and tosses it at me.

"I don't need a bill. That should take care of it."

I put the bundle into my pocket without counting the notes. I'd better not push my luck. After all, it's not every day someone pays you for your time while you're having sex with his wife.

"On the other little matter," I say, "you know, the one involving dead farangs? Any progress in tracking down the foreign backers for that Lamai building project?"

The Chief shakes his head. "We're still working on that. However, I should be able to get you something on the Carroll forensics in the next couple of days."

I wonder whether Kat will be doing the translation again, but I don't ask.

"I've noticed the murders seem to be getting a lot of press coverage. Investigator Katchai is having a hard time of it I imagine. You must be pleased."

Charoenkul curls his lip. "Hardly," he sneers. "Katchai's bumbling is

252

reflecting badly on the Royal Thai Police. While I don't want him coming out of this a hero, I'd rather he failed more discreetly. He's making us all look like clowns."

I say nothing.

"Oh, by the way," he says, changing the subject, "I have a little bonus for you."

"What's that?"

"The car that was parked outside your house the other night: one of my officers took down the registration number."

He hands me a slip of paper with the number and make of car on it.

"We checked it out. It's registered to a company based here on the island called Smiley Cars. I thought you might like to know."

"Thanks." His boys have just gone up in my estimation.

"Let me know if you want me to do anything further. Though this is really a private matter."

"It's OK. I'll take it from here."

Papa Doc stands up to indicate the conversation is over and presumably to give his bottom a rest.

As I reach the door he speaks to my back.

"Of course you do realise, Braddock, that if I ever found out that my wife *was* having an affair, I'd kill the fucking man involved."

I look back at him over my shoulder.

"That's really not my concern," I say.

*　　*　　*　　*　　*

The brutal sun has long since called it a day as I park the jeep in Chaweng's main street, but the effect of its sizzling presence lingers. There is a distinct electrical crackle in the air, although some of this may stem from the upcoming election or the approach of the Chinese New Year as the

Monkey readies himself to give way to the Rooster.

All day the markets have been busy as people stock up on food and other offerings. Decorations are appearing on balconies, porches and street furniture, and the island is taking on a red and gold hue. On one occasion today I glimpsed dragon dancers in rehearsal, and witnessed the scolding of some waifs who had been letting off fireworks prematurely.

Vehicles equipped with loudspeaker systems have been jamming the narrow roads, the election wagons competing with those advertising Muay Thai. Commercial interests have however been fighting back against the democratic tide, and some election posters appear to have been covered with flyers for drinking competitions and something that looks like a wet t-shirt contest judging from the accompanying picture. Either that or some blonde girl with large breasts is standing for political office. Well, I'd vote for her anyway.

My adolescent employee (and sometime drug-dealer) having finished his homework, he meets me at a local bar. Puffing on a Marlboro, I exchange the pre-agreed amount of Baht for the safe return of my second-best camera, which he assures me has plenty of pictures of Jingjai in it. He further informs me that the *Ocean Pearl* is having a few evenings of special events, since the bar is closing this weekend for 'renovation'. I thank him for his information while politely declining his request for me to buy him a beer, explaining that it is against my principles to corrupt the young of the island.

Strolling casually past the Pearl I see my young informer is correct. There is a hastily-painted sign announcing that Saturday will be the last night before the remodelling of the establishment starts. Jingjai is on duty inside but doesn't see me: the place is already busy with customers taking advantage of the 'special' prices. Presumably the girl with the diamond tooth will shortly be out of a job. I don't know whether that will please Vogel or not.

Someone else I recognise is also on duty tonight. The old tramp, showing superhuman powers of resilience, is still on the island despite the intimidation I've already witnessed from the local representatives of law enforcement. He seems to me like a talisman, poking a begrimed finger in the eye of uncaring authority; a symbol of the indomitability of the stinky human spirit. As usual I hand him some Baht, and as usual he treats me to his decayed smile.

"Hey, Braddock, I see you have new friend," says a large man with gold in *his* smile.

"Hello, Vlad," I reply leaving the beggar to his night among the cardboard boxes.

"We go for a drink."

It wasn't a question. I accompany the bald giant to one of the less respectable bars in town.

Vlad is relishing the opportunity of a rematch with the Polish fighter, and his moroseness from our last meeting has entirely evaporated. The scratches on his face are, however, still highly visible.

He tells me in graphic detail exactly what he is going to do to his opponent, as if he is addressing a connoisseur of the kick-boxing sport rather than a PI that just wants a few beers to forget his troubles. But I don't care. I'm glad of any company, even that of a psychotic Russian.

"Hey, Braddock, maybe I come to see you soon for some business, yes?"

"What kind of business *exactly* are you engaged in here, Vlad? You never did tell me."

"Ah, we Russians are taking over the world, my friend."

"And you're starting with *Thailand*?" I ask sarcastically.

"You might say I am in the import-export business," he says. "But *special* products. Very special, if you understand me."

"I don't, but never mind. Come and see me whenever I can help." *Like bailing you out of jail, probably.* He nods and asks for one of my business cards, although I'm sure I've already given him one.

"We need a man who can speak good Thai, and who understands how local people think."

"Then it sounds like I'm your man," I reply and order more beer. I neither know nor at this point care who 'we' are.

Walking back up the main street later someone steps out in front of me and asks me if I want a taxi. I recognise Sinclair's employee, Kwanchai Ramsuwan, and he apparently *doesn't* recognise me. He is also clearly moonlighting with one of the Smiley Cars hire vehicles – that is not an official taxi. I give him a polite 'no' and move on, before unobtrusively noting the details of the car he is standing beside.

Some memory of a taxi tickles in the back of my head. Wasn't there a Sherlock Holmes story where the murderer turned out to be a cab driver? *A Study in Scarlet*, was it?

My main conundrum about the burning murders is how the murderer transported his victims to the killing site. How he persuaded them to go there. How he avoided their suspicions being raised. Why the dog didn't bark.

Getting into a taxi, no-one would feel threatened by that, would they?

Even if the driver was about to beat your head in.

*   *   *   *   *

When I arrive home Wayan has already turned in but Claire is sitting waiting for me in the study reading Henry James' *Turn of the Screw*.

"Ah, so her ladyship is back," I say.

"Looks like we both are. I take it no-one is outside watching the house tonight?" she asks.

I deposit the camera bag on the desk and slump down on the chair.

"No."

"Any idea who it was? Should we be worried?"

"As to the first question," I reply reaching into one of the desk drawers to take out Sinclair's box file, "I may be able to tell you in a couple of minutes. As to the second –" I hesitate a moment, "– I don't think so."

"You don't *think* so. That's reassuring."

I stop unpacking the box file and look at her.

"I'm not in the mood for banter tonight, Claire," I state bluntly. "Would you care to tell me how long you'll be staying with us this time? Just so that I know."

"You usually enjoy a bit of banter," she responds evasively.

I go back to the file and find the sheet showing the details of the Smiley Cars fleet.

"What's wrong?" Claire persists. "Did things go badly in Bangkok?"

"Not at all," I respond casually. "In fact it was all pretty good. I had a big raunchy sex session with Kat Charoenkul. Biting, scratching, the lot."

"Well, that was entirely predictable, David. Anything else?"

"And a rather nice blow job from a working girl in Patpong." I can feel my irritation rising at her coolness.

"Didn't you put her on her back too?"

"No. I couldn't. She was having her period."

"Shame. Although I'm surprised you'd let a little thing like that stop you."

I crack. "Don't you give a fuck about anything anymore, Claire?" I say, suddenly furious.

"Times have changed, David. And *yes*, I've changed. Does my being here give you anything? No, it doesn't. Does your being here give me anything? No, it doesn't. Whoever you choose to screw is no longer of any concern to me. How can it be? It's not like you and I are ever going to have sex again, is it?"

"Just shut up, Claire."

"Well, is it?"

I stare at her then look down at my hands. They are shaking. I am too angry to speak. I don't trust myself to say anything more.

Claire stands up and walks slowly to the door.

"I guess that just about wraps it up. For tonight, at least. Yes?" She sounds sad.

I can't look at her. I nod. When I lift my head she has gone.

I get up and fling open the door to the terrace. I need fresh air but the night tastes bitter and overcooked. I take some deep breaths nonetheless and light a cigarette to calm the fluttering in my ribcage.

Once I am semi-calm I go back into the study and sit down at my desk. I am thinking about Kwanchai Ramsuwan moonlighting in rental cars.

I take out the paper that Charoenkul had given me this afternoon and compare the car registration number on it with the list of Smiley Cars rental vehicles. I check it twice, but it is not on the list. And that can only mean one thing.

The car parked outside my house was Kenneth Sinclair's private vehicle.

11

"I've got a red hot heart
And your heart's as blue as the blood in your veins
I say there's fire down below
You say it's only smoke and ashes baby"
Tracy Chapman, Smoke and Ashes

While I'm eating breakfast Wayan hands me a white envelope she says she found under the door early this morning. It's one of *those* envelopes. I can visualise the twice-folded A4 sheet inside it. This does not infuse me with feelings of unmitigated delight.

Since I'm not about to read the contents in front of Wayan, I leave the envelope on the table propped up against the croissant basket. It looks at me disdainfully while I finish my coffee, but I ignore it as best I can.

I can handle the suspense for about five minutes before I have to take my second cup of coffee and the odious missive to the study. I close the door behind me and tear the envelope open without bothering to dust it. No point unless I'm going to ink Wayan's fingers to compare prints, which I'm not.

The letter says

IT HAS BEEN FUN WITH MR. AND MRS. C AND IT MIGHT BE AGAIN
BUT THE WIFE I'M MORE INTERESTED IN IS YOUR WIFE

This writer is some piece of work, that's for damn sure. He's been leading me and the Charoenkuls up the garden path and back down again. Whatever is the reason behind this campaign of psychological warfare, this guy – or girl – has identified systematically where my weak spots are, and how to exploit them.

It's either someone who knows me very well or is an outrageously lucky guesser. I'd be foolish to assume the latter.

Who are my enemies? Who is so pissed with me that they would resort to premeditated acts of malice? Who do I know with that sort of warped mind? Who can possibly know this sort of stuff about me?

Wait a minute. What do they actually *know*? How much am I reading into this?

I take out the four letters and look at them all.

The first one, *HOW DO YOU SLEEP AT NIGHT?*, is a fairly common English phrase, as is the second, *WIVES CAN BE A PROBLEM*. The letter to Charoenkul which the Chief took away, (*YOUR WIFE IS UNFAITHFUL*), the one to Kat, (*THE INDO-CHINA INTERNATIONAL, BANGKOK, IS DAVID BRADDOCK'S FAVOURITE HOTEL*) and today's missive, all on reflection look like they could have been cut and pasted out of some language phrase book, merely substituting the odd word.

Is the writer even an English speaker? Maybe not.

Does the writer really know about my affair with Kat? Almost certainly.

What does he/she know about *my* wife? Or is he/she just shooting in the dark? No idea.

So to summarise: one 'maybe not', one 'almost certainly' and one 'no idea'. I suppose that's progress. But I'm still just reactive, waiting for the next move.

Based on the people who know or might have reason to suspect my affair with Kat, that makes the letter-writer most likely either Charoenkul or Kat herself. Charoenkul is just sadistic enough to have cooked up something like this as a mental torture prelude to a more physical torture. And Kat's general behaviour recently has been reckless in the extreme: I can't even imagine what has prompted it.

I suppose the only other person who might know is ...

No, that's just plain ridiculous. If the anonymous writer is *her*, then I might as well just top myself straightaway because there really is no hope left for humanity.

Now I really am in a bad mood. I need to vent my spleen on someone, and I know just the person.

I call Sinclair and tell him I'll meet him at his house in an hour.

When I pull up on the Northern Neanderthal's drive I take a moment to check the registration plate on the black SUV. As I surmised, it matches the numbers on Charoenkul's paper.

The doddery maid shows me into the garden where the man himself is taking a late breakfast in his sala. His head is wrapped in a bandana, in the style of Willie Nelson. He appears done in but perks up when he sees me approaching.

"Ah, David, good morning. Would you like a coffee or something?"

"No thanks."

The maid shuffles off and I light a Marlboro. Sinclair pushes his half-eaten plate of rice to one side and looks at me expectantly.

"Your voice sounded urgent on the phone," he says. "What's up?"

I take a long draw on my cigarette and feel a momentary impulse to beat his face in.

"You tell me."

His eyebrows and forehead wrinkle in a pantomime of puzzlement but there is wariness in his eyes.

"I don't understand."

"Well, to kick off," I say calmly, "let's talk about why you were parked outside my house the night before last."

At first I think Sinclair is going to deny it and claim some egregious mistake; but his resolve withers and a look of profound weariness takes possession of his face. He stares at me while the fan whirrs above us.

"Particularly," I go on, "as you *knew* I was in Bangkok at the time."

He clears his throat and utters a quiet, "Yes."

"Unless you'd like to come clean first on this charade of an assignment you're employing me on."

I wait. The Geordie heaves a big sigh, rises unsteadily to his feet and appears to come to a decision. He slumps heavily against one of the sala's support posts and passes a tired hand across his face. Then he raises his head and surveys the garden as if he hopes to find the appropriate words written on the greenery.

"If I was a smoker," he begins, "I suppose now would be the time for a cigarette."

I offer him my packet. "Be my guest," I say. "Never too late to start."

He gives a small shake of the head before glancing quickly at me than away again.

"How much do you know about me? About my history, I mean?" he asks shyly.

I offer a non-committal shrug.

He scratches his neck nervously, then launches off.

"I can tell you that when I first came to this island I was a very angry man. A very angry man," he reflects. "You see, I'd been badly burned by my first wife who ran off with another man. Then she made it hard for me to see the kids. Looking back, it made me very bitter and distrustful of people." He pauses before continuing. "So I came to Samui to start over. But what I found here initially just made me more cynical: girls who are sweet to your face but are really only interested in your wallet.

"I've never really been that good with women. I get tongue-tied, don't know what to say. My first wife, Joy, was my childhood sweetheart. She was a bit of a bunny-boiler but I married her anyway. When I came here ... well, I don't need to tell *you*. You know how the girls are. Hookers were not what I wanted." He stops again.

"I'm listening," I prompt.

"Anyway, then a miracle happened. Or at least it seemed like a miracle to me. I met Nok. She was different. She was kind and sincere and she really cared about me. And I fell for her. I mean I really did. It wasn't like with Joy. This was ... *love*. Not a word I've used very often," he adds.

"Within a year we were married, and then our boy came along. I'd never been happier. Life was good. I was alive again. Everything that had gone before, all the disappointments didn't matter."

"And then –" Sinclair rips the words from some dark place within himself. "It all ended."

"How?" I ask, although what I've heard so far chimes with Charlie's story. I know what's coming next, but I need to hear him say it.

"Nok died. She was killed in a hit-and-run accident. The bastard didn't even stop. He was never caught. I put adverts in the papers to try and find the driver, offered rewards, everything. All that produced was a load of slime balls coming out of the woodwork to squeeze Baht out of me. It made me crazy. And nothing, nothing came of any of it.

"Things settled down for me after a while. I needed to think about my boy. I'd lost the love of my life but he'd lost his mother. I buckled down, worked, tried not to think about things."

"But then a few months ago it all started again, right?" I say.

Sinclair looks at me sharply. "I don't know how you know, but yes. Some Thai guy got in touch with me, said he knew about the accident, that he could help. All the craziness started again in my head. I knew it was all nonsense, that it had always been nonsense before. But I kept thinking *what if.*

And then –"

He breaks off and shakes his head.

"What?"

"Then I met someone who put things into perspective. I decided to stop torturing myself. I told myself that whatever happened Nok wasn't coming back. What good could it do now dragging over old dead coals? I started to think maybe I could put my wife's death behind me. I would never find another Nok; I knew that. That would be impossible."

"You met someone?"

"Yes. Someone kind and open. Someone who took care of my little boy when I was late collecting him from school one day; who took an interest in him. Someone *normal*."

"You're talking about Wayan."

He hesitates before answering. Then he nods.

"Go on," I say.

"I started thinking that maybe my boy could have a mother again. Perhaps I could have a companion. All sorts of notions."

"Sounds like your next word is going to be *but*."

"I didn't know what the arrangement was between you and Wayan. I didn't know whether, well –"

"Whether I was fucking her?" I say brutally, and watch him wince.

"I came up with this scheme that maybe I could get to know her better and make sure I didn't make a fool of myself if you were –" He makes a gesture of hopelessness.

"If I were conveniently out of the way some evenings? Like if I was sitting on a porch in Bang Rak watching your damn car compound?"

"I also thought that maybe if I talked to you, got to know you better then I might be able to sense whether you and Wayan were romantically involved."

"What a quaint way of putting it," I fume. "So you must have been delighted when I told you I was going to Bangkok. It meant you could stalk Wayan without any hindrance. Skulking around outside my house at night, scaring the poor woman half to death."

"Hey, wait a minute," he interjects. "I'm not stalking her. I'd never do that. Never. I've far too much respect for her. Listen, the fact is I was outside your house trying to get up the courage to ring the bell and talk to her."

I sneer at this.

"It's true. Look, you've no reason to believe me, I know. I know I've behaved badly. I've gone about this all wrong. I've tried to be clever and just ended up looking like an idiot. I'm sorry. I'm really sorry."

"And you rope your employee in on the scheme too to act as a decoy. He must think I'm a real mug."

"What do you mean?" he asks, looking puzzled.

"Oh, come on," I say. "Are you telling me you didn't send Kwanchai to follow me in Chaweng yesterday evening to make sure I saw him offering his services as a taxi driver?"

Sinclair looks gobsmacked. "I swear I don't know anything about that. I'd never take him into my confidence on anything private like this. If Kwanchai is touting for taxi business then that means the little shit really is taking my cars out and moonlighting. I had no idea."

"Well there's dramatic irony for you. Life imitates art; or in this case, *artifice*. Anyway, never mind about Kwanchai," I continue not wishing to get sidetracked, "if you wanted to know about Wayan's relationship with me why not just ask her? Why go through all this elaborate pretence?"

He puts up his hands in frustration. "And what exactly would I say? It's not exactly something that you can easily drop into a casual conversation outside the school gates."

He has a point there.

"Besides," he sighs. "I told you. I have no small talk with women. I feel awkward around them. I never know what to say."

"So it's more natural for you to hang around in the dark watching them through binoculars."

"That's not fair," he objects. Then he sighs deeply. "But I know what you're saying and I know how it looks. You're right. I surrender. I should never have tried to deceive a private detective. I'm a fool."

"And what is more you've tried to make me look like a fool too."

"That was never my intention."

I take my time lighting a second cigarette and look at him as if I'm weighing things in my mind.

When he realises I'm not about to speak he sits down and says, "So what happens now?"

I flick my ash and lean forward. "Two things," I reply. "First, I'm going to send you a whopping bill for wasting my time; and I'll be including the cost of the hotel I had to book Wayan into after your night-prowling gave her the jitters."

"That's fair. And the second thing?"

"You're going to go and see Wayan, tell her everything and apologise."

His face drops. "She'll think I'm some kind of creepy weirdo."

"No, she'll understand you're more of a pathetic saddo than a creepy weirdo. Actually," I add more kindly, "she is a very understanding lady, particularly where people are honest with her. You might come out of this none-too-badly. Better than you deserve in fact. And for the record, Wayan is my housekeeper and a valued friend, but *nothing else*."

Sinclair takes a deep breath and capitulates. "I'll go and talk to her. I don't know what I'll say, but you're right. I owe her an explanation."

"Then we're finished here." I rise from the chair.

"Just before you go. Did you *really* see Kwanchai touting for taxi business with one of my cars?"

"I did," I say. "But don't even *think* about asking me to tail him."

*　　*　　*　　*　　*

Kat has SMSed me while I've been with Sinclair: *Can I come and see you on Sunday morning while DC is playing golf?*

I wonder whether this was prompted by my call to Rattanakorn yesterday, but I'm not going to think about this now. I have other stuff bouncing around in my head that I have to resolve first. I send a quick reply: *OK 11.00am my office*

The Sinclair line of inquiry has turned out to be a dead end. He's no murderer, just another lovelorn farang; and a rather sad one. I need to check up on the Nikom Promsai angle otherwise as far as the burning murders are concerned I'm out of leads.

I call Prasert.

"Have you heard anything from your brother?" I ask.

"Nothing. Nothing at all. I can tell you I'm worried."

"He'll turn up, Prasert, I'm sure."

"I hope you're right."

"Where are you now? I'd like to talk to you."

"I'm in Lamai. I've just finished a meeting with a client. I'm just about to have something to eat."

"Can you meet me at the abandoned building project site today? You know, the one you and your brother were involved in?"

"I can," he says sounding mystified. "But why there?"

"I'll explain later."

"OK. I can meet you at the coffee shop there. Say around two o'clock?"

"*The coffee shop?*" I ask. "There's nothing at the site but rubble and coconut trees."

"I don't know which site you're talking about, but at *our* old site they've built some shops, and there's a very nice coffee shop."

"Never mind, Prasert. Listen, forget I suggested a meeting. Let me know if your brother calls."

I ring off.

Bollocks.

In less than one hour all my carefully-constructed hypotheses have collapsed.

Coincidences and fanciful thinking. That's all it's been. The building project, the mysterious foreign investors, the Rhino beetles, Sinclair's dead wife, the parked car outside my house, the lot. I've been imagining associations where none exist. Curse that Old Monk and his interconnectivities. My brain is so gummed up with my own problems that I'm not thinking straight. Indeed I'm barely thinking at all.

Bollocks.

Bollocks.

Bollocks.

So far as the burning murders are concerned I'm back to square one. I've got nothing at all. Nichts. Niente. Rien. Zip. Sweet FA. Nada.

*   *   *   *   *

The attentional practices of Theravada Buddhism stress that in our approach to reality we do not observe closely enough. The Zen schools conversely might argue that our problem lies in the fact that we have not engaged ourselves unequivocally: that the observer and the observed remain separate.

Whatever.

If attaining wisdom, or *prajna*, means realising no-mind, then today I must be very wise indeed, because my head is so scrambled I'm barely capable of thought.

The Old Monk tells me he prefers me this way.

We are back at the clearing on the hillside, sitting cross-legged in the shade of the trees. Despite the slight breeze rising from the sea, my body is running with sweat and I feel slightly giddy. Whether this is due to the fact that I have had no lunch or to the intensity of the guided meditation that the Old Monk has just put me through is hard to say. I have no sensation in my limbs and real misgivings as to whether I will ever be able to move them again. A vertiginous lightness swirls around in my skull.

My orange-robed companion studies me and makes the observation, "You seem less opinionated today, less cocky. That is progress."

I laugh mirthlessly.

"Progress? You must be joking."

"I would doubt that. I rarely joke."

He hands me a bottle of water and to my relief I discover my hands are still capable of functioning, even though unscrewing the top is unusually tricky. The water is warm and my tongue feels like some fat slug twisting around slowly in my mouth.

"Are you still involved in the murder investigation?" he asks.

"Yes, but I might as well not be. I'm out of ideas. I'm afraid your suggestions on interconnectivity haven't produced a useable lead. I've just been blundering down one blind alley after another, over-indulging my rather lurid imagination in the process."

"Why is solving this problem so important to you? Surely this is a matter for the police?"

"It's a long story, and a rather inglorious one on my side. But perhaps you are right. Perhaps I should just let it go. I'm only supposed to be helping with profiling, after all."

"You should be concentrating on Your Problem."

"Ah yes, My Problem. And what exactly *is* that?"

The Old Monk mimes that he wants a cigarette. We both light up.

"Your Problem," he says exhaling a deep lungful of Marlboro, "Is that you spend too much of your time on things that are unimportant."

Oh yeah. Like, for instance, my wife, vindictive anonymous letters, Kat Charoenkul's body, murdered farangs, and making a living. All of them unimportant.

"A monk's life is simple," I retort. "You don't have the complications and responsibilities we non-holy folk have. You can devote your whole life to becoming a Buddha."

"You don't know what you are talking about. *You* think a raven is like a writing-desk," he states with a sly grin.

"That's just a riddle," I say gruffly, "a sort of joke."

"You treat too many things like a joke. You are not serious enough in your practice. You will never achieve enlightenment the way you are going."

"Me achieve enlightenment?" I laugh. "I don't think so, not with my track record. I have more skeletons in my closet than I have coat-hangers."

"It is irrelevant what you have done. It is what you *are doing* that matters."

"Won't my past misdeeds have created bad karma that will hold me back?"

The Old Monk snorts. "Karma means 'action'. Like many, you misunderstand its nature. Past misdeeds can be corrected before your karma ripens: it is not some pre-determined fate. It is what you do *now* that counts."

"Forgive me, Old Monk, but my sins are multitudinous. You wouldn't understand."

"What makes you think I wouldn't understand?" he says with an edge to his voice. "Do you suppose that I have always been a monk and am therefore ignorant of the ways of the world?"

"I didn't mean to –"

"I will tell you how I spent my time as a young man, shall I? I was a person for whom violence was always the answer. The power of the gun: that was the shrine at which I used to worship. For years I was an enthusiastic member of the Thai security services. That way of living culminated in my taking part in the massacre at Bangkok University in the 1970s. Afterwards I was so sickened with myself that I became a monk so that I could purge away all that I was responsible for. What do you think of that? Do you imagine you have done worse things than I have?"

I am struck momentarily dumb. The 1976 massacre was the beginning of the chain of events that led to the suicide of Bee's father in the coconut grove. The same grove where the two Westerners died; all of which in turn brought me into the investigation of the burning murders. *Interconnection* ...

"And even if you had," he continues quietly, "that would not matter *now*. Have you heard the story of Milarepa?"

I shake my head.

"He was a black sorcerer and murderer, whose life was changed through the teachings of the Buddha. He became a great practitioner, a Buddhist saint. All things are possible."

The Old Monk stubs out his cigarette and looks at me meaningfully.

"Have you ever wondered why local people come to see you, a farang, at your offices? Does it not strike you as strange that Thai men and women are prepared to confide their deepest fears and hopes to someone who is not from our culture?"

"I have thought about it."

"And?"

"I have no answer."

He begins tracing strange shapes again in the dust as he talks.

"It is because they sense something within you, something that you cannot see, and that they themselves do not understand. But they are aware of *something*. I tell you it is a potential within you. Unrealised, but present nonetheless. You cannot feel it yet, but *I* can. When I call you the White Tathagata, you imagine I am joking, but as I have said I rarely joke."

"You're saying I have the makings of a Buddha?" I smile, but a stern glance from the Old Monk stops me.

"Everyone has the Buddha Nature," he says carefully, "but with some people – not many – the latent capability of attaining enlightenment is closer to the surface. Why do you think I spend time with you? Why do you think I persevere through your self-pitying episodes?"

271

"I don't know," I reply simply.

He traces more shapes in the dust. They are incomprehensible to me. Almost as incomprehensible as this conversation.

"And yet," he continues after a moment, "there is something that holds you back, something strong. I do not mean your obvious lack of self-control or your cynical attitude; these can be corrected in time. Buddhism first requires great doubt, if there is to be great realisation."

He studies me carefully, and chooses his words.

"You have compassion but by itself it is not enough. It is almost as if you carry around inside you some dead thing. Some heavy black cinder in your heart that burdens you; a ponderous anchor that tethers you to the past. Until you can burn it away, you can never truly live in the present, in the *now*. Until you can live in the now, you cannot see things as they really are. Meantime you are a man who is wilfully blind. You have eyes and yet you will not use them."

If he is correct, if I have compassion, it is a circumscribed and conditional compassion. I help Yai, the wilfully blind, to see while I myself remain stubbornly sightless.

I ponder on Yai's self-imposed darkness. I realise that what angers me about him is the qualities we share.

He presents to me a mirror. And I do not like the image that is reflected back.

* * * * *

After my time with the Old Monk I went to see Yai to make my peace with him. It was easier than I thought. He was like a man reborn, having made peace with his family and himself. No trace remained of the black cinder in *his* heart. Within days he would be able to see again, to view the face of his beloved grand-daughter. Looking at the old man, it was almost as

272

if he already had his sight back.

I envied him that he had been able to break the chains of bitterness and regret that had held him prisoner. It made me aware of the chafing of my own chains, and since my hours at Wat Son today I had begun to feel a building-up of tension inside me, an increase in pressure which would soon have to find an outlet or a rupture at some point of weakness.

This sense of looming catharsis is however put aside as I walk the darkening streets of Chaweng, and hear a ruckus in one of the bars near to the Ocean Pearl, which had been my intended destination.

All eyes in the Destiny Bar are on an extremely belligerent and very drunk Englishman holding court by one of the pool tables and waving his half-full beer glass menacingly. He is (I guess) in his late thirties, not especially tall but built like a brick shithouse, his hair a severe crew-cut, and something about him suggests ex-armed forces. He is in mid-stream roundly cursing the locals, and indeed anyone within earshot. Spittle flies from his mouth. The veins in his neck bulge out and his face is red and angry. I judge he is going to take a pop at someone any moment.

"You fuckers," he bellows. "You slant-eyed yellow-brown fuckers. First you kill my brother and then you have the cheek to nick my fucking cell phone."

"Nobody here has killed your brother, my friend," says a nervous middle-aged backpacker. "Please just calm down."

"Somebody on this rat-infested island killed my brother," he asserts loudly. "Fucking set fire to him. Not enough just to kill him, oh no. And it never even got into the papers. Some slimy little Thai bastard knows what he did. And as for the fucking police –" Words fail him.

The customers are half-horrified and half-fascinated by this impromptu circus. I notice the barman reach carefully under the bar and grasp the handle of a baseball bat.

The drunk lurches to one side and turns his attention to the ladyboys.

"What a pissing degenerate country this is. Men with *tits*. It's a bloody freak show."

Two of the katoeys are already reversing their grip on their pool cues, and it's about to get really ugly.

"*Peter Ashley*," I call to the inebriate. "Peter Ashley, I need to talk to you."

He swivels around in confusion and tries to focus on me.

"Who are you?" he says forcefully. "I don't know *you*."

Taking a chance I put my face close to his ear and say quietly, "I know about your brother. I know about Anthony. I know about how he died. Come with me. We have to get out of here. Now."

He half-hears me. "You knew Anthony?" he asks, sounding less pugilistic and more like a whining drunk.

"Peter, we have to leave before the police arrive."

"But I want to see the police," he says. His voice rises again as he addresses the whole bar. "They've stolen my cell phone. I go for a piss and they steal it. And my cell phone had pictures of *her* on it. Pictures of that *bitch*." He spits out the word. "They're the only ones I have, the only ones. I'll never find her without my pictures."

Somehow I get him out of the Destiny Bar and onto the street. People are watching us and pointing. I hail a cab and help him into it. Then I climb in beside him.

"Which hotel are you staying at?"

"What's your name?" he slurs drunkenly, but not aggressively.

"David Braddock. Which hotel are you staying at, Peter?"

He can just about get his mouth around the words Lotus Blossom Villas. The same place he stayed with his brother. Nothing like a trip down Happy Memory Lane.

My half-formed resolution to disengage myself from the burning murders investigation has dissipated over the last few minutes. I need to get Peter Ashley rested and sober, so that I can pick his brains on his brother's death, while at the same time keeping him away from the tender embrace of the local constabulary.

I want to hear Ashley Junior's account of what happened. There may be stuff in his head that was not on the file. And that means stuff that Katchai doesn't know.

But first I drag him out of the taxi – not a straightforward matter – and put my shoulder under his arm to help him to his room: which fortunately is not far from the reception.

Eventually he finds his keys and I dump him on the bed.

"They stole my phone," he repeats emptily.

I tear a page from my notebook, write my name and cell phone number on it and put it on his bedside table.

I speak slowly and into his face. "Listen, Peter. Here is my name and phone number. Have a good night's sleep then go out tomorrow and buy a cheap cell phone and a SIM card. Then call me or SMS me. We'll meet up later. Tomorrow."

His eyes look like blood has been poured into them.

"Do you understand, Peter? Don't go out. Stay in the hotel. Yes?"

He nods.

As I reach the door he lurches quickly to his feet, and scuttles to the bathroom. There is the sound of loud violent vomiting. Apparently not all army types can hold their booze.

I walk out of the hotel and into the hot night.

I light a Marlboro. Bad idea. A dull throbbing begins in my temples.

*   *   *   *   *

Although I have had the aircon blasting away in the jeep, my body is covered in perspiration and my head is pounding on the way home. The day, perhaps everything, is catching up with me. The cars, the street-lights, the

275

trees; all have a sense of unreality about them. I have to concentrate hard on my driving to stay on the road. There is buzzing in my ears and my thoughts are spinning like broken pool cues.

Finally I park the car on my drive and take a deep breath. I am unsteady on my legs as I climb from the vehicle and almost fall. My hands are shaking and there is no strength in my fingers. I drop the front door key twice before I manage to turn it in the lock.

Wayan is waiting for me in the hall. She looks anxious and immediately puts a hand to my forehead.

"Mr. David, you are hot. I think you are not well."

She brings a cold towel and gently rubs down my face and neck, then my wrists, while I sit in the chair in my study trying to gather my scattered attention. I'm concerned that I'm going to black out. Although my flesh is feverish, something icy is chewing at me inside. It feels like *fear*.

"You should go to bed," Wayan says.

A black flying demon circles the fringes of my imagination.

"Drink some water. Please, Mr. David." Wayan hands me a glass and I drink. I see concern, almost panic in her brown eyes; and I know I need to make an effort.

I smile and squeeze her arm. "I'm all right, Wayan, really. I've just had a bit of an emotional day. I'll go to bed soon, I promise. Just let me sit here quietly for a while."

She says she will wait up with me, and that she will be in the kitchen until I turn in. She is reluctant to leave the study, but I pat her hand to reassure her. She is not reassured, and leaves the study door open – presumably so she can hear the thud if I faint.

Then my cell phone rings.

I am about to ignore it but then I see the caller is Anna. I take a gulp of water and wipe my clammy face with a handkerchief.

"Hello, Anna,"

I do my best to sound normal, but after a couple of minutes Anna picks up on my state.

"David, you sound odd. Are you all right?"

"I'm running a little fever," I reply.

She has heard this before.

"You're ill," she says, "I can tell from your voice."

She is silent awhile and we listen to each other's breathing.

Finally she says quietly, "Is it Claire?"

"Claire," I say flatly. I find myself laughing softly. "Yes, Claire. Anna, you know better than anyone, it's always Claire. One way or another, always."

"David," she says, "oh God, David. You have to stop. You have to stop this now."

"You mean I have to stop talking to my dead wife?" I say angrily. "You mean I have to stop acting like a crazy person? Stop living with a ghost? Stop communing with the dear departed?"

"It's been four years, David. Claire is gone."

"Don't you think I know that, Anna? Don't you think I understand that all my conversations are with a ghost? That it's all in my head?"

I can feel tears running down my face, but I don't stop.

"*I know*, Anna, believe me *I know*."

"I should have done something different to help you," she says. I can hear her choking back her own emotion. "I shouldn't have encouraged you to continue with *this*, but I thought it would help you to work through your loss."

"It's not your fault. You've been there for me. You've been the only person I could talk to about Claire. It's not your fault."

I feel something break inside me, and can imagine my pursuing furies slowly gaining ground. I see myself tire. I am on the precipice now.

"My wife is nothing more than cold ashes." It is as if I understand for the first time.

"What can I do?"

"Just be there, Anna. Like you always have been there for me. It is enough."

I cut the line.

I reach into the bottom drawer of my desk and remove a small cardboard box. I take off the lid and examine the contents, as I have many times before. There is a scuffed and dog-eared photograph of Claire and myself at Foxton Locks in our early days, wedding pictures, Claire in a silly hat at my fortieth birthday party. There is a bundle of letters tied in a ribbon, some old Valentine's Day cards, a lock of Claire's fiery hair, her engagement and wedding rings, a necklace, and a host of other mementoes; the residual debris of a lost life. The detritus of my marriage, the things I could not let go.

At the very bottom of the box are some very personal poems I wrote for Claire, and one I wrote perhaps for myself, after her death in England, entitled *Ghost*.

I saw you this evening
Walking along a street in Stratford
Your flame hair waving in the breeze

You were in the bookshop
I wanted to call out
As you turned your back
But when I reached you
You were not there

You were on the steps with friends
But quickly gone as the rain came

EVERYONE BURNS

And later
In the dimness of the theatre
An arcing spotlight caught your profile an instant
Leaning forward, in frozen gaze
Then the glare was gone
And you became someone else
Someone else's lover

I see you everywhere
I scan the faces in the crowd
Looking for your face
Because I long to see it

I see you so often
My heart roars at me
The expectation of seeing you
In impossible places
In parks, in high streets, in cars
In strange towns where you cannot possibly be
In the aisles of a supermarket
In the darkness before sleep
Everywhere

Everywhere you are with me
Everywhere I am alone

And I know now why the man Sinclair fills me with deep revulsion. It is because he carries around with him his grief, as I do; because the smell of loss emanates from him like a sickness, as it does with me. It is because he is I, and I abhor what he is and what I have become. And I weep, clutching these relics of burned-out time. Because at the end and forever I am alone. Because in the face of death all the joking and the bravado eventually ends. Because I can never run fast enough or far enough away. Because the loss of Claire is too great for me to bear, because it is insufferable, because it is absurd. And I know now why a raven is like a writing-desk; because neither of them matter, because nothing matters, because in the darkness all is one and all is nothing and everything converges to a point, to a kind of emptiness, to a zero.

And Wayan hears my distress and comes to me as she has other times before, and she raises me gently to my feet and takes me upstairs, and she helps me to undress and she puts me into my bed. She knows this sad routine, it is her burden and it is the reason she is with me. She is kindness and comfort, and she is my nurse and she is my angel. And she lies behind me on the covers, and she presses her body against my back, and she holds me tight, and nuzzles my hair, and she waits with an infinite patience until exhaustion and the shadows take me.

12

"All things are intertwined with one another;
United by a sacred bond;
And there is scarcely any thing unconnected to any other thing."
Marcus Aurelius, Meditations

I am back in the forest of charred trees. On the horizon a mountain is belching forth flame and acrid smoke. Scores of black winged creatures circle and swoop in the red light some distance away. Ash falls around me like snow. Ahead of me in a clearing is a long table set for tea, sitting at which are skeletons clothed in rotted Victorian garb. The bones in the host's chair wear an oversized top hat. Everything is coated in the grey powder.

I move beyond the clearing and see again the white-boarded house. With the passage of time it has become a ruin. The roof has fallen in, the front door hangs lopsidedly on its hinges and the windows are broken and dirty. The deck-chair in the garden is unoccupied, torn and stained; the rag that bound the old man's eyes lies draped across it.

I squeeze past the door and enter the house. As I make my way across the dim hallway, the dusty wooden floorboards creak beneath my feet. Against a peeling wall stands an ancient ornate mirror, its glass cracked and clouded. I gaze at my reflection and see a gaunt, stooped figure with burning eyes. I realise that I have become the old man.

I go back out into the garden and take my place in the deckchair.

I wait for the circling demons to see me.

When I awake it takes me a few moments to register I am in my bedroom and it is morning. The imprint of Wayan's body is still apparent on the bedcovers, and on the pillow she has left a trace of her scent.

Whenever I have had one of these cathartic episodes in the past, I have woken up feeling different, but this time *everything* feels different. I am slightly dehydrated, but calm and more clear-headed than I have been in weeks; almost *purged*. I can hope that perhaps I have finally re-emerged from the rabbit hole. In my personal version of the Mad Hatter's Tea Party the clock has been motionless for the last four years. I sense that time may be starting to drag itself forward again, albeit slowly. The ceiling fan whispers above me stirring the air.

I resolve myself to action, climb out of bed, and shower away the night-sweats. Shaved and dressed, I feel almost euphoric. It could be just another manic upswing, but I think not.

When I go downstairs Wayan examines my face closely and decides she likes what she sees.

"Mr. David, you look better. You have come back to me."

"I feel better."

It appears as if she is going to hug me, then she changes her mind, then she changes her mind again and does hug me.

I put my arms around her.

"Welcome back," she says into my shoulder and squeezes me tight.

I step back from her and notice the wetness sparkle in her eyes. Holding her arms I say, "Come upstairs with me. We have something to do."

"Don't you want some breakfast?" she asks, not sure where this is leading.

"Afterwards."

We go back up into my bedroom and I indicate Claire's perfumes and lotions on the dressing table.

"I am having a clear-out today," I say. "Do you want any of this stuff?"

Wayan is not sure whether to be happy or fearful. She shakes her head.

I fling open the wardrobe door where Claire's clothes hang.

"How about any of these? Any good for you?"

She shakes her head again. "I do not think I should be wearing any of

Miss Claire's clothes, Mr. David. It would not feel right."

"I understand," I reply. "Inappropriate. Anyway, your bum is probably too big."

"Is it?" she says concerned.

"Not at all," I laugh. "You have a lovely bum, Wayan. Now help me with all this. We're going to have a bonfire."

We sweep up all the cosmetics and drop them into a box: this can go out with the refuse.

In big armfuls we carry all of Claire's dresses downstairs and deposit them in a pile in a corner of the garden. I fetch some lighter fluid and pour it over them. I hear Wayan catch her breath.

"Mr. David," she says in a concerned voice, "Are you sure –"

"I'm sure, Wayan. It's time to let go."

I start the fire, and watch as it consumes my dead wife's clothing. It is as if I am bearing witness to her cremation for a second time. Wayan stands beside me and says some prayers or incantations quietly in Balinese. Her fingers lock into mine and we stare at the burning pyre. Images of the murdered farangs flick through my mind, although my thoughts are mainly of past days with a flame-haired girl. The hot bright sky looks down on this impromptu ritual as the smoke rises upwards and the green leaves wobble distortedly in the haze.

After a few minutes the fire dies and Wayan wipes my cheek tenderly. We go inside to breakfast together.

*　　*　　*　　*　　*

An unfamiliar number comes up on my cell phone.

"Hello, this is David Braddock."

"Ah, hello," says a hung-over English voice, "This is Peter Ashley. I'm calling on my new phone as you asked."

"Good. How are you feeling today?"

"I feel like crap. I'm afraid I don't remember too much about yesterday evening. I do remember however that you mentioned my brother's name, and that you got me back to my hotel in one piece. Thank you for that."

"Listen, Peter, I need to talk to you about your brother. I'm a private investigator and I'm looking into your brother's death. I'll explain it all later." I'm not about to go into details now about how I'm assisting the police in case he goes off on one.

"You're a detective?" he asks hopefully.

"I'm what passes for one on Samui anyway. We'll discuss it later, but in the meantime I'd suggest you stay at your hotel. Do some sunbathing or swimming. Have a massage. Do something non-aggressive. Keep your head down, just for today. Will you do that?"

He sounds reluctant.

"I suppose. Although I do need to find this girl –"

"I may be able to help you there. In my line of work I know lots of girls. But you need to stay out of trouble, Peter. The authorities here won't hesitate to boot you out of the country if we have a repeat of last night's floor show. You can't go around getting pissed out of your brain *and* slagging off the police and the whole of the native population. If I hadn't arrived when I did you'd be in a cell now. Probably with internal haemorrhaging."

"OK, OK. I'll lay off the sauce as well. But you'll come and see me later today?"

"Yes. I've some errands to run first, but I'll be over to your hotel later this afternoon. I'll call you if there's any change. I've got your number now."

"I'll wait for you."

*   *   *   *   *

284

The American educational psychologist Patricia Alexander has expressed the view that fear paralyses and curiosity empowers. Accordingly, she reasons, we should always be more interested than afraid.

Mind you, she's probably never found herself driving to an appointment with a Crime Godfather.

However, although I'd have to be brain-dead not to feel some apprehension at the forthcoming meeting, I do confess to feeling a certain curiosity at seeing Kat's *other* lover. I am also aware of a small twinge of jealousy nibbling at me. While I am hardly in a position to object to sharing her with her husband, I do feel slightly resentful of being number *three* in the queue for her favours.

Be curious, not fearful.

Not that curiosity did the cat any good.

Rattanakorn's office is a modernistic steel and glass building outside Lamai, set inside a high-walled compound. Security guards scrutinise the underside of my car with a mirror on a pole and look inside. My passport is checked against a list before the barrier is raised.

One of the guards escorts me inside the structure. I'm taken up two flights of stairs where two other large guards – this time in suits, not uniforms – frisk me intimidatingly, before knocking on the door of their boss' office.

I am admitted into a large bright room whose walls are adorned with modern artwork and antique statuary. In the centre of the room is an enormous carved mahogany desk behind which sits Thongchai Rattanakorn. He dismisses the bodyguards with a nod and indicates for me to sit.

"Mr. David Braddock," he says appraising me as if I am some curious *object d'art*.

"Mr. Rattanakorn."

The businessman is wearing a white tailored shirt with his initials on the breast. His cufflinks look to be made of real diamonds. The tie is red and wide with a dragon motif. His sharp pinstriped jacket hangs on the chair behind him.

He is a handsome, beautifully groomed bugger, and his face puts me in mind of the heart-throb actor Jet Li – maybe he has some Chinese ancestry. But his most striking feature is his piercing eyes. His whole persona exudes confidence and power. He should be stroking a white long-haired cat and plotting the death of James Bond. As I look at him I feel my peripheral vision shrink, my reality collapsing to a tunnel which ends in his unblinking gaze.

The contrast with Charoenkul could hardly be more striking. *Here* is real authority and intensity, compared to which Papa Doc appears as a jumped-up and anodyne bureaucrat.

Rattanakorn indicates for me to sit.

"Would you prefer us to converse in English or Thai?" he asks in my native tongue. "I am given to understand that you are fluent in my language."

"I have no preference."

"Then we will stick to English."

Silence. Rattanakorn smoothly raises a china teacup to his lips, takes a delicate sip and sets down the cup; his eyes never leaving mine. He sits unmoving and waits for me to speak.

"Well, first let me reassure you I have not come here with any malicious intent. I realise my telephone call to you may have caused you some concern, but I felt it was necessary to meet you in person."

There is another silence. When he speaks it is as if I had not said anything.

"Do you know who I am?" he asks. There is a touch of menace in his voice and I feel the hairs rise on the back of my neck.

Before I can answer he goes on. "It's just that –" he pauses, picks up the teacup again, sips thoughtfully and replaces it carefully in its saucer. "It's just that on occasion people seem to get the wrong idea about me. I have even come across individuals who seem to have a notion that I am some kind of *Crime Lord* here on Samui, that I am somehow an Underworld figure. Have you heard anything of this, Mr. Braddock?" His voice is mild, but all the more frightening for that.

"I have heard that you are well-connected," I say carefully, "and from a very powerful Thai family; that you were educated at Cambridge and in the United States; and that you go about your business affairs in a very private – some might say secretive – fashion."

"Anything else?"

"Also that wherever you go you are accompanied by bodyguards. And this to most people is a sure sign that you are a jâo phâw."

"On that reasoning," he says, "that would make most wealthy people gangsters."

"Most wealthy people *are* gangsters."

He opens a drawer of his desk, casually takes out a pistol, flicks off the safety catch and points it at my head.

He says almost sorrowfully, "Do you believe me to be a gangster, Mr. Braddock?"

"I suppose I do, Mr. Rattanakorn," I respond in the same tone.

"Then I suppose at this point you would expect me to shoot you."

"No, actually I wouldn't."

"And why is that?"

"Two reasons: one practical and one artistic."

"Please explain," he continues in an almost friendly fashion, although the barrel of the gun remains aligned with the centre of my forehead.

"First, you don't really know why I've come here. You probably suspect a blackmail motive, but you're not sure. Also I may have protected myself by leaving some incriminating document with a trusted person.

"Secondly, if you were to pull that trigger not only would the bullet pass through me and a rather splendid abstract canvas behind me, but also my ensuing blood loss would completely ruin the marvellously intricate and expensive Kashmir rug that is underneath my chair.

"But quite aside from those two reasons; why would you bother? You just have to snap your fingers and the two heavies outside would come in, beat any required confession out of me and then crush me like a bug without the need for any damage to your art collection.

"So, no, Mr. Rattanakorn, I don't think you are going to shoot me. At least not yet. However, the gun *is* a nice touch, and your point is well made."

He looks at me for a moment, then puts the safety catch on and drops the gun back into the drawer

He sighs. "Many businessmen have guns today, Mr. Braddock. These are dangerous and violent times. And while I can understand why people might think I have criminal connections, I can assure you they are mistaken."

"As am I."

"Every man is entitled to his delusions." He leans back in his chair. "So why *are* you here exactly?" he asks.

"If the theatrics are over, may we talk hypothetically for a while? I have a story I'd like to tell you."

Rattanakorn indicates a *go ahead* with his hands.

I take a deep breath and launch off.

"OK. For the purposes of illustration, let's suppose that once upon a time there was a certain English private detective – let's call him David – who had been making his living on an island in the Gulf of Thailand. Furthermore, let's describe David as a man who … had a certain difficulty in reining in his sexual appetite. Put simply, he just couldn't keep his hands off attractive women.

"Then one day David met a very, *very* attractive lady and the inevitable happened. And not just once either, but several times," I add somewhat ill-advisedly.

"Now this may have been all well and good, but unfortunately the lady in question happened to be the wife of the top policeman on the island; and so David would spend much of his time looking back over his shoulder, waiting for the consequences of his bad behaviour to catch up with him. Are you with me so far?"

Rattanakorn nods, but his face remains expressionless.

"Anyway, one sunny afternoon in January, our detective received a call summoning him to meet the Police Chief. As you can imagine, he thought the game was up, started checking his will was up-to-date, etcetera.

"Picture his surprise therefore when the Police Chief told him that he wanted to employ him to follow his wife because he suspected she was having an affair.

"Not feeling able to refuse the Chief, the detective first went to the wife and told her of his assignment. He then followed her to Bangkok and found that she was indeed having an affair – with a prominent, married businessman from the same island.

"Appalled by the woman's reckless behaviour, David now has a dilemma. He obviously can't tell the Police Chief what he has discovered in case the story of his own affair comes out. On the other hand, if he tells the Chief his wife is innocent but she continues her rash affair with the businessman and the Chief finds out *some other way*, the detective is also in trouble. Do you see David's quandary?"

"I'd say your detective was screwed," says Rattanakorn leaning forward with a slight smile on his lips.

"Perhaps. But he does see one possible way out. He reasons that there is a good chance that the wife has *not* told the businessman that her husband has employed a private detective. Furthermore – he thinks – there is also the possibility that if the businessman *did* know the whole story, he might be unhappy at the wife's risky behaviour which is putting his *own* marriage and standing in jeopardy. At that point he might end the relationship.

Naughty wife keeps quiet: no reason not to, provided the businessman lets her down gently. Detective is off the hook. Everyone lives happily ever after. In the Chief's case, in blissful ignorance.

"Of course," I continue slowly and meaningfully meeting his gaze, "there is a downside to this course of action. The detective would be taking a real risk in going to see the businessman, since the latter has something of a reputation for employing – shall we say – rather ruthless methods to fix his problems."

"So what does your detective choose to do?"

Rattanakorn looks at me. I look back.

"He goes to see the businessman. And he keeps his fingers crossed the businessman understands his true intentions."

I wonder what cogs are turning in his mind. Is he thinking about Kat's behaviour, his marriage, his social position, Charoenkul's reaction if it all goes public? Is he considering whether I should be allowed to leave the building alive?

The jâo phâw strokes his chin reflectively then he leans forward across his desk and pushes a gold cigarette box towards me.

"Cigarette?" he suggests.

I take one and light it. He doesn't. Instead he leans back in his chair.

"Changing the subject," he says, "I gather my wife Nittha has been to see you. In a professional capacity, I mean."

"I never discuss my clients, real or imaginary."

"You just discussed our Police Chief," is his riposte.

"You are mistaken," I say drily, "that was a hypothetical situation."

"Touché."

He continues to look at me as I smoke. He waits for me to say something. I don't say anything. When he has stretched the silence out as far as it will go, he asks nonchalantly, "Do you have many married ladies come to you for advice on their husbands? And do they come to see you as a counsellor or as

290

a private detective?"

"I have married *and* single ladies come to me for advice on all sorts of things. Usually it is as a counsellor. Most married ladies here wouldn't need to employ a private detective to find out if their husband is having an affair. *They would already know.*"

"I see."

"I might also add that, in my experience, what such ladies really want is simply for their husband to stop fooling around. That's all."

I wonder how much this Godfather knows about me. I'm sure he'll have done his research as thoroughly as possible since my initial call. So far as Nittha's association with me is concerned he could just be guessing – maybe his impression is that Nittha had hired me to follow *him*, rather than Papa Doc's employing me to trail Kat. Impossible to tell from his face, the man is unreadable.

And of course if he's *not* guessing about Nittha's meetings with me, then it presumably follows that someone is engaged specifically to watch *his* wife.

He takes a cigarette from the box and lights it.

"You are an interesting man, Mr. Braddock; discreet *and* understanding. Although quite how you have gathered the impression that I am some kind of gangster, I don't know." The trace of a smile.

I shrug. "Urban myths tend to cluster around powerful men," I volunteer enigmatically.

Then I ask him, "So how would *you* see my hypothetical story ending? Do you think the fictional businessman would believe the private detective and so end his affair with the Police Chief's wife? Or do you think he would continue the liaison and maybe arrange for some unfortunate accident to happen to the detective?"

"I think," he says cogitating on the matter, "that if the detective is as smart as I suspect he is, he would have taken out some form of insurance against that happening. Say, leaving a document and some pertinent photographs in an envelope to be opened in the event of his death or disappearance, perhaps?"

"The detective *could* certainly have done that," I reply, "but in my story he's not that kind of man. He operates on a basis of persuasion, not on the basis of blackmail. So, no, he hasn't left any such envelope."

Rattanakorn gives a small nod of the head.

"I think I like this detective," he says evenly, "even if he is a little naïve. He has a certain charm. I feel sure the fictional businessman would like him too. He may even consider himself somewhat indebted to the detective."

I relax slightly in my chair.

"The detective is no saint, as I've explained. He's really acting out of self-interest."

Rattakorn gives a dismissive wave of his hand.

"Everyone acts out of self-interest," he observes. "I wouldn't trust anyone who doesn't."

"You appear to have a rather pessimistic view of humanity, Mr. Rattanakorn."

"A realistic view rather." He pauses before continuing. "I may have some work for a man of your talents, Mr. Braddock. Are you interested?"

"I'm always open to discussion."

"Provided it doesn't involve anything deeply criminal, of course," he says with a twinkle in his eye.

"Naturally."

"What cases are you working on at the moment?"

"Well, I am doing some confidential profiling work for the police on the farang murders."

"Hmnn. Interesting," he muses.

"I don't suppose, with your extensive knowledge and network of people here on Samui, you would know anything that could be helpful to me on this?"

His body language signals regret. "It's not my field, I'm afraid. I know nothing about it, other than what I have read in the newspapers. And newspapers are not inherently reliable sources of information, in my experience."

"Nor mine. Other than that, it's just my bread-and-butter business. I'm in the process of wrapping up a routine assignment on a bargirl in the Ocean Pearl then I'll be watching another girl. And so it goes."

Rattanakorn suddenly looks interested.

"The Ocean Pearl, you say?"

"Yes."

"That wouldn't happen to be Wiwattanee Lamphongchat, would it? Known as 'Jingjai'?"

"Why yes," I say surprised. "Do you know her?"

He laughs. "Yes, I know her. The question is: do *you* know her? Do you know who she *is*, I mean?"

I'm taken aback.

"Well, she's a very talented young musician who is clearly over-educated for what she's currently doing," I improvise lamely.

"She's far more than that," Rattanakorn announces smugly.

"You have my attention, Mr. Rattanakorn. I'm all ears."

"Wiwattanee Lamphongchat is the niece of a Bangkok business associate of mine. She was partly educated in Switzerland and holds a Batchelor's Degree in Music. To my knowledge she is fluent in English, German and French. Her father died about ten years ago while she was still at school. The Lamphongchat family is rather wealthy."

"So what's she doing working in a bar on Koh Samui?"

Rattanakorn chooses his words with care.

"Miss Wiwattanee somewhat disapproves of the family business, and consequently there was a falling-out a few years back."

"You're telling me her relatives are all gangsters?"

"Given your prejudices they are wealthy and therefore gangsters by definition."

"Never mind about that."

"Anyway, Wiwattanee wanted to pursue a career in music, but she does *not* want her family supporting her – she thinks of it as 'blood money', and won't accept their help. The girl wants to make her own way in the world: commendable in its own way, I suppose. She thought if she stayed in Bangkok the family would interfere, so she packed her bags and came to Samui. Hardly the place to start a musical career, I'd have thought; but I guess a musician has to start *somewhere*."

"I've seen her performing. She's good. But how do *you* come to know all this?"

"The family likes to keep an eye on her – just to make sure she's not getting herself into trouble, or associating with undesirables. So they employ a 'minder' here on the island to look out for her. As a favour to Lamphongchat I organise the payment of the minder's retainer."

"I see," I say cynically. "So Jingjai's uncle has some other paid gangster spying on her."

"Hardly a *gangster*," Rattanakorn retorts. "In fact the man is a local policeman, although a rather unpleasant one. You might know him: Chaldrakun is his name."

"*Preechap* Chaldrakun?" I ask. "Otherwise known ironically to the ex pats here as 'PC'?"

"Yes. Something of a gorilla, and not terribly sophisticated." He wrinkles his nose. "I gather that's why he's never been promoted. So the minder money must come in handy for him."

"Does the girl know about him?"

"I shouldn't think so, although it depends how discreet Chaldrakun has been about observing her. A policeman hanging around a bar shouldn't really attract suspicion. That's why he was chosen in the first place. *You*, of course, will *not* be enlightening her on the arrangement," he adds. It's not a question.

I shrug. "It's really none of my business. Although as far as PC is concerned, this information might be useful leverage if ever I need to get that big ugly bastard off *my* back in the future.

"I don't suppose you have any other titbits of local gossip for me? That Police Chief Charoenkul is a cross-dresser, perhaps?"

"No."

He stubs out his cigarette, and I follow suit. I take it this signals the end of our conversation. I might *look* calm but I can't wait to get out of the room. I stand up.

"Thank you for your time then, Mr. Rattanakorn," I say with a deferential bow of the head. "I won't be troubling you again."

He remains seated. "Thank you, Mr. Braddock," he replies. "However, I will say that I may be troubling *you* at some point." He picks up on my unease and smiles. "But in a *good* way."

*　　*　　*　　*　　*

On my drive home to change out of my damp, fear-smelling clothing I reflect *that encounter went as well as could be expected*.

With luck, Rattanakorn will gently disengage from Kat and I'll be back to number *two* in the queue. Maybe even number one if Charoenkul is still distracted elsewhere.

When I decided to meet the jâo phâw it was supposedly on the basis that I was seeking to de-risk my personal situation vis-à-vis Papa Doc. I wonder now whether I was really looking to rid myself of a rival for Kat's attention. If that is the case, then I am even more reckless than my mistress.

Wayan is pottering around when I arrive at the house.

As is the custom after one of my episodes, we first become very close and then start to feel self-conscious about touching each other, even casually. Having had her in – or rather *on* – my bed for the night, with her arms around my almost-naked body, it is a strange tightrope of repressed intimacy that we tread in the days that follow. It's almost like the awkwardness that teenagers feel in the presence of the opposite sex; trying not to cross an invisible line.

It also occurs to me that Wayan must have seen the scars and bruises on my torso from my Bangkok wrestling match with Kat. I wonder what my Balinese Princess made of *those*.

She seems shy and avoids direct eye contact as she tells me an envelope has arrived while I was out. My first thought is *another anonymous letter*, but then she passes me a large official-looking manila envelope which I'm guessing contains more burning murders stuff.

I sit down in the study and pull out the contents of the envelope: slim pickings, only two sheets of paper.

The first is typed, not even addressed to me and with no preamble. Although it's clearly from Charoenkul, he is covering himself – there would be credible deniability if it ever fell into anyone else's hands.

It reads:

Lewis Carroll
Forensics show traces of benzodiazepines
which suggests victim was drugged.
Cause of death trauma to the head.
No usable DNA or trace samples.
Tyre tracks inconclusive.

That's *it*.

As it happens I know a bit about benzodiazepines ('BZDs'), owing to a case I was involved in a couple of years back where a backpacker's drink had been spiked by a bargirl who subsequently robbed him. BZDs have an unsavoury reputation as date rape drugs, although their *intended* use is for anxiety conditions and insomnia. One of the BDZs – temazepam – is a major recreational drug in parts of South East Asia, and is a Schedule II controlled drug in Thailand; making possession and distribution illegal. Another BDZ – midazolam – is water-soluble and is also available in a liquid form. This latter drug has a rapid onset, and has the advantage that, although it only works for a short time it becomes undetectable in the blood after a few hours.

Forget *Rohypnol*, which popular culture holds to be the date rape drug of choice. Based on my research, BDZs are second only to alcohol as the most common way of putting your victim out. *Combined* with alcohol, they are even more potent and dangerous.

(If BDZs are not up your street, incidentally, you could instead try gamma-hydroxybutyric – 'GHB' – but if so, you'll have to slip it into something with a bit of flavour, otherwise your intended mark might notice the salty taste. And, since you need relatively higher doses to induce unconsciousness, be cautioned that detection is easier.)

I wonder if drugging is part of our murderer's usual MO. Carroll's body was relatively 'fresh' when discovered which may be why forensics found the drug: or maybe they just didn't test the other bodies. I don't recall anything about this in Charoenkul's extracts.

If the victims were all immobilised, then they probably weren't brought to the sites of their death voluntarily. Which means they might *not* have known their killer. So much for some of my earlier theories.

The second sheet of paper is a photostat copy of Lewis Carroll's passport.

Wait.

Hold on.

Wait a minute.

I know this face.

I've spent time sitting next to this man at the bar in the *Ocean Pearl*. It's the guy who was trying unsuccessfully to chat up Jingjai. The uncommunicative Mancunian.

I'd stood over his corpse and I hadn't recognised him. Hardly surprising though, considering he had no face. His own mother wouldn't have recognised that obscenely destroyed, burnt thing.

And with a start I realise something else. If I hadn't taken the call from Nittha Rattanakorn that evening; and if I hadn't been so eager to leave the bar prematurely and meet up with her; then perhaps Lewis Carroll might still be alive. Because *that* was the night he died.

Other thoughts begin crashing inside my head in big, ugly waves.

I snatch up my second-best camera bag and rush past a surprised-looking Wayan on my way to the front-door.

I haven't even changed my sweaty shirt, but there's no time.

I must talk to Peter Ashley *now*.

*   *   *   *   *

The late afternoon sun casts long shadows across the pool and sunbathing deck of Lotus Blossom Villas as I make my way through the surfeit of blubbery human skin flopped across the loungers. Not all the bathers are fat, but most of them are. Obesity: our true *Zeitgeist*.

Peter Ashley, by contrast, is looking trim, muscled and worried, in equal measure. He is wearing swimming trunks, sitting hunched over what looks like a fruit-juice and gazing unhappily into space. He has lots of tattoos, I notice, and he probably has yet more beneath the faded hotel towel draped across his shoulders. A look of relief floods his face when he sees me.

"Let's go to the bar, Peter, and find a quiet corner to talk. You might want to change first; the mosquitoes will be out now."

He grabs his clothes, slips on some flip-flops and shuffles off hurriedly into the toilets.

I set up a couple of beers and borrow some insect repellent from the barman. He lights a coil under the table as an added precaution.

Ashley arrives quickly, clad in a khaki tee-shirt and cargo pants: he still looks army, in spite of the fact that he is wearing flip-flops. He is clearly very impatient. Sitting around the pool most of the day waiting for me has made him fidgety. I hope he's not going to be difficult.

"Before we go any further," I say, "I need you to clarify some things for me."

"Well, I've had some time to think today and I need *you* to clarify some things for me," he says tersely. "Like what exactly is your interest in my brother's death? And why would *you* be investigating it? If you're a private detective that means somebody must be paying for your time. I know I'm not, so who is? How do I know you're not some journalist or something?"

"All fair questions. OK, let me tell you what I know about Anthony's death. Then you can judge for yourself whether I'm just some interfering busybody."

I try to sound and appear patient, although I'm not. My thoughts are racing, making connections. I'm itching to move on to the meat of the discussion.

I recount speedily what I remember of the circumstances of his brother's murder, endeavouring all the while to sound professional and non-judgmental. He listens intently, nodding occasionally as I talk.

"That's pretty much right," he says. "But you still haven't told me why *you're* involved in any of this, or how you got to find out all these details. None of it made the papers."

"I owe a favour to a senior policeman here on Samui. He's asked me to help out on the investigation with some psychological profiling and other stuff; so I've seen extracts from the case files. This policeman's career may well depend on how the case is resolved."

At the mention of the police Ashley snorts derisively.

"Listen, I met the policeman heading up the investigation at Bophut Police Station two days ago. What's-his-name? Katchai? A right smug bastard."

"I'm not talking about Katchai. He's not the one I owe a favour to. But before we get any further into Thai police politics, there are a couple of things *I* need to know from *you*."

He looks like he might become objectionable but instead he shrugs.

"Fire away then."

"First, what are you doing back on Samui? And how long have you been here?"

He takes a large swig of beer, and I light a Marlboro.

"A few days ago," he begins, "I saw the reports in the international news about the murder of two Europeans on the island, and an inference about the bodies being burned. My first thought was that one must be my brother, and that *finally* they were going to carry out a serious investigation. But then I learned that the two dead guys were a Dutchman and some other Brit – which meant there was *still* a cover-up going on over my brother's murder.

"So I caught the first flight out here that I could and pitched up at Bophut Police Station. I made a loud nuisance of myself until they eventually let me meet the policeman in charge of the investigation. I told this guy Katchai who I was and that I might have information to help him in his search for the murderer."

Ashley twists his mouth in contempt.

"Do you know what that bastard said to me?"

"No," I say quietly.

"He had the fucking cheek to say that my brother's death was in no way related to the other two murders, and that effectively no active investigation was currently going on into Anthony's killing. He also practically threatened me that if I made any waves I would be – how did he put it? – 'dealt with severely'."

"The police are in a double bind. They can't talk about Anthony's death now, it's been too long. They have to pretend there have only been two burning murders."

"It's a bloody disgrace."

"Never mind about that now, Peter. Tell me about the photograph of the girl on your phone. Did you mention it to Katchai?"

"No. I didn't get the chance. Now it's too late. The phone's gone. Stolen."

"Who is she? Is it someone Anthony was sleeping with here?"

Ashley shakes his head.

"No. He spent a lot of time with her in the evenings, but it never got that far. He never introduced me, although he must have taken a few photos of her on my phone. I remember there was one evening he borrowed my phone because there was something wrong with the SIM on his. That must have been the evening he snapped the pictures. I didn't realise I had them on there until later. And I can't even recollect the girl's name. I was more interested in getting laid than in Anthony's chats, you see," he adds regretfully.

"Do you think you would recognise her if you saw her?"

He looks at me.

"I've only ever seen her photograph," he says, "but yes, I think I would."

I take my second-best camera from its bag, and fast-forward the viewer through the digital images until I reach the photographs taken by my teenage helper a few days ago.

I show the pictures of Jingjai to Ashley.

"Is this the girl?" I ask.

His mouth drops open and then he swallows hard. His eyes are bulging out of his head.

"Yes," he stammers, "it is. But – but – how did you find her? How did you *know*?"

"Now listen to me very carefully, Peter. I don't *know* anything. Not yet. I have a number of suppositions and some very tenuous connections. But I have no *evidence*. And what is more, I have already made lots of foul-ups and errors so far on this case; which could have resulted in one or two completely innocent men ending up in the police cells."

"But you know who the girl is. You can take me to her."

"So you can do *what exactly*?" I say with a hard edge to my voice. "Beat her up? Get yourself arrested? *No*, you need to wait."

"You must be fucking joking. Wait for what?"

I realise I have to keep Ashley away from the Ocean Pearl tonight; its last night before it closes for refurbishment. I need to make sure he doesn't bump into Jingjai. That could wreck everything. The last thing Samui needs now is an angry English vigilante prowling its streets.

"Wait for *me*. Wait here until I talk to a man about a dog."

"What sort of a dog?" he asks suspiciously.

"A dog that doesn't bark," I say.

Why would a dog not bark at a stranger in the night-time? Answer: because the person he detects is not a stranger. For the same reason, in fact, that a policeman on night duty in the police box outside Lamai might not remark on a police car driving by, even one with a slumped figure in the back seat.

And why might a spinning pool cue haunt my subconscious? Perhaps because of who came into the Mosquito Bar after the cue had been spinning; because of the violence represented by both the broken cue and that person.

And finally, why might the murderer of the farangs choose *that* particular coconut grove in which to dispatch his victims?

I phone an old blind man, and I ask him, when his son died, does he remember any of the policemen who came to investigate? And he tells me, yes, there was one *particular* policeman. One who was morbidly obsessed with his son's death by fire; a very large, thick-necked policeman. And I ask him if he remembers the man's name. And he does.

*   *   *   *   *

I double-check DTs' address from the paper that Charoenkul gave me which I had stuffed in the back of my notebook.

I have parked the jeep in a run-down and badly-lit area on the outskirts of Chaweng, a stone's throw from a cluster of cheap massage joints which glow red in the darkness. Dust alternately hangs and swirls in the air, kicked up by the steady stream of bikes and battered vehicles bouncing over the rutted road.

I walk up a quiet unsurfaced side-road, light a cigarette and prop myself against a weathered wooden post while I watch what I take to be the policeman's home. As my eyes become accustomed to the dark, I scrutinise the house which looks old and careworn, its walls stained, its small garden neglected. Lights are on inside and I can see movement.

It had taken all my persuasive powers – and then some – to convince Ashley to stay in his hotel *again*. Unsurprisingly, trust is a scarce commodity with him these days. I told him there was someone I needed to see, that I had to go alone, that his presence would likely hinder my investigation. For a while his stubbornness held sway, and I thought he might try to pummel Jingjai's details out of me. In the end he capitulated with bad grace, but only after extracting from me a promise that I would return later and give him a full report.

"I will likely be *very* late," I'd warned.

"Do you think that matters?" he'd asked sarcastically. "It's not as if I've got anything else to do."

I take in a deep lungful of cigarette smoke and remember Rattanakorn's description of Jingjai's minder: *a local policeman, although rather an unpleasant one. Something of a gorilla.*

But I have no *proof* of anything. I've merely connected some dots: perhaps the picture that has emerged is still the wrong one.

I'm on my second cigarette of the watch when I see the weasel-frame of DTs illuminated in one of the downstairs windows. The master of the house is at home.

I stub out my cigarette, walk the short distance to his front door and knock on it loudly.

There are some raised voices from inside then DTs cautiously opens the door, just wide enough so he can look out. He is wearing an old Manchester United replica football shirt, and some shapeless grey pants. I catch a whiff of alcohol from his breath. A snot-nosed, dirty-faced little boy is hanging onto his legs, looking up at me as if I've climbed out of a spaceship.

When DTs realises it is me at the door, he looks alarmed.

"Good evening, Officer Tathip," I say smoothly in Thai. "I'm sorry to interrupt your evening, but I need to speak to you on an urgent matter."

"Can't it wait until tomorrow?" he asks in a high-fluted voice which takes me by surprise. Thinking about it, I'm not sure whether this is the first time I've actually heard him talk.

"I'm afraid it won't wait. It concerns the farang murders." I look at him pointedly and register satisfaction at the barely-suppressed panic I see in his eyes. "Is there somewhere we can go to talk privately? I wouldn't wish to intrude on your family." The little boy is mining one of his nostrils with an index finger.

Seeing I'm not about to leave DTs says reluctantly, "There is a sala at the back. I will be out in a couple of minutes."

As he tries to close the door I put my foot in it. "Excellent," I reply, "but please don't make any phone calls in the meantime. It would not be in your or your family's interest. If you understand me?"

He nods and I remove my foot from the door. With a trembling hand the policeman ushers his son back inside and pushes the door shut.

I walk around to the back of his property and make my way through the dark overgrown garden to a sad, semi-dilapidated sala. After a moment a fluorescent light comes on casting a harsh glare over the squadrons of flying insects. I am glad I've sprayed up: this looks like Mosquito Central. I take a seat in the most serviceable of the rickety wooden chairs.

DTs closes the back door behind him and joins me, sitting with some reluctance. His pock-marked face looks even more unhealthy than usual in the unforgiving strip-light. A child's face is pressed curiously against one of the house windows until an adult arm pulls it away and the curtain closes.

"I think," I say trying to emulate Rattanakorn's understated menace, "That you are in a lot of trouble, Officer Tathip."

He squirms in his chair, and pleads ignorance in as unconvincing a fashion as I have ever seen. He is clearly terrified. For months he has held out waiting, presumably petrified, for the axe to fall. On reflection, I'm surprised his rodent nerve hasn't already snapped. I guess he fears his partner's retribution more than he fears discovery. That's a hard place to be. My main concern now is whether he will have a heart attack or some form of seizure before we've finished our little talk.

That would be *unhelpful*.

"I know who murdered the farangs and set them alight, Tathip." I pause for effect, although that's probably unnecessary. I'm sure I already have his attention. "Your partner did. Officer Preechap Chaldrakun. And he did it with your help."

"That's ridiculous," he pipes. "We are police officers. What you say is an outrageous accusation –"

"Shut up," I hiss at him, "or I will have to slap you hard."

He looks at me in shock.

"Chaldrakun killed the farangs because they were paying too much attention to the girl in the Ocean Pearl; the one he was minding for the Lamphongchat family. He took the first two to a coconut grove outside of Lamai that he knew from a suicide investigation he was involved in. Perhaps the method of that suicide – self-immolation – was what gave him the idea for setting fire to the farang corpses."

DTs' face is deathly pale; and not just because of the lighting.

"In any event, Chaldrakun used his position as a police officer to get the foreigners into a police car, and then he took the men to those remote sites, and he killed them by beating their heads in. He probably 'arrested' them on some local technicality to get them into handcuffs and after that they would have been helpless. Whether he drugged them initially, or only after he arrived at the killing sites I don't know – probably before."

Tathip starts to gabble something, but I raise my hand.

"When I want you to talk, Tathip, I'll let you know. For now, I want you to know what *I* know."

He sits panting and trembling. I almost feel sorry for the little squit. But not quite.

I continue. "He burned the lower arms of his victims to conceal any marks that might have been left by the handcuffs, and he made the face unrecognisable to buy time, not ultimately to conceal the man's identity. He just couldn't take the chance of the girl in the bar seeing a familiar phizog in the next day's newspaper.

"And of course Chaldrakun couldn't have done all this alone. He needed to be on duty, in uniform, with the police car. And that means, as his partner, you must have been with him."

I look into DTs' eyes.

"*You* helped him."

"You're mad," he squeaks. "Even assuming what you say is true. Why would I do that?"

306

"Because you're shit scared of your partner," I say casually lighting a cigarette. "And I suppose I can hardly blame you. He's a scary man."

"That's just nonsense –"

I cut him off. "I do, however, know an even scarier man. His name is Peter Ashley, and he's the brother of your first victim. Ashley, being ex-army, is a *professionally trained* killer. What is more, he's here on the island. Would you like me to introduce you to him? By the way, I don't think he's too particular about following legal due process. It was all I could do to stop him coming here tonight and breaking your neck."

OK, so I'm improvising a bit. But I need Tathip to be more frightened of my threats than those of Chaldrakun. Tricky, but let's see how we go.

DTs puts his head in his hands. Then he sits up and looks at me wildly.

"What are you going to do?" he asks.

I take a draw on my Marlboro, and blow smoke in his direction in what I hope is a gangster manner.

"Well, that depends on you?" I reply languidly.

"What do you want *me* to do?"

"First, tell me about the girl. What does she know about all this?"

"Nothing," he says decisively, "nothing at all. I don't believe Preechap's even spoken to her. He's just become ... obsessed with her. He told me once she reminds him of his ex girlfriend, the one who ran off with a farang. That's why he hates you all so much," he adds a little spitefully.

Charlie Rorabaugh's words come back to me. *Everyone falls in love with Jingjai.*

Somewhere in the twisted head of the gorilla some attachment had grown, some hopeless yearning for a tender relationship way beyond his reach. Or maybe it was just plain lust, of the unrequited variety. He had taken his resentment and his futile longing and mixed them into a lethal Molotov cocktail. The spark that had finally ignited the conflagration was not some cheap cigarette lighter.

It was a love *match*.

"And the drugs? Chaldrakun did drug all three victims, right?" DTs nods. "What drug was it and where did your partner get his hands on it?"

"I don't know the name of it. But he injected them with it. He said he got it from his brother in Bangkok."

"What a charming family." I remark drily. "And the burning of the bodies … that wasn't solely about destroying evidence, was it? There was contempt there too."

Tathip looks at his feet.

"I need a drink," he croaks.

"In a minute. What did he use to beat in their heads and faces?"

"A tyre wrench," he replies quietly.

"The wrench *from the patrol car?* That sounds like an improper use of official police equipment. He could get into trouble for that."

"No, not from the patrol car. He has his own wrench."

"Especially for these occasions, presumably. Nice."

I study Tathip.

"So what exactly was your role? Helping him carry the unconscious body into the trees? Keeping lookout? Or something a little more hands-on with the deaths, perhaps?"

He looks like he's going to throw up.

"I never hit them, I never burned them. What could I do or say? *You've seen him. You know him.* He's a violent man, with a violent temper. I have a family. What could *I* do?"

"You could have grown some balls, Tathip," I say contemptuously. "Three men are dead. How long were you prepared to go along with this killing spree? Four men? Five? Ten?"

"Please," he whimpers pathetically. "What are you going to do?" he asks again. "I'll do anything."

I lean forward. "You will say *nothing* to Chaldrakun about our talk. You will say nothing to *anyone*, do you understand? I will be in touch again soon. Until then you will act normally."

I look at the quaking wreck before me and wonder how easy that's going to be for him. Not very.

"Whatever you want," he says.

After I've finished with Tathip I consult Charoenkul's paper and take a drive to see where PC lives. Unusually, he lives among what is primarily a Chinese community off Mae Nam 4.

His apartment is on the top floor of a small grubby white block; his front door and landing being accessed via two flights of concrete external steps. The whole shabby structure looks like it hasn't been maintained in years, and none of the lights on either the stairs or the landings appear to be working. Some of the windows are boarded up: I guess only a few of the flats are occupied.

From the street below I can see that the lights in PC's apartment are on, so I presume he is in although I don't see anyone moving around. I don't intend paying him a social call.

It strikes me as unreal that while Chaldrakun's neighbours go about their preparations for the Chinese New Year, unbeknown they have among them a brutal man with a terrible passion.

I look at the red lanterns, the golden cut-outs of roosters, the jolly streamers hanging over the road. I think of the celebration to come, and it feels weird, like some sick cosmic joke.

I light a cigarette and contemplate the discussion I'll be having shortly with Peter Ashley.

I wonder what to do next.

13

By the time I left Peter Ashley's hotel last night I was completely drained of coherent thought.

I told him everything I knew about the murders except the addresses of PC and DTs, and where to find Jingjai.

I had worried that he would want to grab the first blunt object to hand and beat his brother's killer – and his dumb accomplice – to a pulp. Recounting my findings to him was a calculated risk, but one I had to take. His brother *had* been murdered, after all.

To my relief, however, with the facts before him his reaction was more considered and less angry than anticipated. I think his main feeling was relief; that closure might at last be near. Ashley even started calling me 'David' towards the end. Much more of this and people will say we're in love.

The former army man also appreciated immediately the dilemma we had: *as the killer is a policeman, how will the police themselves react to this news?*

Before we parted we agreed to sleep on it, although I didn't sleep much. I was anxious that Tathip might panic and squeal to his partner despite my implied and specific threats. Consequently I imagined every night noise outside my house to be Chaldrakun trying to break in and kill me.

I started to fret about how I may have exposed Wayan to danger too. But what could I do? Knock on the door to her room and say, "I'm worried we might have an intruder. Can I sleep with you in your bed tonight?" Sounds like the most feeble attempt at seduction ever.

However, it was not a killer that arrived eventually but the dawn. And I was happy to see it.

Sunday, 6th February. National Elections Day.

Yippee.

I take breakfast in the sala. Wayan brings out a tray with scrambled eggs, toast, papaya juice and black coffee.

While I eat and smoke I doodle in my notebook.

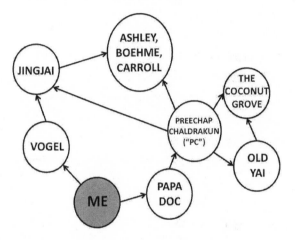

Connections and interconnections. The Old Monk was right after all.

The muddled Braddock psyche had just over-elaborated on its original jewelled net.

But today my mind is clear as a choirboy's conscience, even if the rest of me feels like the Swamp Thing. I have no need to meditate to focus my attention. The way is open but my long march to Buddhahood will have to be put aside for now. I have a tricky non-spiritual decision to make.

I consider my options in the hot light of day.

I could contact Rattanakorn to ask for his advice. A jâo phâw should be adept at making life and death decisions. But what can *he* tell me to do? He's not going to want to get involved in something like this. Why would he? He's the guy who pays Chaldrakun's wages.

Second option: do nothing. *Yeah, right.* And wait around for Tathip's nerve to snap and for me to end up a smouldering corpse in some coconut grove.

There's only one real option.

*   *   *   *   *

"There's only one real option," I tell Ashley.

We're sitting at a driftwood table on the beach at Chaweng, having a mid-morning soft drink. I've had one of the restaurant staff put up an umbrella for us because the sun is especially scorching today. A family is creaming-up with sun-block not far from us and a dark-skinned hawker is trying valiantly to get them interested in some seashell jewellery. The sea looks calm and inviting. Kids splash in the water. An old Smokey Robinson number plays quietly on a nearby sound system. The incongruity between the holiday tableau before us and the subject of our discussion could hardly be greater.

"I'm going to have to talk to the Koh Samui Police Chief, Charoenkul. He's the guy who got me into all this in the first place."

"How do you think he'll take it?" asks Ashley.

If I knew that, I'd be a very wise man indeed. As it is, I'm still not sure whether he knows about my affair with his wife; whether he's playing me along. And Chaldrakun *is* one of his trusted 'boys', even if he's never promoted the ape. On the other hand, resolving the burning murders would fix his career problem, and it would be a poke in the eye for Katchai. Or would the natural lure of the police to close ranks prove too tempting?

"Well, if he's minded to do the right thing, I don't think there'd be too much of an issue with getting a conviction if the police act fast. There's Tathip's testimony which I'm sure could be obtained with a promise of clemency. Even if the inside of the police patrol car has been cleaned thoroughly I'm confident a decent forensics team could still find trace evidence of the victims' presence there. The tyre wrench must be around Chaldrakun's place *somewhere*, and I'll bet he has a stock of the incapacitating drug in his apartment."

"But that's only if the Police Boss is minded to do the right thing. The way you say it, it sounds like a big *IF*."

I shrug.

"Anyway, I'll go talk to him today. No point in delaying."

"Then I'll come with you."

"That's not a good idea."

"For fuck's sake, David," he says in frustration. "I've been sitting around on my arse for two days. I think I've been *very* patient. Do you seriously expect me to go on hanging around like a spare prick at a wedding? It's my brother who was killed, remember?"

"Peter, listen to me. You're a man who acts first and thinks later. That is *not* what is needed here."

He tries to interrupt me, but I go on, "Charoenkul knows you. Or at least he knows *of* you. He thinks you're a nuisance and a trouble-maker, and he said as much to me. You're loud and bad for the tourist trade. It's better that I go alone. I can talk to him, reason with him if necessary."

He looks at me and his eyes are angry.

"You can't *stop* me going to the police," he announces stubbornly.

"That's perfectly true," I reply, "but consider what the point of all this is: *to bring your brother's killer to justice*. Not to satisfy your personal rage. You want revenge, fine. But let's go about this in a way that will maximise the chances of the right outcome."

I hand him the parcel I've had lying on the chair next to me.

"Besides," I say, "you're my ace in the hole."

"What's this?"

"All the files and transcripts Charoenkul has given me relating to the murders, including the one on your brother. If, for whatever reason, I don't come back to see you later today, I suggest you get out of Thailand, take that with you and do whatever is necessary."

Ashley looks shocked. "That's a bit melodramatic, isn't it? What do you imagine might happen to you?"

"Actually, I don't know."

"You've thought all this through, haven't you?"

"Yes."

He sighs and looks at the parcel, then back to me.

"Are you going to see Charoenkul now?"

"No, he's playing golf this morning. I'll see him this afternoon if I can. Anyway," I add consulting my watch, "I have a lady to see first."

Kat. Charoenkul's wife.

*   *   *   *   *

The police are much in evidence during my short drive to the office: election day duties. The voters, queuing for their opportunity to influence destiny appear hot but in a good temper. Some new food stalls have appeared from nowhere for the occasion, and they're all doing brisk business. Trust the Thais to make a festival out of it. I wonder what Khun Thaksin is doing right now. Some last minute photo opportunities kissing babies, I guess.

Just after the hour I hear Kat's heels on the stairs to my office.

She looks bewitching, as always, but perhaps a trifle more reserved than usual. Almost coy. She wears a cream and pink dress, but little jewellery, and her makeup gives her a demure quality.

She stands in the doorway and asks, "Can I come in?" *That's a first.*

"Please. Would you like something to drink?"

"No, I'm fine, thanks."

She sits down.

"What time was the Chief teeing off this morning?"

"Deng isn't at the golf course."

"Oh?"

"No, he had a call before he was due to leave, and he's had to go into the office. He seemed very excited about it."

"Excited stressed or excited happy?"

"The latter. Actually," she reflects, "he looked happier after the call than I've seen him in weeks. I guess it must be good news."

"Bully for him."

She looks at me meaningfully and indulges in a small pout.

"I had the feeling the last time we spoke that things were not right," she says. "You were cross with me, David. I wanted to know why."

I decide on the direct approach.

"Maybe I just don't like being lied to, Kat."

"About what?"

"Well, let's start with your condition, shall we?"

She says nothing.

"Look, Kat," I say in a conciliatory tone. "I figured it out. I may not be the best private detective in the world, but I'm not an idiot.

"That trip to the hospital with your friend Sumalee. You weren't accompanying *her*, were you? She was accompanying *you*. Something's wrong, isn't it? With you, I mean," I add gently. "Just how serious is it?"

She looks at her hands, then at me.

"Can I trust you, David?" she asks.

"Yes."

"Then it's pretty serious," she says. "My specialist tells me that, technically-speaking, I'm suffering from a malignant neoplasm originating in the cervix."

"Jesus, Kat. You have *cancer*? And that's the reason for your 'shopping trips' to Bangkok in recent months."

"That's the reason. I didn't want to talk to any doctors here. Samui is too small an island."

"Have you told your husband?"

"No. The only one who knows is Sumalee. And now you."

"But you *have* to tell him."

"I will. But not for a while yet."

"But surely you don't think you can keep any surgery and chemotherapy treatment secret from him. That would be absurd. It will be ... obvious."

"You mean when my hair starts falling out."

"Hey, I think bald chicks are sexy," I proffer in a weak attempt at humour.

She shakes her head and smiles sadly.

"It's too late for all that," she says. "They found it too late. I'm Stage IV, and the cancer has metastasized. Treatment at this point would be a painful waste of time."

Not knowing what to say the investigator in me blurts out, "Is that why you've been so reckless lately? Because you think you're dying?"

"I *am* dying, David," Kat states simply. "And yes, why *not* have some fun while I can, while men still find me attractive?"

She raises an eyebrow.

"I presume you do know about the *other* man?"

She takes my silence as a 'yes'.

"Of course you do. That's why you were in a huff with me. Well," she goes on, "that's over now."

"Good," I say. "I'm glad about *that*. So when can you and I get back to having sex on a regular basis?"

This takes her aback.

"You still want to have sex with me? Knowing I have cancer?"

"Why not?" I reply. "There's nothing unethical about it. You're not a client of mine, after all."

"But I *am* married."

"But I'm *not*. So that makes it unethical for you, but not for me."

Kat looks grave for a moment.

"Can we keep this between ourselves for now, David? I really *don't* want Deng to know. Not yet."

"All right," I respond. "I won't say anything so long as you continue to have sex with me."

"You are incorrigible."

"I'm also entirely serious."

Mrs. C studies me closely.

"Yes," she says, "I do believe you are."

She becomes suddenly businesslike and stands up.

"We'll discuss this some other time, Mr. Braddock. I have to leave you now for a lunch appointment."

"Not with a man, I hope."

"No. With a woman friend of mine. With Nittha Rattanakorn, as it happens. I gather she's been availing herself of your professional services. She tells me you're very good. Although, of course, I knew *that* already."

*   *   *   *   *

My jeep is parked on the waste ground next to Bophut Police Station. I'm trying to summon up the enthusiasm to go inside, to recapture the resolve I showed to Peter Ashley this morning. But that seems like a long time ago now. That was before my meeting with Kat.

After Kat left I sat in the East Office feeling numb, my superficial jollity gone, my energy seeping away like ash through a grate. I took the whisky bottle from the West Office and downed a couple of shots; hardly a wise action on an empty stomach but I needed it.

I'd thought about Charoenkul and our impending confrontation. I don't like him. In fact I *dislike* him. But it is hard not to be touched in some way by his situation. He is, after all, about to become a member of the Widower's Club; a select society which includes myself and Kenneth Sinclair on its roll. The Club doesn't have many perks, but the subscription is free and membership is for life.

Moreover the Chief has no idea that his application has already been submitted by his wife on his behalf.

I'd picked up my cell phone and called him.

His voice was animated. He was delighted to hear from me. He didn't even ask why I was calling.

"Come in to my office, Braddock," he'd said. "Something truly amazing has happened. Come straightaway and I'll tell you all about it."

Then he'd rung off before I could think of anything to say.

I climb out of the jeep and trudge slowly to the reception wishing I'd had another whisky. A few more even. Five minutes later I'm entering Charoenkul's office.

"Ah, Braddock, come in, come in," warbles Papa Doc cheerfully. "Take a seat."

His obvious elation makes me feel even more despondent. I want to say, *Your wife is ill: your world is a chimera, a fantasy. Go to her.* My ode to epistemology: knowing can be a toxic blessing.

"I think a celebratory drink is in order. Normally I wouldn't indulge in the office, but this is a special occasion." He takes two spirit glasses from his cabinet and a bottle of whisky from his desk drawer. It's even the same brand as I have in my office.

What shall we drink to? Your wife's health?

"What are we celebrating?" I ask, endeavouring to sound positive.

He hands me a glass.

318

"To the dogged determination of the Royal Thai Police and to Lady Luck. The burning murders case is solved."

Papa Doc sees the shocked expression on my face and laughs.

"Drink up, Braddock," he says.

I knock back the whisky quickly and ask, "You mean the killer is in custody?"

"Better than that," he replies. "The killer is *dead*. No need for an expensive trial and ensuing media circus. Isn't that great news?"

I need to sit down, so I do. He pours us both another whisky.

Something tells me I'm not going to like the answer to my next question, but it has to be asked.

"So who is it?"

"Who *was* it?" he responds with a twinkle.

"Whatever."

"His name is – or rather *was* – Arthit Bussakiam, an itinerant from Phayao. He'd been on Samui for months, supposedly looking for work."

"You mean he is – sorry, *was* – a tramp? A vagrant?"

"That's right. He was known to a couple of my officers. I believe they had previously spoken to him about his begging activities."

"It seems like a long way from begging to murder," I interject.

"I'm getting to that," he replies slightly miffed. "Apparently seeing all the wealthy farangs around made him resentful, and it started to eat away at him. He couldn't get any work, and there were all these foreigners running around with money to burn. After a while it tipped him over the edge and he started killing."

"So how did all this come to light?" I ask, trying to keep the sarcasm out of my voice.

"Well," says Charoenkul warming to his theme, "by the most amazing stroke of luck. Late last night one of my officers was driving through Chaweng and this figure suddenly fell out into the road. It was too late for my officer to swerve and so he hit the man. Since he was in mid-fall, the man's head was struck hard by the front of the vehicle."

"Doesn't sound too lucky so far."

My irony is lost on the Chief. "Ah, but it *was* lucky for us. An ambulance was called and the man was rushed to hospital in a serious condition. He died this morning of his injuries."

"Who was driving the police car?"

"I don't see why *that* is relevant," Charoenkul replies indignantly.

"Never mind," I say. "Go on."

"Anyway, the man – Bussakiam – was passing in and out of consciousness. He realised he was dying and said he wanted to clear his conscience. He told my officer in attendance that he'd committed three murders. When it was realised that these were the farang killings I was called. I was actually *there* in the hospital today when he made his statement," he says proudly. "Worth missing a round of golf for, don't you think?"

"Absolutely," I say trying to process all this.

"I have already spoken to Surat Thani, and they, naturally, are delighted. Everyone is delighted," he beams happily, "Except for poor Katchai, of course. He and his team should be going back to the mainland this week." He looks like he wants to say some derogatory comment about the Investigator, but he thinks better of it and instead clinks my glass. "Cheers."

"So," I summarise, "you're saying a tramp killed the three Europeans."

"That's right."

"And how did he get his victims to the murder sites?" I ask. "I presume, as a tramp, he didn't have a vehicle."

Charoenkul smiles condescendingly. "Braddock," he purrs, "I realise you must be disappointed that your efforts for me eventually came to nothing. Nevertheless your work *is* appreciated, believe me. I wouldn't hesitate to consult with you again if ever the need arose. Your insights were very valuable. But please, don't worry yourself about the *details* of the case. Alas, some of these I cannot share with you. Just be happy it's over. I know *I* am."

"It's not that, Chief. I was just thinking how awful it would be if it turned out that you'd got the wrong man. If the murders continued, that is."

Papa Doc looks me in the eye. "We *don't* have the wrong man. But if we did, and I was the *real* murderer, I'd take the hint and stop now, while I was in the clear. Wouldn't you?"

How appropriate that one of the victims was named Lewis Carroll. Because this is all *nonsense*. Worse than that, I'm left with a deep unease that Charoenkul might know the *real* truth and that the Police Chief, our bulwark against the forces of crime and chaos, is perpetrating a whitewash.

I wonder if the dead tramp was the one I'd given money to. I wonder if he was even alive when he arrived at the hospital, or whether the doctors there are also complicit. I wonder who was driving the police car – presumably not PC who I know was home last night – and whether the 'accident' really an accident. I wonder how I could ever have felt sympathy for Charoenkul, even if his wife is dying.

"By the way," he remarks as an afterthought, "what was it you were phoning me about earlier?"

"Oh, it was just about the forensic summary you sent me on Carroll," I reply. "It hardly matters now."

*   *   *   *   *

I sit in my jeep and chain-smoke.

With the announcement of Charoenkul's successful conclusion to the burning murders and Ashley's eventual departure from the island, my hold over Tathip will be gone. It won't be very long before the little canary sings to Chaldrakun. David Braddock's prospects of a long and happy life are not looking great.

Everyone burns, as the Buddha says, in their own way. Some burn with anger, some with lust, some with a desire for vengeance, some with fear. But inside us burn many fires, not just one. We are legion, we contain a multitude.

Yes, everyone burns. However, human beings are not the *only* things that burn.

I start the engine and drive into Chaweng.

The streets are full of people; voting, gossiping, shouting, flirting, selling, and stocking up for the New Year celebrations. I move among the throng unnoticed. A white ghost. A dead man walking. Just another unremarkable European face.

I make some purchases and call ahead for Peter Ashley to meet me in his room at the Lotus Blossom Villas.

When I arrive he asks, "How did it go? By the look on your face, I'm assuming not well."

"Charoenkul has already fitted up somebody for the murders. It's ludicrous, but the police will run with it. He couldn't *wait* to tell me. I didn't get the chance to say anything; not that it would have made any difference if I had.

"I don't even know whether the Chief suspects what has really been going on, and this is pre-emptive to close the files and get everybody off the hook. One thing is clear to me, however. Chaldrakun is never going to stand trial."

"So what's our next move?" Ashley asks grimly.

I empty onto his bed the contents of my shopping bag: firecrackers, rockets and other assorted fireworks. He looks at me quizzically.

"You're ex-army, aren't you? Do you know how to make a slow-burning fuse?" I ask.

"Of course I do," he replies. "Why? What do you have in mind?"

"What I have in mind, Peter, is killing Preechap Chaldrakun," I say. "Are you up for that?"

14

"How tedious is a guilty conscience!
When I look into the fish-ponds in my garden,
Methinks I see a thing arm'd with a rake,
That seems to strike at me."
John Webster, The Duchess of Malfi

Thaksin Shinawatra's Thai Rak Thai Party won the election by a landslide, no longer requiring the support of the former coalition partner to govern. The polls had closed at 3.00pm on Sunday, and the Monday edition of the *Bangkok Post* carried the headline *Single Party Rule*, with the *Nation* announcing *One Party Rule Looms*.

Initial results showed that out of 500 seats in the House of Representatives Thaksin had taken 375, with the Democrat opposition collapsing humiliatingly to a mere 96. Bangkok had fallen and only in the South was there any resistance to the landslide.

Today, Thursday, there is still too much political coverage in the national papers for them to hold my attention. *The Island Daily*, however, does have an interesting little piece on the inside page entitled *Local Policeman Dies in Bizarre Accident*.

I put down my saxophone and wipe my sweaty brow. Although the fan is going full tilt in the sala, it's fighting a losing battle against the relentless heat. Still no rain.

On a whim I'd pulled out my instrument to see just how rusty my playing has become; it being two weeks since I last picked it up. The answer is: pretty rusty. But then a sax is not really at home in the tropical daytime, it's more a creature of the night. Like me, I guess.

Wayan knows telepathically it's time to bring me a cold beer.

She's been pensive and a little withdrawn since Sinclair pitched up, as promised, to make his stumbling confession and apologies. She had listened quietly and assured him this would not affect their friendship. I know this because I was eavesdropping, naturally.

After the old boy left, I felt a little guilty so put in a good word for him. He's not such a bad stick really, all things considered. For a Neanderthal, anyway.

I suggested to my Balinese Princess that she should think about a serious relationship with someone; that she was not going to want to look after me forever.

She'd given me a somewhat hurt look and explained that, as she'd told me before, her *karma* was to be alone. I'd squeezed her shoulder and suggested she at least *think* about it.

Klaus Vogel had meantime returned to the island for a quick stopover en route for Europe, and to clear up for me the mystery of his interest in Jingjai. It turns out his attention was not romantically-based. He's in the music business and he'd shortlisted Jingjai for a contract and upwards career move to Germany. Unfortunately for the girl with the diamond tooth, Vogel's subsequent scouting in South East Asia had thrown up a Filipina beauty who had pipped her at the post. So no contract for Wiwatanee Lamphongchat, who will have to make do with Monday evenings at Charlie's place for the time being.

As an interesting coda, the charmless Vogel had slipped me some extra cash to convey the bad news to Jingjai, explaining that *it might upset her more* if it came from him. It seems that some Germans – though not all – could use lessons in interpersonal relations and empathy.

Do you know, by the way, that German is the only language in the world that has a word for 'pleasure derived from the misfortune of others'? *Schadenfreude*. That must tell you something.

In truth, I undertook the assignment willingly. I wanted to see Jingjai again; the girl whose mere existence had unwittingly put in motion a firestorm that had engulfed the lives of three people.

Talking to her quietly and privately I could see how PC might have become obsessed with her. I'm the obsessional type myself: I can recognise the *leitmotif*.

For a girl who'd just lost her job at the *Pearl* and whose dream of a musical career was – at the very least – postponed, she took it stoically.

"Well, I'll just have to keep at it. No-one told me it would be easy," she'd said.

I hope she never finds out about Chaldrakun. I don't know what it would do to her. In any event, she certainly won't *ever* find out from me.

Of the other people in my life, Da has *still* not produced that damn baby yet, and is confined to bed with high blood pressure. Although that hasn't prevented her from ringing me to enthuse about the piece in the local paper on my sponsoring Yai's eye operation. I resolve to take her some flowers tomorrow, and possibly an enema.

Prasert's brother Nikom is meanwhile still AWOL, and Vlad is back to his unbearable best after a narrow points victory over the Polish fighter. He's still promising me work of some murky and unspecified type. We'll see.

Yesterday I spent a few hours with the soon-not-to-be-blind Yai and his family, joining in their Chinese New Year festivities. It turns out his daughter-in-law – a tubby and rather bossy woman, if the truth be told – has Szechuan ancestry which she's quite passionate about.

The occasion had a quality of domestic normality about it: exchanging red envelopes, seeing friends drop by, performing prayers to the ancestors, burning paper money for good luck, watching the dragon dancers in the street outside, and listening to the noisy drumming and cymbals. All this was punctuated by the extremely loud bangs of firecrackers and other exploding gunpowder ushering in the Year of the Rooster. My *own* Chinese horoscope year in fact.

Chinese tradition dictates that this is a time to be nice to everyone and to cause no harm; otherwise bad fortune will follow you for the whole year.

If that is correct then the Year of the Rooster is going to be a real stinker for me.

Wayan interrupts my ruminations.

"Mr. David, the Police Chief, Mr. Charoenkul is here to see you. I thought it best to show him into the study."

"Is he alone?"

"Yes," she says, looking apprehensive.

"Good. He can't be here to arrest me, then," I respond with a grin.

I ask her to put my saxophone away and to bring some green tea.

I knew Charoenkul would turn up at some point. Best to get it over with today.

When I enter the study he is examining a large, well-crafted woodcut depicting a naked female being entered simultaneously by two men; one at each end, as it were. The piece had arrived this morning, a gift from Rattanakorn, with an accompanying card: *As a memento of our shared experience*. Who says gangsters don't have a sense of humour?

"This is a bit explicit, isn't it?" he asks.

I'm tempted to reply, *Yes, but I don't feel the artist has properly captured your wife's eyes. What do you think?*

Instead I say, "A gift from a client who is something of an art collector."

Papa Doc drops himself into a chair and begins drumming with his fingers. He seems uncertain how to begin. I help him out.

"So, Chief, to what do I owe the pleasure?"

"I was in the area, and thought I'd drop by and pick up those files I sent over to you. Best we get them back into the police archives for safe keeping."

"Sure."

I unlock the drawer, take them out and hand them to him. Fortunately it hadn't proved necessary to leave them with Ashley.

The policeman shows no sign of leaving. Wayan brings in the tea.

Charoenkul appraises her arse as she leaves the room.

"Attractive woman, your maid," he says approvingly.

"She's my *housekeeper*. And yes, she *is* a very attractive lady."

He sips his green tea.

"I suppose you saw the article in t*he Island Daily* about Chaldrakun's death, did you?" This said casually.

"I did. It was a bit short on detail though. What happened exactly?"

He looks at me.

"It was all rather odd, in actual fact."

"Odd?" I ask with a straight bat.

"Mmnn. Well, it happened late on Tuesday evening; the eve of the New Year. Chaldrakun was on his cell phone to Officer Tathip at the time when some children started setting off loud firecrackers outside his apartment. Tathip said he could hear the bangs distinctly. Chaldrakun rushed outside to chase the children away, slipped and fell down the concrete stairs leading up to his apartment. Broke his neck on the wall at the bottom."

"Wow."

"Tathip heard a thud then the phone went dead. He raised the alarm, and one of our patrol cars found Chaldrakun's body a few minutes later.

"The patrolman said there was no lighting on the landing or stairs; all the bulbs were either burnt-out or missing. Chaldrakun must have lost his footing in the dark. His cell phone was in pieces beside him; his front door still open. The landing was strewn with spent firecrackers.

"We've been questioning the neighbours, but naturally they all deny that *their* children were out letting off fireworks. I doubt we'll find the spawn responsible."

Charoenkul shifts slightly in his seat.

"There are a couple of puzzling aspects to the death, however," he remarks.

"Oh?"

"First, the position of Chaldrakun's hands."

"His hands?"

"When someone is falling, the natural reflex is to put out the hands for protection. Like this." He illustrates. "Yet there was no indication that my officer had done that from how his body was lying."

"Maybe he'd been drinking; slowing the reflexes, or whatever."

"There was a glass of whisky on his side table, that's true," he says, "But still."

I keep quiet and watch him.

"And curiously," Papa Doc goes on, "the large spent firecracker on his landing had an abnormally long fuse, a home-made one by the look of it. What do you think of *that*?"

I shrug. "Who knows? Maybe the kids were experimenting. Boys will be boys."

"Perhaps." He continues to look at me.

"And to think," I say, "while all this excitement was happening, I was having a boring evening parked up in my jeep in Girly Bar Heaven snapping time-stamped photographs of the latest unfaithful bargirl."

He holds my gaze for a couple of seconds then announces, "Well, I must be going. Thank you for the files and for the tea." He stands. "Don't forget to behave yourself in the Year of the Rooster, Braddock. Remember, *I'll be watching you.*"

After he's gone I send the pre-arranged SMS to Peter Ashley: *Case closed*

The price of DTs' clemency had been his participation in Chaldrakun's killing.

Ashley and I had knocked on PC's door that evening with a spurious request for assistance in my investigations. Grudgingly, and with obvious suspicion, the big lug had admitted us to his apartment. When Tathip called PC's cell phone at the appointed time, and the gorilla turned his back to answer, Ashley sprang to his feet and twisted Chaldrakun's neck. PC was dead before he hit the floor. I had thought that thick collar would be difficult to break, but the former army man snapped it like a twig, and with an efficiency that made me shudder.

After checking outside, we each took an arm and a leg, and after a few swings and considerable exertion, threw the corpse down the steps. He flew like a black demon descending into the depths. I tossed the phone down after him.

Ashley then lit the long fuse on the monster firecrackers, giving us enough time to make our escape before the bangs started. We walked quickly, but not too quickly, back to the car hired by Ashley for the occasion. My jeep had already been parked for some hours in Girly Bar Heaven while my teenage drug-dealing employee unwittingly established my alibi by taking photos of 'Ching Ching' Ting.

The following morning, Peter Ashley was on a plane heading for Bangkok, and thereafter England.

Ironic to think three days before this I was concerned Ashley might turn into a vigilante. Now we were both vigilantes, for our own different reasons.

On my path to Enlightenment, clearly I've taken a diversion. The Old Monk would be disappointed if he knew. But then again, perhaps he wouldn't. He understands that some fires are difficult to extinguish.

I had destroyed a mad dog; a lonely, bitter and dangerous one. I had put the demon down where he belonged; at the bottom of a dark stairwell that smelled of urine and dirt.

In karmic terms, perhaps that had merit. Although as the monk Bodhidharma observed to the Emperor nothing *really* earns you merit; and there is *nothing* holy. His answer to the question 'Who are you?' was the same as the Mad Hatter's to the riddle of the raven and the writing-desk: *I haven't the slightest idea.*

Which is exactly where I still am on the identity of the anonymous letter-writer. Many issues seem to have been cleared up in the last few days, but this isn't one of them.

His most recent missive, now stowed in the file in the locked drawer, was at least direct:

DAVID BRADDOCK, I KNOW YOU KILLED YOUR WIFE

I wander out into the garden and light a cigarette.

Wayan's shapely figure is attending to the spirit house. Despite the perturbations of the world, life goes on.

The sky presents an endless canopy of translucent blue. The still air is suffused with sunshine.

Perhaps tomorrow the beneficent clouds will gather and it will finally rain. The earth will cool and revive and in that seminal moment all our sins perchance will be washed away.

It might happen.

But somehow I doubt it.

David Braddock returns in

HUNGRY GHOSTS

The second book in the *Time, Blood and Karma* series.

For the last half-hour my mind has been playing games with me. I keep thinking I see Claire at the periphery of my vision, but when I turn my head she vanishes. But then of course she would. She is a ghost, after all.

It is the spring of 2005 and the macabre 'burning murders' have ended. Life has apparently returned to normal for the Thai island of Samui.

For private investigator David Braddock 'normal' means finding a missing drug smuggler, sleeping with the Police Chief's wife and ensuring his office manager's latest money making scheme doesn't bankrupt him.

For Police Chief Charoenkul it means resuming his seemingly-endless wait for that elusive promotion to Bangkok.

However, the peace is destined to be short-lived. Unbeknown to both men, karmic storm clouds are gathering and murderous forces are about to be unleashed which could destroy them both ...

Made in the USA
Middletown, DE
06 April 2015